Praise for *Shelf Aware*

'Richly illustrated and meaningfully premised, V.R. Ferose's *Shelf Aware* captures the author's exciting journey of discovering himself through the magical world of books. Writing about the world of words, illustrated with sketches by autistic artists, Ferose ensures that his readers are in for a pleasant surprise – for they soon learn that they are discovering themselves, too!'

Shashi Tharoor, Member of Parliament for Thiruvananthapuram, Lok Sabha, and bestselling author of *The Great Indian Novel* and *Inglorious Empire*

'Books are like Aladdin's lamp. If you don't rub the lamp, the genie doesn't come out. Writers need readers to awaken the genie within. V.R. Ferose is an author's ideal reader. Extending his guiding hand to us through his exemplary book, we – his lucky readers – are inducted into the alchemy of literature itself.'

Steve Wasserman, former editor of the *Los Angeles Times Book Review* and publisher of Heyday Books

'Beyond the avid reader lies the secret realm of the bibliophile who is bound to books in inexplicable ways. From the physicality of the book to its history, the bibliophile sees in books what many readers do n't perceive. *Shelf Aware* is a compilation of essays of one such bibliophile V.R. Ferose, where his deep abiding regard for books reigns supreme. *Shelf Aware* also has the distinction of being illustrated by five artists on the autism spectrum whose interpretation of the writing is both magnificent and inspiring. A must-have for anyone who loves books.'

Anita Nair, author

'Ferose will be your guide to the world of wisdom. You will seek out this book when you need answers. I am waiting for one for my shelf.'

Adil Hussain, actor

shelf
AWARE

First published in 2023 by Hachette India
(Registered name: Hachette Book Publishing India Pvt. Ltd)
An Hachette UK company
www.hachetteindia.com

2

All authorial proceeds of this book will go to Sense Kaleidoscopes – a unit of Ayathi Trust, a non-profit school based in Bengaluru that focuses on providing art classes to individuals on the autism spectrum.

This four-colour production has been made available to readers at an accessible price owing to a print subsidy.

Regular Hardback edition: 978-93-5731-249-3
Limited Collector's edition: 978-93-5731-255-4

Hachette Book Publishing India Pvt. Ltd
4th & 5th Floors, Corporate Centre,
Plot No. 94, Sector 44, Gurgaon - 122003, India

The paper used for this book has been made from responsibly sourced wood fibre.

Typeset in Open Sans
Designed by The Other Design Studio

Printed and bound in India
by Manipal Technologies Limited

Shelf Aware

A Love Affair with Books

With Art by Artists on the Autism Spectrum

VR Ferose

hachette INDIA

Outside of a dog, a book is a man’s best friend.
Inside of a dog, it’s too dark to read.

— Groucho Marx

(i)

FOREWORD

Nicholas A. Basbanes

On those occasions that I am invited to talk with kindred spirits about my fifty years of roaming among people, I have come with great affection to call the 'gently mad', I like to point out that the passion to ferret out, acquire and amass books in wild abundance is the only pastime I know of that has a recognized malady named to characterize it. Bibliomania, I go on to explain, has been rampant through most of recorded history, yet there is very little in the clinical record that documents an appropriate therapy or even offers any advice on how to keep it under control. And the reason for that, I surmise, is that nobody who has ever had the condition has expressed the slightest interest in being cured, much less being treated, and therein lies a paradox that I leave for others more versed in the foibles of human nature to figure out.

What I do know is that book people come in all shapes and sizes and from every demographic station and every point of the compass. They cut across all cultural and ethnic lines and find satisfaction at every level of activity, regardless of how little or how much money they have to spend. Indeed, wonderful collections are put together on a shoestring. Some of my very favourite books are kept together in what I like to call my 'orphan corner', an area I have designated to shelve titles that for one reason or other have been withdrawn from institutional collections, many with the word 'discarded' stamped boldly on the inside flyleaf, their 'read by' dates, apparently, having expired, rendering them expendable. Some are sold at secondhand book sales, others go off ignominiously to shredding plants or landfills, others, of surprising importance and value, often wind up in rare book catalogues, while others still find new lives in other institutional libraries.

Many hundreds of these deaccessioned books also find their way to what is known as the Open Library, a component of the Internet Archive, a non-profit initiative based in San Francisco that scans these orphaned copies and allows anyone to 'borrow' them online for varying periods of time at no cost, which is a wonderful resource

– one, in fact, that I use often – but controversial in that a good many of these selectively deaccessioned books are not yet in the public domain, and thus, still protected by copyright, including several of my own books, none of which is out of copyright. Nevertheless, I recently found a hardcover copy of *A Gentle Madness: Bibliophiles, Bibliomanes, and the Eternal Passion for Books* – my first book – listed on Open Library, and checked it out to see if there was any provenance that might document its prior ownership.

Sure enough, the scanned copy was marked 'withdrawn from circulation' on the front flyleaf, pulled, it further notes, from the shelves of the San Rafael Public Library, in San Rafael, California in 2007, though clearly not because it hadn't been read over the previous twelve years since there is ample evidence there, stamped directly beneath the 'withdrawn' notice, that it had been loaned out no fewer than twenty-six times over that period, proof positive that this copy enjoyed a pretty solid record of active circulation. So why was it pulled from the stacks if the good people of San Rafael were still reading it? Maybe it was worn from overuse, though it looks fairly healthy and intact to my eyes. Where it went from there is anyone's guess, too, but in 2022, this copy was acquired by the Internet Archive and digitized for the Open Library. I won't argue the legal propriety of its being there; that's the subject of an ongoing lawsuit brought by a group of American publishing houses against the Internet Archive alleging unauthorized infringement of copyright, but since this particular work of mine is no spring chicken – it will observe its thirtieth birthday in 2025 – my feeling is that if someone wants to read it in this electronic fashion, fine with me, I'm flattered – writers write to be read, after all; that is the ultimate satisfaction in what we do.

What certainly pleases me, too, is that this copy – be it worn from repeated use or merely discarded for unspecified reasons – has found a new life where many more people will be able to read it. Cast out from one place, it has found renewal in another. To that, there is the added satisfaction in knowing that 1,454 other

(ii)

libraries, in dozens of countries throughout the globe – my source for this figure is the WorldCat online catalogue of library holdings worldwide – still have copies of *A Gentle Madness* in their collections, so the book retains, in a much grander sense, a pretty decent shelf life.

And now, dear reader, this copy that you hold in your hands, aptly subtitled by my friend and colleague, V.R. Ferose, to be 'a love affair with books', is a subject I know a bit about. With a clear eye for beauty and significance, Ferose is a book person in the truest sense, a collector of imagination and taste who is guided by a profound respect for the book as material object as well as cultural artifact. Books, he makes clear, are much more than sheets of paper bound between hard covers. They are, in a much deeper sense, touchstones with the past, companions of the present, legacies for the future. And his passion for the subject, as readers of the biweekly column he writes for the *New Indian Express* can readily attest to, is palpable.

Apparent throughout this eclectic selection of his pieces – and they truly do 'cover the waterfront', as the classic Johnny Green jazz lyric goes – is a distinctive voice rendered with wisdom, along with a light and gentle touch. The accompanying illustrations, produced exclusively for this edition by a group of talented autistic artists, are a wonderful addition. You will enjoy the entire package, of this I have no doubt. It is a gem of the genre.

(iii)

PREFACE

What is being 'Shelf Aware'? It is not just being aware of all the books on your shelf... It goes much beyond that. Here is how I came up with the title of the book, or rather, how the title came to me.

The title is, without any doubt, the most important aspect of a book as it captures the essence of the entire book in a few words. You have to live with the idea for a very long time for the title to appear – and once it does, you know it deep within you, and then, it sticks. You just cannot think of an alternative.

When I started thinking about the book, I started with 'Just Books' as a placeholder title because it was about nothing else but books. Halfway through the editing process, I settled on the title 'Shelf Life', connecting it to the idea of 'self life'. When I reached the final stages of the book, I realized that 'self life' is limiting in its meaning and wanted a more open, deeper and introspective word. That's when 'self-aware' came to mind, and I decided to go with *Shelf Aware* to represent a sense of higher awakening with books.

I had commissioned five artists on the autism spectrum to illustrate every essay in the book. The idea was not just to 'recycle' my previous essays but 'upcycle' them – the quality of every essay being enhanced by the artwork of these incredible artists. In the journey of working with them, I grew more self-aware. As a parent of a child on the autism spectrum, I could see my son's life projected into the future through the artworks. Some illustrations were extremely detailed, some strokes in the work were continuous, some broken and some abstract. The art allowed me to introspect – I became more attuned to my thoughts, emotions and behaviours. Just like the artwork, we are all connected and broken at the same time.

Through the journey of writing this book, I started to recognize patterns and habits that were no longer about serving my own needs but in service of the world around me. Self-awareness is a crucial component of personal growth and spiritual evolution. It allows individuals to take responsibility for their lives and empowers them to make conscious choices based on their true desires and values. Self-awareness is probably the most powerful tool for personal growth and transformation. By being self-aware, we can unlock our full potential and live a more calm, fulfilling and purposeful life. Hence the title of the book, *Shelf Aware*, inspired by the notion of self-awareness and the love of books!

ACKNOWLEDGEMENTS

I always wanted to be a writer, but I never thought I would become one. Hence, this book is dedicated to everyone who made that happen. As with all good things, there are many people behind the scenes who play a bigger role than you, people who believe in you more than you believe in yourself.

First and foremost, let me confess that I have neither been trained in writing nor hold any degrees to justify my being the 'literary' type. I have only attended a couple of weekend classes at Stanford University, just to fine-tune my practice of writing columns. So, my entire education is thanks to my habit of reading during every possible free moment I get. My biggest role model and inspiration is my wife Deepali, who is a much better writer than I am – she was my first editor and remains my biggest critic. She was always the first to spot mistakes and correct them – for which I am eternally grateful. While we both have very different tastes in reading – she loves fiction and I, non-fiction – we share the same passion for reading and writing. We both consider ourselves as accidental engineers – in another life, we would have loved to become full-time writers.

(iv)

Since this book is about books, I must thank my friend and India's topmost scholar on books – Pradeep Sebastian. It is thanks to him that I got an education about books – not only is Pradeep a treasure house of knowledge, but he also shares his vast knowledge selflessly and unhesitatingly. The first column I wrote on books for *Swarajya* magazine titled 'The Chase for my Alice' was made possible solely by Pradeep. Of the rare books I mentioned in the column, he procured one from a dealer in New York and all the rest from an auction house. I would not have written about books but for his guidance and constant support. Pradeep was also responsible for giving me an introduction to the legendary bibliophile Nicholas A. Basbanes. Over the years, I have become something of a 'Basbanomaniac', reading his works and collecting books from his personal library. People like Nicholas A. Basbanes are as rare as some of the rarest books in the world, and it is an honour that he agreed to write the foreword for this book.

My friend and co-author C.K. Meena deserves all the gratitude for being my editor. She persistently reminded me how mediocre my writing was but always with the intention of making me a better writer. I hope she will be pleased with this book as she has edited most of my columns and improved upon what I have written.

Two editors to whom I owe my biggest debt are Sandipan Deb (formerly with *Swarajya*) and Vidya Iyengar (*The New Indian Express*). Both Sandipan and Vidya gave me the opportunity to express myself regularly through columns. Both of them constantly nudged me into making writing a habit – writing a regular column is all about muscle memory.

The book became a reality because I wanted to offer something unique to the reader instead of publishing yet another of those anthologies. That's when I thought of adding art to my column, but art by those on the autism spectrum, sourced from Sense Kaleidoscopes. After my first meeting with the co-founders of Sense Kaleidoscopes, Akshayee Shetty and Anima Nair, I was convinced that I could have uniquely portable magic in my hands! The beautiful illustrations would not have been possible without Angie and Upesh from The Other Design Studio. For over a year, I have had regular calls with Angie, and many a time, we have debated about the artwork. Angie is probably the only person who has read my columns more than I have read them myself.

There cannot be anyone more praiseworthy than the artists themselves – Adarsh, Anshika, Pranav, Rohit and Tanush. When I met them for the first time in Bengaluru, they were already diligently working on the artwork for my columns and were as overjoyed to meet me as I was to meet them. I wanted to not only share their talent but also explain the unique process of maximizing the potential of artists on the autism spectrum. The artwork in this book is visual proof that the brains of people with autism are not inferior but distinctive. I hope this book becomes one more platform to share the talent and creative output of the amazing artists at Sense Kaleidoscopes. All author proceeds from this book will go towards supporting them.

And finally, to my friends at Hachette India. This being my first solo book (and my fifth overall), I knew that only Hachette would do justice to it. I am grateful to Thomas Abraham, MD at Hachette India, for unquestioningly supporting all my crazy ideas; I hope I can repay his trust through the success of this book. Abhivyakti Singh has been an incredible partner in this project by gently but firmly steering me towards the finish line.

While this book is about my passion for books, it is also about my global travels and the ideas that have shaped me. The talent of people on the spectrum is what led us to this book in its current form. I hope readers will make the connection to a larger truth: magic happens at intersections – of people and minds, of business and technology, of art and the humanities. Creating inclusive environments that embrace the beautiful diversity of human lives can lead to better outcomes for all.

CONTENTS

What's Special

Philosophical Pages

Guide to a Better Self

Scientific Scripts

Portrayed Pages

Flipping the Pages

The Joy and Art of Collecting

Places Through Ages

Glossary of Genres

How Do You Read?

Scribbling Stories

Films and Fiction

Lore of Legends

Insights

Bonus

COLLECTOR'S PIECE

I have been a compulsive collector – starting with stamps, like most kids those days, and then moving on to matchboxes, rubber stamps underneath Cola caps, and comics.

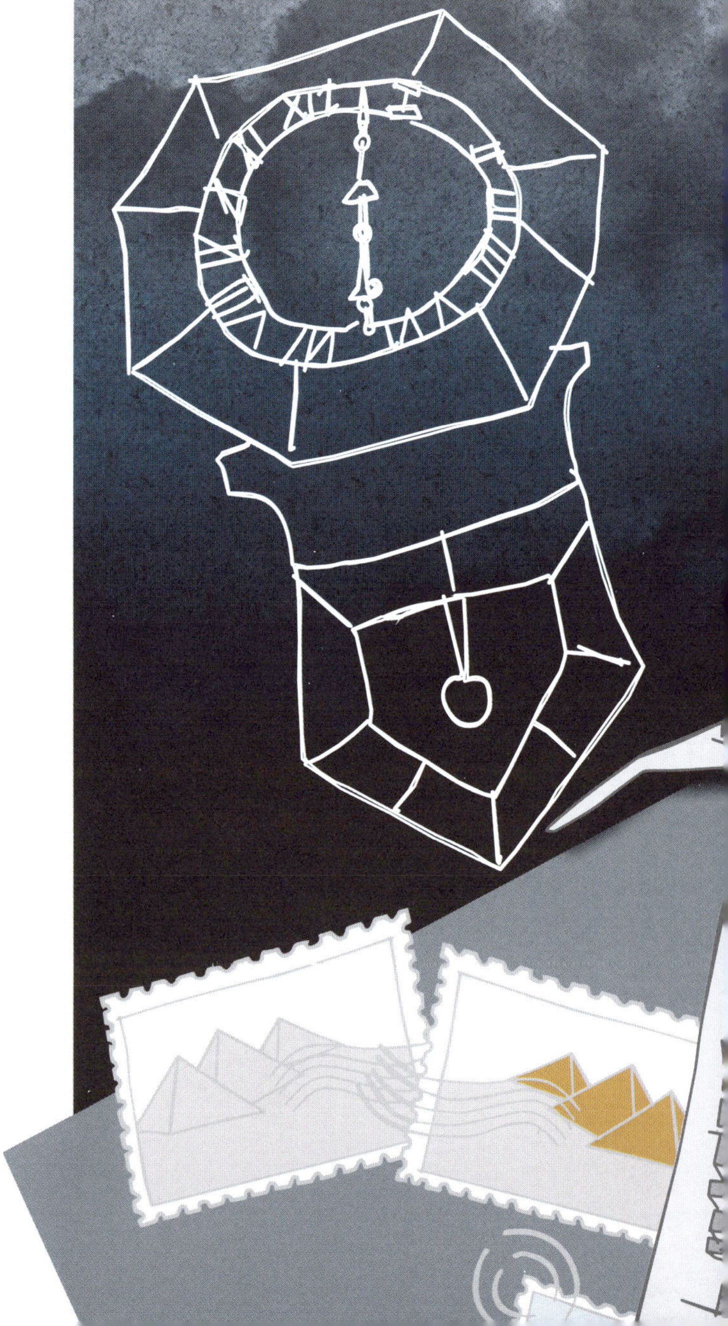

Stamps were peeled off letter envelopes, matchboxes were picked up from the neighbourhood streets and Cola caps were collected during trips to the market. Only the comics were bought, but none were collectibles at the time. I sometimes saved cutouts of cricket images from newspapers and pasted them into a book.

From the ages of fifteen to twenty-five, studies took priority for me. It was only after that I dived deep into collecting with greater passion and obsession as my resources and finances improved. When I travelled internationally, I collected coins, postcards, masks and model cars. For the past two decades, though, I have been a serious book collector, specializing in rare and signed books.

So why do people collect something? Why is collecting things the world's biggest hobby? Why are television shows such as *American Pickers, Antiques Roadshow, Bargain Hunt* and *Pawn Stars* so popular? Why are there more male collectors than female? Here are some of the books where you can find the answers.

One of my favourite books on collecting is Hunter Davies's *Confessions of a Collector*. It is a perfect introduction to and a personal celebration of the strangely compelling world of collecting. I felt at peace after reading the book, knowing that there was a reason behind my madness.

Another of my favourites is *On Collecting* by Susan Pearce. Academic in nature, this book is invaluable to museum professionals, students and cultural historians, and also to any reader who is curious about this social phenomenon. Pearce, in her book, explores the psychology of collecting – why do we bestow value on certain objects and how does this add meaning to our lives? But if you want to know the range of things people collect, you must read *Men and Collections* by Brian Jenner. Apparently people collect everything from beer mats, bean tins and lawnmowers to airline sick bags!

My current book collection serves multiple purposes – reading in order to write, sometimes reading for pleasure, and at other times, buying a book only because it is a rare collectible. Every collector will tell you that the joy is in the hunt, and that often, once you get the object, you lose interest.

Collectors also collect for the joy of completion. I often buy a sub-category of rare books (signed books by Nobel laureates) and then spend time and energy trying to complete the collection or reach a landmark (such as hundred books signed by Nobel laureates). Once a category is completed, I move to the next, grateful for the immense learning that occurs in the process of collecting. I must admit, my collecting has also become my escape and distraction in an otherwise busy schedule. My wife may be best suited to share the downsides of my obsession – we will keep that for another occasion.

Susan Pearce writes that every third person collects something. Famous collectors include President Franklin D. Roosevelt (stamps), Andy Warhol (anything interesting), Ian Fleming (first editions), Tom Hanks (typewriters) and Rachel Whiteread (doll houses). Every collector collects for their own reason. With rapidly changing technology, many items have become instantly collectable – typewriters, mechanical clocks and telephones. And as people's disposable income and leisure time increase, collecting will continue to flourish and grow.

As John Windle, the famous antiquarian bookseller told me: 'People collect to stay alive and have a reason to live.'

Fine Press Books

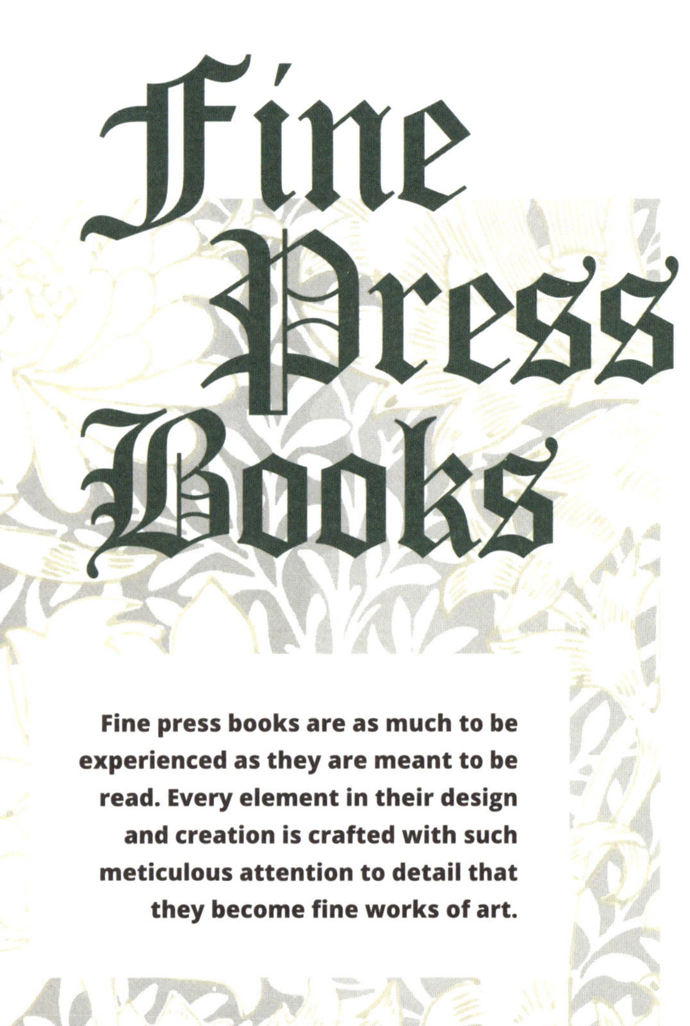

Fine press books are as much to be experienced as they are meant to be read. Every element in their design and creation is crafted with such meticulous attention to detail that they become fine works of art.

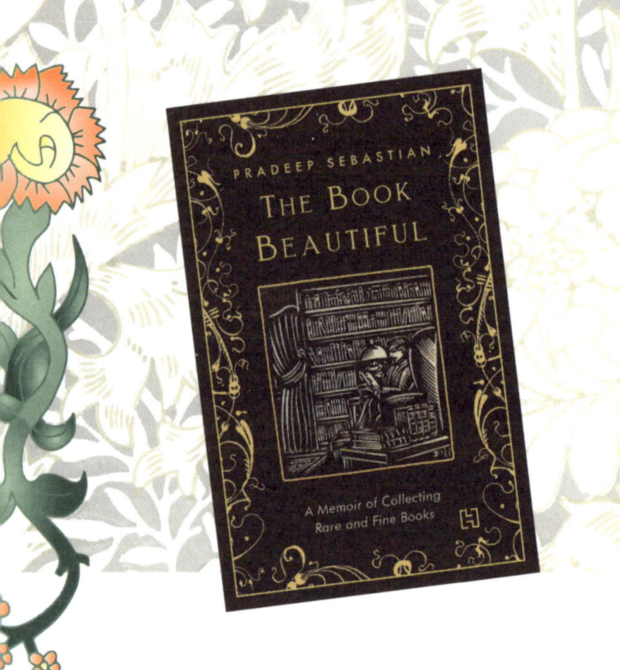

These books are produced in limited quantities using high-quality materials and refined techniques, and are prized by collectors and bibliophiles for their beauty and craftsmanship.
The mid-nineteenth century saw the birth of the arts and crafts movement in the UK, which was a reaction to the perceived decline in aesthetic standards that was associated with factory-made products. A major influence on the movement was the English designer William Morris, who founded the Kelmscott Press in 1891 towards the end of his life. During its seven-year operation, the private press (another term for fine press) published fifty-three books printed by hand in limited editions of around three hundred copies. Morris designed the typefaces and ornamental borders, chose the inks and handmade paper, and involved himself in every aspect of production. Inspired by the Kelmscott Press, Elbert Hubbard from East Aurora, New York, founded the Roycroft Press in 1893.

One of my favourite fine press books is Arion Press's *Sea of Cortez* by John Steinbeck and Edward F. Ricketts. First published by Viking Press on 5 December 1941, the book remains an overlooked masterpiece. In honour of the authors' landmark 1940

voyage, Arion Press brought new life to a monumental collaboration – part detailed scientific study, part philosophical and spiritual exploration. Steinbeck and Ricketts set off to investigate the narrow gulf between Baja, California, and mainland Mexico (now referred to as the Gulf of California), which encompasses over nine hundred islands and remains one of the most biologically abundant and biodiverse ecosystems in the world. Written with lush description and wry humour, *Sea of Cortez* is at once a journal of an intimate friendship and an ecological rallying cry. What makes the Arion Press edition special is that it incorporates into its design, reclaimed wood from the *Western Flyer*, the vessel on which the two men travelled.

While there are less than hundred private press publishers in the world today (e.g., Limited Editions Club, Folio Society, Term Press and Black Sparrow Press), Arion Press is considered one of the best. It is the last printing facility in the US where books are made from start to finish – from the type to the binding – by hand, under one roof, employing the letterpress printing technique (all letterpress printed books are considered fine press, but not all fine press books are printed via letterpress). One of their masterpieces is *Moby Dick*, which came out in 1979, and was sold out before publication. I was fortunate to see and feel a copy of this landmark book. The paper is watermarked with an image of a whale – you see it when you hold it against the light. Today the book costs 30 times the initial price.

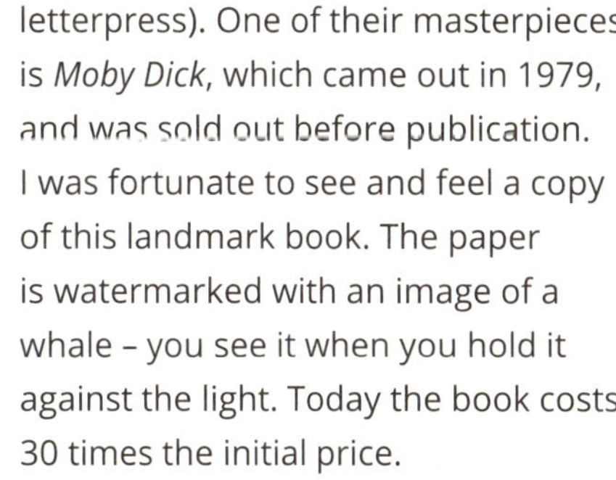

The two standard reference books about fine presses and their books are *The Private Presses* by Colin Franklin and *The Private Press* by Roderick Cave – the latter is more wide-ranging, although the former is more interesting. I will also recommend *The Book Beautiful* by Pradeep Sebastian. Though the book is not just about Pradeep's love for fine press books, it gives a great overview for every book lover to discover these rare fine press copies. The special edition comes with a letterpress keepsake from the celebrated fine press of Robert LoMascolo.

Fine press books offer sensory transcendence – whether it is a connection with the binder who glued the pages together carefully, a wistful affection for something delightful and unusual, or an examination of a fragile thought. Fine press books are vehicles that feed a bibliophile's passion.

It is not surprising that some readers buy a book just for the uniqueness of its cover. It is why my wife has often bought multiple copies of the same Agatha Christie book, especially vintage editions.

Studies show you only have eight seconds to persuade the reader to take a chance on your book. How do you make it count? The answer lies in the book cover.

Classics such as *Gone with the Wind, Pride and Prejudice* and *Wuthering Heights* are often released with new covers. The novel *1984* by George Orwell has seen more than forty-two different covers, my favourite being the one with the 'Big Brother' eyes, designed by Adronauts Berlin (Patrick Pichler and Wolfgang Warzilek).

Classic examples of a cover reinforcing the message of the title are *Made To Stick* by Chip Heath and Dan Heath that has an aptly placed, sticky duct tape on the cover while *The End of Food* by Paul Roberts has an image of an empty styrofoam package.

Some covers of Vladimir Nabokov's *Lolita* have managed to take 'suggestive' to a whole new level. In fact, there are many book covers that show sexually explicit content in subtle but provocative ways, like that of *Tampa* by Alissa Nutting that has a buttonhole turned into a vagina, and of *Sex and the Citadel* by Shereen El Feki, which shows how sex is all wrapped up in religion, tradition and culture.

Artist Archie Ferguson makes a visual pun on the title of Kevin Brockmeier's *The Brief History of the Dead* with his cover design of disembodied hands, their creepiness accentuated by the black-and-white colour scheme. A book I bought for the sheer genius of the cover was *Look Who's Back* by German writer Timur Vermes, a satire about Adolf Hitler and twenty-first-century Germany.

But as hard as it is to imagine, there was a time when books had no covers. Up to about the mid-eighteenth century, hardcover books only had boards. Later, publishers began issuing these books wrapped in plain paper covers, their function merely to keep the hardboards of the book free from dust – which is how it probably came to be called the dust wrapper. In the nineteenth century, when publishers began to compete aggressively to sell books, the idea of making such plain wrappers attractive came into being. Interestingly, these blank covers were initially imprinted with not illustrations but advertisements for future books from the publisher.

The book jacket has evolved into a variety of styles. One significant transition was what Chip Kidd brought into being – the photographic collage. Kidd began experimenting with a marriage of letters and photographic objects and has since become one of the most famous book-cover designers. His most notable was for Michael Crichton's novel *Jurassic Park*, which was so successful that it was carried over into the marketing for the film adaptation. *Chip Kidd: Book One* is a collection of all his book covers and designs, as well as hundreds of developmental sketches and concepts. It is annotated by Kidd and many of the best-selling authors he's worked with. One study of Kidd's work notes that he 'uses every surface of a hardcover jacket – the spine, the back, the flaps – to escape the two-dimensional world of graphic design'.

When it comes to magazine covers, the *New Yorker* is unbeatable. I have over the years collected issues of *TIME* magazine that have Indians on the cover. *Cover Story* by Steven Heller and Louise Fili showcases memorable magazine covers that are the result of successful collaborations between graphic designers, writers and marketers. This is commercial illustration at its most alluring and sophisticated. Hence, it is no surprise that many collect rare magazine covers in addition to rare and unique books.

Some even collect yellowbacks. A yellow-back or yellowback was a cheap novel published in Britain in the second half of the nineteenth century. Developed in the 1840s to compete with the 'penny dreadful', they were marketed as entertaining reading and had brightly coloured covers.

Among Indian books, I had always loved the simplicity of the covers of Ruskin Bond and R.K. Narayan books; their colours and artwork resonated with the characters in the stories. Speaking of Indian books, I spent considerable time with my graphic artist, Sriram Jagannathan, when we were developing the cover of *GRIT: The Major Story*. A book cover cannot be an afterthought; it should stir the curiosity of potential buyers and lead readers through the story. It is heartening that there are several talented book designers working in India today, some as full-time, in-house graphic artists for our major publication houses and others who freelance. While many of them are influenced by the work done at the US and the UK publishing houses, they also bring their own desi slant to their design work.

There are so many books being published that to keep track of all the covers is simply impossible. But the real good ones will remain with a reader for a long time. It was Orhan Pamuk who famously said: 'Book covers are like people's faces: either they remind us of a lost happiness or they promise blissful worlds we have yet to explore. That is why we gaze at book covers as passionately as we do faces.' And whoever said, don't judge a book by its cover!

'A book fanatic like you needs to have the smallest book in the world: *The Lord's Prayer* in seven languages, produced by the Gutenberg Museum in my home town, Mainz.' That was the farewell gift from my colleague, Michael Depner, after I took on a new role.

MINIATURE BOOKS

TREASURES

Considered the smallest book in the world at the time of printing, the 5 mm × 5 mm, 16-page book, *The Lord's Prayer*, was produced as a fundraiser for the reconstruction of the Gutenberg Museum.

That gift was the trigger for me to understand more about miniature books – publishing history and the fascination they evoke, especially among book collectors. If you want to know all about miniature books, a must-read is Anne C. Bromer and Julian I. Edison's *Miniature Books: 4000 Years of Tiny Treasures*. The very first miniature book that I procured was a signed copy of the rare *At the Feet of the Master* by J. Krishnamurti. Another of my favourites was Rabindranath Tagore's *Fireflies.*

No bigger than 3 inches in length, breadth and width, miniature books are not just intricately designed but are also important artefacts in the development of books through history, reflecting some of the finest examples of various binding styles. High-quality editions include the exquisite 1896 leather-bound *Galileo a Madama Cristina di Lorena*, published by the Salmin Brothers in Padua. In 'fly's eye' 2.5 type, it reportedly took an entire month to print its 30 pages and is considered the smallest book to be set by hand.

Pushing the limits of what a miniature can be, Robert Chaplin, in 2007, printed *Teeny Ted from Turnip Town* using an ion beam. It fits nicely on the width of a human hair. The book's size is 0.07 mm × 0.10 mm and is certified by the Guinness World Records as the world's smallest reproduction of a printed book.

Faith as a subject is the Goliath in the world of diminutive volumes. The sacred writings of the religions of the world, with an emphasis on Judeo-Christian scriptures, serve as content. Excerpts from the Old and New Testaments with special editions of the Psalter are popular texts. But there are Jewish, Muslim, Hindu and Zoroastrian religious texts, too, in the form of miniature books, most of them brought out by Bryce Publishers Ltd. They have even issued a microminiature edition of the Bhagavad Gita in Sanskrit. Rarest of all Bryce religious miniatures is the *Khordeh Avesta*, the prayers and texts of Zoroastrianism, in Gujarati.

One of the most interesting events that the miniature book is associated with is the moon landing. When Apollo 11 landed on the moon on 20 July 1969, crew member Edwin E. 'Buzz' Aldrin had taken a miniature book along for the momentous event. It was the autobiography of Robert Goddard (roman), considered the father of modern rocketry.

Later, three hundred copies of an approximately 1 inch × 1 inch (2.5 cm × 2.5 cm) Bible flew on board NASA's February 1971 Apollo 14 mission. Each printed with 1,245 pages and 7,73,746 words of the Christian holy scriptures, they were not the space agency's official cargo, though. Rather, they were carried by moonwalker Edgar Mitchell as a favour to a group of faithful NASA employees who prayed for the safety of the astronauts. Two hundred copies were kept aboard the orbiting Apollo 14 command module while the remaining hundred descended to the moon's surface with Mitchell and mission commander Alan Shepard on board the lunar module. Collectively, the copies became known as the 'First Lunar Bible'.

Miniature book collections have been owned by famous people such as Queen Mary of England and US President Franklin D. Roosevelt and displayed in institutions including The British Library, The Library of Congress, and the Harvard and Yale libraries. Clubs and societies, such as the Miniature Book Society, which began in 1983, hold annual conferences attended by enthusiasts from around the world and bring out magazines devoted to this form, as well as newsletters that keep the community informed of what's happening in this 'small' world.

There are some publishers that specialize in miniature books; Miniaturbuchverlag Leipzig (Miniature Book Publishing House) is one. Their books are entirely manufactured and assembled in Germany and comes in their own custom-made, protective slip cases. I got Lewis Carroll's *Alice's Adventures in Wonderland* from here.

One of the most charming aspects of miniature collecting is shelving them – you can't put them on your bookcase with the other books because they would simply disappear among all the large spines. Thus, another tradition has been to own custom-made miniature bookshelves; there are shelf makers devoted to doing just this.

I was pleased to learn of a silk screen printer in Chennai who has begun printing their own miniature books. Eswar Kumar recently received a Limca Record for the smallest Tirukkural book, also winning a Limca Record in 2006 for the smallest screen-printed book. Apparently it took him two years to finish his latest miniature book of the Gita.

I was just as excited to learn of an Indian collector of miniatures, Siddharth Mohanty in Bhubaneswar, who has over four thousand miniature books not only in English but in several Asian languages. The oldest in his collection is from the sixteenth century. One of his focuses has been collecting various miniature editions of the Gita. Well, good things do come in small packages!

It was by a complete accident that I first came across a Big Little Book (BLB). One of the collectors in Bengaluru was selling his collection of rare books, and I was interested in acquiring them.

When I looked at the big little book lot, I came across an odd-sized book titled *The Man from U.N.C.L.E.: The Calcutta Affair* by George S. Elrick. It did not interest me at that point, until I came across a huge collection of similar-sized books at Bells Bookstore in Palo Alto, California, many years later. That's when I found myself interested and bought a rare copy of Edgar Rice Burroughs's *The Son of Tarzan*, signed by Gordon Scott, the actor who played Tarzan in five movies released between 1955 and 1960. Big Little Books have now become collectibles and are prized for their impeccable design and classic illustrations.

The Great Depression gave rise to inexpensive forms of entertainment: ten-cent motion pictures, free radio programmes and cheap reading materials. They came from the few industries that prospered during the decade, and their influence was felt deeply and is warmly remembered by millions. The ten-cent BLBs and other forms of entertainment provided escapes from reality and stirred people's hopes and fantasies of what an ideal world would look like.

The first BLB, *The Adventures of Dick Tracy, Detective #707,* was published in December 1932 by the Whitman Publishing Company of Racine, Wisconsin. It was released in time for the Christmas season, marking the beginning of the BLB's golden age: 1932 to 1938. In mid-1938, Whitman and several competing companies changed their copyrighted logos: Whitman's Big Little Books became Better Little Books. From 1938–1950, the books slowly faded away due to economic and societal changes, and stiff competition from comic books. The series continued until its end in the 1960s.

BLBs were small, compact books designed with a captioned illustration opposite each page of text. A BLB was typically 3 inches wide and 4.5 inches high, with 212 to 432 pages, making an approximate thickness of 1.5 inches. Inside the book, the design usually displayed full-page black-and-white illustrations (later books had colour) on the right side, facing the pages of text on the left. Stories were often related to ongoing radio programmes. Some of the biggest stars in these series include Buck Rogers, Dick Tracey, Betty Boop, Alley Oop and Mickey Mouse.

Over one thousand and one hundred BLBs were published by various publications. They seem to transcend being just books. Small, blocky and colourful, the books have the aroma and sepia glow of old newsprint, and they hold the promise of adventure, laughter and love. Some BLBs, such as the *The Return of the Phantom*, were flip books where the character appears to move when the pages are flipped in quick succession.

'Make mine a small one' was an essay published in the *New York Times* where author Powell Lawrence Clark talks of the pleasures of small books. Apart from the fact that they occupy less space in your home, one advantage is that you could hold it in one hand and read while holding a cup of tea in the other.

If you need to read one book about BLB, I would recommend *The Big Book of Big Little Books* by Bill Borden, which features jacket art and illustrations from rare BLBs. Needless to say, the author has been a lifelong collector of BLBs. I wonder if the pandemic saw the return of cheap forms of entertainment, similar to BLBs.

Arion Press is one of the hidden gems of San Francisco. As a book lover, I am embarrassed that I only discovered it (thanks to Nicholas A. Basbanes) after living in the Bay Area for eight years.

IS THE LAST HANDMADE BOOK THE ANTITHESIS TO TECHNOLOGY?

Arion Press is one of the hidden gems of San Francisco. As a book lover, I am embarrassed that I only discovered it (thanks to Nicholas A. Basbanes) after living in the Bay Area for eight years. Mentioned in the book *111 Places in San Francisco That You Must Not Miss* by Floriana Peterson, Arion's historic production facility includes a letterpress print shop with a one-of-a-kind collection of historic metal typefaces, the foundry of Mackenzie & Harris (M&H) that has continuously operated for over hundred years, and a complete hand book bindery, all housed in a fourteen thousand square foot industrial building in San Francisco's Presidio National Park. The press is designated an 'irreplaceable cultural treasure' by the National Trust for Historic Preservation. I was fortunate to get a personalized tour and talk to some of the people who worked there.

Arion Press pairs great artists with great literature to create beautiful books by hand. The entire experience seems like the antithesis to technology. But, is it? Technology is defined as 'a discourse or treatise on an art or the arts'. The root of the word technology comes from the Greek word techne which means art, craft or skill. Seeing a letterpress machine at work, as we did on our visit to Arion Press in San Francisco, makes the word come alive. Running since the 1940s, the presses are an engineering feat and a marvel of human ingenuity.

It used to be that everyone working with technology was a technologist in the sense of being a craftsperson. Every member of the Apple Macintosh team was picked specifically because they were artists and craftspeople. Steve Jobs even encouraged them to think of themselves as artists and sign their work. It used to be that technologists knew what they were making and why.

By comparison, today's engineer knows only his narrow slice of code. The machine is too intricate for any one person to fully grasp. The technologist has become the assembly line worker, focused only on the throughput of his part.

What does it do to engineers to lose their connection with the larger purpose of their work?

We (Rana Chakrabarty and I) visited Arion Press to seek some answers to this question. Every bookmaker we met had worked there for ten years or more – the current typecaster had taken over from a person who had worked in the foundry for sixty-five years. When asked why he did this, day in and day out, he answered simply, "Oh, I enjoy it. I also do this in my spare time." Chris Godek, a veteran typecaster in the foundry, replied: 'I enjoy the craftsmanship aspect and keeping a craft alive'. Rochelle Youk, the bindery manager, responded: 'I enjoy repetitive manual labor'.

These responses are the opposite of what you would expect to hear from an engineer in 'high-end' technology, who might say, 'it's cutting-edge' or 'it pays very well' or 'the level of automation increases my productivity'. Yet, when engineers from large companies visit Arion Press, they are entranced by the manual nature of the work. They recognize that in giving up craftsmanship in the pursuit of technology, productivity and efficiency, something has gone awry between the head and the hand.

By all counts, Arion Press is not efficient. It produces only three books a year. Each book, however, is breathtakingly beautiful and awe-inspiring to the extent that it embodies the spirit of 'allusive typography' and the book's essence. The cover for Steinbeck's *Sea of Cortez*, for example, has a piece of wood sourced from the very ship mentioned in the book.

Ge Wang, who heads the Stanford Center for Computer Research in Music and Acoustic (CCRMA) says, in his book *Artful Design*, that technology should create calm. He advocates that engineers should be responsible not for making the best widget but for creating 'needlessly beautiful' experiences that give us a glimpse of the sublime – like Arion Press's books do.

The lesson from Arion Press, if there is one, is that speed disconnects us and moves us into our heads. We become more efficient and productive but also joyless. And joy comes from slowing down and performing the labour of love with our hands.

We may not be able to stop the growth in platforms any more than automotive manufacturers can stop the growth in the assembly line. There are real benefits to millions of consumers that accrue from the efficiencies of scale. We can, however, choose whether the assembly line makes machines out of engineers, or as we are seeing in Tesla, makes engineers technologists again, responsible for the machines but not a part of them.

For those engineers who feel trapped inside the machine, there is a way out. Technology has severed our connection to humanity, but humanity is like a weed. Give it a little space, and it'll grow right back and take hold everywhere.

Make a little time, every day or every week, to work with your hands on something you of love. If you're not a technologist, work with wood. If that's not possible, make a meal. Pick any material that requires you to work with your hands. Make something that creates calm. Make something sublime.

Is it not ironical that Silicon Valley, which is at the centre of all technology change, also houses the last hand-printing press that, in its own small way, is pulling humans in the opposite direction.

the origin of illuminated manuscripts

I discovered very recently that illuminated manuscripts were the origin of Western painting. Those European Renaissance masters didn't create their oils on canvas from out of the blue.

The art form of illuminated manuscripts took root in the sixteenth century when illustrators who created miniature landscapes and figures on the pages of manuscripts decided to branch off into making 'paintings' as we know them, and then decided to sell them.

Before the invention of printing in the fifteenth century, books were painstakingly copied by hand (hence called manuscript). The finest were illuminated with brilliant colours and real gold. They weren't just for show; gilded illustrations decorated important passages to highlight their significance. In addition, when light reflected from candles or sunlight, it would make it seem that the whole book was glowing. It would take a team of illuminators several years to complete a single book. Many medieval manuscripts still survive today, fully preserved, with their colours just as vivid as the day they were illustrated. Of all the illuminated manuscripts from this period, the *Book of Hours* was, by far, the most popular and the most frequently commissioned by both the aristocracy and the middle classes. It clearly was the bestseller of its time.

A selection of these splendid pages is presented in *Time Sanctified* by Roger S. Wieck, along with a detailed discussion of their importance and their contents. The *Books of Hours*, a prayer book for the laity, contains, at its heart, a series of prayers devoted to the Virgin Mary, which were meant to be recited at seven specified times during the day. Highly skilled calligraphers and painters were commissioned to execute the finest decoration with the most luxurious materials, such as gold, silver and lapis lazuli.

If you are a beginner to the illuminated manuscript (just like I was), *The Illuminated Manuscript* by Janet Backhouse is an excellent introduction. It's not too long, so it won't overwhelm you. This book provided the foundation for my first steps into researching medieval illumination for my column. What is illumination? Why were books illuminated, and what types of books were considered worthy of illumination? Who were some of the most famous medieval illuminators?

A book that I read to my thirteen-year-old son that I enjoyed was *Marguerite Makes a Book* by Bruce Robertson and illustrated by Kathryn Hewitt. This book, set in fifteenth-century Paris, is about Marguerite, the young daughter of a manuscript illuminator, who has to help her ageing father illuminate a *Book of Hours* for a very important lady or her father will lose both his commission and his reputation. This beautifully illustrated book follows Marguerite through each step of her illuminated book's creation. You will be transported to medieval Paris and Marguerite's workshop as you read and gaze the pictures. This book was inspired by a rare collection of illuminated manuscripts held by the J. Paul Getty Museum.

Two of my prized possessions are a twentieth century facsimile of *Book of Hours* in colours and gold and an 1842 Henry Bohn deluxe edition of twenty-five copies of Joseph Strutt's *A Complete View of the Dress and Habits of the People of England.* The *Book of Hours* reproduction is considered one of the finest modern facsimiles for its colour reproduction and the use of 22-carat gold illumination. Printed to a limited edition of 980 copies, it has 157 colour miniatures highlighted in gold with 714 pages. The 1842 Bohn edition of Strutt's *A Complete View of the Dress and Habits of the People of England* with the extra hand-coloured plates and illuminated in gold is scarce and is absolutely gorgeous.

I have often wondered what the point is of holding on to these illustrated manuscripts. I suppose it is the thrill of owning something as beautiful and rare as the Taj Mahal or the Pyramids, with viewing access granted only to me.

Perhaps the most touching instance of marginalia - the jottings or scribbles of readers found in books—is in the novel *S* by J.J. Abrams and Doug Dorst.

CHATTING IN THE MARGINS

Two readers - a man and a woman using the same library reference copy - meet and fall in love because they began reading each other's margin notes. Not only do they discover each other, but they also stumble on a mystery that only marginalia can decode. *S* beautifully exemplifies the notion that reading each other's marginalia can be a form of vital communication, a code or shortcut to someone's mind and heart.

Perhaps the most famous book on the subject is H.J. Jackson's *Marginalia: Readers Writing in Books*. This bestseller made the study of margin notes popular, escalating an interest in marginalia. Jackson tells us that it was possibly Samuel Taylor Coleridge, the Romantic poet, who first suggested the word 'marginalia' to refer to the exchange of notes between him and essayist Charles Lamb. They had a wonderful conversation going in the margins of books - each would borrow the same copy, and when it was returned to the other, the scribbles of both would be read.

The most recent book on margin jottings illustrates the intimacy and depth of even anonymous 'leavings' in library books. *Letter to a Future Lover* by Ander Monson is an anthology of very short essays on marginal inscriptions from borrowers of library books. The subtitle of the book says it all: 'Marginalia, Errata, Secrets, Inscriptions and Other Ephemera Found in Libraries.' Monson makes a striking point in one of the essays: 'of the thousands of books in a library, you pick one, a heavy tome printed in the 19th century, and you realize as you hold it that the author has spent a lifetime researching and writing it. And yet if no one checks out the book, and it remains unread, so much labour has gone waste.' However, this is the glorious point he makes - if someone were to borrow it that very day and read it, suddenly the library has made it possible for that book to have a new life. Now if that reader were to scribble in the book and return it, the book's life is extended. Monson

CHATTING IN THE MARGINS

notes: 'What you write in response to the book – how you mark it up or how you take it with you and reproduce it – that's a part of the book too.'

Marginalia becomes a collectible when it comprises annotations by a hand that belongs to a famous person. Bibliophiles often find books with the margin notes and scribbles of authors, artists, thinkers, activists, world leaders and so on. Imagine if you were to come upon an ordinary edition of a physics textbook in a rare-book fair and open the pages to find Einstein's pencil notes in the margins! One of the most prolific marginalists was Vladimir Nabokov. A collector came across an anthology of short stories once owned by the Russian-American master of prose. He discovered that Nabokov, who was also a renowned professor, had actually graded each story in the book with a B minus or C plus or just a B, and so on. Only two stories had an A plus: a J.D. Salinger story and a story by himself. Other famous margin-jotters have been John Donne, Ben Jonson, Emily Dickinson and Virginia Woolf.

But perhaps, equally interesting are the margin notes of ordinary, anonymous, previous owners or readers of a secondhand book. Very often there is violent disagreement – 'No! No way!' – or sometimes hearty approval – 'Absolutely true!' In *Used Books* by William H. Sherman, he asks: 'What if we saw the marginalia of readers from previous centuries? Would they not reveal a lot about how ordinary people felt and thought then?'

The marginalia of today's reader is most likely found not scribbled in the physical copy of a book but instead as 'shared' comments on social media platforms. What is lost is the visibility of handwritten notes. We know that Kindle now provides for margin notes, so we have to factor in digital marginalia as well. The thrill of marginalia for me is that it is private, quiet, uncommented on. Once you've shared it with others digitally, they are not personal anymore.

Critic Sam Anderson writing in *New York Magazine* said that marginalia were 'not just to passively read but to fully enter a text, to collaborate with it, to mingle with an author on some kind of primary textual plane.' Not everyone likes to scribble inside books, though. Some are horrified at the thought. The famous children's book illustrator Maurice Sendak once recounted a funny incident during one of his book signing tours. He was in a bookshop signing copies children were bringing to him, and one boy said he didn't want Sendak to sign it as it would spoil the book. Sendak readily agreed and gave the book back to him without daring to autograph it.

It was Anne Fadiman, American essayist and reporter, who said all readers are made up of only two classes: those who scribble in books and those who don't. Those who make margin notes turn the whole exercise into a conversation. It could become an argument between the reader and the writer. Or just the reverse: a dialogue between the writer and the reader.

AN ODE TO ODD BOOKS

What attracts you to high concept books is that even after you've read them, you can still look forward to taking them out of your shelf and exploring their external features.

As a fan of printed books, I am drawn to their physical shape as well. I am fascinated by books whose form communicates their intent as much as the content does. I prefer to call these odd books 'high-concept books' since the book's shape is based on an underlying notion.

I didn't know that the 'Abrams' in the novel *S* written by Doug Dorst and and conceptulized by J.J. Abrams is the Hollywood sensation J.J. Abrams who created the *Star Wars* and *Star Trek* reboots. The real surprise was waiting inside the book, though. With faded covers – a design that resembles something created in the 1920s – and a library accession number across the spine, it appears like a used book discarded by a library. The design concept becomes clear only when you start reading the story. The plot revolves around a man and woman who borrow the same copy of a library book, leave margin notes on the pages and become interested in meeting each other. The book they borrow is *Ship of Theseus* by V.M. Straka, a pseudonym. The man and woman then try to figure out the author's real identity. And here is where surprises galore begin to emerge in the physical make-up of this extraordinary book.

Laid into the book are all manner of inserts: postcards, photocopies, handwritten pages from legal pads, newspaper clippings, a hand-drawn map on a napkin, letters, margin notes in two different handwritings and even an old book slip-cased inside a box. To prevent these objects from slipping out, the publisher has ensured that all copies sent to bookstores are shrink-wrapped. Abrams said the book is 'a celebration of the analog' in our digital era.

Another book that plays around with its appearance is Mark Z. Danielewski's *House of Leaves*. It is amazing how the shape of the text on the pages mimics the plot. A man enters a strange house, and as he explores it, the house changes shape and contour. To suggest the shape-shifting nature of the story and the house, the text as it is laid out changes shape.

Yet another book that makes a striking impact in how it presents its material is *The Gorgeous Nothings*, where the poetry of Emily Dickinson is magnified using photographs to present them in actual size. This is also a facsimile of the poet's original manuscripts. Dickinson mostly wrote on envelopes, often scribbling her poems as they came to her. This book presents all fifty-two of those scribbled covers.

Lastly, a mention must be made of *Building Stories* by Chris Ware, a box containing various text objects that you, the reader, can assemble in any fashion to make a story out of. Writing about this graphic novel with avant garde elements, *Booklist* describes this as a 'box containing 14 differently sized, formatted, and bound pieces: books, pamphlets, broadsheets, scraps, and even a unfoldable board that would be at home in a Monopoly box... this graphic novel (if it can even be called that) mimics the kaleidoscopic nature of memory itself – fleeting, contradictory, anchored to a few significant moments, and a heavier burden by the day'.

Every time you open a high-concept book, you end up exploring new features whether it is looking at the strange pages inside *House of Leaves*, or poring over all the inserts in *S* by taking them out of the book and putting them back in, or shuffling the text in *Building Stories* according to your fancy.

I would really like to see such high-concept books coming out of India, too. They might be priced a little more than the regular trade edition, but to a lover of the book as an object, they would be a delight.

A visit to Morgan Library & Museum in New York gave me a chance to view many landmarks in printing history. Pierpont Morgan, the most influential financier in US history, was a voracious collector, acquiring art objects in virtually every medium.

LANDMARKS IN PRINTING HISTORY

To fulfil his father's dream of making the library and its treasures available to scholars and the public, Pierpont Morgan's son J.P. Morgan transformed it into a public institution.

I spent most of my time in the Morgan Library, which had several volumes of European literature from the sixteenth through the twentieth centuries. The walls, reaching 30 feet, are lined floor to ceiling with triple tiers of bookcases. While Shakespeare's *First Folio* (one of the three Morgan copies of the Folio is always on public view in the East room) and the Gutenberg Bible are the most famous collectibles, my favourite was an Albert Einstein-signed version of the formula E=mc2.

While I was thinking about what would be worth collecting, facsimiles of landmarks in printing crossed my mind. Why just facsimiles? Because notable examples of printing since its invention are simply beyond the budget of most individual collectors. The first printing landmark facsimile I got was a reproduction of a page from the 'Genesis' chapter in the Gutenberg Bible that the Library of Congress had made in 1972. It came in a specially made, large orange folder and laid within was the page printed in three colours. There are so many facsimiles of the various Shakespeare folios that acquiring one was easy enough (I bought *As You Like It*).

Rather than only looking at early examples of landmarks in printing, I turned to the nineteenth and twentieth centuries. Victorian printing is known for an explosion of decorative and colour printing – in fact, the idea of the sumptuous 'gift book' began here. A landmark book in this century was Henry Shaw's *Dresses and Decorations of the Middle Ages*, published by William Pickering. This book faithfully reproduced several aspects of the Middle Ages by hand-drawn engravings. It was published in two editions, one black and white, and the other, a deluxe edition in colour. I was lucky enough to find both editions (though, I have only volume one of the deluxe version).

From the twentieth century, my first acquisition was something called *Liber Librorum*, an international project from 1955, which invited the world's best graphic designers to create their own version of setting a page from the Bible. This project was undertaken to celebrate the five hundredth anniversary of the Gutenberg Bible in Stockholm, Sweden. The challenge was that each designer was given the same page from the Bible, a page from Genesis, and they each had to come up with a different way of setting the page. About two dozen printing samples from famous designers were laid into a cloth portfolio and though fifteen hundred sets were printed, only five hundred were for sale to the public, making it scarce. The rest of the portfolio sets were given rather than sold to institutions and libraries around the world.

Another wonderful and impressive set of twentieth century printing examples I managed to ferret out was a boxed set from the Society of Printers containing the best works of American printers to celebrate hundred years of the society. This came in a large black box with samples printed through various methods and in many colours.

There were several such examples of printing that I have bought – for instance, National Audubon Society's famous *Birds of North America* and the *Nuremberg Chronicle*, which the first great example of colour printing and the use of colour wood blocks in books.

A facsimile, if faithfully reproduced, can help us recall and celebrate great examples of the printed book and give us a glimpse into its finer aspects. For me, it has been a way of acknowledging the genius and labour of printers and illustrators.

when POLITICIANS write MEMOIRS

Former US president Barack Obama's memoir *A Promised Land* published by Penguin Random House sold a record 8,90,000 copies in the US and Canada within twenty-four hours of its release and 3.3 million (its initial print run) in the first month.

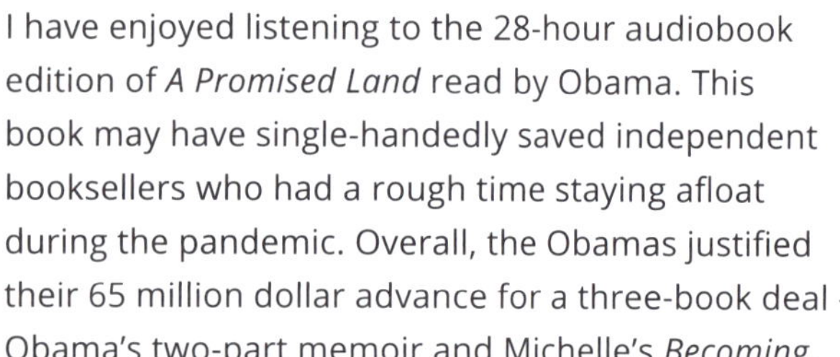

I have enjoyed listening to the 28-hour audiobook edition of *A Promised Land* read by Obama. This book may have single-handedly saved independent booksellers who had a rough time staying afloat during the pandemic. Overall, the Obamas justified their 65 million dollar advance for a three-book deal – Obama's two-part memoir and Michelle's *Becoming*.

As a literary genre, a memoir forms a subclass of autobiography. Although the terms 'memoir' and 'autobiography' are often used interchangeably, there is a subtle difference – an autobiography is your life story from beginning till the present day and a memoir focuses on a specific period (for Obama, it was his presidency). There are many subgenres of memoirs, such as, the travel memoir which foregrounds the places the author has visited, or the celebrity memoir, which is mostly ghostwritten.

Of all the presidential memoirs, *The Personal Memoirs of Ulysses S. Grant* (by Ulysses S. Grant, the eighteenth president of the US) is considered among the finest military memoirs. Written primarily to pay back a loan and support his family, the book focuses on the general's actions during the Civil War. It was published shortly after his death and is still in print today.

Diaries: In Power by British Conservative Member of Parliament Alan Clark is one of the best political memoirs because of its engaging writing, acute observation and dashes of insanity. *The Path to Power*

by Margaret Thatcher, on the other hand, became a bestseller but was boring (and had been written by her assistants).

The first political memoir I read was *The Insider* by P.V. Narasimha Rao, which had invited widespread criticism from all the political parties of India. It is neither an autobiography nor a work of fiction but is a semi-autobiographical work of Rao written in a fast-paced narrative style. It not only describes the dark side of politics but also sheds light on the evolution of India and Indian politics. This book details events from his childhood, all the way up to the early 1970s. His plan was to continue the rest in a sequel which, unfortunately, never materialized. A more objective biography of Narasimha Rao, *The Man Who Remade India*, was written by Vinay Sitapati in 2018.

Compared to the West, where practically every US president and British prime minister pens a memoir after his term, very few Indian prime ministers have followed that path – after Narasimha Rao only I.K. Gujral wrote a memoir, which was called *Matters of Discretion*. I would have loved to read a memoir of Dr Manmohan Singh as it would have given us the perspective of a man who was much admired yet misunderstood. Sanjaya Baru's controversial *The Accidental Prime Minister* was harsher to him than how history will probably judge him. However, he may have been more comfortable writing academic books than dwelling on his prime ministership, or his private life.

Then there are autobiographical works by leaders of national importance such as L.K. Advani's *My Country, My Life*, P. Chidambaram's *Speaking Truth to Power* and Pranab Mukherjee's multi-volume memoir. I also look forward to reading *Furrows in a Field: The Unexplored Life of H.D. Deve Gowda* by Sugata Srinivasaraju this fall. It has been on my to-read list for a while. I hope the book has done justice to someone who has been in public life for nearly seven decades and rose from the very bottom to the very top.

POLITICAL SATIRE IN THE AGE OF TRUMP

Donald Trump's presidency will remain the golden era of political satire. Those presidential tweets provided ample fodder for cartoonists every single day of his four years in the White House. I have been diligently following *The Daily Don* by artist Jesse Duquette who has unfailingly come up with a cartoon daily since the very first day of the Trump administration.

At the end of four years of Trump's presidency, it may well become the best historical evidence of one of the strangest of times in the history of the US. Satire is a literary technique of writing or art which ridicules its subject, often as an intended means of provoking or preventing change. It uses humour, irony, exaggeration or ridicule to expose and criticize people's inanity or vices, particularly in the context of contemporary politics and other topical issues. It is, however, different from parody.

Parody is easy, because it is the laughs that matter, whereas satire is harder because the truth is deeply embedded in it. We should not forget that while humour is important, it is just one of the tools in the toolbox of a satirist. Political satire, of course, has existed almost as long as politics. When people with power act in ways that seem to run counter to good sense or commonly held ethical principles, people with less power find ways to revolt.

In many ways, satirists are visual columnists who stimulate an intellectual discussion, tell uncomfortable truths and talk about topics that are sensitive to people. Satire is a very effective medium as imagery as a language predates the invention of the written word by thirty thousand years with cave paintings and other forms of art. There are so many Trump-related satirical books that picking the best is a hard task.

Garry Trudeau, creator of *Doonesbury* (the first comic strip to receive the Pulitzer Prize in 1975), has three books on Trump – *Yuge!, Sad!* and his latest, *Lewser!* As Trudeau points out, 'With other presidencies, you could forget who was in office for whole stretches of time: weeks, even months. But with Trump, the powerful stench is refreshed daily. There's no escaping it.' And then there's Christopher Buckley's rollicking novel, *Make Russia Great Again*, which has a devoted White House Chief of Staff called Herb Nutterman as the narrator.

The iconic *Punch* was a British weekly magazine of humour and satire established in 1841 by Henry Mayhew and wood-engraver Ebenezer Landells. It was most influential in the 1840s and 1850s, when it helped to coin the term 'cartoon' in its modern sense. It eventually closed down in 2002 but its cartoons are timeless. In India, R.K. Laxman's world-class political cartoons remain the benchmark for political satire. Political satire on Rahul Gandhi is best captured in the short story 'Brunch' by Parvati Sharma, although she does not spare the current dispensation either.

'Making fun of the Gandhis (and the Congress as a whole) has become something of a cottage industry,' said Sharma in a recent interview, adding that her story 'isn't just about the Gandhis, it's also making fun of the age of Modi'. Political satire is an important aspect of democracy, even if it, at times, outrages people. As America's premier political cartoonist, author of *Drawing the Line*, Paul Conrad said, 'Good political cartoons are indeed critical. Sometimes they amuse, sometimes they infuriate. But... the best political cartoons allow us to see the truth more clearly.'

Fascism combines totalitarianism and authoritarianism; it involves an extreme devotion to one's nation over all others and a belief in racial purity.

The Rise of Fascism

FASCISM
A WARNING
MADELEINE ALBRIGHT
New York Times Bestselling Author

Totalitarian, authoritarian, fascism, majoritarianism – these words are used a lot, but what do they really mean? The first three are forms of government characterized by a strong central rule that attempts to control and direct all aspects of individual life through coercion and repression. A totalitarian state has unlimited power and controls virtually every strand of public and private life.

An authoritarian state is characterized by a strong central government that allows people a limited degree of political freedom, but controls individual freedom and the political process without constitutional accountability. A majoritarian government, meanwhile, is run by the majority community, disregarding the views and wishes of the minority.

Modern dictatorships, such as Venezuela under Hugo Chávez and Cuba under Fidel Castro, typify authoritarian governments. While the People's Republic of China under Chairman Mao Zedong was a totalitarian state, modern-day

China is more accurately described as authoritarian because its citizens are allowed limited personal freedoms.

Sri Lanka, where Sinhalas rule the country, opted for majoritarianism. Following the attack on Ukraine, a growing number of analysts called Vladimir Putin's regime 'fascist', meaning that Putin's Russia genuinely resembles Mussolini's Italy or Hitler's Germany where fascism first sprouted.

The recent Ukraine crisis forced me to look back in history to understand what the future may look like. I started by watching the 10-episode documentary *Evolution of Evil* (available for free on YouTube).

It is a great historical summary of Mussolini, Stalin and Hitler in Europe; Gaddafi, Saddam and Osama in West Asia; Mao, Tojo and Kim Jong Il in Asia; and François Duvalier or Papa Doc dictator from Haiti. Will Putin join this list?

Here are some of my insights into the current Ukraine-Russia war. Of the nine nuclear countries, Russia has the largest stockpile of nuclear warheads (6,250) and if Europe and the US sense a real threat, World War III is around the corner. Maybe the only way out is to arrive at a bargaining position where Putin's survival is assured. Or, if his own people turn on him and he gives up his leadership voluntarily, which is impossible to conceive.

The Dictator's Handbook: Why Bad Behavior is Almost Always Good Politics by Bruce Bueno de Mesquita and Alastair Smith has turned conventional wisdom on its head. They introduce a groundbreaking new theory of the real rules of politics: leaders do whatever keeps them in power, regardless of the national interest. While there are many biographies of dictators, I want to focus on what gives rise to authoritarianism.

The Origins of Totalitarianism by Hannah Arendt is a 1951 classic and is profoundly relevant and thought-provoking. From her personal experience of escaping Hitler and the Third Reich, she details the preconditions for the rise of Nazism and Stalinism.
In the 2018 book, *Fascism: A Warning*, Madeline Albright, the first woman to serve as the US Secretary of State, mentions that there is a more virulent threat to international peace and justice now than at any time since the end of World War II. As Primo Levi said, 'Every age has its own fascism' and we are living through ours now.

In one of the oldest books on politics, Plato's *Republic*, written in 375 BCE, a passage describes a dialogue between Socrates and his friends on the nature of different political systems, how they change over time and how one can slowly evolve into another.

In Plato's *Republic*, Socrates makes a shocking statement: 'Tyranny is probably established out of no other regimen than democracy.'

Plato's description of how a demagogue emerges bears an eerie resemblance to Trump's rise: 'A visually appealing demagogue is soon lifted up to protect the interests of the lower class. However, with too much freedom, no requirements for anyone to rule, and having no interest in assessing the background of their rulers, the people become easily persuaded by such a demagogue's appeal to try to satisfy people's common, base, and unnecessary pleasures.'

The Trump years have shown us how fragile the notion of democracy is, and that any constitution is only as good as the people who uphold them. India has had its share of elected autocracy, starting with Indira Gandhi's draconian Emergency rule in the mid-1970s when she ruthlessly but 'legally' undermined civil liberties. In recent times, India fell to its lowest-ever ranking in the Economist Intelligence Unit's democracy index, a drop largely caused by the erosion of civil liberties.

In the book *How Democracies Die*, Steven Levitsky and Daniel Ziblatt remind us that no constitution by itself is enough to save democracy. It is reinforced by two principles: mutual toleration – our dislike of the other party shouldn't mean that we view our opponents as enemies; and forbearance – an elected leader's strength comes from under-utilizing, not over-utilizing his power.

The last few years have seen the rise of demagogues around the world. History has repeatedly shown us that they come to power through elections and are enabled by established mainstream politicians. Hugo Chávez in Venezuela opened an authoritarian door and Nicolás Maduro walked right in. Similarly in Italy, Benito Mussolini came to power by forming an effective government before declaring himself the dictator in 1925. And it was the conservatives who enabled the rise of Hitler in Germany.

Sarah Kendzior is a scholar who has studied autocratic regimes in countries such as Russia. In her book *The View from Flyover Country* she wrote (and warned) about the rise of Trump even before he became president. Her latest book, *Hiding in Plain Sight*, outlines how Trump's rise coincided with the degradation of the American political system and the continual erosion of civil liberties in the country by foreign powers.

CRACY

However, demagogy is not new to America. Larry Tye, author of *Demagogue*, chronicled Senator Joe McCarthy's infamous smear campaign in the 1950s. McCarthy's wild allegations of Communists having infiltrated the US government led to the destruction of many lives. Tye said, 'Trump owes a lot to McCarthy's playbook'.

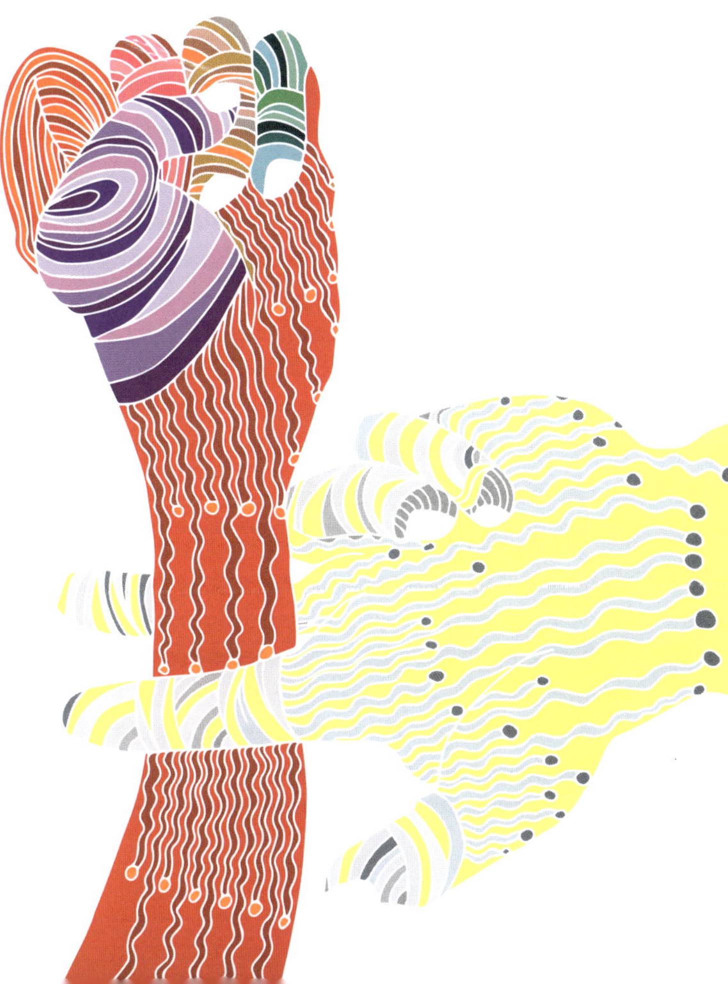

Timothy Snyder, a professor of history at Yale University and historian of the Holocaust, has carefully dissected the events and values that enabled the rise of Hitler and Stalin, and the execution of their catastrophic policies. In his book, *On Tyranny*, he wrote, 'Americans are no wiser than the Europeans who saw democracy yield to fascism, Nazism and communism. Our one advantage is that we might learn from their experience.'

We should remember that Donald Trump is not the cause but the symptom of a deeper problem. While Trump is out of the White House, Trumpism is not. We continue to live in a highly polarized world and that can be the single biggest reason to kill any democracy.

Books have been banned primarily for three reasons – religion, politics and sex. Such bans have often had the opposite effect: the books get so much publicity that owning and reading them becomes an act of rebellion.

WHY reading BANNED BOOKS becomes AN act of REBELLION

On 5 October 1988, India became the first country to ban Salman Rushdie's *The Satanic Verses*, a book that paints unflattering portraits of important figures in the Quran. The ban was invoked by the Finance Ministry, which prohibited importation of the book into the country under the Customs Act of 1962. Though, possession of the book was and is not a crime.

By early 1989, Ayatollah Ruhollah Khomeini, then Supreme Leader of Iran, issued a fatwa calling for Rushdie's death, forcing him into hiding for several years. Bangladeshi author Taslima Nasrin is another writer who has spent decades in exile. Her novel *Lajja* (Shame) is about a Hindu family being attacked by Muslim fanatics. Nasrin suffered a number of physical and other attacks for her graphic language, demand for women's equality and critical scrutiny of Islam. Her book *Dwikhandito* was banned in West Bengal.

Other books that have faced some form of censorship in India for fear of offending religious sentiments are *The Hindus: An Alternative History* by Wendy Doniger and *The Land of the Lingam* by Arthur Miles. The history of a banned book is often a good indicator of the culture of that country.

America's first officially banned book, Thomas Morton's *New English Canaan*, published in 1637, contains the author's compassionate observations about Native Americans and satirises the Puritans. Adolf Hitler's *Mein Kampf*, banned in Germany since 1945, was republished for the first time in 2016, prompting public debate and divided reactions from Jewish groups. Dan Brown's runaway bestseller, *The Da Vinci Code*, was banned in Lebanon because it was considered offensive to Christians.

In China, *Winnie the Pooh* is censored. References to the little yellow bear were blocked on social media after bloggers compared him to China's premier. Lewis Carroll's *Alice's Adventures in Wonderland* was originally banned in China and other parts of the world due to objections to the animal characters using human language. *And Tango Makes Three* by Justin Richardson and Peter Parnell has been widely restricted because it tells the true story of two male penguins in Central Park Zoo who adopted a female chick and created a family. In Singapore, the book was removed from state libraries and destroyed. Even a bestseller like Jay Asher's *Thirteen Reasons Why* (now a Netflix series) was temporarily removed from school libraries after some critics claimed that it romanticized suicide.

Lady Chatterley's Lover (first published in 1928), a novel by D.H. Lawrence became notorious for its story of the physical relationship between a working-class man and an upper-class woman, its explicit descriptions of sex, and its use of then-unprintable words. Bookseller Ranjit Udeshi in Bombay was prosecuted under Sec. 292 of the Indian Penal Code (sale of obscene books) for selling an unexpurgated copy. The book could not be legally published in full in the UK until 1960; Penguin Books won publishing rights following a famous court case, and two-hundred thousand copies were sold on the first day.

Banned books also end up being endorsed and celebrated. In the US, the annual Banned Books Week was launched in 1982 (typically in the last week of September) to celebrate the freedom to read. The mission is to bring together the entire book community – librarians, booksellers, publishers, journalists, teachers and readers – in shared support of the freedom to seek and to express ideas, even those some consider unorthodox or unpopular.

LITERATURE THAT SPROUTED FROM PRISON CELLS

As a genre, prison literature refers to literary work created by authors while they are incarcerated.

I have been fortunate to call two individuals across the Atlantic, who played a pivotal role in prison improvement, as mentor and friend: Dr Kiran Bedi, whose work in Tihar Jail won her the Ramon Magsaysay Award in 1994, and Jason Bryant, who spent twenty years in a California prison and founded Creating Restorative Opportunities and Programs (CROP) – a non-profit that works for former inmates' re-entry into society. These friendships led me to a better understanding of the prison system and to reading some of the most profound works of prison literature.

The genre of prison literature includes memoirs, autobiographies, essays, poetry and fiction. They provide deep insights as the experiences of these inmates are often traumatic, isolating and psychologically challenging. Through their writing, the authors offer a window into a human experience that most of us would never have encountered in our lives, and hence, it expands our understanding of what it is to be human.

One of my favourite books in this genre is *The Buddhist on Death Row* by David Sheff. It explores the transformation of Jarvis Jay Masters, who was locked in a cell on death row, into one of America's most inspiring Buddhist practitioners. The book allows us to understand how meaning can be found even in – perhaps especially in – adversity. It is a study of Buddhism, of criminal justice and of the ways in which people connect with one another.

To understand the American prison system and the high rate of incarceration, two must-read books are Jessica Mitford's *Kind and Usual Punishment: The Prison Business* (first published in 1973) and Shane Bauer's *American Prison* (The *New York Times* Book Review 10 Best Books of 2018). Mitford opens our eyes to the lunacies, the delusions, the frauds and the sheer grotesqueness of what is euphemistically called 'correction facilities'. Bauer's book is not only a blistering account of the private prison system but is also a thoroughly researched history of for-profit prisons in the US from their origins in the decades before the Civil War.

Some books that are considered classics are *The Gulag Archipelago* by Russian novelist and Nobel Prize-winner Aleksandr Solzhenitsyn, *Letter from Birmingham Jail* by Martin Luther King, *In the Belly of the Beast* by Jack Henry Abbott and *The Autobiography of Malcolm X* as told to Alex Haley. The prison has also been the birthplace of many narratives such as Mahatma Gandhi's *The Story of My Experiments with Truth* (1927) and Jawaharlal Nehru's autobiography *Toward Freedom* (1936).

Another example is the 2003 novel *Shantaram* by Gregory David Roberts, which was a bestseller (now with a television adaptation for Apple TV to boot). Roberts is a convicted Australian bank robber and heroin addict who escapes from Pentridge Prison and flees to India. His novel offers a vivid portrayal of life in Bombay (now Mumbai) in the 1980s.

And, finally, a book that offers solutions is Dr Kiran Bedi's *Its Always Possible*. Kiran was forty-four when she was appointed inspector-general of Delhi Prisons on 1 May 1993. In just a couple of years, she turned a hellish institution into a humane one. Tihar Central Jail was a cesspool of drugs and gang wars, corruption and extortion by both guards and powerful inmates. Bedi transformed the jail into a place where inmates gather for morning prayers and meditation, for vocational training, legal aid and even entertainment. *It's Always Possible* captures that journey of transforming one of the largest and most notorious prisons in the world.

Prison literature is one genre that allows us to see two contrasting perspectives: one that displays what is fundamentally wrong in our prison system; and the other shows that humans have the miraculous capacity to find redemption, and even joy, no matter who or where we are, and that we are all united by suffering.

I was an ardent fan of Sunil Gavaskar; when he was batting in his 90s, I would not go for a toilet break until he crossed his century. Gavaskar's batting was thus sometimes physical torture for me. When he finally scored his century, there would be joy, followed by relief.

Cricket and books have played important roles in my life. Reading was a culture I grew up in. I recall how eagerly my brother and I would wait for the newspaper delivery person and then pounce on the sports pages. Growing up in Kharagpur, a small town in West Bengal, meant that football competed with cricket in our affections. Chima Okorie, the Nigerian footballer, had as many fans as Sunil Gavaskar. At least an hour was spent reading the newspaper. One of my earliest memories is building a scrapbook of players with cuttings from the *Statesman* newspaper, and later the magazine, *Sportstar.*

The black-and-white photos on newsprint looked so fuzzy that it was impossible to make out who was who. The cover of my scrapbook (it was a school notebook) had Kapil Dev in his famous 'Nataraja' hook shot. I was an ardent fan of Sunil Gavaskar; when he was batting in the 90s, I would not go for a toilet break until he made a century. Gavaskar's batting was thus sometimes physical torture for me. However, when he finally scored his century there would be joy, followed by relief.

At one point, I wanted to own a small bookshop so I could read all the magazines without having to pay – a wish that I still haven't given up on! Going to College Street in Kolkata to buy books was a high point. That was where my passion for collecting old, rare and secondhand books started. During my teens, cricket books were as rare as Maninder Singh reaching double figures in batting. The first two I bought were Gavaskar's *Sunny Days* and Sandeep Patil's *Sandy Storm*. I lost count of the number of times I re-read them. My first salaried job was in Chennai, which had its share of fine booksellers, and now, I finally had the resources to buy the books I wanted.

(v)

After I moved to Bengaluru, my passion for reading cricket literature took a huge leap. Ramachandra Guha's writings had a huge influence. I learned that Guha would often drop by Premier Bookshop, which I was a patron of. So one fine day, I gathered the courage to ask Shanbagh, the shop's owner, if he could call me when Guha was in the shop next. Anyone who knew the reticent Mr Shanbagh would be surprised to know that he actually called me to say Guha was in the shop just then. I rushed from my home in Victoria Layout (on my girlfriend's Kinetic Honda). I had brought along *A Corner of a Foreign Field* and got it signed by Guha. That started my journey of collecting signed copies. Ten years later, on my birthday, a colleague gifted me *The Oxford Companion to Australian Cricket*, and with it, I completed my collection of the fifty best books on cricket. There are, of course, many such 'best lists' on cricketing literature, but the one that I followed was recommended by Guha.

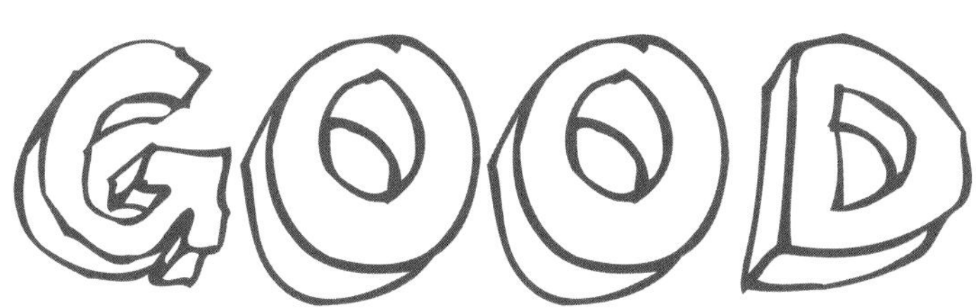

cricket book

It's been a journey that has taken me from the bylanes of Bengaluru's secondhand bookstores to J.W. McKenzie Cricket Books in Surrey, England. And then there was eBay and scores of online specialist book dealers. My most prized possession is a signed first edition of Don Bradman's *Farewell to Cricket* – which I got through the graces of a collector who was willing to part with it.

Hunting for each book has been an adventure. I have been lucky to get a copy in the most unexpected places. JW McKenzie supplied eight of these books while Premier in Bengaluru (now closed) managed to get me a couple of scarce titles. On eBay, I got some at throwaway prices. The most expensive has been the biography *Ranji* by Simon Wilde. Owning a signed copy of Neville Cardus's *Autobiography* probably ranks up there with my other prized possession, the signed Bradman. My personal favorite is *10 for 66 and All That* by Arthur Mailey while my all-time favourite is David Frith – though not part of the canon, I loved *Bodyline Autopsy.*

The one book that I could not afford to buy was Bradman's *The Art of Cricket* signed by Neville Cardus (which was priced at a whopping `2,50,000), while the signed book that cost me just two dollars was Cardus's *Autobiography.*

Everyone can create their own list. Here's mine: *Bodyline Autopsy* by David Frith; *Chinaman: The Legend of Pradeep Matthew* by Shehan Karunatilaka; *A Lot of Hard Yakka: Triumph and Torment* by Simon Hughes; *Pundits from Pakistan* by Rahul Bhattacharya; *A Corner of a Foreign Field* by Ramachandra Guha; *The Art of Captaincy* by Mike Brearley; *Harold Larwood* by Duncan Hamilton; *On Cricket* by Michael Parkinson; and *On Warne* by Gideon Haigh.

I have been fortunate to have met some of the legends of the game. The high point was meeting my childhood hero Sunil Gavaskar, who visited my workplace, SAP Labs in Bengaluru (as part of a promotional activity). I had prepared myself well. I had brought multiple copies of *Sunny Days* and had all of them signed. I even got the deluxe editions of *Idols*, *Sunny Days* and *One-Day Wonders* (signed only once). Life had come a full circle!

Japan's ex-deputy prime minister (Tarō Asō) has said the Games are 'cursed' with a forty-year jinx: the 1980 Moscow Olympics was boycotted by sixty-six countries because of the Soviet-Afghan war, and the 2020 Games had to be postponed because of the pandemic. With the 2020 Tokyo Olympics finally taking place in the summer of 2021, here is a round-up of titles that capture the Olympic spirit at its best.

> **Japan was the first Asian nation chosen to host the Olympic Games in 1940, but World War II forced the cancellation of both the summer and winter Games it had planned to host.**

The Games: Global History of the Olympics by David Goldblatt is an insightful, anecdotal history of the modern Games. The first Olympics in Athens in 1896 was an all-male, all-white affair; women began to enter the arena in 1900; and in 1924, William DeHart Hubbard became the first African American to win a gold medal. It was the 1932 Los Angeles Games that first introduced theatrical touches such as the Flame and the national anthems. Athletic success was linked with nationalistic fervour in the 1936 Berlin Olympics when the Nazi organizers initiated a torch relay that began in Olympia.

the Spirit of the games

The Boys in the Boat by Daniel James Brown is an irresistible story of how nine working-class boys who comprised the University of Washington's eight-oar crew team triumphed in the 1936 Games. Drawing on the boys' own journals and memories, Brown has created an unforgettable portrait of an era. The book was later made into a PBS documentary *The Boys of '36*.

The story of Eric Liddell, a Scottish sprinter, continues to inspire generation after generation. Liddell was immortalized in the Oscar-winning *Chariots of Fire*; however, if you want to know him not just as the fastest man on earth but as a force for good in the world, then read Duncan Hamilton's *For the Glory*.

I remember flinching while watching Greg Louganis, American Olympic diver, hit his head on the diving board at the 1988 Seoul Olympics. Watching him return to triumph was a tremendous experience. *Breaking the Surface* by Greg Louganis is a deeply moving yet inspiring book that describes the abuse he suffered growing up, and how he never felt like he truly belonged, having been given up for adoption as a baby.

Milkha Singh, 'The Flying Sikh', is one of India's greatest Olympians. Singh is best remembered for his fourth-place finish in the 400 metres final at the 1960 Olympic Games. The movie *Bhaag Milkha Bhaag* was inspired by *The Race of My Life*, an autobiography co-written by Singh and his daughter Sonia Sanwalka.

It was a single shot at a target smaller than the seed of an apple. Despite imperfect vision, Abhinav Bindra shot a perfect ten at the 2008 Beijing Olympics. The autobiography, *A Shot at History* captures Bindra's tough training schedules and much more.

India's Olympic journey has been best captured by Boria Majumdar and Nalin Mehta's *India and the Olympics* (followed by *Dreams of a Billion*). *India and the Olympics* explores how and when the Olympic ideology took root in India and its relation to India's quest for a national and international identity. India surpassed its highest Olympic medal tally (six medals at the London 2012 Olympics) at Tokyo with a tally of seven.

I have been fortunate to know India's greatest athlete and Olympian P.T. Usha, who made it her mission to get a medal for the country long after her time on the track. My hope is to see a new and updated full-length biography of this legend!

I have lost count of the number of times I have hit a tennis ball in my verandah to an imaginary goal post during my years growing up in Kharagpur (West Bengal).

Playing five-a-side football (it was called footer) with a tennis ball and a miniature goal was a craze. Football has been, without doubt, a popular game in India, which was once called the 'Brazil of Asia'. In fact, the rivalry between East Bengal and Mohun Bagan is ranked amongst the top 50 club rivalries in the world. Novy Kapadia's *Barefoot to Boots* is a thrilling account of the incredible journey of Indian football.

CAPTURING ALL SIDES of a BEAUTIFUL GAME

Football craze reached its pinnacle during the 1986 World Cup when an entire generation began to idolize Diego Maradona. It thrilled me to watch a match in Maradona's own Boca Juniors stadium, La Bombonera in Buenos Aires, which was built in 1940. In his *Touched by God: How We Won the Mexico 86 World Cup*, Maradona details every game. On the field, I tried to emulate Johan Cruyff's total football, practising the famous 'Cruyff turn' but without much success. The late great Cruyff (he died in March 2016) has written a biography that is a must read: *My Turn*.

To football fans everywhere, the 1970 Brazilian World Cup-winning team will remain the ultimate master class in skill, sophistication and style. Garry Jenkins celebrates this team in *The Beautiful Team*, a priceless collection of personal histories. Nick Hornby's *Fever Pitch* captures his love for Arsenal and the obsession, loyalty, depression and joy that a soccer fan goes through.

The Damned Utd by David Peace is a fictional account of Brian Clough's ill-fated forty-four-day tenure as football manager of Leeds United in 1974. It received critical acclaim but drew controversy when former Leeds player Johnny Giles complained about how he was portrayed. He won a libel suit, and the publisher made changes to the text in later editions, turning the first edition into a collectible. Duncan Hamilton wrote a bestseller on the same subject, *Provided You Don't Kiss Me: 20 Years with Brian Clough.*

The Away Game by Sebastian Abbot captures the gripping story of a group of boys chosen in one of the largest talent searches in sports history, the Football Dreams program, which has held tryouts for more than five million thirteen-year-old boys across Africa. The book describes the journey – filled with joys and agonies – of the boys and their families as they chase their dreams.

While there are many books by football coaches (like Alex Ferguson's *Leading* or *My Autobiography*), I particularly enjoyed Stephen Constantine's *From Delhi to the Den.* It is full of anecdotes and opinions from a viewpoint outside of the elite footballing bubble. It also has interesting insights into the type of football coach that we, as fans, rarely get to see and appreciate.

However, my favourite book is *The Illustrated History of Football: Hall of Fame* by the *Guardian* cartoonist and illustrator, David Squires. The book, replete with his hand-drawn cartoons, covers almost all the high points in soccer history and its famous players. One of my prized possessions is an original artwork of Maradona's Hand of God from *The Illustrated History of Football* and this is how David described it to me in writing: '"The Hand of God" was a big football moment in my childhood, perhaps the biggest. I was 11 years old when it happened and, as an English boy, it took me a while to see the funny side! However, my friends and I were soon recreating it in the playground.'

I am fortunate to have visited many of the football-crazy countries (including Brazil, Argentina, Germany and even Russia) and I make it a point to play soccer matches with my local team. To this day, the game remains a great unifier. As Dmitri Shostakovich, the famous Russian composer and pianist of the twentieth century said: 'Football is the ballet of the masses.'

For thousands of years, humans have been asking difficult questions about life and the world.

What is truth?

What is morality?

What is justice? What is a just system of governance?

When one of my friends asked me to recommend good books on philosophy, it got me thinking hard. It took me some time to come up with titles of books that anyone could comprehend and yet would allow the reader to view the world differently. *A Little History Of Philosophy* by British philosopher, columnist and podcast host Nigel Warburton is an easy read that gives a good summary of the thinkers who shaped philosophy over two-and-a-half millennia.

the story of philosophy

Every philosopher from Socrates to Immanuel Kant and Bertrand Russell has tried to provide answers to these fundamental questions. The answers are inspiring yet confusing, sometimes consoling and often challenging.

Philosophy draws indiscriminately from all fields of knowledge and involves endless questioning. Plato pretty much invented what we now call 'philosophy'. *The Republic: A Socratic Dialogue*, authored by Plato around 375 BCE, concerns justice, the order and character of the just city-state, and the just man. It is Plato's best-known work, and has proven to be one of the world's most influential works on philosophy and political theory, both intellectually and historically. He is most famous for his parable, *The Allegory of the Cave.*

One of my personal favourites is the collection of essays in *The Lessons of History* by two prominent modern thinkers, Will and Ariel Durant. The book provides an overview of more than five thousand years of human history. It covers changes in morality, religion and government systems, such as socialism and capitalism, and traces the historical trends of war.

The Socrates Express by Eric Weiner takes us on a voyage of his life-changing pursuit of wisdom and discovery. Weiner explores philosophers and places (from Socrates and ancient Athens to Simone de Beauvoir and twentieth-century Paris) to navigate today's chaotic times. In addition, India's lasting contribution to the world, the philosophical wisdom of ancient and modern India, is best captured in *A Sourcebook in Indian Philosophy* edited by Sarvepalli Radhakrishnan and Charles A. Moore.

The Prince by Niccolò Machiavelli is sometimes claimed to be one of the first works of modern (especially political) philosophy in which the effective truth is taken to be more important than any abstract ideal. The origin of the word Machiavellian is credited to this book. It denotes subtle or unscrupulous cunning, deception, expediency or dishonesty (often to maintain authority).

The Second Sex by Simone de Beauvoir, an 800-page feminist classic, is as relevant now as when it was first published in 1949, and is a must-read for all genders. It explains how the woman has been shaped into the 'other' – the second sex – the negative counterpart to the man. By examining history, myths, biology and life experience, de Beauvoir paints a clear picture of why women are subjugated to men and how womankind should respond.

All the great philosophers have provided unique perspectives. Epicurus recommended a simple, ethical and fulfilling life without fear of death. Rousseau believed that instead of competing with each other for money and status, citizens should obey communal laws while exercising individual freedom. Kant believed our actions are moral when we approve of the universal maxims they embody. Nietzsche showed that atheism undermined some of our most cherished moral assumptions.

Eventually, philosophy reveals to us the reasons behind the ways we act, and in doing so, helps us to understand our inner selves and how we relate to the world around us.

BOOKS ON spirituality

There is a distinction between religion and spirituality. While religion is a specific set of beliefs and practices shared by a community, spirituality is more of an individual's search for purpose and meaning.

The pandemic saw a surge in people who, in the face of fear, actively discussed matters of faith and spirituality. In seventy-five countries in the month of March 2020, internet searches related to prayer skyrocketed to their highest levels in five years. Probably, the COVID-19 pandemic unintentionally created a massive spiritual awakening in humankind. As we were unable to venture outside, we were forced to look inward. During this time, I read (and listened to) more books on spirituality than ever before.

There is a distinction between religion and spirituality. While religion is a specific set of beliefs and practices shared by a community, spirituality is more of an individual search for purpose and meaning. One of the most popular books on spirituality is *Autobiography of a Yogi*, the autobiography of Paramahansa Yogananda, first published in 1946. An introduction to the methods of attaining God-realization, the book is acclaimed as a spiritual classic and has been in print for seventy years and translated into over fifty languages. Steve Jobs, co-founder of Apple, gave this book to family and friends to read at his memorial service at Stanford because it had a huge influence on his life.

Apprenticed to a Himalayan Master is the bestselling autobiography of Sri M. of Madanapalle. Sri M. is a true modern mystic. Born in a Muslim family, he became a yogi in the Himalayas, got married, raised a family and founded two successful schools. He neither offers namaz five times a day, nor prays at any temple. But he can recite texts from the Holy Quran and the Bhagavad Gita with equal command. He teaches Vedanta and Kriya Yoga and is a guru to thousands across the world.

Sadhguru Jaggi Vasudev is one of the most popular gurus of the current generation. His Isha Foundation has thousands of volunteers, and his talks are followed by millions around the world. I was able to listen to his book *Inner Engineering: A Yogi's Guide of Joy* on Audible. In his revolutionary book *Sadhguru*, he distils his experiences with spirituality and introduces the concept of inner engineering, a practice that serves to align the mind and the body with energies around and within.

Jiddu Krishnamurti was a unique philosopher in that he negated the aura and the authority that go with being a guru. Of all his books, *Krishnamurti's Notebook* is one of the few that he wrote himself (others are mostly collections or compilations of texts from his talks). Something that Krishnamurti required us to do, and which I found relevant, was to inquire about religion without aiming for an outcome. By sitting and emptying the mind of all judgement of the surroundings and allowing oneself to be open to any and all truths, one is then able to see things as they truly are.

Of the various spiritual books by non-Indians, I have loved *The Miracle of Mindfulness* by Thich Nhat Hanh, *The Seat of the Soul* by Gary Zukav, *The Secret* by Rhonda Byrne, *Siddhartha* by Hermann Hesse and *Book of Mercy* by Leonard Cohen.

When it comes to spiritual books, it helps to find that one book that connects with you and to read it daily. A piece of advice: read the book slowly, internalize it and let it live with you for some time. And don't be surprised if you end up more confused after you read them. The important thing is to seek answers and introspect.

EYE-OPENING BOOKS ABOUT BUDDHISM

I have been drawn to Buddhism because of its universality – everyone can relate to it and everyone can practise it. I don't consider myself a Buddhist by any means, and my knowledge of it is entirely bookish. I have neither followed a monk, nor done any extensive practice, but the message of Buddhism has helped me overcome my suffering.

The books that opened my eyes and introduced me to Buddhism were gifts from friends and are perfect for beginners – *What Makes You Not a Buddhist* by Dzongsar Jamyang Khyentse and *Instructions to the Cook* by Bernhard Glassman and Rick Fields.

Buddhism is not a religion. It is a very complex belief system that focuses on personal spiritual development. It does not consider Buddha as a god: rather, everyone can become a Buddha. There is no single holy text; instead, several scholars throughout history have contributed to a vast library of concepts. Buddhism is open to change, and it is dedicated only to the pursuit of truth. The central

idea in Buddhism is that evil is measured by how much suffering it produces. The biggest cause of suffering is the ego, and the most important thing is the ever-present now, working on ourselves in the moment, and letting go of the past and future.

His Holiness the 14th Dalai Lama is undoubtedly 'the authority' on the matter, and his numerous books offer a clear vision of the Buddhist path. *Approaching the Buddhist Path* is the first of a trilogy compiled and co-authored by the Dalai Lama and the American Buddhist nun Thubten Chodron. In it, the authors explain every step of the path to enlightenment. It narrates Buddhist history and introduces the fundamentals of Buddhism along with the Dalai Lama's personal experiences.

The Foundation of Buddhist Practice is the second in the trilogy, which explains the key teachings to start the practice of the Dharma. The book offers a simple description of how to structure a meditation session, and of the appropriate relationship between the spiritual mentor and the student. It has a series of chapters on the law of Karma and the concepts of birth and death. *Samsara, Nirvana, and Buddha Nature* is the third volume, which gives information about the Four Noble Truths. The reader will learn how to improve personal practice with insightful and easy-to-apply methods, and learn about the mind's infinite potential through the teachings of Dzogchen.

Thich Nhat Hanh, one of the most famous Buddhist monks and peace activists, has written over 130 books and is considered the father of the mindfulness movement (Little known fact: Martin Luther King Jr. nominated him for the Nobel Peace Prize in 1967). His *The Heart of the Buddha's Teaching* serves as a guide for transforming your suffering into peace and joy. It covers significant Buddhist teachings such as 'The Four Noble Truths' and 'The Noble Eightfold Path'. If you are someone who holds on to anger and hurt, this book will help you find relief.

If you are curious to know about the life and teachings of Gautama Buddha, then I would recommend *Old Path White Clouds.* Drawn directly from twenty-four Pali, Sanskrit and Chinese sources, and retold by Thich Nhat Hanh in his inimitably beautiful style, this book traces the Buddha's life slowly and gently over the course of eighty years, partly through the eyes of Svasti, the buffalo boy, and partly through the eyes of the Buddha himself. *Old Path White Clouds* has also become a classic of spiritual literature since its publication in 1987.

I believe that Buddhism is as relevant today as it was twenty-five hundred years ago. If we understand the truths – that life is full of suffering, and that the path to overcoming suffering is through compassion and wisdom – then we can all find happiness and peace in our lives.

'The Bhagavad Gita is perhaps the most systematic scriptural statement of the Perennial Philosophy,' wrote Aldous Huxley in his introduction to the English translation of the Gita by Swami Prabhavananda and Christopher Isherwood.

Bhagavad Gita *and its* TIMELESS APPEAL

The perennial philosophy is a perspective in philosophy and spirituality that views all of the world's religious traditions as sharing a single metaphysical truth or origin from which all esoteric and exoteric knowledge and doctrine has grown.

The Gita has inspired many people, from freedom fighters like Lala Lajpat Rai, Bal Gangadhar Tilak, Bankim Chandra Chattopadhayay and Mahatma Gandhi to intellectuals and scientists such as Swami Vivekananda, T.S. Eliot, Herman Hesse, Ralph Waldo Emerson, Albert Einstein and Dr A.P.J. Abdul Kalam. Some have even advocated for the Gita to be declared the national book of India.

Why does the Gita have a universal appeal? The Bhagavad Gita, or a song of god, often referred to as simply the Gita, is a 700-verse Hindu scripture that is part of the epic, Mahabharata (chapters 23–40 of 'Bhishma Parva'). It has been translated into more than seventy-five languages worldwide, and has over three hundred translations in English alone. The Gita is about a way of life – it teaches us better concentration, self-control, the art of right action, true happiness, devotion, overcoming anger and so on. Here are the three English translations that I would recommend.

The first one I read (or rather, heard on Audible) is by English professor, meditation teacher, Hinduism scholar and spiritual leader Eknath Easwaran. It is the best version to start with for its simplicity and readability.

The Bhagavad Gita According to Gandhi is based on talks given by Gandhi between February and November 1926 at the Satyagraha Ashram in Ahmedabad. I read this version, curious to know how Gandhi came to the idea of non-violence. I wondered how he reconciled the violence advocated in the Gita (where Krishna recommends that Arjuna fight his relatives in war because it is his sacred duty) with his own non-violent position.

During the time that Gandhi translated the Gita from Sanskrit to his native tongue Gujarati, he had withdrawn from mass political activity. This holy book became Gandhi's most dependable spiritual guide and a constant companion through all the trials and tribulations of his life. He considered the Gita as the universal mother who turns away nobody; her door is wide open to anyone who knocks. As Gandhi famously said: 'When doubts haunt me, when disappointments stare me in the face, and I see not one ray of hope on the horizon, I turn to Bhagavad Gita and find a verse to comfort me; and I immediately begin to smile in the midst of overwhelming sorrow.'

And finally, the book I want to read is Lokmanya Balgangadhar Tilak's magnum opus, *Shrimad Bhagvad Gita Rahasya,* popularly known as *Gita Rahasya*. Written while serving his six-year prison term in Burma (now Myanmar) from 1908 to 1914, it must rank very high in the body of prison literature created anywhere in the world. The book is Tilak's heroic attempt to show that the Gita – and Indian spiritual tradition in general – was not a call for renunciation and inaction but essentially a guide that preached 'Karma Yoga', a path to desireless action to achieve a lofty goal.

Having read numerous books on leadership, I can, with conviction, say that if you can internalize the Gita, you don't need to read any other leadership book in your life. And as Gandhi said: 'Those who meditate on the Gita will derive fresh joy and new meanings from it every day.' Don't postpone it, read it now.

Mental health impacts every aspect of our lives, affecting how we think and feel, guiding us in our decisions and governing how we act around other people.

One of the most important lessons I learnt from Aparna Piramal, author of *Chemical Khichdi*, was to 'separate the person from the illness'. In the book, Piramal, who has been wrestling with bipolar disorder for years, presents a helpful pathway to those with a mental health condition and their loved ones. The book offers the message that one can live and thrive with a severe disorder. Another book that captures the struggles with the manic highs and depressive lows of bipolar disorder, and its impact on caregivers, is Jerry Pinto's *Em and the Big Hoom*.

KEEPING A HEALTHY MIND

Mental illnesses have been around for as long as humans have. Our society is only now beginning to understand the importance of discussing mental health. When actor Deepika Padukone spoke about her struggles with depression, it brought the topic to the mainstream. The numbers are depressing. Globally there is a suicide every forty seconds; in India it is every seventeen seconds. India has one-third of the world's cases of depression, alcoholism and suicides while only 0.6 per cent of our overall health budget is dedicated to mental health. About 60–70 per cent of those in jails have a mental health problem, which indicates that early intervention could have nipped crime in the bud.

In a survey on mental health in the workplace (conducted in 2019, with 829 respondents whose average age was thirty and most of whom had full-time jobs), one in two people answered yes to the question on whether they had a mental health issue – anything from worry and stress to diagnosed illnesses such as anxiety and depression. Two out of three said they knew someone at their workplace with a mental health issue; however, most of them said they rarely or never discussed mental health among themselves (some of these discussions have just started in major corporations). A report by the WHO estimates that depression and anxiety disorders cost the world economy US$ 1 trillion annually in lost productivity.

Mental health impacts every aspect of our lives, affecting how we think and feel, guiding us in our decisions and governing how we act around other people. Poor mental health also directly affects our physical health, making us more susceptible to certain chronic physical conditions.

The deeply-researched book *This is Depression* by psychiatrist Dr Diane McIntosh is considered the go-to on this topic. She takes readers through common causes of depression, how it is diagnosed and the many possible treatment options. For a more scientific understanding of depression, Siddhartha Mukherjee's new book, *The Song of the Cell*, shows that depression could possibly be traced to abnormalities in neurons in the brain.

I recently met someone suffering from long-term effects of past trauma, which led me to read the *New York Times* bestseller *The Body Keeps the Score* by renowned trauma expert Bessel van der Kolk. The book offers a bold new paradigm for healing. Trauma is all-pervasive: veterans and their families deal with the painful aftermath of combat; one in five Americans has been molested; one in four grew up with alcoholics; one in three couples have engaged in physical violence.

This insightful book transforms our understanding of traumatic stress, revealing how it literally rearranges the brain's wiring. Dr Bessel shows how these areas can be reactivated through innovative treatments, including neurofeedback, mindfulness techniques, play and yoga. Sometimes, the worst place you can be is in your head. And there should be no shame in discussing mental illness and seeking support and intervention.

There are more books on leadership than real leaders! On an average, at least four books are released every day with the word 'leadership' in the title, but hardly any of the bestselling ones are written by women – a glaring omission.

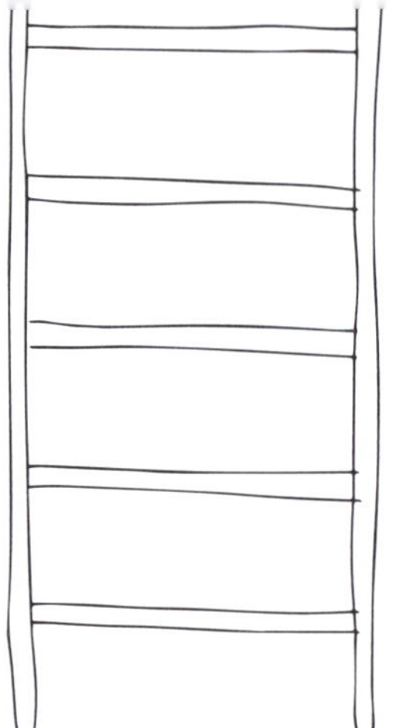

The practice of leadership has evolved over the years and so has the understanding of it. Writers now apply concepts of neuroscience, evolutionary biology and behavioural economics to the study of leadership.

The traditional model of leadership has produced hierarchies that do not work any more. The new environment of interconnectedness has created a fundamental shift, where leaders are at the centre of the circle and not the top of the pyramid. Today's leaders are comfortable operating at the edge of chaos and ambiguity, where the ability to ask questions, to think in non-linear and non-binary ways, is more important than having concrete answers. The new-age leaders are an amalgam of yin and yang.

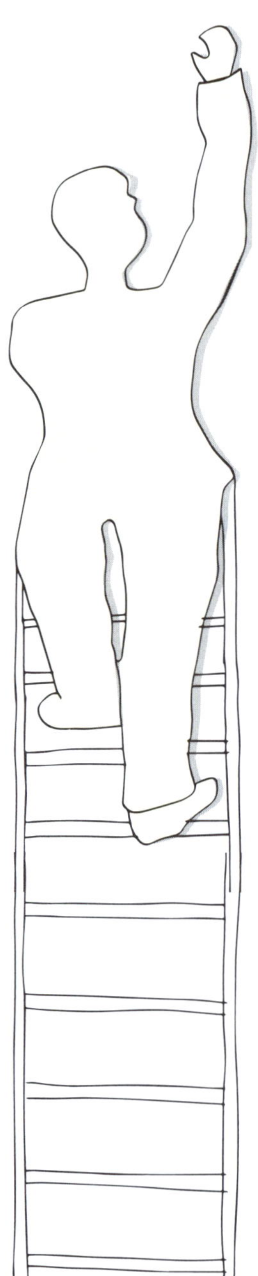

As Daniel Pink, author of *When: The Scientific Secrets of Perfect Timing* says about leaders: 'They are humble but not too humble. Confident but not too confident. The very best strike that right balance between humility and confidence.' Instead of trying to emulate what exceptional leaders do, we need to understand and emulate how they think. This is a list of leadership books that have had an impact on my life, books with compelling ideas and best practices.

The Art of War is a must-read leadership book. Published in the fifth century BCE by Sun Tzu, each of the book's thirteen chapters is devoted to an aspect of warfare and how it applies to military tactics. The book remains the most influential strategy text in East Asian warfare and has influenced both Eastern and Western military thinking, business tactics, legal strategy and more. Another ancient guide to effective leadership is *How to Be a Leader* by Plutarch, second century Greek philosopher. Blending pragmatic advice with historical anecdotes and political history, this book lays out a timeless vision of the qualities of all great leaders have in common.

Stewardship by Peter Block, published in 1993, remains one of the most provocative and revolutionary books written on leadership, business and organizational design, and shows us how we can transform our organizations for the common good of the wider community.

Marshall Goldsmith's *What Got You Here Won't Get You There* is essential reading for anyone in the ascendancy to leadership. One of Goldsmith's interesting insights is that while smart people know what to do, they need to know what to stop doing. His advice is to create a 'to-stop list' rather than a 'to do list'.

Rajeev Peshawaria's *Open Source Leadership* argues against some common myths and that 'positive autocracy' must replace democratic leadership; talent and innovation are abundant, not scarce; early identification of high potentials is counterproductive; and setting employees free to do as little as they want will increase productivity. Liz Wiseman's *Multipliers* focuses on leaders who use their intelligence to amplify the smarts and capabilities of the people around them. This book will show you how to harness all the energy and intelligence around you.

One book that has had a great impact on me, and I believe, is a model for organizations and leadership in the future is *Reinventing Organizations* by Frederic Laloux. One of its case studies is about Buurtzorg, a healthcare company in the Netherlands with more than ten thousand employees but with no management and no organizational structure in the classic sense. I was fortunate to meet the CEO, Jos de Blok, and his talk was an eye-opener that encouraged people to break away from traditional structures. To this list I would add popular bestsellers like *7 Habits of Highly Effective People* by Stephen Covey, *True North* by Bill George and *The Five Levels of Leadership* by John C. Maxwell. The list goes on!

When the SAP Academy started a programme for managers, our central theory was that the best managers kept 'empathy at the core and ambition at the edges'.

Satya Nadella, Tim Cook, Sundar Pichai and Dara Khosrowshahi are 'new age' corporate leaders who demonstrate a unique quality – empathy. They have used this characteristic to drive their companies to growth. Unlike leaders who have a 'dog eat dog' attitude and 'winning at all costs' mindset, these leaders are thoughtful, open to criticism and work towards the success of others. All of them are good listeners first, before being good orators.

Tim Cook, in his 2017 Massachusetts Institute of Technology commencement address speech, warned graduates, 'People will try to convince you that you should keep empathy out of your career. Don't accept this false premise.' While Cook will always remain in the shadow of Steve Jobs, there's no disputing the fact that he has made Apple a nicer place to work, with his empathetic style of leadership.

When we at the SAP Academy for Engineering started the programme for managers, our central theory was that the best managers kept 'empathy at the core and ambition at the edges'. The programme had Jamil Zaki, Stanford professor and author of *The War for Kindness*,

the art of empathy

Organizations are now shunning corporate politics and turf wars and chanting the mantra of empathy. Satya Nadella, who reads voraciously and has eclectic tastes, says, 'Without books, I can't live.' One of his favourites, *Nonviolent Communication* by psychologist Marshall B. Rosenberg, played a starring role in Microsoft's transformation. The book is all about how to communicate with empathy.

among the faculty. In his book, Zaki calls for concerted action to build empathy in a world he sees as fractured and threatened by escalating tribalism, cruelty and isolation.

The Age of Empathy by Frans de Waal views empathy from an evolutionary perspective. Empathy, de Waal says, is an innate capacity that likely evolved from mammalian parental care. His research shows ample evidence that our ability to identify with another's distress is deeply rooted in the origin of our species. This view has been independently reinforced by recent biomedical studies showing that our brains are built to feel another's pain.

In *Compassionomics: The Revolutionary Scientific Evidence that Caring Makes a Difference*, physician–scientists Stephen Trzeciak and Anthony Mazzarelli uncover the eye-opening data that compassion could be a wonder drug for the twenty-first century. This is a great book that focuses on medical empathy but has implications beyond it.

Karen Armstrong's thoughtful and thought-provoking *Twelve Steps to a Compassionate Life* taps into spiritual traditions' views of empathy and connectedness and shows us how we could lead a more compassionate life. Armstrong believes that while compassion is intrinsic to human beings, each of us needs to diligently cultivate and expand our capacity for compassion.

Dev Patnaik, a leading business strategist, insists that people are hardwired to care and so are some of the most successful companies. His book *Wired to Care* takes us inside big-name brands like Target, Intel and IBM, showing us how powerful empathy can be in a business context.

However, if you want to hear an alternative (though, I feel, misguided) perspective, *Against Empathy* by Yale researcher Paul Bloom is a provocative account of empathy's pitfalls. Blooms suggests that empathy might stoke inequality and immorality, and shows how, when it comes to both major policy decisions and our everyday individual choices, limiting our impulse towards empathy is often the most compassionate path we can take.

Finally, the election of Joe Biden and Kamala Harris signalled a return to empathy in 2021. But mere emotion will not do; it should lead to action. What we actually need is actions centred on empathy.

BOOKS ON SCIENCE FOR THE LAY PERSON

We have grown up learning science broadly categorized as physics, chemistry and biology (mathematics is closely related but considered a separate category).

Between 1920 and 2020, the average human lifespan doubled, from approximately thirty-five years to seventy years. More than hundred million people died from the Great Influenza outbreak that circled the globe a century ago. In comparison, roughly six million have died from COVID-19, on a planet with four times as many people. In all these situations, science has played a huge role. The word 'science', which comes from the Latin word *scientia* meaning 'knowledge', is a systematic enterprise that builds and organizes knowledge in the form of testable explanations and predictions about the universe.

I loved physics and hated chemistry and biology in equal measure. Over the years, though, I have started to develop a deeper appreciation of science with a broader understanding of the natural world. An introduction to physics from the subject's greatest teacher is now captured in the book *The Feynman Lectures on Physics*.

The legendary American physicist and Nobel laureate Richard Feynman taught a two-year introductory course in physics in California Institute of Technology, or Caltech for short, from 1961 to 1963. His famous lectures were not based on any textbooks, so they were sourced entirely from students who had written them down.

One of the first science books that I read like a novel was *Longitude* by Dava Sobel. For centuries, sailors, lacking the ability to measure longitude, had been literally all at sea. John Harrison was the eighteenth-century genius who solved the problem. Sobel's book, which narrates the story of Harrison's forty-year obsession with building his perfect timekeeper called the chronometer, is also a fascinating history of astronomy, navigation and clockmaking. *On the Origin of Species* (1859) by Charles Darwin is considered the most important science book. Darwin challenged many of the most deeply-held beliefs of the Western world. Arguing for a material, not divine, origin of species, he showed that new species are achieved by 'natural selection'.

A Brief History of Time: From the Big Bang to Black Holes, a book on theoretical cosmology by Stephen Hawking, has sold more than twenty-five million copies, but it is often considered the least-read, most bought book ever! Hence, I would recommend the illustrated version, which is an easier read. Lest I be accused of playing favourites, let me also recommend popular books on chemistry and biology: *Understanding Chemistry* by C.N.R. Rao, which is an elementary introduction to the subject, and the recent book of biologist and Nobel laureate Paul Nurse called *What Is Life?* Nurse illuminates five ideas that underpin biology.

Gene Machine by Nobel laureate Venki Ramakrishnan is an engaging and witty memoir about his contributions to the discovery of the structure of the ribosome. In doing so, he tells a story that highlights how science actually works. *Reinventing India* captures the fascinating evolution of India's science, technology and innovation (STI) landscape through some of Dr R.A. Mashelkar's most inspiring and insightful lectures and essays. I was fortunate to meet him and was drawn towards his optimism about India's future. India lags behind other countries when it comes to research in basic science. We need more bright young minds to take an interest in research. Equally, we need to spark an interest in science among the general population. And none do this better than popular books on science.

Technology literature for the masses is relatively new. Non-academic technology books are now widely read with passion and interest.

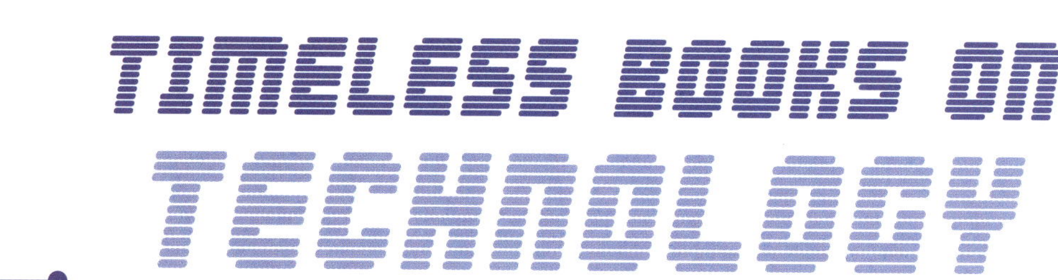

TIMELESS BOOKS ON TECHNOLOGY

Tracy Kidder's *The Soul of a New Machine* (1981) is a Pulitzer Prize-winning bestseller. This page-turner describes how a team that shares a detailed understanding of a complex problem (and even a shared all-black wardrobe) can create breakthrough solutions.

Futurist Ray Kurzweil's *The Age of Spiritual Machines* (1999) predicted that low-priced computers could match the power of the human mind, and that the difference between man and machine would begin to blur, with positive benefits to humanity. Several predictions he made for 2020 are materializing today.

In 2006's *Invisible Engines*, authors David S. Evans, Andrei Hagiu and Richard Schmalensee explain: 'Software platforms are the Invisible Engines that have created, touched, or transformed nearly every major industry for the past quarter century.' Airbnb owns no real estate; Lyft owns no cars; Facebook creates no media. Underlying them are platforms, which 'provide enormous value to consumers', and have created great fortunes.

Steve Blank and Bob Dorf's 608-page *The Startup Owner's Manual: The Step-By-Step Guide for Building a Great Company* (2012) is used by thousands of entrepreneurs. The book is a guide to Silicon Valley's best practices,

which were tested in many organizations. It was also validated by the National Science Foundation (NSF), and is taught at Stanford, Berkeley, Columbia and many more universities worldwide.

The Wisdom of Crowds: Why the Many are Smarter than the Few and How Collective Wisdom Shapes Business, Economies, Societies and Nations, by James Surowiecki (2004) explains a big idea that overturns conventional wisdom: mob rule is usually right. If you guess the weight of an ox at a county fair, odds are you'll be wrong. But the average of all guesses will often be quite close to the truth. This kind of aggregation of information by groups often leads to better predictions and decisions than those made by individuals, even experts.

Chris Anderson explains in *The Long Tail: Why the Future of Business is Selling Less of More* (2006) how the infinite 'shelf space' of the internet and the efficiency of search engines together allow obscure products to sell in small quantities. While blockbuster items receive the bulk of marketing attention, a larger share of sales for any product category is in the 'long tail' of a distribution graph. This translates into a massive profit opportunity for many companies, even for products that sell in small quantities. Eventually, the result for consumers is a new universe of choices.

Fred Brooks's 1975 project management classic *The Mythical Man-Month: Essays on Software Engineering* discusses counter-intuitively, how 'adding manpower to a late software project makes it later' – a rule that has come to be known as Brooks's Law. It is based on the author's experience at IBM while managing the development of the OS/360 operating system.

I am fortunate to have met many tech gurus when I worked in Silicon Valley, and I had the opportunity to work with Geoffrey Moore and his team. Moore's *Zone to Win* (2015) is a practical manual to address the challenges that large enterprises face when they seek to add a new line of business to an already established portfolio.

Amazon lists hundreds of books on innovation, but Clayton Christensen's *The Innovator's Dilemma* stands out. It illustrates why listening to customers can cause executives to misread the market. Too many are afraid to disrupt their own products, and so they are disrupted instead. At the same time, businesses that routinely improve their products often miss the boat when a new technology comes along.

Michael Lewis is an incredible storyteller and his *The Big Short* and *Moneyball* are highly entertaining yet classic stories that teach important lessons about technology and how it interacts with society.

Together, these titles weave a fabric of ideas that are critical for navigating technology towards maximum value to humanity in the twenty-first century.

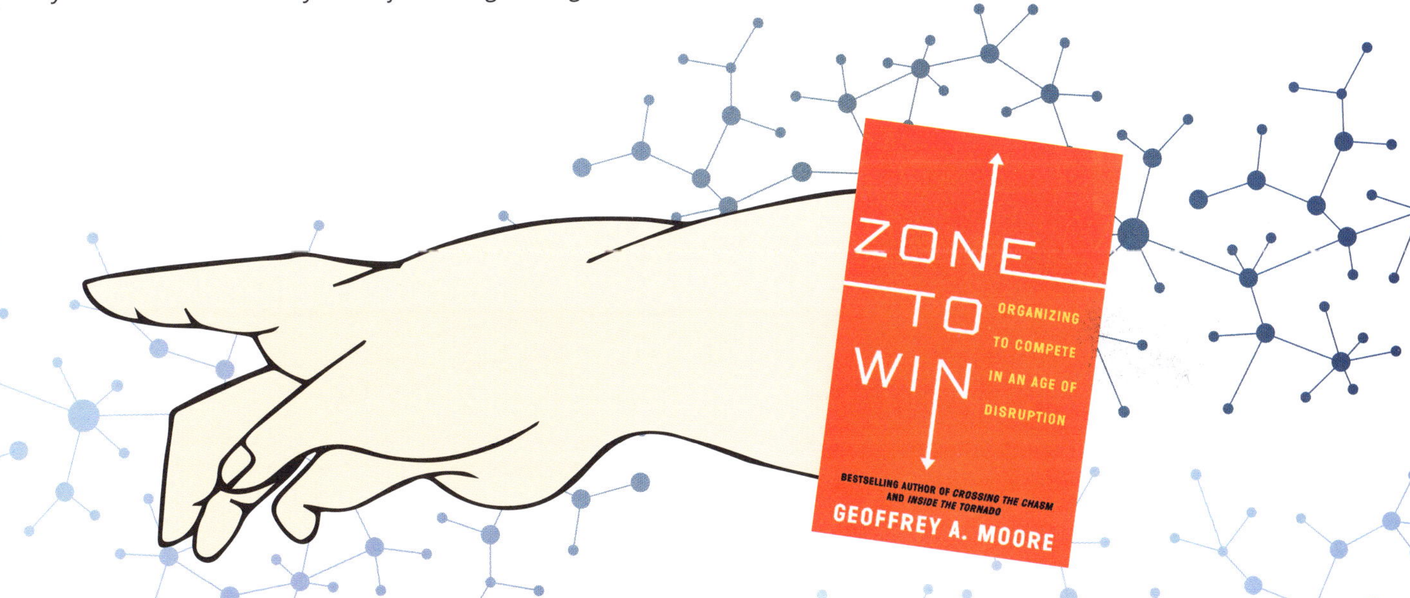

Every day, Analog Sea receives around twenty letters by post from readers. Not a lot but not a small number either. It proves that in just five years, Jonathan and his colleagues have moved the needle away from robots towards humans, even if only a tad.

Analog Sea is a publisher that releases just one book a year, sells uniquely through independent bookstores, prints only hardback editions and communicates with its readers through snail mail. Whether this is a viable business model or not is beside the point: Analog Sea is, above all, about principles, not profit, and its mission is to promote 'the human right to disconnect'.

Based in Freiburg, Germany, and Austin, Texas, Analog Sea sells its literary journal, *The Analog Sea Review*, through over two hundred and fifty independent bookstores, mostly in the United States and Europe. Its website has only one simple page displaying a postal address (no phone number, email address or social media handles), and you cannot buy their books from corporate online retailers. A cheque sent to the publisher with a request for a copy will be politely returned with an encouragement to the reader to head to their nearest independent bookstore.

ANALOG SEA

A COUNTER TO THE DIGITAL WORLD

(vi)

I encountered *The Analog Sea Review* in my local bookstore, Kepler's in Menlo Park, California. I picked up a copy of the third edition, and everything about it felt just right – its beautiful cover art by painter Joseph-Antoine d'Ornano, its pocket-friendly size, its hardcover binding, the quality of its paper and its smell.

I later met Jonathan Simons, founding editor of Analog Sea, in Walldorf, Germany. A dreamer and idealist to a fault, Jonathan was born in the US but has lived and studied in six countries. He was once a 'practitioner of Buddhism' and a touring musician, but now he runs an offline publishing house in an increasingly digital age. When I met him, he was also a visiting scholar at the Max Planck Institute for Human Development, Center for Humans and Machines, Berlin. Chatting with him over dinner, I felt a meeting of minds in our common vision and desire for a more human-centric world.

We live in a world of digital pervasiveness, always connected, with endless entertainment and stimulation only a quick tap away. At a time when AI is becoming the new electricity, we need reminding that we were equally in awe of social media during its heyday – until we realized that democracy was at stake. While we should of course celebrate the success and value of shiny new AI tools, we must also look critically at the challenges these present and the harm they can do. Jonathan jokes, half seriously, that future editions of *The Analog Sea Review* will need to include a note: 'ChatGPT was not used in this publication.'

When I asked Jonathan what gave him hope, his response was, 'If digital takes over every part of our lives, an analog life is what we will yearn for.' When there is no room for idleness, where every moment is filled with 'pixelated madness' and we lose our ability to imagine and wonder, he argues, we will crave the physical spaces where "humans look other humans in the eye, where civil dialogue and undivided attention are privileged, where thoughts and imagination have space to meander and roam'. Hence, we must decide today, for ourselves and for our communities, which parts of our lives and culture to preserve – by keeping them offline. As he mentions in the opening lines of the latest volume of *The Analog Sea Review*, 'The question is no longer whether our future is digital but to what degree we want it to remain human.'

A desire for a deep connection with the natural and physical world still exists, and organizations like Analog Sea certainly help to nurture it.

One of my concerns with the education system was that it never emphasized how mathematics can be applied to our day-to-day lives.

I have gone from having nightmares about maths to being in love with it. I assume many of us have felt nervous before a maths exam (even when we were very well prepared) and dreaded the outcome.

The first time I started enjoying maths was entirely because of my incredible maths teacher – Mr S.K. Banerjee. However, it was a long time before I read a maths book like a novel. And that book was Simon Singh's *Fermat's Last Theorem*. The theorem is the most notorious problem in the history of mathematics and surrounding it is one of the greatest stories imaginable.

Around 1637, Pierre de Fermat scribbled this proposition in the margin of a copy of *Arithmetica:* no three positive integers a, b and c satisfy the equation an + bn = cn for any integer value of n greater than 2. It took 358 years of effort by mathematicians before the first successful proof was released in 1994 by Andrew Wiles and formally published in 1995. Singh's book not only explains the theorem but also tells the fascinating stories of mathematicians whose lives were tormented by this intriguing problem. I loved the book so much that I sent a copy to Mr Banerjee!

Seventeen Equations that Changed the World by Ian Stewart is both informative and entertaining. From Newton's Law of Gravity to the Black-Scholes model used by bankers to predict the markets, equations are omnipresent and fundamental to everyday life. This book examines seventeen ground-breaking equations and explores how Pythagoras's Theorem led to GPS and Satnav (satellite navigation); how logarithms are applied in architecture; why imaginary numbers were important in the development of the digital camera and what is really going on with Schrödinger's cat!

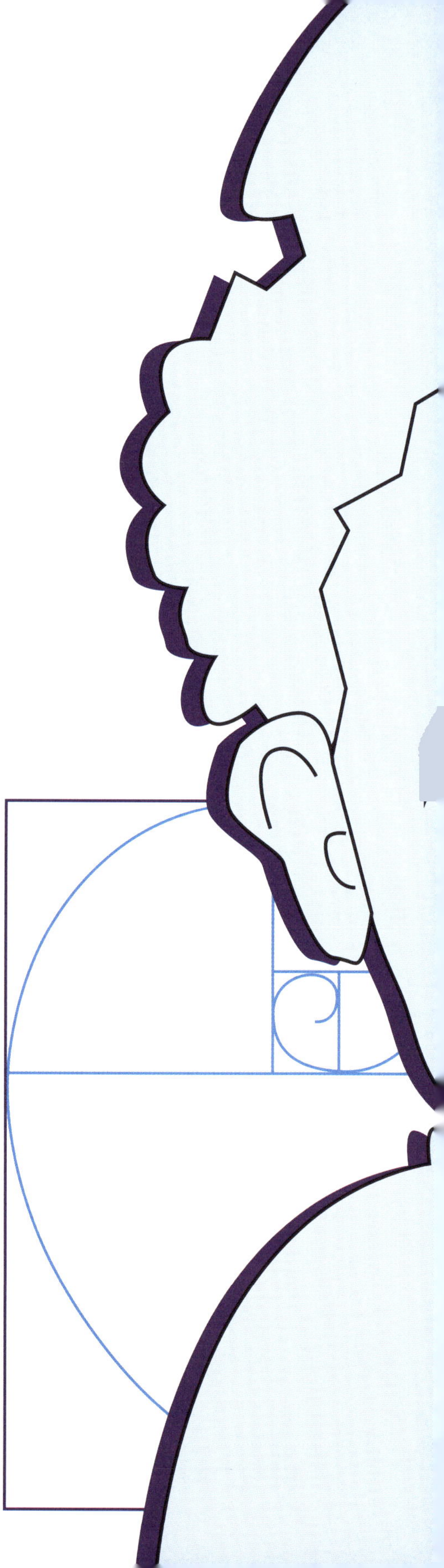

For many Indians who have grown up hearing the story of the genius Srinivasa Ramanujam, *The Man Who Knew Infinity* by Robert Kanigel is a must-read (it was later made into a movie). Ramanujam died at thirty-two but left behind a magical and inspiring legacy that is still being plumbed for its secrets. A similar book is *Finding Fibonacci* by Keith Devlin. The author has delved into the life of Fibonacci (famous for the Fibonacci number, which, ironically, he did not invent.). His book, *Liber Abaci* (the book of calculation), in 1202 introduced modern arithmetic to the western world.

Zero by science journalist Charles Seife is an entertaining look at a number that is both nothing and everything. The book follows the number from its birth as an Eastern philosophical concept to its struggle for acceptance in Europe, its rise and transcendence in the West, and its ever-present threat to modern physics. Today, zero lies at the heart of one of the biggest scientific controversies of all time: the quest for a theory of everything.

And finally, I would urge everyone to read *Weapons of Math Destruction* by Cathy O'Neil. It is important to know how the decisions that affect our lives – where we go to school, whether we get a car loan, how much we pay for health insurance – are being made not by humans but by mathematical models. The models being used today are often opaque, unregulated and uncontestable even when they're wrong. Most troubling, they reinforce discrimination. This important book empowers us to ask tough questions, uncover the truth and demand change.

MATH matters

When I started working in Chennai, my desire to buy books was largely fulfilled by settling for the pirated versions from the pavements of Mount Road (now Anna Salai). While the act was illegal and not to be spoken about publicly, I realized that these books made up a kind of unofficial 'bestseller' list!

The Dancing Wu Li Masters was Gary's first book (published in 1979), and while he was confident of its success, his publishers were not. There were several rejections, and most of the notes from the editors said the same thing: there were no categories for it in bookstores. After it was published, it received a rave review covering almost a full page in the *New York Times.* The book went on to win the American Book Award, and Gary wrote a series of books after that: *Authentic Power, The Heart of the Soul*, *The Mind of the Soul*, *Soul to Soul, Spiritual Partnership*, *Universal Human* and many others.

The AUTHENTIC and POWERFUL GARY ZUKAV

One of the books that I was introduced to back then in its pirated version was *The Dancing Wu Li Masters*. Considered a cult book about physics and consciousness, I re-read the book many times but never fully understood it. Never did I imagine that one day, the book's author, the legendary Gary Zukav, would become a dear friend.

The Dancing Wu Li Masters is timeless because it is based on the history of quantum physics and its relationship to consciousness. It is hard to believe that Gary has no formal educational background in physics! His core idea is that human beings are becoming multi-sensory and that we are acquiring perception beyond the five senses. He believes that an unprecedented transformation of human consciousness is occurring now. It is a matter of looking at the origin of our negativities and then using our knowledge to grow spiritually, which means creating authentic power.

The intention of love is very important in creating authentic power. An intention is a quality of consciousness that infuses a deed or word. Your intention is the cause that creates consequences when you act or speak. If creating fear is your intention when you act or speak with anger, jealousy, resentment, superiority and entitlement or if your intention is the need to please and you act or speak from a position of inferiority – you create painful and destructive consequences. But when you act with an intent of love, with gratitude, appreciation, patience or contentment you create healthy and constructive consequences.

What gets Gary excited is physics. He can speak at length about how ingenious Thomas Young's double slit experiment is, how it eventually became part of the famous wave-particle duality of quantum mechanics, and along with Albert Einstein's famous photon experiment, led some founders of quantum mechanics to realize that scientists could never reveal nature 'the way it really is'. He points out that quantum physics does not predict individual results but probabilities of events, and this is why Einstein never accepted it.

About the future, Gary thinks it is pregnant with possibilities. 'We are living in two worlds,' he says. 'We have one foot in the five-sensory world of the dying consciousness and another foot in the multi-sensory world of the new consciousness that is being born.' He says that children suffering from cancer or dying young are tragedies from the perspective of five-sensory perception but experiences like these are opportunities to grow spiritually from a multi-sensory perspective.

At my first meeting with Gary, I told him that his books were popular in India. He could not believe it. 'I have never received any royalty from India,' he said shockingly. I wasn't surprised, having been guilty, like thousands of others, of buying a pirated copy! But Gary wasn't worried about this practice. He likes his books to be read by many people.

The Tokyo Olympics nudged me to rediscover the world of manga. The nine Olympic ambassadors featured on official Tokyo Olympics merchandise created a greater interest around the world of manga characters.

The nine Tokyo Olympic ambassadors were Son Goku (from the 'Dragon Ball' series), Usagi Tsukino ('Sailor Moon'), Naruto Uzumaki ('Naruto'), Monkey D Luffy ('One Piece'), Astro Boy ('Astro Boy'), Cure Miracle and Cure Magical ('Pretty Cure'), Shin-chan ('Crayon Shin-chan') and Jibanyan ('Yo-kai Watch'). Manga was used at the opening ceremony of the 2020 Tokyo Olympics in multiple yet subtle ways: the placards for the country names for the parade used manga speech bubbles, and the costumes for the placard bearers and assistants had manga touches in their design.

Manga's roots can be traced back to twelfth-century Buddhist monks who created scrolls depicting animals that behaved like humans. The word 'manga' in Japanese means whimsical pictures; it is used to refer to comics and graphic novels from Japan, while 'anime' is Japanese (film or television) animation. Manga is read from right to left, is almost always published in black-and-white, and has numerous genres (action, adventure, business, romance, science fiction, horror, sports, erotica) and subgenres.

The first manga I read was *Ichi-F* by Kazuto Tatsuta, an amateur artist who signed on to the dangerous task of cleaning up the Fukushima Daiichi Nuclear Power Plant after it was destroyed by the devastating earthquake in 2011. One reason why manga fascinated me was its ability to create new epics; it has its own gods, fantastic creatures, histories and invented futures.

Manga stands out for the sheer volume of content it produces with titles running into hundreds of volumes and thousands of pages – so collectors beware! Tito Kube's Bleach series has seventy-four volumes and over 120 million copies in circulation; Noriyuki Abe has directed four animated feature films based on it. Bleach incorporates the traditional

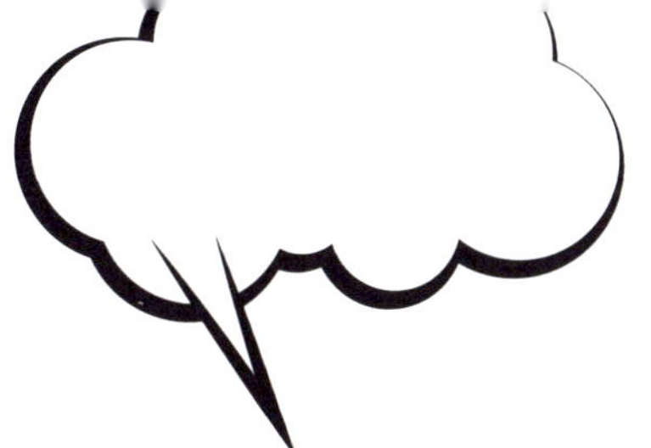

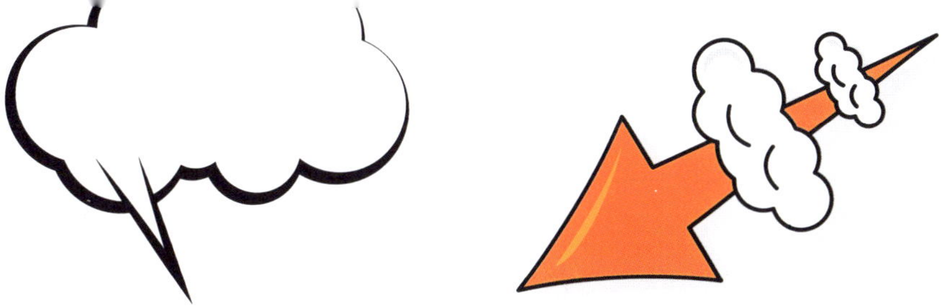

Japanese belief of spirits coexisting with humans. It follows the adventures of the hot-headed teenager Ichigo Kurosaki, who journeys to various ghostly realms while defending humans from evil spirits and guiding departed souls to the afterlife.

Goku, a naïve but determined warrior, is the main character of 'Dragon Ball Z'. Usagi Tsukino, whose alter ego is Sailor Moon, welcomed many women into what had previously been a predominantly male fan base. Naruto is a quirky teenager determined to become his village's strongest ninja. Astro Boy is a compassionate kid robot from the first popular televized anime series in the 1960s that inspired the genre; his creator, Osamu Tezuka, dubbed the 'Father of Manga', has been compared to Walt Disney. Luffy is the main character of *One Piece*, the best-selling manga of all time with about 490 million copies sold in fifty-eight countries. Gantz is one of the most expensive manga series (around $2,000).

The artists who create manga are known as *mangaka*. A *mangaka* has to produce a new manga every week, and a weekly reader survey can determine whether you are good enough to be retained or must be replaced. *One Piece* author Eiichiro Oda says that being a manga artist is 'voluntary enslavement'.

I have observed that manga is occupying more and more shelf space in American bookstores compared to DC and Marvel comics. The reason, I discovered, was that besides the rising demand, bookstores found it easy to stock them because they come with serial numbers, in a similar spine design and the same size. As a lover of comics, it took time for me to come to enjoy manga. I won't call myself a manga fan yet, but I won't bet against becoming one.

'A cartoonist is someone who draws the same thing day after day without repeating himself.' – Charles M Schulz, creator of the comic strip *Peanuts*.

There was a comic-swapping ritual when I was growing up that had its own unwritten rules, and one of them was: one Tintin comic book equalled a whole bound book of comics. That's the leveraging power Tintin had: you could trade just one comic for a whole set of Phantom or Mandrake or Marvel comics. And long after it became more fashionable to prefer Asterix, I stuck with Tintin. You can imagine my delight then, years and years later, when I acquired a Hergé-signed Tintin in the original French edition. And hardcover! The only kind of Tintins we came across in India were paperbacks, mostly later reprints.

THE NOSTALGIA OF COMICS

The Adventures of Tintin consists of twenty-three volumes published from 1929 to 1976. Apparently, every ten seconds, somewhere in the world a Tintin album is sold. The best albums are said to be *The Calculus Affair*, *The Red Sea Sharks* and *The Castafiore Emerald*, while Hergé's own favourite was *Tintin in Tibet*. A Tintin museum opened recently in Brussels, Belguim, and one of the largest comic strips in the world is a Tintin strip on display in that city.

In my childhood days, I was blissfully unaware, just as most readers were, that Tintin's reclusive Belgian creator, Hergé (real name: Georges Remi), was a right- winger who worked briefly for a Nazi collaborationist newspaper. Some Tintin editions, such as *Tintin in Congo* and *Tintin in Sovietland* had to be revised by Hergé for his crude ethnic caricatures of the Congolese and vilification of communists. Hergé later gave a statement regretting his stereotyping and explained that as a child he had come under the influence of ultra-conservative Catholics who had indoctrinated him early with the notion of colonialism as a benevolent force and the supremacy of European/Christian culture.

But of course, these controversies have never prevented fans, scholars and filmmakers from exploring the world of Tintin. There is now a branch of learning that is officially known as Tintinology. In the last couple of years, there have been several books on Tintin and Hergé, including a biography of its creator called *Hergé: The Man Who Created Tintin* by Pierre Assouline (translated from French). Another classic work of scholarship, also recently translated from French, is *The Metamorphoses of Tintin* by Jean-Marie Apostolidès.

Assouline's book, while being critical, remains sympathetic to his subject. Hergé, we learn here, moved away from his earlier prejudices, and in his later Tintin albums, shifted his plots from political concerns to psychological themes to avoid further controversy. Apostolidès's book was the first critical work of scholarship to study the comic book in depth and demonstrate how the Belgian artist's obsession with the later comics turned to champion the underdog. Michael Farr is another leading Tintinologist who has written a series of books not only on the character and its creator but also on other major recurring characters, such as Captain Haddock, Snowy, and the Thomson and Thompson twins.

A comic and cartoon creator I have admired is Bill Watterson of Calvin and Hobbes fame. After seeing what the commercial world had done to the strip Peanuts, all because Charles Schultz allowed it, he refused to merchandise his comic strip. He could have made millions if he had said yes, but he held true to his pure vision and did not compromise. And so, one of my treasures in my collection of signed cartoonists is a *Calvin and Hobbes* signed by Bill Watterson. Even to date, there are rumours that *Calvin and Hobbes* could return, that their creator has missed them so much that he could bring them back... we'll just have to wait and see.

The two comic characters that had an overwhelming influence during my early days were Spiderman and Bahadur. I used to eagerly wait for the fifteen-minute *Spiderman* episodes on Saturdays and watch them on my neighbour's TV. For Bahadur comics, I had to wait for my exams to get over until my parents gave me three rupees to buy a copy, which I read and re-read.

The scenes of Bahadur on horseback, along with his friend, police officer Sukhiya, may seem a little dated today, but Aabid Surti, who conceived of Bahadur and started the comic strip in 1976, explains its relevance to those times: 'Bennett, Coleman & Co. wanted me to create an Indian character that could take on the popularity of the four foreign comics that ruled the market in India then —The Phantom, Mandrake, Flash Gordon and Tarzan. During that time, the Chambal Valley was becoming increasingly notorious, and there were exhortations to people to group together to fight crime. So I developed the character of Bahadur as someone who helps create a citizens' police force to fight the dacoits.'

Indrajal Comics was a series launched by Bennett, Coleman & Co. in March 1964. The publishers decided to cancel the series in their twenty-seventh year of production. The last issue was 805, published on 16 April (my birthday) 1990 (Vol 27 No 8: *Dara: The Jaws of Treachery*).

How I wish we had a museum of comic characters so we could retrieve the sense of a childhood that many of us share!

Of late, I've started re-reading some of my favourite books just to check if they still resonate with me the way they did when I first read them. And that gave me the idea of re-reading in a different format – graphic novels of classics.

I first read Kurt Vonnegut's *Slaughterhouse-Five* two decades ago. It covers significant events around the world, including the Vietnam War, as well as the bombing of Dresden, Germany in World War II. I re-read it more recently – the graphic novel version by Ryan North and Albert Monteys. Having visited Dresden as a tourist, I realized the images in the graphic format added to the original. I could imagine what Dresden looked like before and after the firebombing. Although I enjoyed reading the graphic format, the characters sometimes felt a little cartoony.

Re-reading George Orwell's *Animal Farm* by Brazilian illustrator Odyr was more captivating as the animals came to life. I learnt all my Indian mythology from comics.

More recently, graphic novels have come with innovative adaptations. *Ramayan 3392 A.D.*, the brainchild of Deepak Chopra and Shekhar Kapur, is written by Shamik Dasgupta with art by Abhishek Singh. It is an imaginative re-invention of the epic set in a post-apocalyptic future. *Sita: Daughter of the Earth* by Saraswati Nagpal and R. Manikandan is another outstanding graphic adaptation.

For many people who might baulk at reading classic works of literature, graphic novels are an effective way to be introduced to classics in a visual and more digestible fashion. It is a great way for reluctant readers or those with a time crunch to access classics. However, a lot depends on the way the stories are narrated. The retelling should be as close to the original as possible without appearing to resemble a comic book. The true test of a good graphic novel of a classic is whether the graphic adaptation has a long shelf life.

CLASSICS IN GRAPHICS

An unintended consequence is that a graphic novel is easier to translate into languages as it has minimal text. Gareth Hinds is the prolific creator of critically-acclaimed graphic novels based on literary classics, including *King Lear, The Merchant of Venice*, which Kirkus called 'the standard that all others will strive to meet' for Shakespeare adaptation, *The Odyssey*, *Romeo and Juliet* and *Macbeth,* which the *New York Times* called 'stellar' and 'a remarkably faithful rendering'.

Hinds's landmark achievement was a graphic novel of *The Iliad*, a complex endeavour as the epic contains myriad characters. Hinds introduced the characters by dedicating a page to the cast and assigning a colour to each Greek god. He says that he had initially targeted school children, but the book has now reached all age groups.

One of the best graphic novels of a modern classic is Margaret Atwood's 1985 novel *The Handmaid's Tale*, beautifully realized by artist Renée Nault. The novel explores themes of subjugated women in a patriarchal society and the means by which they attempt to gain independence.

Other graphic novels of modern classics that I have enjoyed are Harper Lee's *To Kill a Mockingbird: A Graphic Novel* illustrated by Fred Fordham; Herman Melville's *Moby Dick* illustrated by Christophe Chabouté; *Anne Frank's Diary* adapted by Ari Folman and illustrated by David Polonsky; and Paulo Coelho's *The Alchemist* illustrated by Daniel Sampere.

The challenge will be to do a graphic adaptation of the classic *The Catcher in the Rye*. As Robertson Davies, Canadian novelist and playwright, said, 'A truly great book should be read in youth, again in maturity and once more in old age, as a fine building should be seen by morning light, at noon and by moonlight.' And when it comes to classics, they should be read in different formats too.

The difference between a cartoonist, a graphic artist and a caricaturist is the same as between a Baptist, a Protestant and a Mormon. For a practitioner, there is a world of difference.

GRAPHIC NOVELS ARE FOR ADULTS TOO

A SKETCHY AFFAIR

'Step back and they are pretty much the same, each trying to find meaning by drawing' – this is how the *New Yorker* cartoonist and creator of the satirical superhero Too Much Coffee Man, Shannon Wheeler described to me the difference between a cartoonist, graphic artist and caricarurist when I met him for a book event in California.

When I first began exploring graphic novels, they struck me as comic books for adults. However, you can't just flip through them like you would comics, or glide past the picture panels, which are intricately drawn with dense text. What's more, you must summon up greater focus and concentration for going through a graphic novel. But the rewards are twofold: there's text that's as rich as in any good work of fiction, and graphics that rise to an art form. My introduction to the graphic novel was through my meeting with India's first graphic artist, Sarnath Banerjee. I was amazed by his ability to draw something impromptu and personal.

For someone who is starting his/her journey with graphic novels, here are some landmark titles. *Maus* by Art Spiegelman, which won the Pulitzer Prize, is a classic. Will Eisner's *A Contract with God* popularized the term 'graphic novel'. Perhaps the first-ever novels to be drawn were the Japanese manga comics. They sparked a revolution in the West, with several illustrators reimagining the graphic novel. Foremost among them: Neil Gaiman, Chris Ware, Alan Moore and Frank Miller.

One of the first graphic novels that went mainstream was probably *Persepolis* by Marjane Satrapi. This novel about a young woman in Iran, drawn in black-and-white panels, was embraced globally by even those who had hitherto ignored the genre.

So many graphic novels today can boast literary merit – consider *Blankets* by Craig Thompson, a 600-page black-and-white graphic novel that takes a meditative look at falling in love, or Joe Sacco's *Palestine,* a political memoir of living in the war-torn Gaza Strip and the West Bank.

The genre is also known for how it tweaks iconic themes and characters from the world of pop culture. To give an example: In one desi version of *The Return of Superman*, Clark Kent meets his brown colleague: 'Hello,' she says, 'I'm Lois. Lois Chaudhary.'

An even more welcome development is the turning of modern literary classics into graphic novels. Thus, we have, in graphic form, the stories of Kafka as well as Marcel Proust's epic *In Search of Lost Time* and Paul Auster's postmodern *City of Glass.* Finally, to not mention Osamu Tezuka's Buddha series would be a serious lapse. We wholeheartedly embraced it because it was the beloved story of the Buddha, and also because we hadn't encountered a graphic novel with an Asian or spiritual sensibility before.

For beginners in this genre, graphical adaptations of the classics is a good starting point. My personal favourite is Christophe Chabouté's retelling of *Moby Dick*. The pages swing to and fro with the swell of the waves depicted on them in beautiful black-and-white sketches. Another favourite is the *New York Times* bestselling author Nick Bertozzi's retelling of Pearl S. Buck's timeless classic *The Good Earth*. *Ulysses Seen* by Robert Berry, a graphic adaptation of James Joyce's *Ulysses*, is a very ambitious project. It is available for free online.

Perhaps the most noblest aspect of *Ichi-F: A Worker's Graphic Memoir of Fukushima Nuclear Power Plant* is that the author, Kazuto Tatsuta, did not volunteer at the nuclear plant just to write a manga novel, which is what most opportunistic artists would have done. Tatsuta's intentions were merely to do his bit for this Japanese disaster site where perhaps the most lethal nuclear waste cleanup mission today is in progress. His manga went on to become a sensation in Japan, particularly for the way it revealed daily happenings at the cleanup that the government had not fully disclosed. He took part in the cleanup until his radiation level almost reached the danger mark, and that is when he stopped.

The graphic novel medium has taken off in India too in such fantastic directions, with *Kari,* the lesbian heroine, *Kashmir Pending,* an imaginative story that observes the ongoings in the valley. *Mumbai Confidential, The Barn Owl's Wondrous Capers* and *Moonward* are also a few titles to name a handful.

When my friend Dr Malvika Iyer's inspiring story was made into a graphic novel *Mai* by the very talented Jagannathan Sriram, the narrative struck a chord across generations, finding readers among both children and adults. That's the true power of a graphic novel!

Strokes of creativity

Vincent van Gogh's 'Starry Night' draws thousands of visitors every day at the Museum of Modern Art in New York. It is no ordinary landscape painting but reflects van Gogh's unique state of mind during his stay at a mental hospital in Saint-Rémy.

Vincent van Gogh suffered from epileptic fits, started hallucinating and was suicidal as he plunged into depression. And from that mental landscape came the most famous painting of the nineteenth century.

The lockdowns as a result of the COVID-19 pandemic led to a huge surge in painting as a pastime and way to cope with stress. Art critic Jerry Saltz in the *New York Times* interview titled 'Yes, You Can Channel Your Stress Into Creativity. Here's How', says that creativity is a survival strategy; 'It's in every bone in every person's body; it was there with us in the caves... Right now, people are working over long periods of time at the kitchen table... In many ways, this is closer to what art was for the last 50,000 years than it has been for a long time.'

In *Painting as a Pastime*, Winston Churchill, wartime prime minister and avid painter of the UK, talks about how picking up a paintbrush for the first time at the age of forty brought him peace during his dark days. The unpublished and penurious author Henry Miller was thirty-seven when he began painting in 1928 while he was 'supposed to be at work on the great American novel'. His *To Paint Is to Love Again* is a lost gem, out of print. Former president, George W. Bush Jr, whose *Portraits of Courage* is a collection of oil paintings and stories honouring the sacrifice of America's military, started to paint only in 2012. According to his art teacher, he was the most persistent student albeit not the most gifted.

One of my favourite artists is British. Stephen Wiltshire, whose talent clearly springs from his autism, draws detailed cityscapes, creating accurate impressions of them after having only observed them briefly. *Floating Cities* and *American Dreams* contain such drawings.

India's most well-known artist M.F. Hussain's autobiography written with Khalid Mohamed, *Where Art Thou*, is not just his life story but about the everyday instances in his life. Bengaluru has had some of India's most famous artists, including the late Yusuf Arakkal and S.G. Vasudev. *Vriksha Vasudev* is about the art and times of S.G. Vasudev. With the recently opened Museum for Art and Photography, India's largest privately owned museum, Benguluru is poised to be the epicentre of arts in the country.

When I reflected on my own life, I realized that I gave up painting in my adulthood. Although I was reasonably good at it, my academic pursuits took precedence over my hobby. Painting, like any other skill, requires practice and patience. I have been fortunate to call artists Vilas Nayak and Niyaz Hussain my friends. Both have followed their passion for painting against all odds. Both have recounted numerous stories of friends who trusted their passion and paved the way for the artists they eventually became.

It reminded me of what author Henry Miller said: 'Usually the artist has two life-long companions, neither of his own choosing... poverty and loneliness. To have a friend who understands and appreciates your work, one who never lets you down but who becomes more devoted, more reverent, as the years go by, that is a rare experience. It takes only one friend, if he is a man of faith, to work miracles.' If we cannot become artists, let us become that miracle worker for our artist friends.

Of BOOKS & Bookshelves

My fantasy of a perfect house is one where the library is the centrepiece and the bookshelves with rare books, its masterpiece.

Often, during my visits to libraries and bookstores around the world, I have been fascinated by the bookshelves as much as the books themselves. One bookshelf that stood out was in the Thomas Jefferson Library in the Library of Congress in Washington DC. Throughout his life, Thomas Jefferson (1743–1826) collected books across a vast spectrum of topics and languages. His collection of nearly seven thousand titles was the largest private book collection in North America at the time and went on to become the very foundation of the Library of Congress.

To transport the large collection to Washington DC, the books travelled in their own special shelves that had housed them at Monticello (the name of his estate in the state of Virginia) for Jefferson believed there were no better packing boxes. The shelves were taken down with the books still in them, the waste paper was stuffed into spaces to secure the volumes and boards were nailed across the front to prepare them for the journey that would involve ten wagons.

The origin of portable book boxes is not known; there is no documentary evidence that Jefferson designed them. Each case comprised three specific dimensions to accommodate different sizes of books, from smallest to largest: duodecimos, octavos, quartos and folios. The bookcases consisted of boxes arranged in three tiers. The set of six bookcases, currently on display at Monticello, was made in 1959 to recreate the originals. The specifications were carefully drawn up after compiling all written evidence as well as measuring the volumes from the Jefferson Library at the Library of Congress. The reproductions were made from pine, just like Jefferson's original boxes.

A book on bookshelves titled *At Home with Books* by Estelle Ellis and Caroline Seebohm is the perfect coffee-table book as far as I am concerned. In this book, you'll see a colourful and tasteful display of photographs showing the elegant personal libraries of collectors and writers. There are essays too on how to care for your library, ways to arrange the books and shelves, the kind of furniture you can match them with and the right lighting for them. The photographs are by Christopher Simon Sykes.

Alan Powers's *Living with Books* depicts the kind of bookshelves and libraries you'll see in the homes of people with large collections. Books are everywhere, shoved into nooks and corners all over the house, under staircases, on the landing, on the windowsill and even in the bathroom!

Books such as *Books Do Furnish a Room*, *Decorating with Books* and *Books Make a Home* have more to do with interior design than collecting. They just carry glossy photographs of bookshelves that you can flip through.

A more interesting book on the subject is *Unpacking My Library,* which visits the libraries of a dozen acclaimed architects and examines their relationship to books and space.

My own bookshelves are a combination of order and randomness. I have often provoked my wife's ire for even filling up our wardrobe with books! I suppose most collectors never get around to cataloguing their own collection while admiring everyone else's. Most of my bookshelves are rectangular, and many are just wooden racks on which boxes of books are piled up (each box has books on a specific topic). Looking back, my earliest memories of a bookshelf at the home where I grew up was a simple wooden box, large enough to keep two rows of *Reader's Digest* (sequentially arranged since 1964) and a Murphy radio on top.

When I had hosted Sudha Murthy (Chairperson, Infosys Foundation) for a book reading at SAP Labs in Bengaluru, she had summed it up beautifully: 'The true wealth of a person is measured not by the money in his bank but by the books in his bookshelf.'

As a fan of physical books, I have often wondered how anyone could ever own a digital copy.

When Michelin Star chef Vikas Khanna released his *Sacred Foods of India* on 22 June 2022, it was the first phygital (physical plus digital) book ever published. Only two physical copies, with non-fungible tokens (NFTs), were made and each was sold for $50,000 – one in Dubai and one in New York. The books came in a sandalwood box, which requires official Indian government certification.

Another two hundred copies of *Sacred Foods of India* are available in maple wood boxes adorned with gemstones and crystals, and are being sold via Akshaya, an NFT-metaverse marketplace (the cost depends on the value of Ethereum). The books are printed on paper acquired from 'special sources' in Italy, meant to last for generations. Vegetable glue is used, and the ink is sourced from Japan.

So, what exactly is a phygital book? For the layperson, let me unwrap what a non-fungible token (NFT) is and what it means for a book. Fungibility is the property of being exchangeable for other assets of the same kind without any change in value or usability. For instance, a US dollar is fungible because, at a given point in time, you could exchange any one dollar for any other, and your new dollar would have the same value and usability as the one you traded. The NFT is simply a record of who owns a unique piece of digital content, and hence, cannot be exchanged. That content can be art, music, books, graphics, tweets, memes, games – you name it.

As a fan of physical books, I have often wondered how anyone could ever own a digital copy. When you buy a book on Kindle, you don't really own the copy. Even a first edition or a signed book online is so easy to copy or share. Also, if the platform (say Amazon) ceases to exist, so will your digital book. That's where NFTs can help to make a book unique and provide an equivalent of a certificate of authentication in the digital world. Of course, since it is expensive to mint an NFT, one would only do it for a rare book.

Once you buy an NFT, it becomes your legal property. It's more secure than a typical digital transaction because the records are kept in blockchain, which offers a public record that cannot be hacked or therefore pirated. However, the biggest advantage I see in an NFT for a book is when reselling a rare book. In the secondhand book trading industry, the royalty of the second sale never reaches the author. If we include smart contracts in the NFT, authors and other involved parties can continue to reap a smaller percentage of royalties on those resales, forever.

We now have an answer to owning first editions, special editions or signed copies in the digital world, but its biggest downside is the environmental cost. Whenever a new NFT is minted, it requires huge computing power, which, in turn costs a lot of energy. But like with every technology, over time, if NFTs become a commodity, we may see a surge in its usage. For now, NFTs will be particularly useful for high-end, branded luxury items (e.g., if you want to ensure that your Versace handbag is not a duplicate from China, NFT is the way to go). And for a digital native generation, a digital product is as real as a physical one.

The best version of a book, one that will satisfy all kinds of book lovers, seems to be the phygital copy – both the physical and digital NFT.

For over two decades, I have spent a significant part of my time reading and collecting books. My book addiction has taken me from the bylanes of Chennai to the streets of Buenos Aires.

I have visited everywhere, from the largest libraries to the rarest bookstores; from airport bookstores to the largest independent bookstores; from spending less than a dollar to multiple thousand dollars on some of the rarest books. My book hunt is as much about owning a piece of history as it is about feeling close to the people I admire.

My travel itinerary always included a book activity. Whether it was visiting Neruda's house in Santiago, Chile; driving to W.B. Yeats's grave in Dublin; visiting Karl Marx's house in Trier; or the Hermann Hesse house in Calw in Germany, I have prioritized visiting an author-related museum over any other tourist activity. Even my memorabilia were always bookish in nature.

on the gentle MADNESS of bibliophilia

Technology and e-books have awakened readers to the fact that a printed book is more than just the written text – it's a historical object in itself. Information on the esoteric subject of book collecting is now widely available online. Since it is a broad topic, it is important to have an area of focus; mine has been author-signed books – either personally signed by the authors at book events or traded online.

One of my earliest learnings was to differentiate between an old book and a rare one. Another learning was that the condition of the book mattered the most. While my personal collection does include a wide variety of rare books and ephemera, I believe that anyone can be a collector, and financial resources are not as important as the passion and love for books. I always carry multiple copies of every book written by the author I am going to meet so that I can get them signed for my friends too. I get as huge a kick out of giving away signed books as out of owning them. However, since I buy books faster than I can read them, I am fully aware that I have not read at least 50 per cent of my own library (though I know about all of the books I own).

Book collecting has had some unintended consequences for me. Wardrobes meant for clothes have been stuffed with books. I have often had to smuggle my books into the house, out of sight of my wife, who has warned me of dire consequences. As a bibliophile, my worries have been unique. Every time I relocated, a significant part of my luggage consisted of cartons of books. During my move from Bengaluru to San Francisco, my shipment had hundred and ten cartons, of which fifty-five were of books. This after donating ten cartons and storing another ten at my friend's apartment! To make matters worse, when my friends travelled from India, they were always bringing books for me, many of which were collectibles.

The locker in my bank had rare books. The bank manager was both surprised and amused – this was a first in his career! The only time I removed the books from the locker was when I had to refer to them and diligently take notes when writing an article that dealt with the subject.

If I had to choose between a book and a beer, I would choose a book. Between visiting a bookstore and a historic building, I would visit the bookstore. Between attending a book launch and a rock concert, the book launch for sure. And between buying a rare book and an expensive suit, it's the rare book I would go for.

If I were given a dying wish, it would be to die on a bed of books in my home rather than in a hospital. As my friend, author and bibliophile Nicholas A. Basbanes calls it, book collecting is 'a gentle madness'.

When I recently invited the cultural historian and bibliophile Nicholas A. Basbanes to be interviewed for the short documentary 'Reimagining Bookstores', he readily accepted but mentioned in passing that if we wanted to do the conversation in situ – among his books – then we had better hurry since he was in the process of downsizing his home library, a process that has been ongoing for the last ten years but has been 'picking up steam' now that he and his wife were 'thinking seriously' about selling their home in Central Massachusetts and moving into smaller quarters.

'I am approaching eighty,' he explained, 'and I am heeding the wisdom of one of the more interesting characters I profiled in *A Gentle Madness*, a delightfully obsessive man named Toby Holtzman, who said that every collector reaches a point in life where they begin to think of their books in terms of subtraction, not addition. I'm at that point now.'

I was well aware that Nick's home library was worth a visit, having already taken a virtual tour of his house in a C-SPAN video produced in 2006 when he still had, by his reckoning, about twelve thousand volumes, 'maybe more, who knows'. He had a warren of storage racks double-shelved in his basement, hundreds of volumes occupying shelves in every room upstairs – some even in a bathroom linen closet – and still more in what he called 'offsite storage'. When he told me that he was now culling his holdings down to what he hoped would be about thousand books – a figure he later amended to fifteen hundred – I was determined to get my hands on some of the remaining titles before they were disposed of. Nick had already

A Gentle Madness

For V.R Ferose –

My friend, colleague, and kindred spirit, I wish to have this copy of my first book – the very copy I brought with me for five years or so when on the road talking about, and reading from "A Gentle Madness". I know it will be in warm, welcoming hands,

warmest best regards

Nick Basbanes

Northampton, MA

VIII.XX.MMXXIV

(8-20-2024)

BASBANES library

made arrangements for their removal with Ken Gloss, owner of Brattle Books in Boston and well-known to viewers of the PBS program *Antiques Roadshow*, so there was a bit of urgency on my part. Nick was kind enough to select hundred books he thought I would appreciate, each one bearing his ownership signature, a good number of them inscribed to me with notes explaining their significance to his research and in his writing. He based his choices on what he knew of my interests – biography, history, photography, books on books – and I was overjoyed when five boxes arrived at my house on 27 August 2022. The postman was my Santa, and Christmas had arrived many months in advance.

I wanted to savour the process of opening the boxes; it took me a week to go through each volume carefully. During Nick's career as a professional book reviewer, editor and literary columnist, he had conducted face-to-face interviews with hundreds of authors over thirty years, gathering, in the process, more than nine hundred books inscribed personally to him. He wrote at length about this unique collection in a two-part essay for *The Book Collector* (Autumn and Winter 2021 issues) titled 'Thanks for the Memories: Recalling Authors and Their Inscriptions'. It is an astonishing range of authors, representing all genres, with names that include the Nobel laureates Nadine Gordimer, Doris Lessing, Toni Morrison, Kazuo Ishigura and Czesław Miłosz, among so many others. In 2015, the Cushing Memorial Library of Texas A&M University acquired Nick's research archive, 365 boxes weighing three and a half tons. The boxes contained documents, correspondence, manuscripts, notebooks, photographs and micro cassettes of about thousand hours of interviews, all since converted to digital files, and freely accessible to scholars. As part of the agreement, Nick gifted the inscribed books and thirty other discrete collections of literary first editions and other curiosities – a grouping of pop-up books among them – to the university. A few of the inscribed books were left behind in the process, however, several of which he decided to pass on to me, assured in the knowledge, he said, that they would find a welcoming new home.

Michael Suarez, director of the Rare Book School at University of Virginia and co-editor of *The Oxford Companion to the Book*, has defined every book to be a 'coalescence of human intentions'. The four special books that Nick gifted me were inscribed copies to him from Gerard Goggins, Robert Cormier, Paul Theroux and Robert B. Parker, the significance of each individual, and each title, explained in an added note to me on the flyleaf of each. This qualified them as double-inscribed copies – sort of like a relay race – for examples from 'Paul Theroux to Nicholas A. Basbane' and from 'Nicholas A. Basbanes to Ferose'.

The other books he chose for me – decidedly 'eclectic', he said, 'since I am eclectic' – include a first issue of *A Gentle Madness*, Nick's greatly admired first book, published in 1995, and the copy he carried with him while touring, lecturing and reading from the book for what he said was a period of five years. His message to me read: 'I have been holding on to this copy for a special occasion. From my shelves to yours.' Needless to say, this means a lot to me. There is also a biography by Janet Morgan of Agatha Christie that Nick selected for my wife, knowing that Christie is one of her favourite authors. That means a lot to us as well.

A Gentle Madness is special to me for several reasons. Above all, it gave me, in a way, the permission I needed to follow my passion to collect books. After reading all the crazy stories of book collectors (including the book thief Stephen Blumberg) I realized that I was not the only one obsessed with getting my hands on every book worth collecting. It was a dream come true getting in touch with Nick, thanks to my friend Pradeep Sebastian and the publishing of my article in the magazine *Fine Books & Collections* (for which Nick has contributed to every edition in the column 'Gently Mad'). In my mail correspondence with Nick, he came across as modest and forthcoming. I was prepared to travel all the way to Massachusetts to meet with him in person.

However, I got the chance much earlier and easier than I had expected. An event in October 2016 brought Nick to San Francisco, and as luck would have it, I had just returned from my own travels, so we arranged to meet at the Marine Memorial Club & Hotel on Sutter Street, where he normally stays when in the city. We met for lunch in Cesario's, a small Italian restaurant in the club. Nick was waiting for me when I arrived. Appearing older than I had expected, he was warm and welcoming. Over the next two hours, I had one of the best conversations ever – and I confess there are not too many people I can spend that much time with talking only about books.

Nick spoke about his forthcoming biography of Henry Wadsworth Longfellow and invited me to visit the Longfellow House in Cambridge, Massachusetts (a place that has more than eight hundred thousand items of archival material, twelve thousand books and eleven thousand letters). In 2016, Nick was named a Public Scholar by the National Endowment for the Humanities, one of only four independent scholars to be so honoured that year. *Cross of Snow: A Life of Henry Wadsworth Longfellow* (Alfred A. Knopf) was published in 2020,and named the best book of the year by the *Times Literary Supplement* (TLS), 'exhilarating', in the words of the Pulitzer Prize-winning poet Paul Muldoon, who selected it for that compilation.

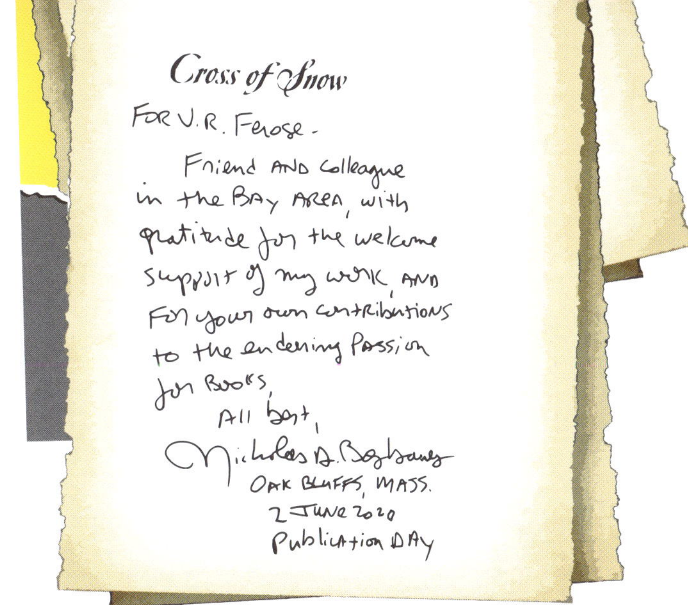
Cross of Snow

For V.R. Ferose -
Friend and Colleague in the Bay Area, with gratitude for the welcome support of my work, and for your own contributions to the enduring passion for books,
All best,
Nicholas A. Basbanes
Oak Bluffs, Mass.
2 June 2020
Publication Day

In our conversation, Nick shared details of how he goes about his work. He starts early in the morning, takes a break for lunch and an afternoon nap and works until 'my eyes give out and its time to stop'. Since he is a non-fiction writer, a significant part of his routine involves research and travel. For Nick, narrative – 'storytelling' – 'is everything'. We talked about the impact of email of future biographies, and how the art of letter writing will soon be lost. We shared some of the most inspiring exchanges through letters. Among Nick's favourites are Vladimir Nabokov's correspondence with his wife Vera. He feels that while collectors are a dwindling population, he is encouraged by what he sees as a committed group of younger collectors – like myself, he noted – who are determined to continue. 'Collecting is something that is innate,' he said. 'And that gives me hope. There will always be a new wave of determined people.'

I had taken two books for him – a signed copy each of *Highway Dharma Letters* and *Seat of the Soul*. He promised to send me signed copies of all his books and took me to the California Book Club just down Sutter Street from the Marine Club, a place that I had never visited before.

When *Cross of Snow* was published, Nick sent me an inscribed copy dated 2 June 2020 – publication day! This is Nick's tenth book and first biography. Every book he has signed for me contains a warm and witty inscription, something personal and meaningful – he never just dashes off a line.

I will always be thankful to Nick for introducing me to Henry Wadsworth Longfellow, an enormously influential poet who was enjoyed and admired by millions of readers throughout the world in the nineteenth century. I am even more thankful that he considers me worthy of sharing a small part of his personal library – a 'custodian', as he put it. I only hope I can pass on the stories from his books to the next generation. As Nick writes in his article for *The Book Collector*, 'It is a fundamental belief of mine that every book collector is at heart a storyteller, and that every treasure in a bibliophile's library is part of a larger narrative with a backstory of its own to tell, one that goes well beyond what appears on the printed page.'

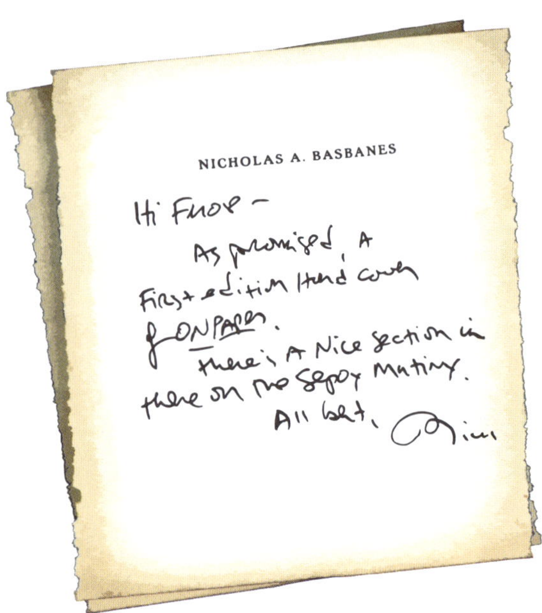
NICHOLAS A. BASBANES

Hi Fnoe –
As promised, a
First edition Hard cover
of ONPAPER.
There's a nice section in
there on the Sepoy Mutiny.
All best, Nick

(viii)

(ix)

(x)

When I say 'living with a collector', I am not talking about being the wife of an officer in the Indian Administrative Services. Nor am I talking about being a gangster's moll extorting money (popularly known as *'hafta'* in gangster lingo) from the unfortunate rich. I am talking about living with a man who literally collects as a hobby.

AN ESSAY BY DEEPALI KULKARNI

Now what might one collect that would actually end up being a whole chapter in a book? Books, yes, but one could also collect coins, stamps and the like. My husband collects mostly books, typically the rare kinds, not something you'd pick up from a random bookshop or the pirated book vendors on M.G. Road in Bengaluru. What makes these collectible books rare could be anything – a first edition, a signed first edition, an out-of-print version of a well-known book, a hardbound version that's not too common and so on.

Years ago, when I met my husband in college and discovered that he, like me, reads books, my joy knew no bounds. I remember introducing him to Erich Segal, my favourite author in those days. Of course, my reading was limited to fiction by Jeffrey Archer, Sidney Sheldon, P.G. Wodehouse and my all-time favourite, Agatha Christie. I had yet to be

introduced to the genius of J.K. Rowling, who might very well have been sitting in the cafe at that time, churning out those brilliant pages which would, in a few years, change my life.

As I got to know him better, I discovered that he gravitated towards non-fiction, something I have never ventured into till date. Although this was slightly disappointing, I didn't care as long as we could both sit in a coffee shop with each of our noses buried in our books and no particular need to have a conversation apart from placing an order. We spent our weekends going to the Strand, Premier, Select, Oxford and other bookshops.

Then the inevitable happened. We got married. I shared a home. Our first home was in Whitefield, and I didn't warm up to the fact that it was 20 km away from my favorite part of the city, M.G. Road. However, we soon discovered that we had enough books to fill our time and space at home. It was a fairly large dwelling with little or no furniture, and I remember spending weekends reading books rather than visiting bookstores.

That was also the phase when my newly minted husband started collecting movie memorabilia and weapons. So the knife that Amitabh Bachchan used in a film to carve off his antagonist's face found pride of place in my bedroom wall right above where I slept. The khukri that we had picked up at our honeymoon in Nepal earned itself a place there too. After a visit to Barcelona, I found some weapons of torture in Ferose's suitcase, and in a few days, they were hung on the same wall. Fortunately, these were never used on anyone, but I still had to uncomfortably share space with them for years, although they were ultimately relegated to the bottom of a storage box still sitting somewhere in Bengaluru.

Several relocations later, we came back to the same house, and this time, our stock of books had reached sizable proportions. Although we now had bookshelves, the books seemed to overflow out of wardrobes and drawers in all the rooms. My interior decorator, who was also one of my best friends, suggested that we decorate each room with books of the colour scheme used in that room. So our bedroom, which was pink/purple, had books with covers in that shade lined up on the dresser and nightstands. Of course, the books we were currently reading ended up being piled up in the same room, not the effect she was going for.

Right about that time, the spouse started taking an interest in cricket bats. He started collecting the ones signed by famous cricketers. And here, I have a funny anecdote to share. Since we were getting some work done at home, there was a carpenter who visited frequently. Ferose decided that a bat belonging to a cricketing legend, which had been a personal gift to him from the legend, should have a place of its own in our living room. So he negotiated with the carpenter about building an appropriate stand where the bat could be displayed. The carpenter wanted to take the bat home for measurements. Despite my warnings, Ferose, the eternal believer in the goodness of people, gave the bat to him. As you can probably tell, we never saw the bat or that carpenter again.

Ferose is also a collector of awards. His hall of fame at home constitutes a shelf full of trophies and wall full of framed newspaper articles featuring him. One of his achievements was the Economic Times' 40 under 40 award. I accompanied him to Mumbai to receive the award. While there, we snuck into Chor Bazaar in search of a specific shop that sold film posters. At that time, I wasn't aware that film posters would become another set of 'collectibles' in Ferose's repertoire. Today we have signed posters of *La La Land*, *The Hunger Games*, *Rock On* and *Kashmir Ki Kali* to name a few of the twenty posters, and it all started in the dingy lanes of Mumbai's Mutton Street.

At our last relocation, this time to the United States, I put my foot down. I refused to carry all those gazillions of books to a home that I had no idea would have any space for them. We started the sad act of categorizing our books into those we would take, store or give away. We ended up giving away three large cartons of books, which, to my dismay, was only one-tenth our total collection. We stored ten boxes at a friend's place and brought back fifty cartons of books. Fifty!

(ix)

The madness continues and has gotten worse after we moved here. Ferose got in touch with several people who aided and abetted this insanity, as I lovingly call it. It's impossible to get mad at a husband who gifts you a signed Agatha Christie and a signed P.G. Wodehouse on your birthday. While he encourages me to take literature and writing courses, he continues his search for rare and unique books.

His interests vary from sports to politics to movies. During the US elections last year, he was deeply into learning about the American presidents and acquired quite a few books on that theme, many of them rare. When I took a Shakespeare course, he found a page from one of Shakespeare's original folios, a very rare artifact indeed. To this day, I do not know, nor do I want to know the obscene amount of money he has spent on it. He has invested in letters written between M.K. Gandhi and other celebrated leaders, and they have found a place along our corridors at home. Every time Ferose is trying to add shelves to a room, I know more books are coming, and I brace myself for that inevitable sound of the shelves falling under the weight of the books.

So what is it like living with a collector, you may ask. It's like living with someone who is constantly passionate, constantly searching, constantly changing. To borrow from the lines that Agatha Christie said about her husband, a collector of artifacts is the best husband a woman can have. The older and rarer she gets, the more interested he is in her.

THE CHASE FOR MY

In my collection, there are many examples of rare books that I have determinedly chased after, but there are also a few that I have missed acquiring.

There is a Limited Editions Club (LEC) copy of Lewis Carroll's *Alice's Adventures in Wonderland* that I passed on when it came my way. What was special about it? The two-volume LEC edition of 1932 is signed by the real Alice – Alice Hargreaves!

'It's sometimes said that Lewis Carroll's Alice books were the origin of all later children's literature,' noted Philip Pullman. 'There were books for children before 1865, but they were almost all written to make a moral point... In Alice, for the first time, we find a realistic child taking part in a story whose intention was entirely fun. Both children and adults loved them at once, and have never stopped doing so. They are as fresh and clever and funny today as they were a hundred and fifty years ago.'

The 150th anniversary of the book's publication was observed around the world. In Japan, for instance, several acclaimed artists made their own illustrations of Alice's Wonderland. And at the Morgan Library in New York, the original manuscript was on display. New translations of Alice's story were commissioned worldwide from one in Egyptian heiroglyphs, an emoji version, to the title in the Afghan languages, Dari and Pashto.

I did eventually acquire a 1932 signed copy of Alice at a price I was prepared to pay. The copy probably belonged to someone who must have had a chance to get it signed by Hargreaves, most likely when she came to Columbia University, New York, to accept an honorary degree. Between the first edition and the numerous editions of *Alice* we have today, there have been several bespoke illustrated editions. There is a 1932 Macmillan centenary edition, done as a facsimile of the original manuscript with illustrations by Lewis Carroll himself. I came to hear of an edition published even earlier in 1872 by Macmillan. While author-signed or Alice-signed copies are scarce, it is relatively easier to locate copies signed by others related to the book, such as Alice's famous illustrator, Arthur Rackham.

Anything signed by Lewis Carroll, of course, was another matter. A copy of a Carroll-signed edition, once in the possession of a family in Oxford that had known him, was to be auctioned privately to raise funds for a collector's circuit book group. I knew I had a fair chance at making a decent bid. Not being able to participate in the auction myself, I placed my maximum bid with a collector, who later informed me that the copy was now mine as soon as the auction was over! The hammer price was not inexpensive, but luckily, it had not skyrocketed.

Now that I had the Carroll–Rackham, I wanted to see if I could lay my hands on anything signed by John Tenniel, Alice's original illustrator. And to my enormous luck, I found an autographed letter signed – what the trade calls an ALS – by Tenniel, addressed to a staff member of *Punch* magazine, to which the illustrator contributed regularly. The previous owner of the ALS had thoughtfully laid it into another early printed *Alice*, an 1899 Macmillan edition, which came as a bonus.

In the space of just a few months, I had experienced a lot – the lows and highs of collecting; regret at missing a highly desirable signed edition that had turned into deep longing; and then unexpected fulfillment. What more can a humble collector and an *Alice* fan wish for? Well, what about the *Pennyroyal Alice* illustrated by the famous wood engraver Barry Moser, or the Dali *Alice*, that fabulous, elusive, expensive limited edition illustrated and signed by Salvador Dali? My chase for Alice, I realized, had perhaps only just begun.

People give away their books because of the 4 Ds – Death, Divorce, Donation and Downsizing – according to Michelle Jenquin, owner of Wilson's Book World in St. Petersburg, Florida. For me, it was a case of relocation-driven downsizing-cum-donation!

the emotional turmoil of de-cluttering

Moving to a new house was hard; decluttering my books was harder. After much emotional turmoil, you realize that you have way more books than you can ever read in a single lifetime and not enough space to store them. Even though I consider myself a minimalist, I've made an exception when it comes to buying books. As a result, I have over three thousand books.

Most of them had been bought for researching the topics I was writing about; several were bought during my travels and reminded me of the time I spent in different cities; while a large number was signed by authors during book events. Now coming to the question: Do I really need them? What if I miss a book after giving it away? Every book has a story, a connection to a point in my life where the purchase of the book indicated my state of mind, my deep thoughts and my response to the world. Books gifted to me or those with an author inscription became that much harder to part with.

There are many books on decluttering and minimalism (for example Marie Kondo's *The Life-Changing Magic of Tidying Up*), but buying a book on the subject would be ironical since it would only add to the clutter and defeat the very objective of the book! Some of my books have travelled across the Atlantic (from India) and have remained in unopened boxes. My wife gave me a stern warning that if she ever saw another Amazon delivery box with a book, she was going to call the lawyer. So I decided to donate five hundred books to my neighbourhood used-books store Book-Go-Round, volunteer-run by Friends of Saratoga Library.

The process of sorting my books took weeks. I realized that I had twelve books on Alaska, including John Green's *Looking for Alaska,* which I had bought without knowing that it was about a girl named Alaska. I decided to part with all except one picture book on Alaska. I had ten books on Israel – all bought before my trip to Tel Aviv. I had 102 books on cricket and decided to part with twenty. Of the eighty-five books on Mahatma Gandhi, I gave away ten. History books were difficult to donate as they were timeless. I also had books that I had no clue why I bought, like the bestseller *I Hope They Serve Beer in Hell*. Older paperbacks were easier to donate.

Since Book-Go-Round would not accept more than one box (typically twenty-five books) at a time, I had to carefully fill up twenty boxes with books and drop them off daily, one by one. What I realized during the decluttering process was that if you think too much, you will never give your books away. So I recommend you speed up the process and remember that the person who is going to read the book will value it as much as you do. With every box of books I handed over, I gave away a small part of me. But the thought that a complete stranger would be connected to me through a book brought a smile to my face!

From Gurugram to Bengaluru to Cupertino to Saratoga, my books have travelled and finally found a home away from mine.

NEW YORK CITY

THE MECCA OF USED & RARE BOOKS

New York was once the Mecca of the used and rare book trade. Between 1990 and 2000, there were four hundred used bookstores. Now there are seventy. Fourth Avenue was once famous as the 'booksellers' row' with sixty-seven shops on just eight blocks with bookstores spilling over on each side street and parallel.

The books at the bookstores on Fourth Avenue were decently priced, and everyone could afford to buy something worthwhile. Now the Strand Bookstore is the last one standing – barely. In 2020, the COVID-19 pandemic almost shut down Strand because of a huge decline in foot-traffic, a near-complete loss of tourism and zero in-store events (compared to four hundred events pre-pandemic). It had to reach out to people, requesting them to buy from their three brick-and-mortar locations and website, and raised $250,000 just to survive.

The used and rare book business is now almost extinct. In the US, it has been an integral part of the American fabric. As Gary Goodman says in *The Last Bookseller,* 'It has been suggested that the humble bookseller by rescuing so many books and manuscripts across so many years have contributed more to western civilization than museums and libraries.' Goodman's book is a must-read to understand the history of the US rare book business. In 2017, Goodman had to finally close his shop in Stillwater after thirty-five years in the used and rare books trade due to the impact of the internet on his business. He shared, 'When the internet came along, for the used and rare bookseller, it was like a lawyer waking up and realizing that all his clients have a law degree!'

Today, even though the numbers have dwindled, New York City still remains one of the last remaining rare and antiquarian book cities in the world. Founded in 1925, Argosy Book Store is one of the founding members of the Antiquarian Booksellers' Association of America and is now in its third generation of family ownership. Overshadowed by the more famous Strand Book Store, Argosy specializes in rare books, prints, maps and autographs.

The James Cummins Bookseller on the seventh floor of 699 Madison Avenue is difficult to locate, unless you specifically look for it. When I rang the bell, even the storekeeper seemed surprised to find a visitor. I then had an hour-long conversation with the very friendly and knowledgeable Alex Obercian (I must admit, I felt elated to be recognized – as Alex had read my profile in *Fine Books and Collections*.). James Cummins has a fantastic collection of rare books and prints in its New York store even though most of its books are in its New Jersey warehouse. Although most of its sales are online, interestingly, 90 per cent of the revenue still comes from serious collectors, who form 10 per cent of the buyers.

Since I started teaching at Columbia University, I tried to spend a couple of hours visiting the nearby bookstores, the closest being the Columbia University Bookstore. I also visited The Westerner and Book Culture, but my favourite was Left Bank Books on West 4th Street (formerly called Asylum Street). While it specializes in First Editions and is strong on fiction, classics and poetry, you can also find some rare gems. It was only while leaving that I realized that the bookstore placed a few books outside for any book lover to take for free.

To understand the rare book trade, a must-read is *Books and Bidders* by A.S.W. Rosenback, and to know the mind of a collector, *Rosenback* by Edwin Wolf and John F. Fleming is an outstanding biography. And finally, I would highly recommend the documentary *The Booksellers* that explores the world of antiquarian and rare book dealers.

Even if a lifetime is not enough to read all the books I want, there is still a possibility for me to visit all the amazing bookstores in New York City.

NORWAY
A Publisher's Paradise

Norway is not just one of the world's wealthiest countries, it is also the world's happiest (yes, it is ranked higher than Bhutan in the Global Happiness Index.).

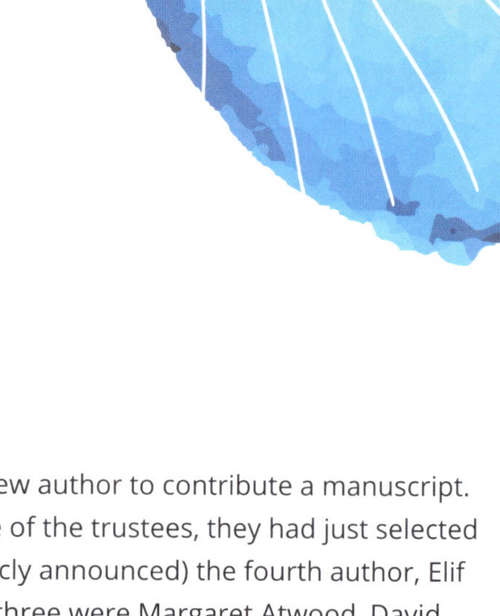

Norway is the home of Edvard Munch and his iconic painting The Scream, which was the most expensive piece of art ever sold at an auction – it went for $120 million. What people don't know about Norway, however, is that it is a writers' and publishers' paradise. It also initiated one of the most innovative projects in the publishing industry – the Future Library Trust.

Started by Scottish artist Katie Paterson in 2014, the project would result in a collection of hundred books, printed hundred years in the future, in 2114, with paper from trees out of a newly planted forest in Norway. Every year, until 2114, the Future Library Trust will pick a new author to contribute a manuscript. The day I met one of the trustees, they had just selected (and not yet publicly announced) the fourth author, Elif Shafak – the first three were Margaret Atwood, David Mitchell and Sjón.

There are many reasons why Norway is a publishing haven. It has a 100 per cent literacy rate, free public universities, and above all, an Arts Council that purchases thousand copies of every Norwegian title for distribution to libraries. The government has also exempted books from Value Added Tax (VAT) and banned deep discounting of new books, thus protecting booksellers from online competition.

During my short stay in Oslo for the Wisdom Together Conference, I managed a quick visit to the bookstore Norli Eldorado, which opened in 2003, and is located on the site of the former Eldorado Cinema. The large store has a great range of Norwegian and international titles and an extensive English-language section. Unusually, publishing companies rent space for their books in the store, allowing Eldorado to retain overall control.

When it comes to books on Munch, *The Rescue Artist* by Edward Dolnick is an entertaining account of Charley Hill, the world's greatest art detective, and his search for 'The Scream' after it was stolen from the National Gallery in Oslo. The graphic novel and part biography *Munch* by Steffen Kverneland explores the artist's relationships and obsessions.

Norway has produced a trio of celebrated authors who have received the Nobel Prize for Literature: Bjørnstjerne Bjørnson, Knut Hamsun and Sigrid Undset. Bjørnson's name is synonymous with nineteenth century Norwegian literature, and his poem, 'Ja, vi elsker dette landet', is also known as Norway's national anthem. Knut Hamsun is regarded as the principal leader of Norway's Neo-Romantic revolution; its notions are articulated in his novels *Hunger* and *Pan*.

My personal favourite is Undset, considered the godmother of Norwegian literature. Raised on her country's profound traditions of folklore and cultural mythology, Undset's fictional narratives are greatly influenced by the framework of national pride and identity. Her critically acclaimed trilogy, *Kristin Lavransdatter* (*The Wreath, The Wife* and *The Cross*), published from 1920 to 1922, is a 1,200-page saga that chronicles the spiritual enlightenment and intellectual evolution of a woman from birth to death. The book supposedly inspired parts of *Gone with the Wind.*

The latest sensation from Norway is Karl Ove Knausgård. His six-volume critically acclaimed *My Struggle* has brought him not only great financial success but bitter blowback from his family and friends. I have personally enjoyed *Autumn*, which is written in the form of letters to his unborn daughter.

Odd, isn't it, that some of the greatest literary works come from a country whose population is half that of Bengaluru, and over 80 per cent of Norwegians speak fluent English, even though it is a foreign language.

When I heard about the death of Mr T.S. Shanbhag, the legendary bookshop owner of Premier, I once again watched Mr Shanbhag's *Shop* on YouTube. It made me nostalgic for the weekends I had spent at Premier Book Shop on Church Street.

DOCUMENTING the bookstore

The grief over the Premier Bookshop's closure in 2009 re-emerged with a pang when book lovers heard that Mr Shanbhag had passed away. It was the end of an era, and Mr Shanbhag's memories will stay with everyone who had walked in between those piles of books and heard the sound of them falling.

(xii)

The short film, *Shop*, reminded me of others that document such iconic places for future generations. A literary tour of New York would include Strand Book Store, Argosy Book Store, James Cummins Bookseller, Housing Works Bookstore and Bauman Rare Books. If you cannot do it in person, then watch the documentary *The Booksellers*, about New York's antiquarian book dealers. *BookWars* by Jason Rosette brings out the perspectives of the street booksellers of New York. I wish someone would make a film on Bengaluru bookstores such as The Bookworm, Blossom, Select Book Shop and Gangarams, which are not just mere bookshops but institutions.

Since many of them closed down or struggled to survive the pandemic, a full-length documentary would capture the spirit of Bengaluru's literary landmarks, including vanished ones like Premier and Strand. The 2015 film *Welcome to the Last Bookstore* is an exploration of the quirkiest bookstore in Los Angeles and the man who brought it into existence. I was fortunate to visit The Last Bookstore (rated one of the most beautiful bookstores in the world) and interact with the owner, Josh Spencer.

(xiii)

(xiv)

When I asked him about the future of the physical book he replied that physical books, like vinyl LPs, were more popular than ever, and perhaps surprisingly, also among the younger generation. Since writers are my role models I love documentaries on them. *Salinger* is about the reclusive and enigmatic author of *Catcher in the Rye* and was one of the top-ten highest-grossing documentaries of 2013. *Mary Angelou: And Still I Rise* reflects on how the events of history, culture and arts shaped Maya Angelou's life and how she, in turn, shaped our worldview through her literature and activism.

I Am Not Your Negro is a 2016 documentary directed by Raoul Peck, based on James Baldwin's unfinished manuscript *Remember This House*. *Becoming* is a documentary about Michelle Obama's life and connections as she embarks on a thirty-four-city book tour of her bestselling memoir.

If there is a documentary that captures the meaning of what a library means to people even in the most harrowing circumstances, it is *Daraya: A Library Under Bombs in Syria.* This is an account of how a group of men decide to build a secret library collecting books from their war-torn neighbourhood in Syria. Delphine Minoui has written about them in her bestseller *The Book Collectors of Daraya*.

My last memory of Mr Shanbhag is of him contemplating re-opening Premier after he read my column about the idea of bookstores being community spaces. He even had a few discussions on this topic with Krishna Gowda from The Bookworm. Unfortunately, the second innings never materialized. But perhaps, I've been paying Mr Shanbhag a silent and unwitting tribute, after all. Because my own room is beginning to look a lot like the interior of Premier Bookshop.

During one of my visits to Toronto to study the Artificial Intelligence ecosystem, I did what I always do – sneak a visit to a local bookstore. The Monkey's Paw is the home of the Biblio-Mat, the world's first randomized vending machine for old books. Here, I had a long conversation with the bookstore owner, Stephen Fowler.

THE MONKEY'S PAW SPRINGS A

Stephen Fowler had always known that he wanted to create a bookstore where people would be surprised by the books they find – books they didn't even know existed. *The Monkey's Paw,* which is the tile of W.W. Jacobs' short story with the message 'be careful what you wish for', felt to him like 'a memorable and somewhat creepy title, which also seemed fitting'.

The Monkey's Paw began in 2004 as an online-only shop, but once Stephen opened in a Toronto storefront in 2006, within a few months he recognized the obvious advantages of in-person bookselling and abandoned online sales entirely. 'Basically, the books we sell (many of them unlikely and forgotten titles) are so obscure that few shoppers on AbeBooks or Amazon would ever even know to search for them,' he said. 'People who buy books online don't really have any sense for where the books come from, so building customer loyalty is irrelevant and impossible.'

Stephen explained how the unique idea of Biblio-Mat occurred to him. He wanted to find a way to get odd or interesting books, which weren't likely to sell off the shelves, directly into people's hands. And he didn't want to give them a choice. 'Having a machine (apparently) make the decision added a sensational carnivalesque twist,' he said. His friend, Craig Small, offered to build the machine. Once it was set up, Stephen was 'flabbergasted by its popularity'. Some people in the book trade dismissed the Biblio-Mat as a cheap gimmick, but Stephen asserts: 'Having seen literally tens of thousands of budding bibliophiles receive books from the Biblio-Mat, I can attest that its users are mostly curious, open-minded, and prepared to find interest and amusement in whatever the machine selects for them. And through it, we've been able to find homes for countless orphaned old books.'

However, Stephen pointed out the increasing difficulty he faced in sourcing interesting and valuable books. He feared that in a decade or two, he might run into a situation where he simply wouldn't find the sorts

(xv) (xvi)

(xvii)

of books he would like to sell, in the quantities necessary. 'To steal a phrase from the oil industry: I feel like we may have reached "peak book",' he told me.

Stephen used to be a book collector, but at some point, he discovered that the real joy lay in finding books that he could put into the hands of new owners – what he calls 'making that "love connection" between people and books'. Unlike many of his colleagues in the field, he doesn't really care about finding super-expensive books.

'I'd rather sell twenty interesting old books for $50 each (or fifty books for $20 each!) than a single elite rarity for $1,000,' he said. Speaking of rarities, he cited the example of a trilingual lexicon he had found; printed in German, Latin and ancient Greek, it was published in Alsace in 1587. 'I happened to find a customer for it on a bitterly cold winter day, when the furnace at my house had broken down; I sold the book for the exact price of a very expensive furnace repair!'

I asked him what his favourite bookstores were other than his own. He names three: 'Brattle Book Shop, Boston... the definition of a stately, old-fashioned antiquarian shop, with a delightful bargain/clearance section in the vacant lot next door. Un Regard Moderne, Paris... mad source for visual culture, crammed with pictorial books of all sorts. Kayo Books, San Francisco... phenomenally entertaining collection of vintage paperbacks (obscure genres and sub-genres), pop culture, and sleaze.'

The Bell Hasn't Tolled for This Bookstore

Bell's Books is one of my favourite bookstores in the Silicon Valley, selling old, new and rare books.

I have often dropped in at Bell's Books with my son, Vivaan, and I found the staff to be very understanding. When I revealed to the owner, Faith Bell, that my son makes noise and accidentally drops books because he is on the autism spectrum, she warmly said, 'Special children are like the sun around which our lives revolve.' Her grandson has cerebral palsy, she shared with me. When my son was undergoing a medical procedure, she wrote to me, 'All the folks at Bell's send their best wishes to Vivaan on his surgery and hopes for a speedy recovery!' There is no way you cannot fall in love with a bookstore like that.

I had just become a huge fan of Arion Press, which produces some of the most beautiful limited-edition (two hundred and fifty to four hundred copies of three books a year), hand-printed books in the world when Faith called me to have a look at a rare collection of signed books from Arion. I bought Seamus Heaney's *The Stone from Delphi*; Lawrence Ferlinghetti's *A Coney Island of the Mind*; Italo Calvino's *Invisible Cities* and William Blake's beautiful watercolour drawings illustrating *Milton's Paradise Lost*. Like all generous booksellers, she gifted me a signed copy of Delia Owens's *Where the Crawdads Sing* and hugged me warmly before I walked out of the store.

Bell's Books was started by Herbert Bell in 1935 as a college bookshop selling textbooks before Stanford University had its own bookstore inside the campus. Faith, who started working in the store as a teenager, showed me books signed by Nobel laureate Linus Pauling, who visited the store over a decade ago. She told me how she spent time with Stephen King when he was signing books while on a bike trip. I am grateful to her for introducing me to the writings of Buckminster Fuller. A signed copy of Fuller's collection of essays *And it Came to Pass – Not to Stay* remains a prized possession till date. In fact, Bell's fine collectable first edition section is where I found a first edition of Agatha Christie's *The Thirteen Problems* – a birthday gift for my wife.

(xviii)

(xix)

One of my visits to Bell's was soon after the death of Harper Lee, when the store paid tribute to both Lee and Umberto Eco, who died on 19 February 2016. As the storekeeper patiently opened the bookcases to explain the uniqueness of each book, I asked him why a pirated copy of *Lolita* would be a rare book. He told me it was collected by a 'completist' (a collector who strives to obtain a complete collection of some type of thing) who bought every possible edition of *Lolita*, including the pirated one from China (where the original ones were difficult to find).

I was contemplating buying a rare, signed book *Sailing Through China* by Paul Theroux and the illustrator Patrick Procktor as I had planned a visit to China (not by boat, though!). That's when the storekeeper mentioned that they had a special, bound, signed first edition of Harper Lee's *Go Set a Watchman.* Well, there were only five hundred copies ever published, so what could be a better buy, even if it meant that I would have to forego buying any other book for months?

After the book was billed and nicely packed, the storekeeper asked: 'Have you visited Feldman's in Menlo Park? You may find some very good rare books there.' A great bookstore never looks at other bookstores as competition.

I asked Faith if there was something about Bell's that hadn't changed since the beginning. She quoted her father: 'People still walk past our bookstore and seem more interested in reading the menu than in the books!' Not surprising if you're located in downtown Palo Alto, famous for its upscale restaurants. But the diehard book lover knows where to look.

As with many brick-and-mortar booksellers, Powell's City of Books is now run by the third generation of the original owners. 'I think the dirty secret of the book business is that people still love to read,' Emily Powell said in an interview with Oregonlive.com. 'People love a physical object and they love to read.'

(xx)

the world's LARGEST independent bookstore

On a weeklong vacation to Portland (Oregon), the high point of our hotel's location was its proximity to Powell's City of Books, which occupies an entire block in the Pearl District. It took multiple visits for me to even scratch the surface of the store's contents: over 1.5 million books divided into three thousand five hundred sections. Good thing it had an unusual closing time: 11 p.m.

Powell's claim to being the largest independent (and thriving) bookstore is founded not just on numbers but also about the quality of its books. Interestingly, from 2008 to 2014, e-book sales seem to have tapered off, and independent bookstores grew in number from sixteen hundred to two thousand.

As I entered the north-west entrance of the bookstore, I was struck by the Pillar of Books. This is a nine-foot column stacked with eight of the world's great books carved in Tenino sandstone: Psalms, *The Whale* the original title of (*Moby Dick*), Mahabharata, *War and Peace*, *1000 Nights and a Night*, *Tao Che Ching*, *Hamlet* and *The Odyssey*. The titles are inscribed in the language in which the book was originally printed. An instant book printer, aptly called the Expresso Book machine, is a clear indication that Powells has adopted technology and adapted to the fast-changing world.

The rooms are named after nine different colours. When I was exploring, I didn't use the store map and preferred to discover the various sections as I ambled through different floors. My wife, though, sought help from the store assistants, who pointed her to the Blue and Gold rooms, which stocked fiction books. The section with signed editions and notices about author visits indicated that there was a book reading almost every day.

As you can guess, my favourite was the Pearl Room, which housed exclusive rare books. This room, which closed at 7 p.m., required a separate badge to enter it. The most expensive book in the bookstore, a first edition copy of the 1814 printed *The Journals of Lewis and Clark*, cost a mere $350,000! From the Books on Books section, I bought a 1917 edition of H.L. Koopman's *The Booklover and His Books* for a humble $18. I also got James Purdy's short story, 'Did I say yes, did I say no', for $25. The Purple Room, in which a section is dedicated to American history and specifically to American presidents, was of great personal significance to me. I found an intriguing book, *Peculiarities of the Presidents*, signed by Don Smith.

(xxi)

(xxiii)

(xxii)

(xxiv)

The unique sections in each floor comprised a vast array of topics – from wooden books to the Rose Festival (as Portland is famous for its Rose Gardens), from Nobel Prize winners in many languages to Pride topics, from a section dedicated to the Kennedy family to summer reading – they had it all.

The souvenir store at Powells deserves a special mention. It had items categorized as Literary Gifts – tote bags, posters, T-shirts and mugs – all related to books and reading. For example, there was a mug that had the opening lines of famous books painted on it. The store also had utilitarian items such as book covers that can be used to safely keep rare books.

At the counter, while checking out my picks, I was surprised to see that the queue in the 'sell books' section was longer than the 'buy books' – a clear indicator that the true bookstore is as much about giving away your books to the right place as about buying them from one.

All in all, a complete experience for any book lover.

THE STORY OF A MULTI-STOREY BOOKSTORE

During my first visit to Detroit, Michigan, I was put up at the Hotel, DoubleTree on Lafayette Street. While driving to the hotel, I happened to see a four-storey building named John K. King Used and Rare Books Store.

During my visit to Detroit, I hadn't done my research on bookstores (that I normally do before visiting a new place), but it intrigued me to see a multi-storey bookstore. I checked on Yelp and was pleasantly surprised to see very positive reviews. So, I made it a point to spend an hour at the bookstore before leaving for the airport.

I must admit that I was a little sceptical in the beginning as the store looked like many of the rundown unoccupied places in downtown Detroit. But even before I entered the bookstore, the smell of books made me feel that I was in for a romantic sojourn. Signboards proclaimed that John K. King Books was Michigan's largest used books store; that CNN had named it 'one of the world's coolest bookstores'; and that it was named the number two bookstore in the world by *Business Insider* in 2014.

When I entered, the receptionist handed me a map of the almost ninety different sections across four floors – I was told there were a million books to select from! There was every topic and category you could imagine: from AfricanAmerican Studies to Eastern Religions, from Military History to Agriculture, from Philosophy to Cooking, as well as Engineering and Fashion. Given the size of the store, employees communicated using walkie-talkies, and there were phones on every floor that one could use by dialling 30 to get assistance.

(xxv)

(xxvi)

(xxvii)

(xxviii)

Since I had limited time on hand, I quickly specified my interests – literature, history and biographies – and was escorted to the third floor, where I found many a treasure. One of the lessons I have learnt over the years while collecting rare books is that it is better to buy one book that adds to your collection than ten that you buy and don't care about. So I went back to the receptionist and said, not very hopefully, that I was interested in books signed by US presidents. I was immediately escorted to the 'Rare Book Room' and asked: 'What is your budget? We have books from $100 to $100,000.'

I was shown the section on books signed by presidents, and there were none they did not have… from Barack Obama to Franklin D. Roosevelt (FDR), there was every piece of history you can imagine, lying right in front of me. Since I was collecting books about FDR, I got a signed book by FDR's personal secretary Grace Tully titled *F.D.R, My Boss* and a signed children's book by his daughter Anna Roosevelt titled *Scamper*. While I secretly wished I had more time, I also knew that if I had stayed longer, I would have spent ALL my money in the bookstore – there were thirty thousand rarest of the rare books to choose from just in this section alone.

John K. King Used and Rare Books Store was started by John K. King, who sold books from the trunk of his 1954 Packard until he bought an old glove factory in 1983. Maverick writer Hunter S. Thompson and music legend David Bowie both have bought books from here for their private collection. This is a bookstore that I would love to revisit and get lost in what seems like an entire kingdom of secondhand books.

While driving past downtown Detroit, I had seen houses up for sale for as low as $1,000, and my mind went back to John K. King Used and Rare Books Store. Here is a bookstore where there are books that are each worth more than a house. The whole bookstore is worth more than all of downtown Detroit!

Before you visit the iconic bookstore Shakespeare and Company in Paris, read *Time Was Soft There* by Jeremy Mercer.

Although I was aware of its legendary status – that James Joyce's *Ulysses* was published by its original owner Sylvia Beach and that Ernest Hemingway borrowed books from the store – I discovered more of its rich history while reading Mercer's book on my flight to Paris.

Time Was Soft There truly captures the essence of the bookstore as it covers the experience of the writer, who spent a year there and became owner George Whitman's right-hand man. You might also pick up the fully illustrated history *Shakespeare and Company, Paris* edited by Krista Halverson, and Noël Riley Fitch's *Sylvia Beach and the Lost Generation*. Hemingway's *A Moveable Feast* evokes the spirit of the 'lost generation', or those who came of age during the First World War, and literary Paris in the 1920s.

Sylvia Beach started Shakespeare and Company in November 1919, and for two decades between the World Wars, altered the course of modern literature. Beach created a literary centre that magnetically attracted artists from across the world. The literary pilgrims to this house of worship included T.S. Eliot, Andre Gide, Ernest Hemingway, Ezra Pound and Samuel Beckett. The bookstore was forced to close in 1941 during the German occupation of Paris. Beach was arrested and even imprisoned for six months by Nazi authorities. She was released towards the end of the war, but her ill health prevented her from ever reopening the store.

In 1951, George Whitman opened the store in its current location as 'Le Mistral' and renamed it 'Shakespeare and Company' in 1964, on the 400th anniversary of William Shakespeare's birth. It comprises three apartments combined into a bookstore on three floors. Movie buffs may remember the opening scene of one of my favourite movies, *Before Sunset*, starring Ethan Hawke, Julie Delpy and Vernon Dobtcheff; it was filmed at Shakespeare and Company.

Whitman was an eccentric bookseller who once walked from Mexico to Panama on foot, and would trim his hair using a burning candle. He invited travellers – usually aspiring writers, poets, and artists – to stay in the shop for free. In exchange, they were asked to help out around the bookstore, read a book a day, and write a one-page autobiography for the shop's archives. An estimated 30,000 guests have slept at the bookstore. Whitman called them 'Tumbleweeds' after the rootless plants that 'blow in and out on the winds of chance', as he described it. The store is now run by his daughter Sylvia Whitman (no surprise that George named his daughter Sylvia!). The ministry of culture at the United Nations has named the bookstore as one of the historic monuments of Paris, and Whitman was awarded the Officier de l'Ordre des Arts et des Lettres, the second highest award in France given to people for their contributions in art. literature and culture, which he promptly discarded.

When I visited the store on 11 September 2022, I had to wait in a queue for twenty minutes just to enter, and for me, that was a first. Luckily, the antiquarian section did not have a queue, and so I spent an hour browsing and talking to Alexendre Freiman, the storekeeper who had spent a decade there. He was friendly and knowledgeable, and we spoke about many things: the COVID-19 pandemic, the terror attacks, the fire at Notre-Dame Cathedral, and how the weather in Paris had changed over the last few years. While browsing, I came across a first edition of *Ulysses*, which, not surprisingly, was not for sale. A few years ago, a signed first edition of *Ulysses* was sold by the store for €15,000, and I believe it would be worth twenty times more today.

Even if you are not book-crazy, to understand the bohemian world of Paris, you must pay a visit to Shakespeare and Company, the bustling bookstore on the left bank of the River Seine, which rests in the shadow of Notre-Dame.

(xxix)

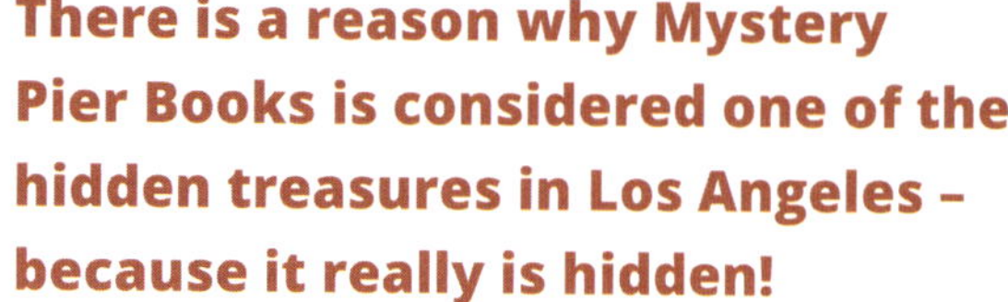
There is a reason why Mystery Pier Books is considered one of the hidden treasures in Los Angeles – because it really is hidden!

A HIDDEN mystery IN LOS ANGELES

After an entire week in LA, I hadn't discovered this place, but when I spent just a day there once, I accidentally stumbled upon it. When I excitedly called my friend Pradeep Sebastian, who is the final authority on antiquarian books and stores, even he had not heard of Mystery Pier Books. What is unique about this store is that every book it contains is a true first edition, making it a one-of-a-kind bookstore. (A true first edition is the one that supersedes all other editions chronologically.)

The entry to Mystery Pier was so narrow that I had to slide my travel suitcase vertically just to reach the doorstep. The door had a poster of the movie *The Martian* with a message 'Bring books home' with a picture of Harvey Jason, the store owner. Harvey spent an hour explaining the uniqueness of every book. Not many bookshop owners run the risk of over-handling and hence damaging a hugely expensive book by showing it to every customer. Perhaps this comes from the belief that every person who walks in is a potential buyer. And looks can be deceptive. Harvey narrated how, once, a ragged-looking woman who he thought was a homeless person came asking for a first edition of Charles Dickens. She bought a 'true first' for several thousand dollars. Talk about never judging a book by its cover!

(xxx)

(xxxi)

The walls of the store have pictures of Harvey and his son, Louis, posing with Hollywood stars; they form a dedicated clientele that often buys rare books as gifts. There are many signed movie scripts here – from *La La Land* to *Fences* and from *Gladiator* to *Good Will Hunting*. Harvey showed me a copy of Michael Crichton's book, *The Lost World*, priced at $10,000. It was signed by ten actors in the movie as well as Steven Spielberg, Stan Winston, and yes, Harvey himself, who has many movies under his belt.

One of Harvey's most famous friends was Kurt Vonnegut, who gifted a self-portrait to Harvey that is displayed in the store. Every true first of Vonnegut is available here – from *Slaughterhouse-Five* to *A Man Without a Country*. There is also a signed photo of Harper Lee with Harvey. Harvey is credited with having got J.K. Rowling to the US even before she became a worldwide sensation and Harry Potter such a craze. A true first edition of Harry Potter costs at least $5,000 because it ran a first print of just five hundred copies, many of which were signed and donated to educational institutions. Every Harry Potter fan should be aware that a true first is the one printed in the UK (origin of the author).

Mystery Pier also has rare magazines. There are copies of an issue of *LIFE* magazine that costs upwards of $5,000 and contains only one piece – the entire text of Hemingway's *The Old Man and the Sea*. This was the very first appearance of the world-renowned novella.

Harvey's business has only grown with time since many collectors find rare books a great investment, even better than art. However, what really mattered and why he loved the profession, he said, was that he only met extremely good people in the bookshop. And Barry Gibb, the Bee Gees singer, was humble, full of gratitude, and a walking ray of sunshine.

What makes the place accessible to every book lover is that it has good, true first editions for less than $50 too. For Harvey's knowledge and love of books and the sense of history you will find here, Mystery Pier in itself is worth a visit to Los Angeles.

(xxxii)

Since my job entails a considerable amount of time spent at international airports, most of which look and feel the same, I went on a quest for bookstores that haven't fallen prey to dreadful homogeneity.

The search For UNIQUE Airport Bookstores

Most airport bookstores do conform to the same template: bestsellers, new releases, magazines, souvenirs and travel accessories (including the omnipresent travel pillow!) but I have found some unique ones.

One could mistake Tanum in Oslo for a space shuttle from the outside. Inside, it is spacious and well-organized, with a sizeable collection of both English and Norwegian titles along with a big section on comics and graphic novels. Good bookstores often reflect the culture and ethos of the cities where the airports are situated. The bookstore in Philadelphia airport has a section on Black authors, hinting at the city's large Black population. Dubai airport's bookshop, titled simply Books and Magazines, is the only one I've seen which sells copies of the Quran; besides books

in Arabic, it has books in Malayalam, as well as a separate section with books about ruling leaders – all of which clearly indicate the political and demographic profile of the city. An unexpected section here was one titled 'General Knowledge'.

The bestseller list in an airport bookstore is an indicator of what is topmost on the minds of people in that city or country. And they vary– the bestseller list at Shanghai airport is very different from the one at Dubai; the Frankfurt list doesn't resemble the one in Los Angeles. AM Bookstore in Shanghai's Pudong airport is the only place where I found a book on Vladimir Putin making its way to the bestseller list. It also has a video playing in the background. The only English books here are the Lonely Planet Guides and a few commonly seen bestsellers.

Sky Harbour airport in Phoenix, Arizona, which calls itself the friendliest airport in the US, has come up with a unique concept: 'Rent and Return' a book. Powell's Books at the international airport in Portland, Oregon, includes used books in its sales stock. I think this is a wonderful idea since it gives travellers an endless choice of titles – those that are quite different from the same old ones they come across in practically every airport bookstore.

My favourite, though, is San Francisco airport's Compass Books, a bookstore with a wide range of choices and staff recommendations. It also has many author-signed books, a feature that more airport bookshops could easily adopt, considering how many authors must be in transit while going on their book tours. I was excited to see an author-signed section as well as a section on Nobel Prize winners at Bengaluru airport's Relay bookstore (part of an international chain).

In the airport at my hometown of Kochi, Kerala, I found four bookstores with practically no customers! When I asked one of the proprietors how he managed to earn any profit, he said the store was a mere prop used for marketing purposes.

Speaking as a somewhat jaded frequent flyer, I am all for creating a lively environment at airports. While most of them have made an effort to provide a simpler and better flying experience, the next frontier would be to make it exciting and cater to personal tastes. What would the airport of the future look like? You needn't stray into the realms of science fiction to imagine a day when you will be driven to the terminal by autonomous cars, bags will have permanent IDs, and your fingerprint or iris may be the only ID that you need. Imagine a day when you choose to reach the airport a few hours early so that you can catch an exciting event – it could be a movie premiere, a live music performance or a book launch – right before you board the flight.

Krishna Gowda, or Krishna as everyone calls him, owner of The Bookworm, has that rare quality that I often look for in my colleagues – PHD – Passion, Hunger and Desire.

When Westland announced its closure, Krishna had his hands full, as orders started pouring in from across the country, and even authors showed up to promote the final print copies of their books. The Bookworm is a firm favourite of writers such as Ramachandra Guha, Anita Nair and Suresh Menon. When former Prime Minister Deve Gowda's biography *Furrows in a Field* was released, he personally spent an hour at the store on 3 January 2022. Rahul Gandhi and former Chief Minister Siddaramaiah took a break at The Bookworm during the Jana Aashirwada Yatre campaign on 7 April 2018.

Krishna Gowda

The Bookman of

As he celebrates his silver jubilee in the world of books, Krishna continues to be driven by his passion for books and his customers, an abiding hunger to learn, and above all, an ardent desire to make the world a better place by throwing his weight behind the right causes.

Krishna is the reason why The Bookworm holds a special place in the hearts of booklovers. To sustain a business for twenty-five years, one must remain relevant and constantly reinvent oneself, and he has done that time and again. The pandemic tested him (like it did everybody else), but he quickly pivoted to taking orders on WhatsApp and delivering books via mobile apps such as Dunzo and Swiggy, as well as Speed Post. To engage readers, he even built a social media presence and held regular author signings.

As someone who has known Krishna for almost two decades, I have seen him grow from selling books on the pavement of MG Road to having the most sought-after address on Church Street. Modest to a fault, success has not changed him a bit. He has not forgotten his roots and supports his extended family back in his village in Rangasamudra (near Mysuru). He knows his customers' interests and recommends books – old and new – that they would like the most.

What makes The Bookworm unique is that it has a huge collection of both old and new books. The store's highlight is its treasure trove of over hundred thousand children's books, most of them priced at ₹50! My own association with Krishna has grown since the publication

of my book *Gifted*, in 2014. It sold briskly, thanks mainly to Krishna's word-of-mouth publicity. He personally added a further 20 per cent discount to the regular 20 per cent, believing that it would contribute to a good cause.

One of the most touching moments was during a visit to his home. After having coffee with his wife, Uma, and eighty-year-old mother, Uma gave me a parting gift – a book signed by Nobel laureate Malala Yousafzai. I did not want to take it as Krishna had gifted it to her. But they would not take no for an answer. Krishna then dropped me back home on his scooter, on which I had arrived. Krishna has enriched my personal collection with some of the rarest of rare books – from a book signed by the Mysore Maharaja to Gandhi's first edition of *My Experiments with Truth* to a signed *The Golden Book of Tagore* and a M.F. Hussain-signed *Story of a Brush*.

My personal highlight was when he managed to get me my childhood favourite, Amar Chitra Katha's first edition of Series Numbers 11 to 69 (from 1969 to 1974). Every time he comes across a rare book, he gives me the first right of refusal – and I have never refused till date. Krishna's vision is to build an institution, to make The Bookworm more than just a bookstore – to also be a place for coffee and conversations.

After the pandemic, he moved to a larger space on Church Street. He hosted an event there in December 2021 around my book on disability, *The Invisible Majority*, making sure to provide wheelchair access. The last time I spoke to him, he said his dream is to build an antiquarian section with rare books. There is one thing you can never fault Krishna for – dreaming big.

THE MYSTERIES WITHIN THE MYSTERIOUS BOOKSTORE

As a subscriber to the newsletter of Mysterious Bookstore, I was aware of its status as the largest bookstore in the world focusing on mystery books.

(xxxiii)

The highlight of my San Francisco to New York travels is that I get five hours of uninterrupted reading time (I avoid watching TV, drinking or eating during a flight). I also make it a point to include at least one literary activity amongst the vast choices you have in New York City. Even after more than ten visits to the city, my NYC literary bucket list is far from complete, as I discovered from reading *A Booklover's Guide to New York* by Cleo Le-Tan, a book I would highly recommend.

Located walking distance from the offices where Edgar Allen Poe imagined gruesome tales while on his day job at the *Evening Mirror*, The Mysterious Bookshop is a haven for any crime, suspense and thriller reader. I was also aware of the founder, Otto Penzler, being a collector himself and a known figure in the bookseller circuit. When I finally did visit the bookstore in July 2022, although Penzler was not in the store, I was not disappointed.

The large store has books stacked all the way to the ceiling. An old sofa and a locked door with the message 'CRIME SCENE DO NOT CROSS' set the appropriate mood. I am not a mystery fan, so I was not expecting to buy much, but alas, the helpful staff led me into temptation. A first edition of *The Hound of the Baskervilles* lured me, but its cost of $1,750 was beyond my means. I struck it lucky, though, when I picked up a book from a box containing signed copies of *Sherlock Holmes in 221 Objects*, a catalogue from the collection of Glen S. Miranker and Cathy Miranker. Fortunately, the store had an extra copy and I wrapped it up for $60. This is a catalogue of 221 rare books featuring Holmes, and it was the best gift I could get for my wife, Deepali, who is a huge fan of the legendary detective.

What amazed me was the huge collection of signed books both old and new. As a collector, I was aware that not all signed books are valuable, and hence, picking the right ones was important. There were signed copies of books by famous modern mystery writers such as Lee Child and Joyce Carol Oates, but what impressed me were the books by many international authors. There were a few by Indian and Indian-origin authors that I had not read or heard of – Harini Nagendra's *The Bangalore Detectives Club* and all the books by Abir Mukherjee. There was a section on the original *Strand Magazine* where *Sherlock Holmes* had first appeared, but I skipped it since I already have a *Strand* copy signed by Arthur Conan Doyle.

(xxxiv)

At the time of my visit, I was researching for my column on books by booksellers and was delighted when a staff member showed me *Mysterious Obsession* by Penzler himself. I managed to finish reading this book in a single sitting. It lists twenty-six of the rarest books in Otto's collection accompanied by the stories of how he acquired them. I had not read any of them except Dashiell Hammett's *The Maltese Falcon.* One of the most interesting stories is about how Otto acquired a copy of *$106,000 Blood Money* inscribed by Hammett to his mistress. Two more staff recommendations were *The Book of the Most Precious Substance* by Sara Gran and *The Memoirs of an Erotic Bookseller* by Armand Coppens.

I was so engaged in browsing that I almost forgot my office bag at the counter. Only hunger would eventually drag me out of the store and into the Benares Indian Restaurant next door. The day cannot get any better than browsing books followed by a fabulous Indian meal in New York City.

(xxxv)

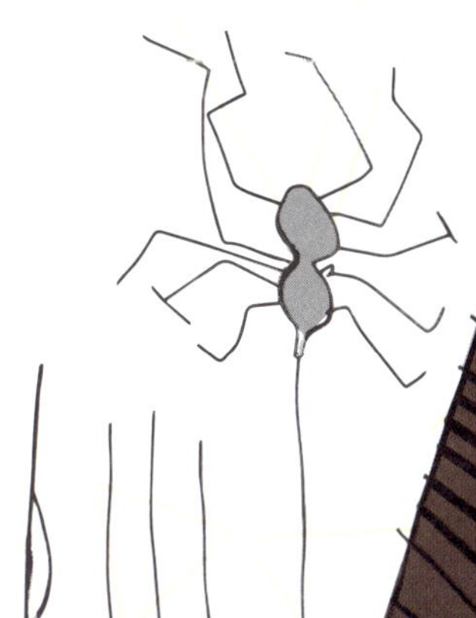

EXPLORING THE GENRE OF BOOKS ON BOOKS

As a bibliophile and technologist, I have struggled with the duality of the physical and the digital book.

When Ray Bradbury wrote *Fahrenheit 451*, his inspiration was the invasion of black-and-white televisions into people's homes. The novel depicts a future American society where books are outlawed, and 'firemen' burn any that are found. If Bradbury had written the book today, it would have been about the impact of social media on our lives. As the virtual world predominates, owning physical books becomes an act of rebellion. And books about books gain importance in this context.

Just a few years ago, you would have been overjoyed at spotting a book-about-books title in a bookshop; in a year you'd be lucky if three to five titles came out. Now, a couple of titles are published every month. But when did this genre originate, anyway? The 14th century! The pioneer was Bishop Richard De Burry, a cleric who wrote *Philobiblon*, a treatise on organising books, in Latin.

There are classics, too, in the genre, and luckily one can read or download them on the internet for free because their copyright has expired. One of the most widely admired classics is Charles Everitt's *Adventures of a Treasure Hunter*, a rollicking tale of this author's quest for 'Americana': books and ephemera dealing with American history. Published around the mid-1950s, it tells of the real adventures of a man who searched high and low for Americana, which he then bought cheap and sold high.

Another classic is Andrew Lang's *The Library*. It examines various aspects that a book lover would find useful, from how to organize your library to commentary on illustrated books. A string of earlier books about books – written as a series that gave impetus to the genre – were those of Thomas Dibdin, in particular *Bibliomania*, and a later title *Reminiscences of a Literary Life* where the author speaks of his great love for books.

John Hill Burton's *The Book-Hunter* is another much-discussed work in the genre. Also published in the nineteenth century, it's a bit controversial because the author satirizes collectors and their mania. Burton's book is not from a collector's perspective but from the opposite side – that of the practical reader. There are numerous other titles from the nineteenth and early twentieth centuries that today's book lovers may not have heard of, and if you keep an eye out for them on Google Books, most of them turn up in free e-book formats.

Turning now to the other end of the spectrum – the absolutely new or new-ish titles – it would be wise to begin with Alberto Manguel's *Packing my Library*, where this literary critic shares his experience of packing his thirty-five thousand books to move them to a new home. In the process, Manguel seizes the opportunity to comment on some of the books in his possession.

The Library: A Catalogue of Wonders by Stuart Kells has already garnered rave reviews. Kells burrows into the history of this greatest of cultural institutions: the library. He remarks that in order to research this book, he and his family toured libraries around the world.

Nicholas A. Basbanes is one of the most well-known scholars who writes about books and book culture. In many ways his book, *A Gentle Madness*, gave me permission to follow my passion to collect books and study about them. After reading all the crazy stories of book collectors (including the book thief Stephen Blumberg) I realized I was not the only one obsessed with getting my hands on every book worth collecting. However, my initial interest in books on books was fuelled by my friend Pradeep Sebastian, one of the finest scholars India has produced. I first met him when I hosted him for a talk on his book, *The Groaning Shelf*, a collection of his bibliophile essays. His most recent work, *The Book Hunters of Katpadi*, is India's first ever biblio-mystery, which delves deep into the world of antiquarian book-collecting.

Finally, I have to mention *The Most Dangerous Book* by Kevin Birmingham, an account of the publishing history of James Joyce's *Ulysses*. I am guilty of never having finished reading *Ulysses*, considered one of the most important novels in the English language. So I decided to read its biography instead.

One of the high points in my bookish journey is a lunch meeting I had with Nicholas A. Basbanes. Of the numerous things we discussed, I asked him about the eight-hundred-plus inscribed books he had collected over years of interviewing authors and how they are now preserved in the Texas A&M institute, carefully documented and catalogued to be used as research material by students. 'As a lover of books,' Nick said to me, 'giving away my lifelong collection for the larger good is the ultimate high.'

I have been fortunate to have travelled around the world and visited some of the most stunning bookstores – big and small; old and new; chain and independent; rare and antiquarian; mobile and personal; in cities and villages. I have seen the world through books and learnt about cultures from bookstores.

BOOKS ABOUT BOOKSTORES

Independent bookstores are central to a thriving local community and are also one of the last truly democratic institutions that are free for all. As Jerry Seinfeld once said, 'A bookstore is one of the only pieces of physical evidence we have that people are still thinking.' Going by the dwindling number of bookstores, it appears we're thinking less. In the US alone, the number of independent bookstores has shrunk from fifty-five hundred in 1995 to seventeen hundred in 2021. Hence, bookstores hold a special place in my heart, and saving them has become a personal mission for me.

Some of my favourite books are true stories of bookstores, and two that top my list are on the ones in Afghanistan and New Zealand. *The Bookseller of Kabul* by Norwegian author Åsne Seierstad, published in 2004, was not just a bestseller but also deeply embedded in controversy. Seierstad entered Afghanistan two weeks after the 9/11 attacks and followed the Northern Alliance, a coalition of militia that operated till 2001, into Kabul, where she spent three months. Disguising herself by wearing a burka, she lived with a bookseller

and his family in Kabul. The experience provided her with a unique opportunity to describe life as ordinary Afghan citizens saw it. *The Bookseller at the End of the World* by Ruth Shaw is a rich, immersive, funny and heartbreaking memoir of the charming bookseller who ran two tiny bookshops in the remote village of Manapouri in Fiordland, in the deep south of New Zealand.

A long-standing item on my literary bucket list was the legendary bookstore Shakespeare and Company in Paris. Before I visited this bookstore in September 2022, I read the memoir *Time Was Soft There: A Paris Sojourn at Shakespeare & Co.* by Canadian reporter Jeremy Mercer. This is a fascinating book on how Mercer, as a wandering reporter, entered the little bookstore, bought a book, and after the staff invited him up for tea, changed his life forever. Within weeks, he was living above the store, working for the proprietor, George Whitman, patron saint of the city's down-and-out writers, and immersing himself in the love affairs and lowdown at the watering holes of the shop's makeshift staff. *Time Was Soft There* is the story of a journey down a literary rabbit hole in the shadow of Notre-Dame, to a place where a hidden bohemia still thrives.

Writer/artist and *Reader's Digest* cartoonist Bob Eckstein's wonderful homage to bookstores that he calls 'temples of thought', *Footnotes from the World's Greatest Bookstores* is full of sweet, funny and poignant stories. I have both the postcards and the book as a reminder of what is essential in our lives.

Two of my current favourites are *In Praise of Good Bookstores* by Jeff Deutsch and *The Last Bookseller* by Gary Goodman. As an experienced bookseller and reader, Deutsch has written an essential book on an institution that is central to a literate society. *The Last Bookseller* is Goodman's desperate yet hilarious account of a career as a used and rare book dealer in Minnesota. In the future, I hope to see a book about a bookstore from India.

The internet has changed the book business forever, but at the same time, preserving the printed word along with the physical space of a bookstore is of great significance. This is where dialogue and undivided attention are privileged and where imagination has space to meander. My dream is to one day own a bookstore, but for now, I am just living my dream through these books about bookstores.

THE SUB-CATEGORY OF EPHEMERA COLLECTING

Maurice Rickards defined ephemera as 'the minor transient documents of everyday life'. Ephemera refers to something that is meant to be thrown away after being used or enjoyed for only a short time, such as tickets or postcards.

Not all ephemera are on paper. They could be matter printed on metal, wood, cloth, celluloid or even plastic. They could be handwritten documents, phrases woven into ribbons or bookmarks, hand-drawn original art works or painted animation cells. Postcards and old trade cards (advertising cards) are hugely popular categories among collectors of ephemera. Old business cards, especially those for businesses that no longer exist, are another favourite. Collecting old passports is an unusual hobby; it is both interesting and educational as you get to learn a lot about the geography, history and politics of a bygone era.

Almost everyone has an old newspaper cover or two stowed away about a significant headlining event in history, and although they are worthless in the collectors' market, they are still fun to collect. Some examples: 'Man Walks on Moon; WAR; Gandhi Assassinated; Nixon Resigns; Kennedy Shot; World Trade Center Collapses.' Being an ardent fan of Mahatma Gandhi, my personal highpoint in ephemera collecting has been getting ten editions of his weekly journal *Harijan*, which he started publishing from 11 January 1933.

Most book collectors like to pick up ephemera in their quest for books because it is an interesting sub-category. More recently, I have taken an interest in literary ephemera such as broadsides, chapbooks, bookplates, booklets and leaflets.

Bookplates or book labels (also known as *ex libris*, meaning from the library of) are little rectangular labels stuck inside a book carrying the signature of the author in a limited-edition book. For instance, I bought a Harry Potter first edition from a bookshop in the UK, where J.K. Rowling's signature was on a bookplate affixed to the page before the title page.

But the earliest usage of bookplates was quite the opposite: to denote ownership of a book. An individual book lover or a library would have a bookplate bearing their name stuck to the book. Some wealthy collectors actually had their own bookplates made, with their symbol. *The Art of the Bookplate* by James P. Keenan is one of my favourite books on this subject.

Broadsides are usually printed on one side only, in different colours, and are illustrated. Collectors keep the best ones framed. One that I've framed has a quotation by Nicholas Basbanes and is even numbered and signed.

Chapbooks, which originated in sixteenth-century Europe, are like booklets but smaller, and therefore, handy. I own a few valuable chapbooks printed by more recent presses as a way to demonstrate how attractive a smaller format can be.

Another kind of ephemera that I acquired recently is 'Grolier Club Notices', a portfolio of printed announcements, notices and invitations from the Grolier Club, a pre-eminent bibliophile society in New York founded in 1884. It was issued in 1924 in a marbled cloth folder and holds some of the club's scarcest ephemera from that period. This originally belonged to one of its earliest members, Harry C. Goebel, with his bookplate. Several of the pieces here are printed in letterpress, probably by one of the club's most famous co-founders, the esteemed scholar–printer Theodore Low De Vinne.

Collecting Printed Ephemera by Maurice Rickards is a good reference book for starters. *Paper Jewels: Postcards from the Raj* by Omar Khan is the first book on postcards printed in the colonial era in India, Pakistan, Sri Lanka and Burma, and features hundreds of professionally-restored images in original format.

Going after ephemera can be frustrating because they are not easy to find, but it is fun because you never know what you might come across. You might buy a box of books, and tucked away inside, you might find a treasure. But you know what they say: finders keepers!

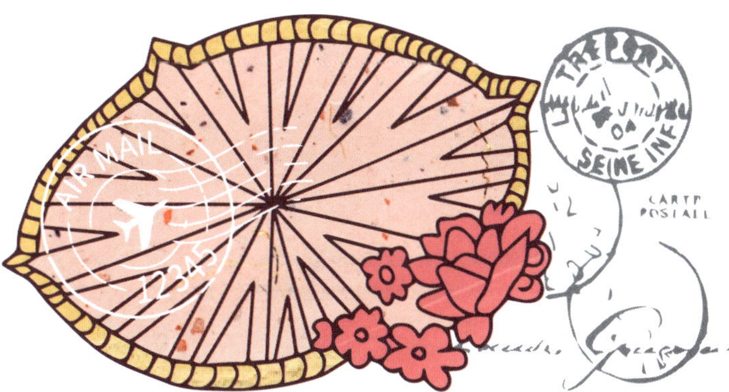

When I relocated to a new house and was arranging all my books, I realized that I had an unintended bias.

women and writing

Over time, I realized that most of my books were by male authors. So I decided that in 2022, I would read mainly books by women authors, preferably those I hadn't read before, and in as many genres as possible. I realized that magic happens when you leave your comfort zone!

I started the year by reading Nisha Susan's *The Women Who Forgot to Invent Facebook and Other Stories*, which was hilarious. I could relate to it because many stories were based in Bengaluru and Kerala – both places that I have lived in. Similarly, I related to *Letter from New York* by Helene Hanff, which my bibliophile friend Pradeep Sebastian gifted me. Since New York is a place that I visit at least thrice a year, descriptions of the city resonated with me although they were from 1978.

Looking for the Good War by Elizabeth D. Samet is one of the best military books I have ever read. The book re-examines the literature, art and culture that emerged after World War II. It looks into American beliefs about the use of military force throughout the world and our inability to accept the realities of the twenty-first century's decades of devastating conflict.

I have been fortunate to have worked with two outstanding co-authors Sudha Menon and C.K. Meena. So, it was obvious that I read their books. Menon's most

recent *Recipes for Life* recreates the memories of the foods we have grown up with. Meena's *Seven Days to Somewhere* is a reflection of our education system that does not allow children to follow their hearts.

I also realized that most of the popular women authors wrote fiction, my least favourite genre, and that those who veer towards non-fiction seem to write personal essays or memoirs, the most recent ones being Kiran Bedi's *Fearless Governance* and Indra Nooyi's *My Life in Full*. In contrast is a book I look forward to reading – *The 1619 Project* by Nikole Hannah-Jones. This title is a long-form journalism endeavour developed by Hannah-Jones, writers from the *New York Times*, and *New York Times Magazine*. It aims to 'reframe the country's history by placing the consequences of slavery and the contributions of Black Americans at the very center of the United States' national narrative'.

As one would guess, there are plenty of books on feminism written by women. My reading list for 2022 included Chimamanda Ngozi Adichie's *We Should All Be Feminists.* Graphic novels are one of my favourite storytelling formats, which have long been dominated by men, so I picked *The Story of My Tits* by breast cancer survivor Jennifer Hayden. Friends have recommended to me books by writers as divergent as Jan Morris and C.S. Lakshmi (Ambai).

One of the highlights of my last visit to London was visiting the bookshop, Persephone Books. This independent publishing house specializes in reprints of forgotten fiction and non-fiction from the mid-twentieth century, mostly by women writers like E.M. Delafield, Diana Athill and Frances Hodgson Burnett. Each book is reprinted with a dove-grey cover and beautiful endpaper inspired by vintage fabrics. After spending a happy hour browsing, I purchased *Fidelity* by Susan Glaspell, *An Interrupted Life and Letters from Westerbork* by Etty Hillesum and *Few Eggs and No Oranges* by Vere Hodgson. Now that I have decided what to read in the future, I have cleared my desk and kept these books in front of me. They are now calling out to me to be read.

When poet Amanda Gorman spoke at the inauguration of Joe Biden, people instantly fell in love with the power of poetry. Gorman's words resonated across the world, and she became an instant phenomenon. Her unpublished book *The Hill We Climb and Other Poems* reached the number one spot eight months before it was released!

While Amanda Gorman had a worldwide audience at the inauguration, Catherine O'Meara alias Kitty O'Meara's poem about the pandemic 'And the People Stayed Home' went viral. At first, it created confusion with people crediting the poet Kathleen Omara, before realizing it was posted online by a lesser-known poet.

The power of poetry is that it often cuts through the noise and clutter, and touches people's heart in ways that is hard to explain. We have all learnt poems in school, but there are a few that we remember. My personal favourites are Rabindranath Tagore's 'Where the Mind is without Fear' (from *Gitanjali*), written before India gained independence; Rudyard Kipling's 'If', and Lawrence Ferlinghetti's 'Pity the Nation'. All three poems have a permanent place in my study room.

Though I have never understood the technicalities of poetry and have not tried writing poetry myself, there are some styles that I have been attracted to, primarily that of Pablo Neruda. Neruda was so popular that many parents lovingly named their boys Pablo (his original name was Ricardo Eliécer Neftalí Reyes Basoalto). His poems are simple, universally comprehensible and speak of the everyday. In his poems, he covers subjects ranging from rain to feet to artichokes. By minutely examining what is commonplace – a plant, a stone, a flower, a bird, or an aspect of modern life – Neruda allowed us to examine them at leisure with love, care and attention.

An anthology of six hundred of Neruda's poems arranged chronologically was published as *The Poetry of Pablo Neruda*. The collection draws from thirty-six different translators, and some of his major works are also presented in their original Spanish. Gabriel García Márquez called this the most comprehensive English-language collection of work ever by 'the greatest poet

of the twentieth century in any language'. One of my personal highlights was visiting Neruda's home 'La Chascona' in Santiago, Chile.

India has had a rich history of poetry. From Vedic Sanskrit poems crafted over three thousand years ago to Urdu poetry that flourished, particularly under the Mughal Empire, the sheer variety of poetry traditions in India can be quite overwhelming. Indian poetry has been written in many languages, and some translations do not do justice to the original. Kabir wrote in Hindi, Kalidasa in Sanskrit, Mirza Ghalib in Urdu, Amir Khusrau in Persian and Rabindranath Tagore in Bengali. Sarojini Naidu, Kamala Surayya and Vikram Seth are among the most influential Indian poets who wrote in English.

One of the best-selling poets of all time is thirteenth-century Persian poet Rumi. His poems about love, spirituality and unity speak to people everywhere. His popularity owes much to the modern English translation *The Essential Rumi* by American poet Coleman Barks. Finally, if you want to know the history of poetry – from ancient times to the present, John Carey's *A Little History of Poetry* is a hugely enjoyable guide.

Poetry reveals truth in places you never cared to look. It invites you to take courageous action in difficult times. It creates connections to the past, present and future, with us and others, across all barriers of language. In her essay, 'Poetry is Not a Luxury', Audre Lorde makes the bold claim that poetry, when wielded well, can create the conditions for revolution. Poetry is both path and destination, able to tell us what is real, what is true and also how we might get free. As Paul Engle said, 'Poetry is ordinary language raised to the Nth power.'

The Climate of Crisis

Climate change is real, and it is exploding right now in front of us. And yet, most of us are ignoring it and some are denying it.

We are already suffering the consequences – floods, droughts, cyclones, hurricanes, forest fires – not to mention the migrant crisis and the almost-routine farmer suicides. But the world is split on the way forward. Books on climate change put forth contrasting points of view – Eastern versus Western; political versus moral; technological versus religious; individual versus collective.

Interestingly, fiction too has covered climate change. *The Drowned World* is a 1962 science fiction novel by British writer J. G. Ballard. It depicts a post-apocalyptic future in which global warming has made most of the Earth uninhabitable. The novel is considered a founding text in the literary sub-genre of climate fiction (Cli-Fi).

Amitav Ghosh in his *The Great Derangement* has passionately examined our inability – at the levels of literature, history and politics – to grasp the scale and violence of climate change. He believes that the climate change debate will be decided in Asia, not in the West, but that the solution has to be international.

Canadian author and social activist Naomi Klein's *This Changes Everything* (2014) challenges the current free-market ideology. She argues that capitalism and controlling climate change are fundamentally incompatible. Her *On Fire* is a collection of essays on climate change and the urgent actions needed to preserve the world.

Bill Gates believes that our only chance of salvation is through innovation. His book *How to Avoid a Climate Disaster* is a must-read for everyone. He proposes the ambitious goal of reaching 'zero by 2050' by innovating in every aspect of our lives – from manufacturing to transport to agriculture. Gates's own favourite book for a better understanding of the climate challenge is *Weather for Dummies* by John D. Cox.

What can we do as individuals? We can find an answer in *Being the Change: Live Well and Start a Climate Revolution* by Peter Kalmus. Kalmus, an atmospheric scientist and father of two, embarked on a journey to change his life and the world. He switched to bicycling, grew food and made other small changes through which he was able to slash his climate impact to one-tenth the US average and become happier in the process. His book will inspire individuals who want to take climate action but are unsure of where to start.

The first time I understood the seriousness of the climate crisis was when I had the opportunity to hear former US Vice President Al Gore at the India Today Conclave in 2008.

His passionate appeal to the world on the urgency of the climate crisis was a turning point that initiated a widespread debate on a topic that few were willing to spend their resources on. His advocacy work and his documentary (and book *The Inconvenient Truth*) won him the Nobel Peace Prize (jointly with Intergovernmental Panel on Climate Change [IPCC]) in 2007. IPCC mentions that climate change is rooted in the idea of justice.

Do we have time to build a social movement around climate change? Can we galvanize everyone to rally behind it or have we yielded to the West's idea of what constitutes a 'good life'? In the 1944 existentialist play *No Exit* by Jean-Paul Sartre, three deceased characters are punished by being locked in a room together for eternity. Are we similarly compelled to become the wardens of our own prison, guardians of an empty future? The question is: Can the pace of human ingenuity outrun our hubris? Time will tell.

Of Mystery & Magic

Johannes Gutenberg, born in the city of Mainz, Germany, is considered one of the most influential figures of the last millennium.

Ironically, Johannes Gutenberg is also one of the great mysteries of history. Not much is known about his personal life – when he was born, whether he married or had children, where he is buried or even what he looked like. His major work, the *Gutenberg Bible* (also known as the 42-line Bible), was the first printed version of the Bible.

Most of the information about Gutenberg comes from legal and financial papers, which reveal that the printing of his Bibles was a particularly tumultuous affair; he was driven to financial ruin by a lawsuit filed by his business partner Johann Fust. It's unlikely that he ever turned a profit off his most famous work. I have been fortunate to have visited the Gutenberg Museum in Mainz, Germany, a must for anyone interested in books and the printing world. The two original *Gutenberg Bibles* (kept inside a bulletproof room) are among the museum's most important treasures.

By studying the size of Gutenberg's paper supply, historians have estimated that he produced around hundred and eighty copies of his Bible. Of these, only forty-five are known to exist today (of which twelve are in the US). Not surprisingly, there are numerous books about these surviving Bibles. *The Lost Gutenberg* by Margaret Leslie Davis tracks the journey of one copy as it passed through several hands over five centuries to arrive at a Tokyo steel vault. *Gutenberg's Apprentice* by Alix Christie places Gutenberg's former assistant, Peter Schoeffer, at the centre and takes us through the fraught journey of the printing of the Bibles.

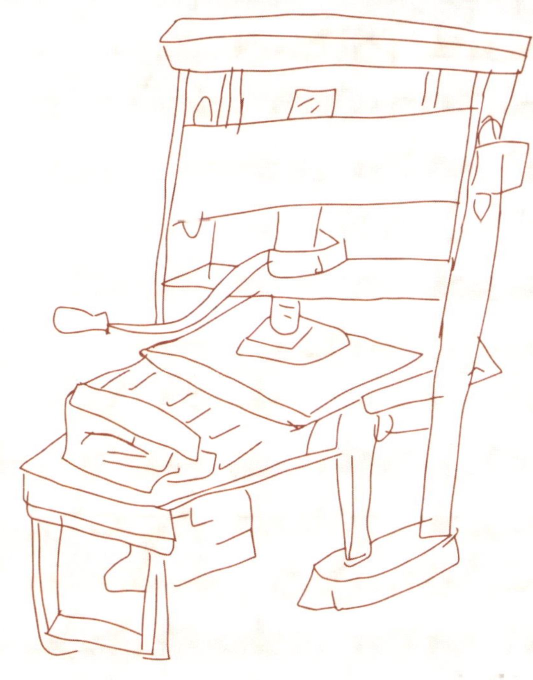

I have bought a facsimile copy of the 1454 Bible – the closest ever to the original. I also managed to acquire a mounted and framed original leaf from 1478, printed in two colours by Johannes Nider, a contemporary of Gutenberg. Another of my possessions is a facsimile of a leaf from a *Gutenberg Bible* – not a mere print, but a leaf reconstructed with type in Germany in the 1950s.

How did Gutenberg arrive at the idea of not writing out a book by hand but mechanically reproducing it? Actually, a form of printing did exist before Gutenberg. From as early as the twelfth or thirteenth century, China (where paper was invented) and Korea were using inked letters carved on wooden blocks impressed on to paper. This early printing process eventually found its way to Europe by the late fourteenth century, and some documents, though not books, were being produced this way.

One wonders how Gutenberg, originally a goldsmith, hit upon the idea of using movable type with individual pieces of metal instead of wooden blocks that can each only accommodate a few lines of text. While Gutenberg pioneered the technology of printing, the printers who came after him – Nider, Anton Koberger, Nikolai Jessen, Aldus Manutius and Erhard Ratdolt – improved on and finally perfected it. I have even managed to get an original leaf from some of these great printers.

Schoeffer partnered with his father-in-law, Fust, both closely associated with Gutenberg in the past, to refine the process and print many beautiful books, including the *Mainz Psalter* of 1457. This is the first book to have a colophon – the printing date and printer's emblem often accompanied by a brief statement. It is amazing that even after five hundred and fifty years, Gutenberg evokes such interest in researchers and technologists alike. Probably because he has had the greatest impact on humankind, or simply because printing is considered the most groundbreaking invention since the wheel.

The oddity of cult books

When it comes to books that have gained a cult following, *The Catcher in the Rye* is the very definition of a cult book. On the night Mark David Chapman shot dead former Beatle John Lennon, Chapman was caught with a copy of this book, in which he had written 'This is my statement.' He identified with the novel's narrator to a degree that he wanted to change his name to Holden Caulfield.

So, what exactly is a cult book and how is it different from a bestseller? The word 'cult' first appeared in English in the seventeenth century, derived from the French 'culte' meaning 'worship'. So cult books can be considered books that are worshipped. All bestsellers don't achieve cult status, but all cult books eventually become bestsellers. It is similar to how some videos go viral – they have an inexplicable 'something' that sticks with certain individuals or groups.

Fans of *A Confederacy of Dunces* by John Kennedy Toole will swear that it is the most hilarious book ever written. This book was a cult classic first and a widely popular novel second, even winning a Pulitzer. The fact that Toole had died by suicide eleven years before the book caught the public eye enhanced its cultish appeal. Although all cult books have a devoted fan following, not all are well-written. Some classic cult books that are great reads include *Catch-22* by Joseph Heller, *The Hitchhiker's Guide to the Galaxy* by Douglas Adams, *The Alchemist* by Paulo Coelho, *One Flew Over the Cuckoo's Nest* by Ken Kesey, *Siddhartha* by Herman Hesse and *Atlas Shrugged* by Ayn Rand.

Of the Indian books that achieved cult status (though not categorized as such), Upamanyu Chatterjee's *English, August* (1988) surely ranks first. A comic masterpiece, it is both an inspired and hilarious satire and a timeless story of self-discovery. It's the story of a privileged young man, Agastya Sen, nicknamed August, and his year of living languorously.

Other books with cult status include Nirad C. Chaudhuri's *Autobiography of an Unknown Indian* (Churchill thought it one of the best books he had ever read), Khushwant Singh's *Train to Pakistan*, Vikram Seth's *A Suitable Boy* and Paramahansa Yogananda's *Autobiography of a Yogi.*

A book that has quietly achieved cult status is Usha R. Prabakaran's twenty-year-old cookbook *Usha's Pickle Digest.* Crammed with a thousand pickle recipes from home cooks (I never knew so many varieties of pickle existed!), the book is simple, text heavy and minimally designed. Prabhakaran, a former lawyer, now living in Chennai, spent a decade researching and testing recipes, and had an initial print run of just thousand copies. The book is available on Amazon.com.

My personal favourite is *Zen and the Art of Motorcycle Maintenance* by Robert M. Pirsig, written the year I was born. I got introduced to this cult classic very late in life, and yet, it had a profound impact on me. The fact that Zen can be found in everyday activity (I found my 'motorcycle maintenance' while dishwashing) and that the best writing happens in moments of pure boredom were notions particularly relevant to the pandemic season in which the book entered my life. I heard it on Audible along with my son on my daily drives – like the author who wrote it during his motorcycle journeys with his son.

Eventually, a cult book should have the ability to alter a reader's life or influence great change, and so, it is not surprising that most of them are a bit odd and a tad obscure.

For once, let me infringe on this unwritten boundary and share the books that inspired me to write my book, co-authored with C.K. Meena, *The Invisible Majority: India's Abled Disabled.* Here are some of the books that helped me formulate my ideas about disability.

Special tales

If you are a columnist writing about other people's books, do you have permission to write about your own? Personally, I would say a loud NO. But for once, let me infringe on this unwritten boundary and share the books that inspired me to write my book, co-authored with C.K. Meena, *The Invisible Majority: India's Abled Disabled*.

Among Indian authors, I came across Arun Shourie's *Does He Know a Mother's Heart?* Through his personal journey with his son who was born with cerebral palsy, Shourie introspects on suffering and critiques religion. I read memoirs by persons with disabilities (PwDs) such as Malini Chib's *One Little Finger* and Siddharth Jayakumar's *Simply Being Sidds!*. In fiction, there was T.G.C. Prasad's *From the Eye of My Mind*, in which the protagonist is a teenager with autism.

However, most of the books I read were by authors from the US, a country that is at least half a century ahead of India in providing an inclusive environment for PwDs. At the top of the list is Andrew Solomon's

Far from the Tree, a ten-year labour of love that involved Solomon going deep into the lives of families of children with disabilities. This thoroughly researched, sensitively and brilliantly written book has been made into an equally noteworthy film. I decided to try something similar, though on a lesser scale, in the Indian context by capturing the life stories of PwDs and their caregivers.

No Greatness Without Goodness by J. Randolph Lewis struck an obvious chord in me since I too, like Lewis, have a son with autism, and like him, I belong to the corporate world. Lewis, who used to be the vice president of one of the fastest growing retailers in the US, went about building an inclusive workspace, which became a model for other companies.

I read all the books written by Temple Grandin, a renowned professor with autism and the subject of a biopic TV show. Joseph Shapiro's *No Pity* gave me an overview of disability in the US. It led me to some key topics that I picked for my book: the status of disability policy, laws in India and the progress of our own disability rights movement.

About Us is a compilation of the *New York Times* essays that were part of the newspaper's disability series. Written in first person, these essays reveal the lives of persons with different disabilities as they navigate a world that is not made for them. The title, incidentally, reflects the slogan of the global disability movement: Nothing about us without us. I knew that the mainstream Indian media would hesitate to carry such a series, but at least my book could reflect the voices of PwDs and record their intimate stories.

While preparing to write *The Invisible Majority*, I also read novels with a disability theme. The graphic novel *Nobody's Fool* by Bill Griffith is an eye-opening true-life story of Schlitzie, a man with intellectual disabilities who was displayed as a 'circus freak'. In an entirely different vein, *The Rosie Project* by Graeme Simsion is a hilarious romance where the protagonist is a scientist who appears to have Asperger's Syndrome.

The working of a mind that is wired differently actually creates material for humour. These books revealed the manifold shapes, sizes and colours of a subject close to my heart and inspired me to bring it close to home through my book on disability in India.

ESSAY ON ESSAYS

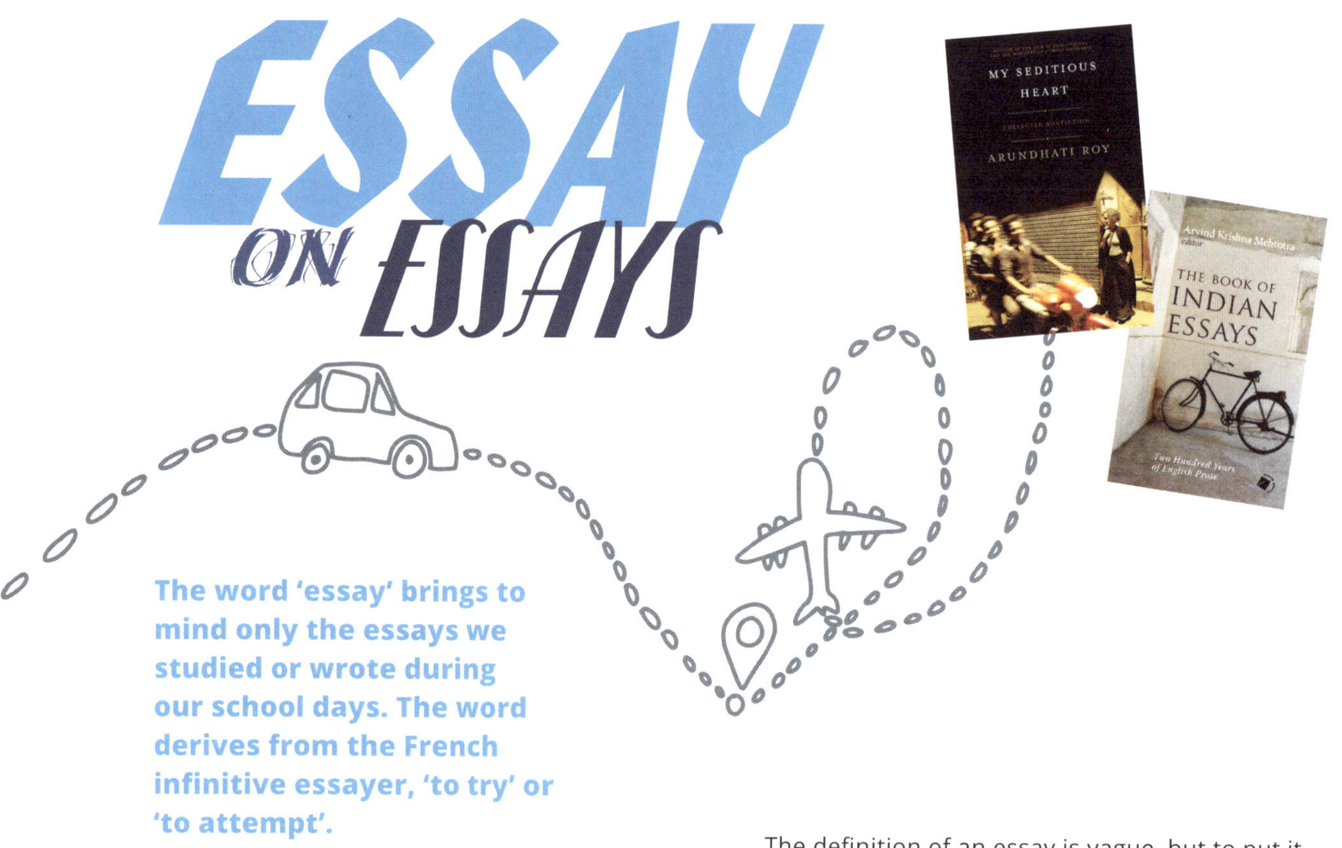

The word 'essay' brings to mind only the essays we studied or wrote during our school days. The word derives from the French infinitive essayer, 'to try' or 'to attempt'.

The sixteenth-century author Michel de Montaigne was the first to describe his work as essays, characterizing them as 'attempts' to put his thoughts into writing.

The essay is my favourite genre, especially the shorter form, which goes back to Greek philosopher Heraclitus, Roman philosopher Seneca, and Japanese author and poet Sei Shōnagon. But the modern notion of what we now call flash non-fiction was kick-started in 1990 by Bernard Cooper's elegant and unusual *Maps to Anywhere*. One of my favourite collections of flash non-fiction is *The Best of Brevity*, an anthology of eighty-four essays.

The definition of an essay is vague, but to put it simply, it is an argument made by the author on a specific topic that could range from a political manifesto to a personal reflection. An essay might offer an answer, but it is just as important for it to leave you with questions. A good essay promotes conversation. According to Aldous Huxley, 'The essay is a literary device for saying almost everything about almost anything.' He adds that it is almost by definition a short piece.

I find Arundhati Roy's long essays, pieces of art and a joy to read, even if, at times, I disagree with her point of view. Her *My Seditious Heart* is a collection of two decades of writing political essays as a way of opening up space for justice, rights and freedom in an increasingly hostile environment. *The Book of Indian Essays*, an anthology of Indian short prose edited by poet and literary critic Arvind Krishna Mehrotra, is a must-read.

One of my favourites is the philosophical long essay *The Myth of Sisyphus* by Albert Camus, published in 1942 in French. Camus uses the Greek legend of Sisyphus, who is condemned by the gods for eternity to repeatedly roll a boulder up a hill only to have it roll down again once he got it to the top, as a metaphor for the individual's persistent struggle against the essential absurdity of life. He argues that with the joyful acceptance of the struggle against defeat, the individual gains definition and identity.

The political essay *The Power of the Powerless* written in 1978 by Czech dramatist Václav Havel became a manifesto for dissent in Czechoslovakia, Poland, and other communist regimes. The essay dissects the nature of the communist regime and discusses ideas and possible actions by loose communities of individuals linked by a common cause. Havel talks of a post-democratic system that should provide hope for a moral reconstitution of society.

James Baldwin's brilliant and provocative essays made him the literary voice of the civil rights era. They continue to speak to us with the same powerful urgency as they did decades ago. Audre Lorde's *Sister Outsider* contains fifteen essays and speeches that take on sexism, racism, ageism, homophobia and class, and propound social difference as a vehicle for action and change.

Essays have the ability to both amuse and surprise us. The feelings and ideas in them provoke thought, compassion and a sense of wonder. As Mehrotra wrote in the introduction to *The Book of Indian Essays*: 'The essay, like a penknife, can be put to many uses; like a newspaper aeroplane, it can fly and crash and fly again; as a literary genre, it is unfussy. The essay gathers no dust.'

World War II engulfed every continent on Earth and inflicted more death and destruction on people and nations in one of the most recorded events. Even though most of the current generation has not lived through the war, everyone is aware of it due to museums, movies and books.

I happen to have visited some of the most prominent World War II museums such as the Holocaust Remembrance Center (Yad Vashem, Israel), the Dachau Concentration Camp Memorial Site (Germany), Anne Frank House (Amsterdam, Netherlands) and the Pearl Harbor National Memorial (Hawaii, US). Most of us have felt the intensity of the war through powerful movies such as *Schindler's List*, based on the book *Schindler's Ark* by Thomas Keneally. Some other notable movies are based on eponymous books such as *Dunkirk* by Joshua Levine, *Enemy at the Gates* by William Craig and *Escape from Sobibor* by Richard Rashke.

With the current Ukraine–Russia war, there is a growing interest in World War II and the lessons we can learn from it. While there are countless books written about it, every year many more are churned out, providing new perspectives. When I spoke to World War II historian Andrew Nagorski about the reason for the continued interest in the topic even after seventy-five-plus years, his response was, 'World War II is the greatest lab to understand human behaviour.'

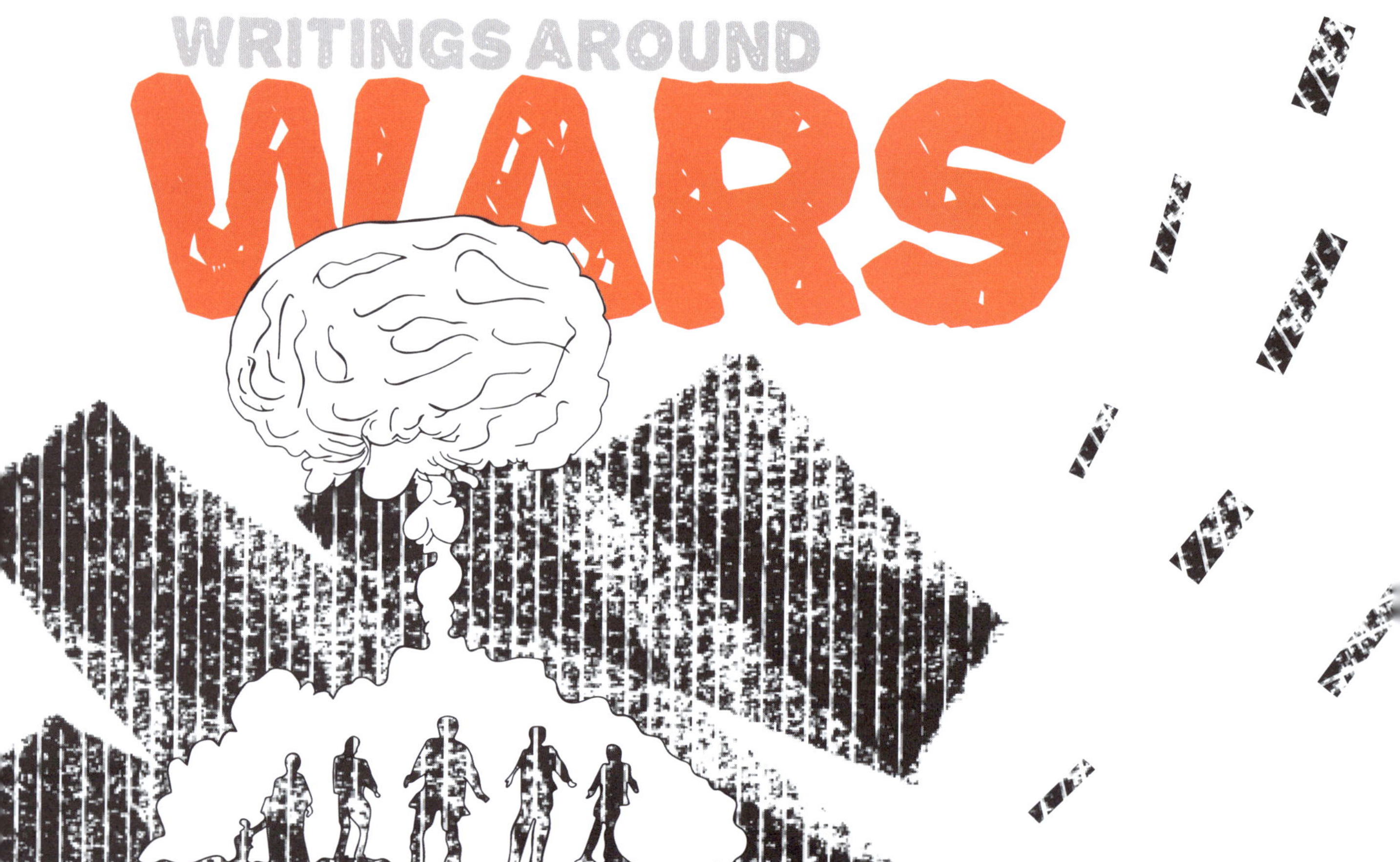

Here are some of my most formative reads about World War II. I read *Hiroshima* by John Hersey in one sitting. In this journalistic masterpiece, Hersey describes what happened on the day the atom bomb was dropped on the city of Hiroshima. Told through the memories of survivors, this timeless, powerful and compassionate document has become a classic 'that stirs the conscience of humanity'. This book was recommended to me by Beverly Potter, the eighty-five-year-old bookstore owner of the Title Page in Philadelphia, USA. She said, 'You should read this book in one sitting, and I would like to see your face after you finish it. I promise you will have tears in your eyes.' And she was right.

World War II: The Definitive Visual History from Blitzkrieg to the Atom Bomb (published by DK) is an all-encompassing book on the topic because of its visual aids and depth of information.

While *Maus* by Art Spiegelman is the most famous graphic novel about this war, one of the lesser-known books that I discovered was the 1999 book *Dr. Seuss Goes to War* by Richard H. Minear. It is a fascinating collection of wartime cartoons from the beloved children's author and illustrator Theodor Seuss Geisel.

One of the recent books that I read was *1941: The Year Germany Lost the War* by Andrew Nagorski. The author takes a fresh look at the decisive year of 1941 when Hitler's miscalculations and policy of terror propelled Churchill, Roosevelt and Stalin into a powerful new alliance that defeated Nazi Germany. The year 1941 forever defined our world, and this book is a lively, opinionated account of this critical year.

When it comes to fiction, some of the best have already been made into movies like *The Book Thief*, *Catch-22* and *The Boy in the Striped Pyjamas*. So, I would suggest *Fatherland* by Robert Harris (which was made into a TV film). It is set in 1964 and imagines an alternative world where Hitler won World War II, the Holocaust is an unconfirmed rumour, and on the eve of Hitler's seventy-fifth birthday, the United States (under President Joseph Kennedy) is negotiating diplomatic ties with the Third Reich. Thank god it is fiction!

DEATH BY THE BOOK

The first book to explore the now-famous five stages of death was *On Death and Dying* by Elisabeth Kübler-Ross.

Death. We generally skirt this subject since it is painful but unavoidable; often unexpected but absolute. And that is precisely why we should talk about death. As American rabbi Joshua L. Liebman writes in *Peace of Mind*, 'Death is not the enemy of life, but its friend, for it is the knowledge that our years are limited which makes them so precious.'

The first book to explore the now-famous five stages of death was *On Death and Dying* by Elisabeth Kübler-Ross. It gives readers a better understanding of how imminent death affects patients, their families and the professionals who serve them.

The Tibetan Book of Living and Dying by Sogyal Rinpoche, which has sold over two million copies in thirty languages, presents the teachings of Tibetan Buddhism based on the *Tibetan Book of the Dead* or *Bardo Thödol*. It explores the message of impermanence; evolution, karma and rebirth; the nature of the mind and how to train it through meditation; how to follow a spiritual path; the practice of compassion; how to care for and show love to the dying; and spiritual practices for the moment of death.

Option B: Facing Adversity, Building Resilience, and Finding Joy is co-authored by former Facebook COO Sheryl Sandberg and Wharton professor Adam Grant. The book advises us to think of resilience as a muscle, one that atrophies in the calm between the storms of our lives, but which can be developed, so we're better prepared when adversity strikes.

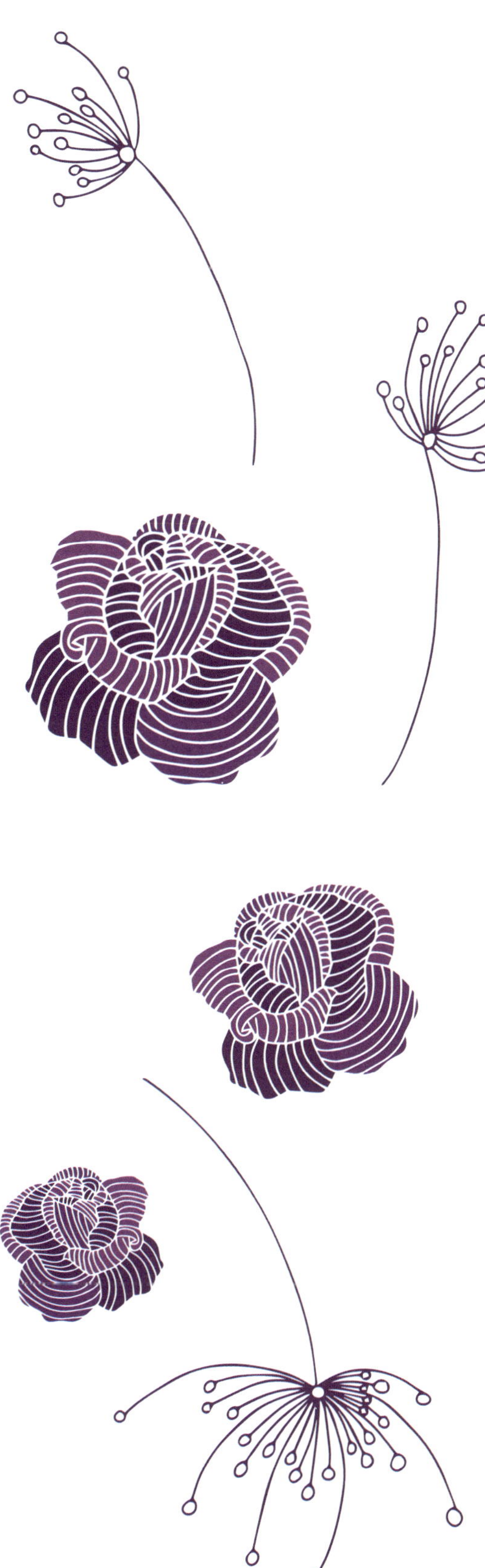

When Breath Becomes Air is an autobiographical book written by American neurosurgeon Paul Kalanithi. This posthumously published bestseller is a moving memoir about his life and battle with lung cancer.

Will My Cat Eat My Eyeballs? is written by author and mortician Caitlin Doughty. She answers real and often funny questions from kids about death, dead bodies and decomposition.

One of my early favourites is *The Last Lecture* by Randy Pausch, which continues to be shared across generations. A lot of professors give talks titled 'The Last Lecture', where they are asked to ruminate on the wisdom they would impart to the world if they knew they would die the next day. When Pausch, a computer science professor at Carnegie Mellon, was approached for such a lecture, he had just been diagnosed with terminal cancer.

But the lecture he gave, 'Really Achieving Your Childhood Dreams', was not about dying. It emphasized the importance of seizing every moment, overcoming obstacles, and enabling the dreams of others. Another bestseller is *Being Mortal* by Atul Gawande, who asserts that medicine can provide both a good life and a good end.

The book is a personal tale of his father's battle with cancer and a public call for a better healthcare philosophy and system that would allow us to die a humane death.

My recent favourite is Arun Shourie's *Preparing for Death*. The section that intrigued me the most is where he documents 'great souls' experiencing the often painful dissolution of their own body – the Buddha, Ramakrishna Paramahansa, Ramana Maharshi, Mahatma Gandhi and Vinoba Bhave, and as a cameo, Kasturba Gandhi.

There is a book for every seeker. Preparing a will forced me to think of my own mortality. All of us will have to deal with the death of a loved one at least once. We need to learn to talk about age, illness and death in realistic terms. I hope these books will guide us to prepare for those days.

During the COVID-19 lockdown, I enjoyed reading books to my son. Since he is an auditory learner, I had to read aloud from a book every day. This introduced me to a genre of books that I had never read when I was growing up. In fact, I feel I started enjoying them more than my son did! My own childhood reading mainly consisted of *Amar Chitra Katha*, *Tinkle* and Enid Blyton's Famous Five series. With an estimated sale of over six hundred million, Enid Blyton has been a bestseller since the 1930s and one of the top-ranked children's book authors of all time.

NOT JUST CHILD'S PLAY

The first book I read aloud to my son was *The Boxcar Children*, created by a first grade schoolteacher in the US, Gertrude Chandler Warner. With hundred and fifty titles in the series, the books are aimed at grades two to six. One of the more recent innovations has been to enable the book using augmented reality, giving children a 3D view of the characters. Roald Dahl's *Charlie and the Chocolate Factory* came next. Dahl, often

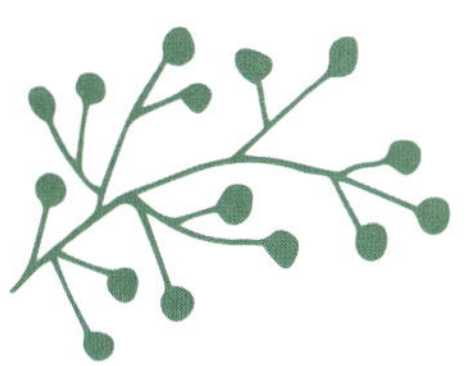

referred to as 'the greatest storyteller for children of the twentieth century', writes books that champion the kind-hearted and feature an underlying warm sentiment.

While Harry Potter, which falls in the 'young adult' category of late teens to early twenties, remains at the top of the list for every child, I personally never got around to enjoying the series. So, when it came to introducing it to my son, I preferred to play it on an Audible rather than read it out myself. The first book in the Harry Potter series is available on the Spotify app; each chapter is read by a celebrity, including Daniel Radcliffe and Alia Bhatt.

Interestingly, according to the Amazon bestseller ranking, children's books sold the most during the lockdown. As libraries and schools remain closed, children were being homeschooled and that made parents buy more books. Drawing books, workbooks, picture books and craft books were among the bestsellers.

In India, Pratham Books has democratized access to books through their engaging storybooks published in various regional languages. Tara Books in Chennai started by Gita Wolf produces handmade books by local artisans. This is one of the most unique and remarkable publishing ventures I have come across. As an example, *This Truck has Got to be Special* by Anjum Rana is a colourful book with such bright and beautiful illustrations that they almost overwhelm the story. If Wolf's aim was to introduce the rich diversity of Indian folk and tribal art into books for children, she has already succeeded. We need more of these in cost-effective ways in as many regional languages as possible.

Children who read more, learn better and are more likely to succeed at school as well as in life. The best gift we can give to our children is the wealth of books. And above all, as I have discovered personally, children's books have something for every age group.

When Eric Carle, author of the classic *The Very Hungry Caterpillar*, was asked where the idea for the book came from, his response was: 'One day, I playfully punched some holes into a stock of paper. Looking at the holes I thought of a bookworm. Then I changed the bookworm into a green worm. With the help of my good editor Ann K. Beneduce, the green worm then became a caterpillar.' Let's hope that all children become like the hungry caterpillar, reading and consuming books aplenty – and evolving into beautiful adults.

What makes a joke? Is it based on a certain formula?

When I met actor and comedian John Cleese of *Monty Python*, *A Fish Called Wanda* and *Fawlty Towers* fame, he said, 'Two different frames brought together creates humour.' His memoir *So, Anyway...* is everything one would expect – smart, thoughtful, provocative, and above all, funny. The genre of comedian-memoirs has been around for a long time. Fred Allen's *Treadmill to Oblivion*, Lenny Bruce's *How to Talk Dirty and Influence People*, Nora Ephron's *I Feel Bad About My Neck* and Tina Fey's *Bossypants* are some of the funniest books by the funniest people.

Another insight that Cleese gave was that comedians are most funny when they speak in a deadpan, mechanical manner. In spoken humour, the trick to being humorous is to know when not to repeat yourself, when not to overkill a joke, when to be subtle and when to leave things unsaid. You should know when a joke is not working, and if it isn't, the most disastrous thing you can do is try and milk it by repeating it again and again.

But what about humour in writing? Is it more difficult to be humorous in print than through the spoken word or in a video or film? My earliest encounter with written humour was through the column 'Offbase' (formerly known as 'Humour in Uniform') in the *Reader's Digest*. The column has appeared for over half a century, with more than thirty-five hundred jokes, quotes and funny stories submitted by more than a million readers.

In my college days, everyone read P.G. Wodehouse, but for Indian humour, alas, we had nothing comparable. All the comedy was in our movies. R.K. Narayan's *Malgudi Days* and *Swami and Friends* are timeless classics while currently, Twinkle Khanna is the most prominent Indian writer of humour with her *Mrs Funnybones*. Post college, I read a lot of Dave Barry and Erma Bombeck. According to Barry, a sense of humour is a measurement of the extent to which we realize that we are trapped in a world almost totally devoid of reason. Laughter is how we express the anxiety we feel at this knowledge. His latest *Lessons From Lucy* about the seven essential life lessons he learnt from his rescue dog is more of a self-help book and yet funny.

A cult novel that gripped many Indians like me was Joseph Heller's biting, anti-war satire, *Catch-22*. Kurt Vonnegut, Kingsley Amis, Tom Sharpe and Woody Allen (the books not the movies) were the other modern satirists who tickled my funny bone. One of the lesser-known classics in humour that I recently discovered is *A Confederacy of Dunces* by John Kennedy Toole. The book centres on Ignatius Reilly, who does odd jobs to make a living and is nothing short of an arsehole (also a slob who constantly farts). You will not only end up laughing at the character but also maybe at yourself too.

My current favourite is David Sedaris, who has written eleven bestsellers. If the size of the audience is anything to go by, then his book release and signings, held in concert halls, indicate that he is nothing short of a rock star. He also has his own MasterClass. His latest collection of essays, *The Best of Me*, is a bestseller, but he doesn't take it or himself too seriously when he says that can you add letters to *Me* in the title so that the book becomes The Best Of Mexico, Mediocrity, Or Meningitis.

Books are intimate possessions, each with its special odour and unique story that lives on in us. When someone asked me why I don't read on a Kindle, my response was, 'How do you get a personalized copy on a Kindle?'

As my friend and owner of Kepler's Bookstore in Menlo Park (California), Praveen Madan told me, 'In the bookselling business, there are only two seasons – December and the rest.' Book sales peak in December because many people buy books as Christmas and New Year gifts. In Iceland, there is a national tradition called Jolabokaflod, or the 'Christmas Book Flood'. It involves giving and unwrapping new books on Christmas Eve, cuddling up with loved ones and reading late into the night. As author Neil Gaiman once said, 'Books make great gifts because they have whole worlds inside of them. And it's much cheaper to buy somebody a book than it is to buy them the whole world.'

With a few exceptions, books are the only gifts I have given. To my wife's dismay, even our wedding gifts have been books! Family and friends who are aware of my book reading/buying habits have often gifted me some unique and special books. Once I spent almost a decade collecting the fifty best books on cricket, a list suggested by Ramachandra Guha in his article 'An Addict's Archive'. Many of the books on the list were rare and some were even out of print. I waited for them to pop up in local bookstores, and after chasing them relentlessly, I managed to get forty-nine of the fifty books. One day, a colleague of mine walked into my office with a gift-wrapped book. When I opened it I found the fiftieth book (*The Great Australian Book of Cricket Stories* by Ken Piesse) that completed my collection!

On another occasion, my friend Nisha gifted me a rare copy of Isaac Walterson's special edition of *Einstein: The Life of a Genius*. While it was neither signed nor inscribed, it was a collector's copy. I took it along with me when I met Walterson at a book event and got it signed by him.

One of my most cherished moments was receiving a book gift from a complete stranger. While browsing at Oxford Bookstore in Bengaluru a few years ago, a youngish guy surprised me by gifting me a book titled *Seven Secrets of Inspired Leaders*. He said he had heard my speech at the School of Inspired Leadership (SOIL, Gurugram), where he'd studied, and wanted to gift me the book out of gratitude. That book still holds a special place for me.

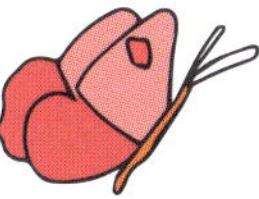

Often, it is the carefully thought-out, inscribed message that makes a book more memorable. After I recently spoke at the Autism After 21 event in Washington DC, the author of *Autism Uncensored*, Whitney Ellenby, gave me a copy of her book in which she wrote: 'You just broke my heart and healed it again.... I hope you will listen to my uncensored voice because you walk in the middle of the story.' Whitney, a champion for the autism community, has now become a dear friend.

The book gift that touched me the most was given to me by my fellow bibliophile friend Pradeep Sebastian, who gave me his most precious gift – a copy of *Keepers* signed by Russell H. Greenan. The book *The Silence of the Lambs* apparently has echoes of Greenan's book. Signed on 6 March 2006, the inscribed message read, 'I flatter myself by thinking that, if I had not written this story, Mr Harris would not have written *The Silence of the Lambs*. Perhaps, you too will see a similarity.' I hope someday I will be able to pay Pradeep back with something equally rare and personal to me.

Books are intimate possessions, each with its special odour and unique story that lives on in us. Once, when someone asked me why I don't read on a Kindle, I asked them, 'How do you get a personalized copy on a Kindle?'

There is something romantic about long train journeys. I spent the first two decades of my life criss-crossing the country by rail; I often joke that I was born in a train!

While the British pioneered rail transport, Indian Railways has become one of the world's largest rail networks and biggest employers, transporting almost 2.5 crore passengers daily and employing close to fourteen lakh people. Not surprisingly, it has spurred books and movies. While there are numerous books about railways, some of the best have been written by British journalists, Christian Wolmar being the most prominent author and railway historian. *Fire & Steam* tells the dramatic story of the people and events that shaped the world's first railway network. The opening of the pioneering Liverpool and Manchester Railway in 1830 marked the beginning of the railways' vital role in changing the face of Britain.

(xxxvi)

My father, who spent thirty years working for the Indian Railways, considered railway stations his second home. My earliest memory is of travelling from Kharagpur to Kottayam in Kerala with an overnight stay in Madras Central (now Chennai) – it took fifty-two hours to reach my grandparents' house. Clothes stained by coal from the steam engine; taking a bath at the Madras railway station guest house; buying food from the platform hawkers; sharing a meal with fellow travellers; exchanging comics and newspapers; reading the railways timetable – they are all etched in my memory.

If your bucket list includes taking the world's iconic train journeys, Paul Theroux's 1975 classic *The Great Railway Bazaar* is a must-read. Here, Theroux recounts his early adventures on an unusual grand continental tour. Asia's fabled trains – the Orient Express, the Khyber Pass Local, the Frontier Mail, the Golden Arrow to Kuala Lumpur, the Mandalay Express, and the Trans-Siberian Express – are the stars of a journey that takes him on a loop eastbound from London's Victoria Station to Tokyo Central, then back from Japan on the Trans-Siberian.

Great Railway Journeys of the World by Max Wade-Matthews contains accounts of nearly hundred of the world's most legendary train journeys. The book has over seven hundred pictures of the locomotives, stations and tracks that link beautiful scenery with bustling metropolises. *The Pictorial Encyclopedia of Railways* by Hamilton Ellis, with over eight hundred pictures and captions running into thirty thousand words, tells the story from the first Babylonian rutways to the 100 mph monorail.

The Penguin Book of Indian Railway Stories by Ruskin Bond remains one of my favourites. *A Short History of Indian Railways* by Rajendra B. Aklekar has many fun facts and stories from the time the first wagon rolled out. For instance, the locomotive engine for the maiden run between Bombay and Thane was pulled by two hundred coolies on the streets. And the maximum speed of India's first experimental train was 7.2 kmph. The more recent *Indian Railways: The Weaving of a National Tapestry* co-authored by Bibek Debroy is an interesting take on the importance of railways in the creation of a national identity.

Platform Souls by Nicholas Whittaker is a classic on the joys of being a trainspotter. Trainspotting was invented in 1942 by a railway publicity officer Ian Allen by publishing lists of locomotives that could then be 'ticked' off when sighted. That started a hobby among many children, who went to great lengths to spot an engine. With traffic jams and global warming on the rise, we may see a resurgence of the romance of the railways. It would be a rejection of the (as Whittaker describes it) 'emotional poverty' of car culture in favour of the 'joyful communism of the trains'.

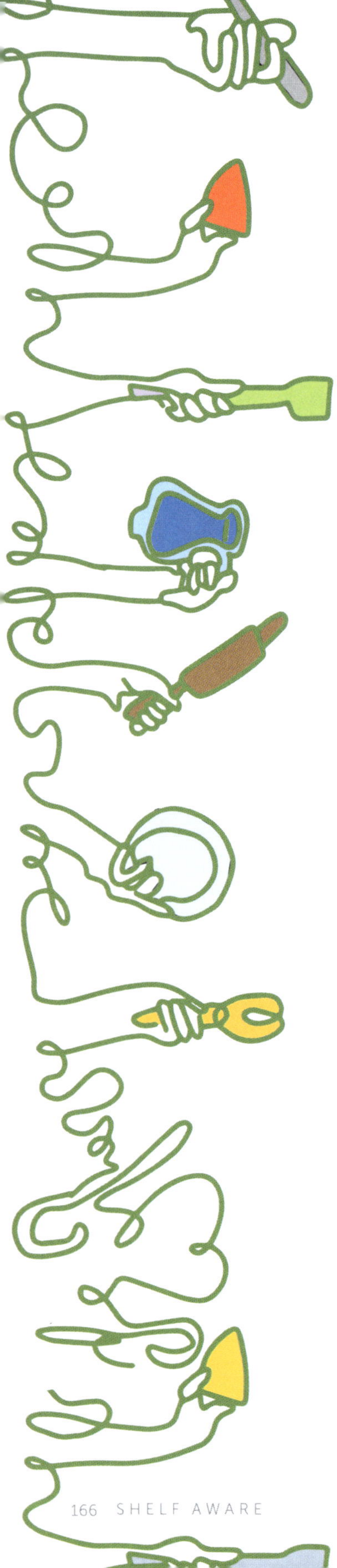

During the pandemic, a mindless task (like peeling onion, ginger or garlic) became a mindful task. I made more phone calls than ever to my mother during the lockdown, asking for recipes, and realized what a wealth of knowledge she possessed.

The COVID-19 pandemic may have caused home kitchens to work overtime. Since restaurants were closed and many were working from home, people started preparing regular meals. We suddenly realized that cooking at home was pleasurable, important and necessary, not just for our existence but also for our happiness. Cooking skills have been passed on orally from generation to generation, and it would be a pity to lose that basic knowledge.

I had rarely bought a cookbook before or watched a cooking show, but during the lockdown, I constantly looked up recipes on YouTube and religiously took printouts of them before I prepping and cooking. It suddenly struck me how much more there is to know about cooking. I started

(xxxvii)

by asking some basic questions: What was the genesis of cooking and how has it evolved over time? What led to the decline of cooking at home? Why is organic food so expensive? What is unique about our mothers' cooking? Why do people spend so much time watching cooking shows about food they never get to eat?

I highly recommend Michael Pollan's book *Cooked: A Natural History of Transformation*, which is also a four-episode Netflix documentary series. It gives great insight into the evolution and history of cooking, how the four classical elements – fire, water, air and earth – transform the stuff of nature into the food that we eat and drink.

Richard Wrangham of Harvard University argues in his book *Catching Fire: How Cooking Made Us Human* that the invention of cooking – even more than agriculture, the eating of meat or the advent of tools – is what led to the rise of humanity. *Homo erectus* (the first human, 1.8 million years ago) evolved when our ancestors learnt to cook; in fact, humans cannot survive on raw food. Cooking also relieves us from chewing a lot. Since monkeys spend half their waking hours chewing, no wonder they don't get anything done!

When my friend, MasterChef India contestant Sadaf Hussain, released his book *Daastan-e-Dastarkhan*, I read and even tried out the recipes to understand the culinary heritage of Muslim communities across India. What makes Sadaf's book so interesting is his ability to tell a story about every recipe. *Cooking at Home with Pedatha* (Gourmand Award winner in 2006 for Best Vegetarian Cookbook in the World) by Jigyasa Giri will make you nostalgic for your grandmother's cooking. In fact, it is one of the first cookbooks that I owned, thanks to being acquainted with her, and is the best book on simple south Indian recipes. Indian recipe cookbooks are legion, but what grips me is the ones that tell interesting stories, and that's why I look forward to reading my friend Query Ferose.

Often, I have wondered why our mothers' recipes are special. Scientifically, the chances are high that we have inherited at least some of our genes from our parents, so what tastes good to them probably tastes good to us too. Maybe it also has to do with the link between memory and taste. Preparing something delicious and nourishing for the people you love is probably the best expression of love itself. There is a reason they say the way to a man's (and woman's) heart is through the stomach. Only so long as the food is cooked at home!

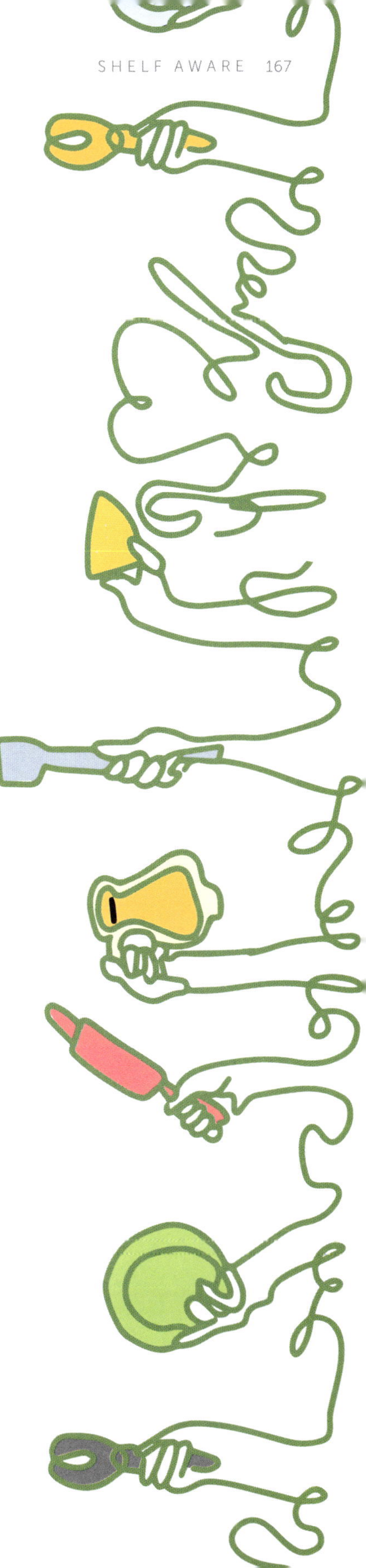

I became suddenly interested in, even intrigued by, regional literary writing when the Kannada translation of a book I co-authored, *Gifted*, won the Karnataka Sahitya Academy Award in 2017.

regional bestsellers IN ENGLISH

Translated by A.R. Manikant and H.C. Natesh Babu, the Kannada translation of *Gifted* opened up a whole new world for me. It had me wondering how much I was missing by not reading more regional or *Bhasha* literature as it is currently known.

But the point is — and this is no excuse — many urban Indians, including me, don't know how to read many of our regional languages, and thus, the only way to access *Bhasha* literature is when it is translated into English. Having grown up reading Tagore's translated works in English, I cannot imagine what I would have missed if the translations were not available. Regrettably, many excellent *Bhasha* novels and short stories seize our attention only when they win awards or turn controversial.

By now, most readers in India and abroad know of the Tamil writer Perumal Murugan who made this earth-shaking announcement on Facebook: 'Perumal Murugan, the writer, is dead. As he is no God, he is not going to resurrect himself. He has no faith in rebirth. As an ordinary teacher, he will live as P. Murugan. Leave him alone.' He instructed his publishers not to distribute or sell his books, and asked that his fans burn his work, and that he would compensate them for the loss. One of his novels had been unfairly targeted by a community, and he and his family had been hounded. A High Court victory gave him the courage to publish again.

Luckily, these instances are few; for the most part our *Bhasha* literature has been winning awards abroad too. Nilanjana Roy, a literary columnist, comments that the enduring literary 'snobbery' of the English-speaking Indians is slowly receding. There was a widely held feeling in the literary community that translations do not capture the style and idiom of the language it was written in. That sentiment or belief has now been set aside as the English translators take great care to capture the flavour of the original, even consulting with the author.

One recent breakthrough novel is the translation of *Ghachar Ghochar* by Vivek Shanbhag, a Kannada novel that was recently published in the US. It made it to the *New York Times* list of recommended books to read in 2017. Translated by Srinath Perur (who incidentally was my college junior at National Institute of Technology, Warangal), the translation has managed to capture the emotions of the original and provide a brilliant social commentary – all in less than hundred pages.

Shanbhag has reminded all of us, 'It is not just English writers that respond to the modern world.' How true. There have been startling postmodern novels in Malayalam, Bengali, Marathi, and Assamese that can hold their own with the best of postmodern literature coming out of Latin America and Europe.

A few years ago, an anthology of Tamil pulp fiction became a runaway bestseller after it was translated into English. Called *The Blaft Anthology of Tamil Pulp Fiction*, its success spurred a second volume. Another groundbreaking postmodern novel was Charu Nivedita's widely acclaimed *Zero Degree*. In fact, many Indian readers were pleasantly shocked that a translated *Bhasha* novel had explored bolder and more audacious themes than our English novels do.

One of the oldest classics in Malayalam, *Chemmeen*, was one of the first southern Indian novels to be translated and find acclaim. Earlier it was largely Bengali (Rabindranath Tagore) and Hindi (Premchand) writers who were being translated, with writers from the northeast and the south being neglected. That changed thanks largely due to the potent literary prowess of Malayalam and Kannada writers: the modern Kannada classic, *Samskara* by U.R. Ananthamurthy that took the world by storm, is a huge example. Or the plays of Girish Karnad, or the poetry of the Vachana devotees. In Malayalam, there was O.V. Vijayan and Basheer, and most widely known of all, Kamala Das (later known as Kamala Suraiyya). Her *My Days* was perhaps one of the first translated novels to become a pan-Indian bestseller.

In Marathi, there was a revolution in modern literature, as too with Assamese writing. Most of the literature had been written decades before they were translated. This means that those who read only English were sadly unaware of the explosion of literary talent among us, within us.

Also, hidden even to a regional audience was our great Dalit literature, often underplayed and overshadowed by the works of 'higher caste' writers. Also, even within Dalit writing, women's voices were not heard as loudly. That has now changed and the works of powerhouse writers such as Bama, Meena Kandaswamy, P. Sivakami, and Urmila Pawar are disrupting and transforming feminist Indian writing. They have been translated into English too, and have found a vast audience hungry for stories that truthfully reflect their lives.

In a country with twenty-two national languages, there are so many unique *Bhasha* stories that deserve a larger audience, waiting to be unearthed. A revolution in regional publishing, however, will be when there are *Bhasha* graphic novels. Translating them would be fun – you don't have to redo or 'translate' the graphics, just the text.

THE CASE FOR LEFTIES

There is a predominantly negative narrative around being left-handed. In *Roget's Thesaurus*, synonyms for 'unskilled' are left-handed, equivocal and sinister, with sinister derived from the Latin for left-hand side.

I grew up observing my mother cut vegetables with her left hand and write with her right hand. Later, she told me that she was born left-handed but was forced to become right-handed; by and by, she became ambidextrous. Statistics show that around 10 per cent of the world's population is born left-handed, but over a period, no doubt due to social pressure, the number is drastically reduced in the same population.

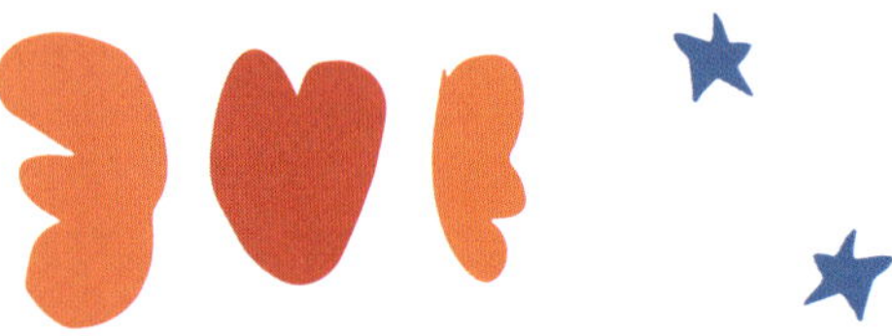

In Hindi, the left hand is called *ulta haath,* which simply means the wrong hand. In French, *gauche* means left and also, of course, awkward, clumsy and socially unrefined. In German, *recht* means right-handed, the law and correct. Left-handedness has long been associated with Satanic influences and witchcraft. In the Bible, the blessed are always sitting at the right hand of God, never the left. The term left-wing in politics, though, carries no negative baggage. It originated in the era of the French Revolution, when the aristocrats sat on the right and the commoners on the left in the National Assembly,

We tend to refer to someone being left-handed only in the context of writing. Famous left-handed writers include Mark Twain, Franz Kafka, Lewis Carroll, Hans Christian Anderson, James Baldwin and Douglas Adams.

However, there are also musicians, painters, actors and other artists who primarily use their left hand to create their art. They include Leonardo da Vinci, Michelangelo, Beethoven, Mozart, Hariprasad Chaurasia, Jimi Hendrix, Paul McCartney, Asha Bhonsle, Lady Gaga, Rajinikanth and Amitabh Bachchan. In the worlds of politics and business you have Julius Caesar, Napolean Bonaparte, Mahatma Gandhi, Barack Obama, Ratan Tata and Bill Gates. Interestingly, NASA found that one out of four Apollo astronauts was left-handed.

The term 'southpaw' in sports was originally used for a left-handed baseball player, but journalists have been using it for other sports too, such as boxing as well as cricket. Tennis is a sport where the left-hander has had disproportionate success. John McEnroe, Jimmy Connors, Martina Navratilova and Rafael Nadal are a few examples. According to tennis experts, the left-hander's forehand serve is equivalent to the right-hander's backhand, and that is an advantage.

Have you ever thought about how hard it is for left-handers to find guitar tutors or golf trainers? While walking on Pier 39 Street in San Francisco, I was pleasantly surprised to see a store called Lefty's, which is entirely dedicated to left-handers. The store is a haven for kitchen tools, basic school supplies, musical instruments and more, specially designed to be used by 'lefties'. Incidentally, to bring the spotlight on to the uniqueness and differences of left-handed people, 13 August is designated as International Lefthanders Day.

There seems to be no good answer as to why people are left-handed. Genetics, which could have been a possible reason, does not explain why left-handers are born in entirely right-handed families. *Left-Hander Syndrome* is an eye-opening book by psychologist Stanley Coren on the causes and consequences of left-handedness. *A Left-Handed History of the World* by Ed Wright carries the profiles of some of the most famous left-handed men and women in history. *The Puzzle of Lefthandedness* by Rik Smits is an enlightening odyssey through the puzzles and paradoxes, theories and myths of left-handed lore.

However, the best book on this subject is *Right Hand, Left Hand: The Origins of Asymmetry in Brains, Bodies, Atoms and Cultures* by Chris McManus. He uses sources as diverse as the paintings of Rembrandt, the sculptures of Michelangelo, the behaviour of Canadian cichlid fish, the story of early cartography, modern cognitive science, the history of the Wimbledon tennis championship and the biographies of great musicians to explain the vast repertoire of 'left–right' symbolism that permeates our everyday lives.

sniffing out some 'PAWSOME' BOOKS

I was not a pet person until I became a pet parent some time ago. It was a well-thought-out decision, and we were fully aware of the lifestyle adjustments we would have to make (especially when travelling) to bring in our new family member.

We had been looking for a service dog for my son with special needs. We finally brought home a four-month-old English retriever, Coco, and our lives have never been the same again!

Once I entered the canine territory, many questions occupied my mind. Are dog people more likely to be extroverts than introverts? Can dogs talk? Why is calling a person a 'dog' an insult in almost every language? Why do we say, 'The world has gone to the dogs'?' So I started reading books with dogs as the subject. Here are some that are meant not just for those who love dogs but those who intend to adopt them.

Classic Dog Stories edited by Nancy Butler is a collection of eighteen enduring tales by an impressive array of authors – from Mark Twain and Rudyard Kipling to Jack London. *The Book of Dog* edited by Hemali Sodhi is a recent collection of forty-five original pieces by some of India's leading writers, outstanding new voices and individuals who have dedicated their lives to animal welfare. I loved every essay, but my favourite was by Sri Lankan author Ashok Ferrey.

Many parents get a dog primarily for their children, and *Harry the Dirty Dog* by Gene Zion is without doubt one of the most beloved children's books. The YouTube video of actor Betty White reading the book garnered more than eight million views! *Lessons from Lucy* is a laugh riot – you can expect nothing less from Dave Barry – but it is also insightful and touching.

A must-read before becoming a dog parent is *Wag: The Science of Making your Dog Happy* by dog trainer and social psychologist Zazie Todd whose dos and don'ts of raising a dog I found extremely useful. When it came to scientific books, I absolutely loved Alexandra Horowitz's *Being a Dog: Following the Dog Into a World of Smell*. Readers will feel that they have broken free from human constraints and understand smell as never before – that they have, however fleetingly, themselves been a dog!

I was immediately drawn to *How Stella Learnt to Talk* by speech-language pathologist Christina Hunger. Since we use augmentative and alternative communication (AAC), which are a range of techniques to help people who struggle with speech to communicate with our non-verbal son, I was curious to know whether the same techniques could be used for dogs. The author shares how she taught her dog to push buttons on a custom soundboard to form phrases up to five words in length – the same method she uses to teach children to speak and read. Finally, a less-known but one of my favourites is *Thurber's Dogs* by James Thurber – a collection of short stories, articles and drawings on the subject.

When it came to fiction, I watched movie adaptations of books instead of reading them. However, *The Friend* by Sigrid Nunez is on my to-read list). *A Dog's Purpose*, *The Art of Racing in the Rain*, *Marley & Me* and *101 Dalmatians* are all wonderful adaptations of bestsellers.

The biggest lesson I have learnt from Coco so far is that dogs overflow with gratitude and never take us for granted. Every time I see her, however brief my absence has been, she greets me with quivering, unbounded joy. It's a wonder how a relationship between two species that began as entirely based on utility was transformed into something based on love. And maybe it's time we rethink the usage of 'going to the dogs'!

(xxxviii)

The Frenchman Henri Cartier-Bresson is regarded as the founding father of photojournalism. Cartier-Bresson, co-founder of Magnum, one of the world's most influential photo agencies, started his affair with photography with a simple Box Brownie camera.

●REC

ZOOMING IN ON PHOTOJOUR

Henri Cartier-Bresson insisted on only using the available light and on editing 'in the camera' rather than in the darkroom. He covered events such as the assassination of Mahatma Gandhi, whom he met just ninety minutes before he was shot, in 1948. His *The Decisive Moment* is a classic, which has influenced generations of photographers. Published in 1952, this collection of the best work from his early years had a collage cover by Henri Matisse.

The first and only reprint is a meticulous facsimile of the original book with an additional booklet on the history of *The Decisive Moment* by Centre Pompidou curator Clément Chéroux. Another legendary photojournalist who captured images of Gandhi a few hours before his assassination was Margaret Bourke-White, who had worked as a staff photographer for *Fortune* and *LIFE* magazines. Her photo of the Mahatma at his spinning wheel is iconic. *The Photographs of Margaret Bourke-White*, edited by Sean Callahan, is a collection of one of America's great photographers. Raghu Rai, a protégé of Cartier-Bresson, is probably India's most well-known photojournalist, who has worked in leading Indian publications and served on the jury for World Press photos. He has produced more than thirty-five photobooks including *Romance of India, Taj Mahal* and *Mahakumbh*.

Many consider Stefan Lorant (co-founder of British picture magazine *Picture Post*) as the godfather of photojournalism. Lorant's pictorial histories of the American presidents include *Lincoln: His Life in Photographs*, a forerunner in the genre of pictorial biography, and *FDR: A Pictorial Biography*. His other works include *The New World* and the photographic book *Pittsburgh: The Story of an American City*. One of my favourites is the *New York Times* fashion photographer Bill Cunningham, known for his candid and street

NALISM

photography. Cunningham led a modest life, bicycling his way through Manhattan and living in a tiny apartment in the Carnegie Hall building.

His life is captured in the documentary *Bill Cunningham New York*. His memoir, *Fashion Climbing*, is the untold story of his education in creativity and style. Ansel Adams is an environmentalist and one of America's most famous landscape photographers. He advocated for 'pure' photography that favoured sharp focus and the use of the full tonal range of a photograph. His photos of Yosemite National Park are best captured in Ansel Adams' *Yosemite*.

My friend Vicky Roy taught me that photography, particularly street photography, is about capturing the essence of the subject. He is on a mission to capture the stories of people with disabilities across every Indian state for the campaign 'Everyone is Good at Something'. In fact, Vicky sold his first photo for just five rupees. His book, *Home Street Home*, captures his journey from his home to living in the streets and then to finding his home again.

The smartphone camera has democratized photography, but can technology turn a mediocre photographer into a great one? Already, it is becoming hard to distinguish between a photograph and an AI-generated image. That is why photojournalism is more relevant than ever.

BOOKS ON CREATING social impact

We need a vision for a new form of capitalism designed to serve human needs rather than mindlessly accumulate wealth.

We need a world where we bring solar energy to millions, have female-owned businesses, lift the underprivileged by providing mobility, shelter and other services, and create a global network to help young entrepreneurs launch their start-ups. This is where I believe social entrepreneurs will play a very important role in driving inclusive growth around the world. I am a huge fan of social entrepreneurs, and I have been fortunate to have learnt from the best – Magsaysay awardees Anshu Gupta (founder of Goonj) and Harish Hande (founder of SELCO).

According to a World Economic Forum report, India has the highest number of social entrepreneurs in the world. So, what are the books that any aspiring social entrepreneur should read? The two books that opened my eyes to radical ideas were *Winners Take All* by Anand Giridharadas and *Utopia for Realists* by Rutger Bregman. *Winners Take All* challenges every entrepreneur to honestly reflect on their efforts: Is that work going to effect positive systemic change, or does it purely appear good while preserving a status quo of inequality and injustice? Rutger's book, on the other hand, is directed at changes in public policy and government intervention and focuses on the role that social entrepreneurs might play in his ambitious call to live in a world that we might consider a 'utopia.'

However, one of the earliest and most important books, considered an introduction to social entrepreneurship, is a book that Nelson Mandela calls 'wonderfully hopeful and enlightening' – *How to Change the World* by David Bornstein. The book was originally published in 2004, and while some of the examples may be a little dated, the concept and ideas are not.

A book that is mandatory reading for social entrepreneurs is *Systems Thinking for Social Change* by David Peter Stroh. It is essential to understand systems thinking so that we avoid unintended consequences even when our intentions are pure. Inspired by some of the social entrepreneurs in the disability space, my foundation has been supporting many young entrepreneurs, and some of them find mention in my book, *The Invisible Majority*.

Two biographies of social entrepreneurs that I would recommend are *Banker to the Poor* by Nobel Peace Prize winner Mohammad Yunus and *Creating Room to Read* by John Wood. The former is the now well-known story of the Grameen Bank credit programme founded in Bangladesh in 1983 by Yunus to provide small loans to the poor. The latter is a spellbinding story of one man's mission to put books within every child's reach. Microsoft employee John Wood left his corporate job at the age of thirty-five to start the nonprofit Room to Read. The book shares moving stories of the people whom Room to Read works to support — impoverished children whose schools and villages were swept away by war or natural disaster and girls whose education would otherwise have been ignored.

Finally, no story of social entrepreneurship is complete without mentioning Aravind Eye Hospitals, the world's largest provider of eye care. The book *Infinite Vision* by Pavithra K. Mehta and Suchitra Shenoy is a must-read for anyone interested in leadership, service and the building of institutions that release the best energies of the human spirit. The book uncovers the radical principles behind Aravind's baffling success. I have often sent my team of engineers to spend a day at Aravind Eye Hospital in Madurai, Tamil Nadu, and it is the best leadership lesson you will ever receive.

(xxxix)

the stories that letters REVEAL

With letter writing a nearly forgotten medium now, a good place to rediscover the joy of letters is in a literary genre that has long fascinated me: epistolary books – that is, fiction and non-fiction showcasing correspondence between two people.

Dracula is a famous example of the epistolary novel, a story told through letters. Others are Alice Walker's *The Color Purple* and Elizabeth Kostova's thriller *The Historian*. But what engages me more are letters exchanged by real people.

Letters of Note, compiled by Shaun Usher, became an instant classic and there are now fourteen volumes in the series. The first book garnered much praise for Usher's eclectic selection of letters – to name a few, Queen Elizabeth II's recipe for drop scones sent to President Eisenhower, Iggy Pop's advice to a troubled fan, Leonardo da Vinci's job application and Virginia Woolf's suicide note.

Highway Dharma Letters comprises correspondence received by a contemporary Buddhist teacher from his two disciples. In 1977, American Buddhist monks, Reverend Heng Sure and Reverend Heng Chao, undertook the ancient ascetic practice of bowing once every three steps and took a two-and-a-half-year pilgrimage up the coast of California, inching along at about a mile and a half a day. They wrote every day to their master, Hsung Hua, describing their journey and the lessons they learnt in compassion and humility. I am fortunate to have met Reverend Heng Sure. 'I'm still amazed that people care to read these letters,' he said. 'The pilgrimage happened three decades ago, and Marty (Reverend Heng Chao) has a white beard!'

On a visit to the Kennedy Library and Museum in Boston, I bought *Letters to Jackie* by Ellen Fitzpatrick. Within seven weeks of President John F. Kennedy's death, Jacqueline Kennedy received more than eight hundred thousand condolence letters. Two years later, the volume of correspondence would exceed 1.5 million letters. Historian Ellen Fitzpatrick selected approximately two hundred and fifty of these letters for inclusion in *Letters to Jackie* – ordinary Americans across generations, regions, race, religion and political leanings expressing their anguish over losing their favourite president.

Then there's Helene Hanff's ever-popular *84 Charing Cross Road*, letters between a book lover and a bookseller. Although it was adapted into a play and then a movie, it is the book that remains a classic. Each letter brings out the personality and literary style of the letter writer. While the staff wrote formal, affectionate letters, Hanff was impish and brazen. Finally, as the letters come to an end, there is nostalgia and tears of both sadness and joy.

However, my all-time favourite book and one that has been central to nourishing my soul is *The Mahatma and the Poet,* private letters between Mahatma Gandhi and Rabindranath Tagore. Written between 1915 and 1941, they are currently preserved in the archives of Visva-Bharati, the university founded by Tagore in Santiniketan, West Bengal. The book gives us deep insights into the relationship between these two giants.

In 1934, after Gandhi made a public statement calling the Bihar earthquake divine retribution for India's sins, an appalled Tagore wrote back to him respectfully but assertively: 'We, who are immensely grateful to Mahatmaji for inducing, by his wonder working inspiration, freedom from fear and feebleness in the minds of his countrymen, feel profoundly hurt when any words from his mouth may emphasize the elements of unreason in those very minds.' The letters offer a poignant example of what it means to be both friends and intellectual adversaries, to stand by one's convictions with equal parts dignity and respect for the other, to seek, above all else, the advancement of the public good.

In a digital world, will we ever have the equivalent of *Letters from a Father to His Daughter* by Jawaharlal Nehru or *The Letters of Ernest Hemingway* or *Graham Greene: A Life in Letters*? Will we have, instead, books about email or social media exchanges?

DIVING INTO BIBLIOMYSTERIES

I am neither a fan of mystery novels nor of fiction, but I do make an exception when it comes to the bibliomystery, a genre introduced to me by my author friend Pradeep Sebastian.

Pradeep's book *The Book Hunters of Katpadi,* considered India's first-ever bibliomystery, revolves around a one-of-a-kind store of rare books in Chennai named Biblio, which specializes in modern Indian first editions. The store is run by two passionate women, whose lives revolve around curious browsers, eccentric book collectors, private-press printers and the occasional thrill of unexpected discoveries of the antiquarian kind.

The famous owner of the Mysterious Bookshop (New York), Otto Penzler, once noted, 'If you go to the dictionary or hit your computer's spell check, you will discover that there is no listing for the word bibliomystery... Nonetheless, bibliophiles who also are mystery fiction aficionados certainly know what the word means… It's pretty clear if the crime involves rare books, or… if much of the action is set in a bookshop or a library, it is a bibliomystery, just as it is if a major character is a bookseller or librarian.'

Bibliomysteries as a sub-genre within detective and crime fiction date back to the nineteenth century. *Scrope* or *The Lost Library* by Frederic Perkins, in 1874, is often cited as one of the earliest titles in the genre.

Modern readers started noticing bibliomysteries only after the success of John Dunning's *Booked to Die* in 1992 featuring Cliff Janeway, an ex-cop turned book collector who solves crimes around expensive modern first editions. As more titles in the Janeway series emerged successfully, other mystery writers tried their hand at this genre.

Bibliomysteries can be broadly classified into Vintage or Classic (from the 1890s to the 1950s), modern (the 1960s to the 1990s) and contemporary (2000 to the present). The conventional bibliomystery is a series featuring a professional or amateur detective who investigates crimes related to books; Kate Carlisle's Bibliophile series is a good example.

Another more complex kind is a one-off novel with books, libraries or manuscripts playing a central role in the plot. This is often a deeply researched work, usually set in the past or the future. You could say that this second type was initiated by Umberto Eco's *The Name of the Rose*, followed by other 'biblio-fables' or 'biblio-novels': *Codex* by Lev Grossman, *The Rule of Four* by Ian Caldwell and Dustin Thomason, *The Shadow of the Wind* by Carlos Ruiz Zafón, *The Club Dumas* by Arturo Pérez-Reverte, *The Dante Club* by Matthew Pearl, *The Nijmegen Proof* by S. Barksworth (pseudonym of Arthur Freeman), *Knock or Ring* by Michael Nelson, and *Mr. Penumbra's 24-Hour Bookstore* by Robin Sloan, to name only a handful. They do not strictly conform to the tropes of the genre, as the conventional type does. Fans of Eco's groundbreaking book badly wanted him to do a sequel, but he refused to oblige them.

Some noteworthy vintage bibliomystery titles published in the first half of the twentieth century are *Murder in the Bookshop* by Carolyn Wells, *Fast Company* by Marco Page, *The Gutenberg Murders* by Gwen Bristow and Bruce Manning, *The Unpublishable Memoirs* by A.S.W. Rosenbach, and *The Colfax Book-Plate* by Agnes Miller. If you are new to this genre, a good place to start would be *Bibliomysteries* edited by Otto Penzler.

Bradford Morrow's trilogy is worth exploring: *The Forgers, The Forger's Daughter* and his final (to be published) book pay homage to three towering figures of mystery and suspense fiction – Arthur Conan Doyle, Edgar Allen Poe and Agatha Christie. Lastly, *The Letter Killeth* by Betty Rosenberg includes three essays that I found very entertaining. For bookworms hungry for a deep dive into the book universe, there's nothing more satisfying than a bibliomystery.

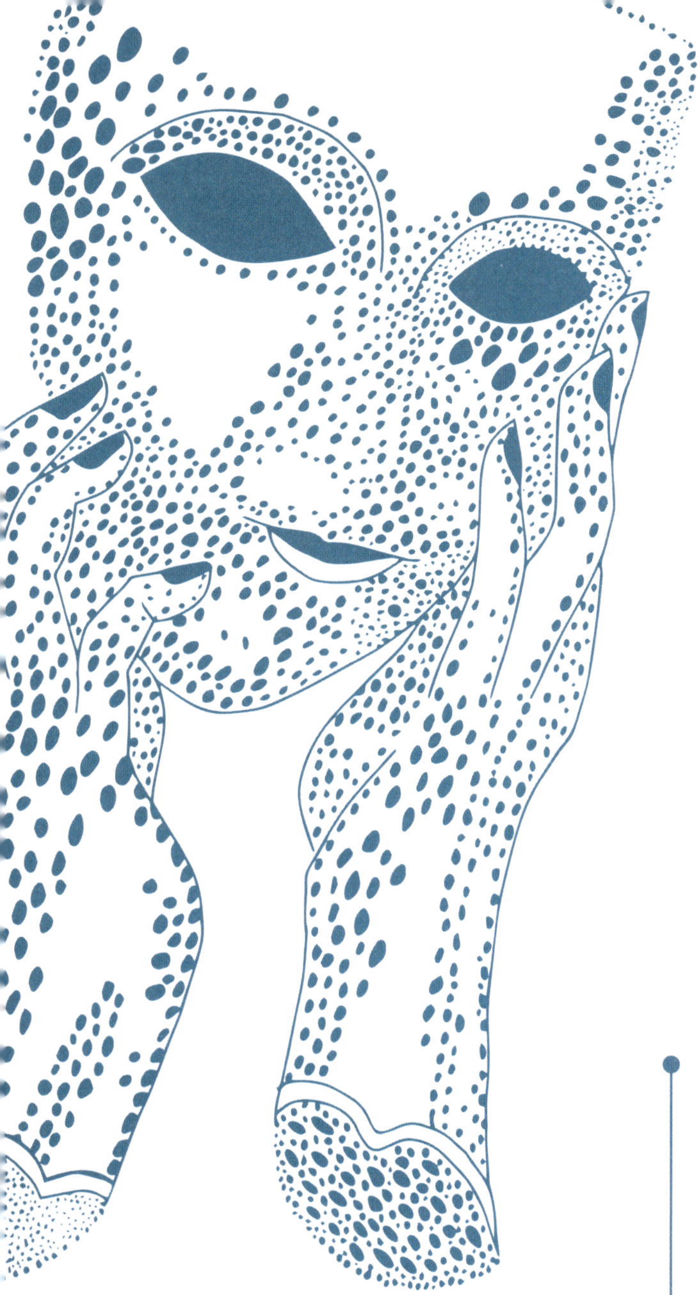

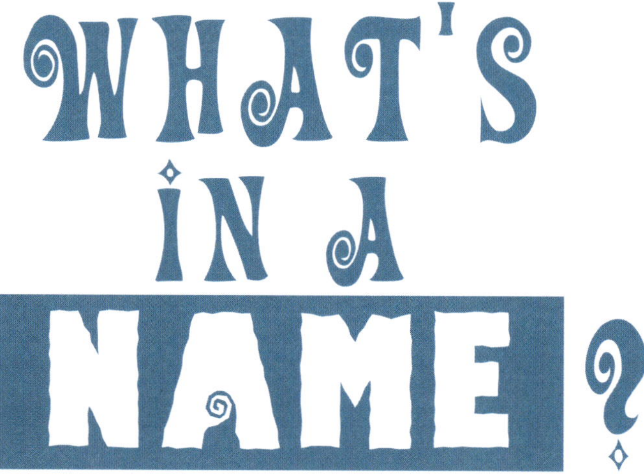

My friend wrote a true story about fearing his wife and disliking his in-laws and published it under a pseudonym. The book became a bestseller, and movie makers were keen to capture it on screen. The author is convinced that if his wife comes to know he wrote the book she would instantly divorce him. Thankfully, he has a watertight agreement with the publisher.

There are many other reasons why writers publish books under fake names or pseudonyms. Stephen King released his book *Thinner* under the name Richard Bachman and even included a fake jacket photo that he claimed was shot by his wife, Claudia Inez Bachman. I was lucky to find this much sought-after edition. At the time when *Thinner* was released, publishers felt that the prolific King's readers may not buy more than one book from an author in a year and therefore he published his 'overflow' as Bachman.

The novel *Primary Colors* created a huge buzz when the author simply called himself 'Anonymous'. The book, an instant bestseller, later made into a movie, is a thinly disguised fictional description of the first Bill and Hillary

A shy Oxford mathematician, Reverend Charles Dodgson, wrote *Alice in Wonderland* as Lewis Carroll. His motive: he did not want to be famous. How many authors today can say the same?

Clinton campaign. Who was the author who possessed so much inside information? The first suspect was Joe Klein, a well-known political columnist, who first denied but eventually admitted that he was the author.

Reverend Charles Dodgson, who was an Oxford mathematician was the one that wrote *Alice in Wonderland* as Lewis Carrol, simply because he did not want to be famous. Fans of Ferrante, the Italian author of the wildly popular series starting with *My Brilliant Friend*, respected her anonymity. When an Italian journalist, using financial records, claimed that Ferrante was Anita Raja, a translator, the journalist was pilloried by upset fans. (The author still hasn't revealed his/her identity, by the way.)

Lars Kepler is the pseudonym of husband and wife team Alexandra Coelho Ahndoril and Alexander Ahndoril, authors of the Joona Linna series that has sold millions in forty languages. The Ahndorils were both established writers, but the pseudonym allowed them to write together without limitations. They also wanted their books to be assessed without prejudice, the same reason why J.K. Rowling wrote her adult thriller as Robert Galbraith. Also, a different identity would give her the artistic license to explore a new genre.

I own the first edition of *The Cuckoo's Calling* by Robert Galbraith, and also a signed first edition of *Joseph Anton*, Salman Rushdie's memoir. Rushdie wrote this autobiographical book in the third person, creating an identity for himself as Joseph Anton.

Patricia Highsmith's reason for using a pseudonym was to write something that was ahead of its time – the first lesbian novel with a happy ending. Those who read the marvelous short stories of O. Henry were unaware that he was William Sydney Porter, who was serving a prison sentence for committing a crime.

Another aspect of pen names is a franchise can be passed off as the work of a single author. Caroline Keene is the collective pseudonym for all those who wrote the Nancy Drew mysteries, and Franklin W. Dixon for the authors of the Hardy Boys books. The Nick Carter books too have different authors.

A pseudonym can conceal a secret personality that can take on a life of its own under this new name. As author Carmela Ciuraru notes, 'Many writers have been lonely outsiders, which is why inhabiting another self offers an intimacy that seems otherwise unobtainable. In the absence of real-life companionship, the pseudonymous entity can serve as confidant, keeper of secrets and protective shield… a pseudonym may give a writer the necessary distance to speak honestly, but it can just as easily provide a license to lie… It allows a writer to produce a work of serious literature, or one that is simply a guilty pleasure.'

Most major newspapers write obituaries in advance, long before the famous person has died. But the obit is not about death at all. It is about life. It is one last chance to make the dead live again.

The obituary page of the *New York Times* is a celebration of extraordinary lives. When I read that paper's obit of ninety-four-year-old Sidney Poitier (the first person of colour to win an Oscar in 1963 for *Lilies of the Field*) by William Grimes on 8 January 2022, it increased my interest in understanding how obits are written so quickly (since it has to appear immediately after the death of the subject).

The obit captures the essence of a person's entire life and makes revealing observations that the subject never gets to read. Writing an obit is an art form. The typical length is 600–800 words accompanied by at

THE LIFE CONTAINED IN AN OBITUARY

least one picture. One of the longest ones written in the *New York Times* was for Pope John Paul II; it went upto 13,870 words! Some obits are on the front page, and the question of who is worthy of a page-one obit is often a matter of debate.

If there is one book that is a must-read in this category it is *Book of the Dead* by William McDonald. It captures the stories of the greatest men and women who ever lived in the form of a collection of obituaries published by the *New York Times*. The paper's obit section has some of the most inspiring, insightful, often funny and elegantly written stories celebrating the lives of the men and women who have influenced our world.

McDonald, who was also an obituary editor for the *New York Times*, was recently featured in the award-winning documentary *Obit*, which selected three hundred and twenty obits of the most important and influential people from the newspaper's archives for the book. In chapters such as 'Stage and Screen', 'Titans of Business', 'The Notorious', 'Scientists and Healers', 'Athletes', and 'American Leaders', the entries include a range of newsmakers from the last century-and-a-half, including Annie Oakley, Theodore Roosevelt, Joseph Stalin, Marilyn Monroe, Coco Chanel, Malcolm X, Jackie Robinson and even Prince. Also included is a Webkey, which allows instant access to an exclusive website featuring ten thousand selected obituaries that are easily searchable by name, theme and even dates.

Another widely read obit column is that of the *Daily Telegraph*. It brought out five books of obituaries that have been both a critical and popular success. Well researched, each life story is told with intimate revelations and very often with great humour. *The Very Best of The Daily Telegraph Books of Obituaries* really lives up to its name. Some of the obits are so captivating that if you didn't know the dearly departed person before reading the *Telegraph* you would wish that he or she had been your life's best buddy.

Another charming and lyrical book is about the people who write obituaries: *The Dead Beat* by Marilyn Johnson. This book answers the question of what makes the obituary page so compelling. On the other hand, Jim Sheeler's *Obit* comprises obits of ordinary people. Most of the people eulogized in *Obit* are unknown, but they will remind you of the variety of humans on Earth and the absolute certainty that no matter how powerful a personality, eventually the body goes, and what remains stays not only in people's hearts but in their stories. If you manage to appear in the *New York Times* or a *Telegraph* obituary column, it meant that your life had been noted and you could really rest in peace!

Why are we obsessed with self-help books? Do they really help? Is there something called self-help? Because if you did it yourself, you did not need help in the first place!

The Thriving SELF-HELP Industry

However vague the idea of self-help may seem (I am a sceptic myself), the fact is that this genre is thriving in the book industry. In the US alone, it rakes in an estimated ten billion dollars and counting. My scepticism comes from the fundamental belief that the people who have written these books – from Paulo Coelho to Viktor Frankl – have spent an entire lifetime building their inner resilience through their struggles in life. While Coelho found his spiritual awakening when he was on his 500-mile walk in Spain, Frankl's learnings were largely from his time spent at the Nazi concentration camp. Most readers, on the other hand, buy these books in the belief that they will find some quick fix for all their problems. They assume that the solution to their life's challenges lies in reading the book, not in practising the message!

Another aspect of it that disturbs me is that because 'self-help' connotes 'self-improvement', the books were aimed at audiences who felt unworthy – those who wanted to lose weight, achieve money and fame, find love as well as happiness. Since most people are average or mediocre performers in all walks of life, this became a perfect business opportunity but had no real impact. Self-help has gone beyond books to workshops, seminars and retreats led by self-help gurus and life coaches (Tony Robbins and Oprah Winfrey being the superstars in the subject). In many ways, self-help has become the modern religion.

The resonance of a self-help book depends entirely on what moment in his life's journey the reader has reached. The same message that may make complete sense when read at a specific time can seem as nonsense or preachy at a different time. Also, the assumption many of us make is that a strategy that worked for the author will work for us too.

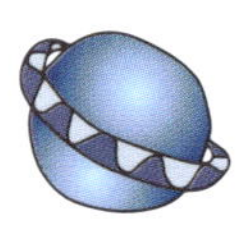

The question is: If self-help has been so helpful, why don't we see more enlightened and better human beings?

While the year 2000 could be seen as the time when the self-help industry took off, the origin of 'self-help' goes back to the eponymous book by Samuel Smiles in 1859. It was the same year that Charles Darwin's *On the Origin of Species* was written – and believe it or not, *Self-Help* was a bigger success than the latter. The core idea was that 'Heaven/God helps those who help themselves'. I have read *Self-Help* and considering that it was written more than hundred and fifty years ago, much of its key message is still relevant. Smiles, a Scottish author and reformer, denounces 'the worship of power, wealth, success, and keeping up appearances'.

Over the years, the key themes have revolved around the idea that 'positive or negative thoughts bring positive or negative experiences', a notion popularized by the movie and the book on which it is based: Rhonda Byrne's *The Secret*. Byrne's book, which became a mainstay of the self-help industry, echoes Wallace Wattles' *The Science of Getting Rich*, published in 1910.

Amongst writers, Coehlo is seen as the leader of the pack, and if you have not read *The Alchemist*, people may look down on you. Personally, I think it is hugely overrated. *The Alchemist* had an initial print run of only nine hundred copies when it was published by a small Brazilian house, before HarperCollins published it in 1994, making it an international bestseller.

Dale Carnegie's *How to Win Friends and Influence People* remains on the bestseller list even after eighty years. It taught readers to become more likable and manipulative at home and in the competitive job market. What specially resonated with me was the first principle, 'don't criticize, condemn or complain', the idea being that 'it is better to speak ill of no man, and speak all the good of everybody you know'. The worrisome part is when people become inauthentic and start gaming the system to influence others.

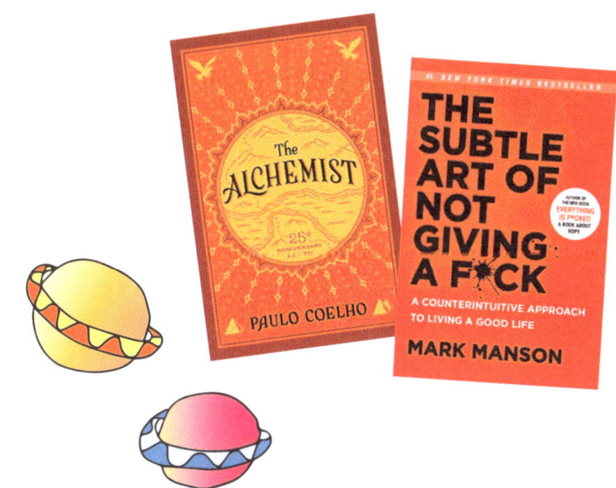

Stephen R. Covey's *The 7 Habits of Highly Effective People* has sold more than twenty-five million copies since its publication in 1989. Covey presents an approach to being effective in attaining goals by aligning oneself to what he calls 'true north' principles based on a character ethic that he presents as universal and timeless.

Another book that has a huge readership is *The Power of Now: A Guide to Spiritual Enlightenment* by Eckhart Tolle. The book is intended to be a guide for day-to-day living and stresses the importance of living in the present moment and avoiding thoughts of the past or future.

The last few years, however, have seen the gradual rise of an anti-self-help sentiment. As Mark Manson, author of *The Subtle Art of Not Giving a F*ck* shared: 'The practice of self-help only highlights the qualities and things you don't have, thus making you more miserable. On the flip side, accepting the fact that you're not successful allows you to be happier with your current state.'

I say, instead of reading multiple self-help books, read the one that connects with you, many times. And then apply the principles at every opportunity – and that is the hardest part. Better still, let's have a new genre called help-other.

why public libraries NEED TO BE REVIVED

Something the British novelist and critic Zadie Smith said about public libraries hit me hard: 'Why do we love libraries? Well-run libraries are filled with people because what a good library offers cannot be easily found elsewhere: an indoor public space in which you do not have to buy anything in order to stay.'

Ah, but this lovely scenario is more valid if we are talking about public libraries in the West, or at least if we exclude those in our country. In fact, to most of us the word 'library' only evokes circulating libraries where you pay a membership deposit and a reading fee for each book borrowed. In the US, you can borrow as many books as you wish for free from your local public library. The only money you fork out is for the bus or subway ticket for the ride to get there.

Like most Indians, I was first exposed to a library in school. I had the opportunity to also access my father's railway club library, which meant borrowing one book and reading the magazines (which we were not allowed to take home). When I was growing up, most families bought only textbooks for their children – that is, if they couldn't get secondhand ones from their school seniors. Children would haunt libraries mainly to unearth material for class 'projects'.

Across the world, budgets for public libraries have been dwindling, and the newer generation prefers their digital devices to physical books. But the great libraries of the world remain extraordinary environments for scholarship and enlightenment. The Library of Congress in Washington, DC is the largest library in the world with over hundred and sixty million books. The National Library in Kolkata is the largest in India with over two million books.

Two impressive coffee-table books, *The Library* and *The Most Beautiful Libraries in the World*, are not merely about book collections but also about the buildings that house them. 'When a library is open, no matter its size or shape,' Bill Moyers wrote in his foreword to *The Public Library: A Photographic Essay*, 'democracy is open too'.

India has over seventy thousand public libraries funded by taxes from local administrative bodies, but not every state has a library-legislation in place, and only five have levied a library cess on its denizens. Very few states have a dedicated Department of Libraries; most libraries are run by education or arts and culture departments. You don't have to look too hard to discover ill-equipped and poorly-stocked libraries; untrained and underpaid librarians; and books borrowed but not returned, or worse, vandalized.

An older friend, an avid reader who frequents the beautiful State Central Library in Cubbon Park, Bengaluru, was astonished to discover a remarkable inventory of books – not only by European and US authors but also Japanese, Australian, South American and Asian authors. How many schoolchildren and collegians know of the treasures that lie within these walls?

I, for one, feel that libraries should not just be places for people to borrow and read but to spend their study time, to soak in the ambiance, to play, do art and meet friends. However, the real benefit of a library is for the less privileged, and above all, for children.

There are 2.6 million functioning libraries in the world, of which 4,04,000 of them are public libraries. In *The Library: A Fragile History* by Andrew Pettegree and Arthur der Weduwen, the authors state: A repeating cycle of creation and dispersal, decay and reconstruction, turns out to be the historical norm. And that while growth and decline are part of the cycle, so too is the recovery.

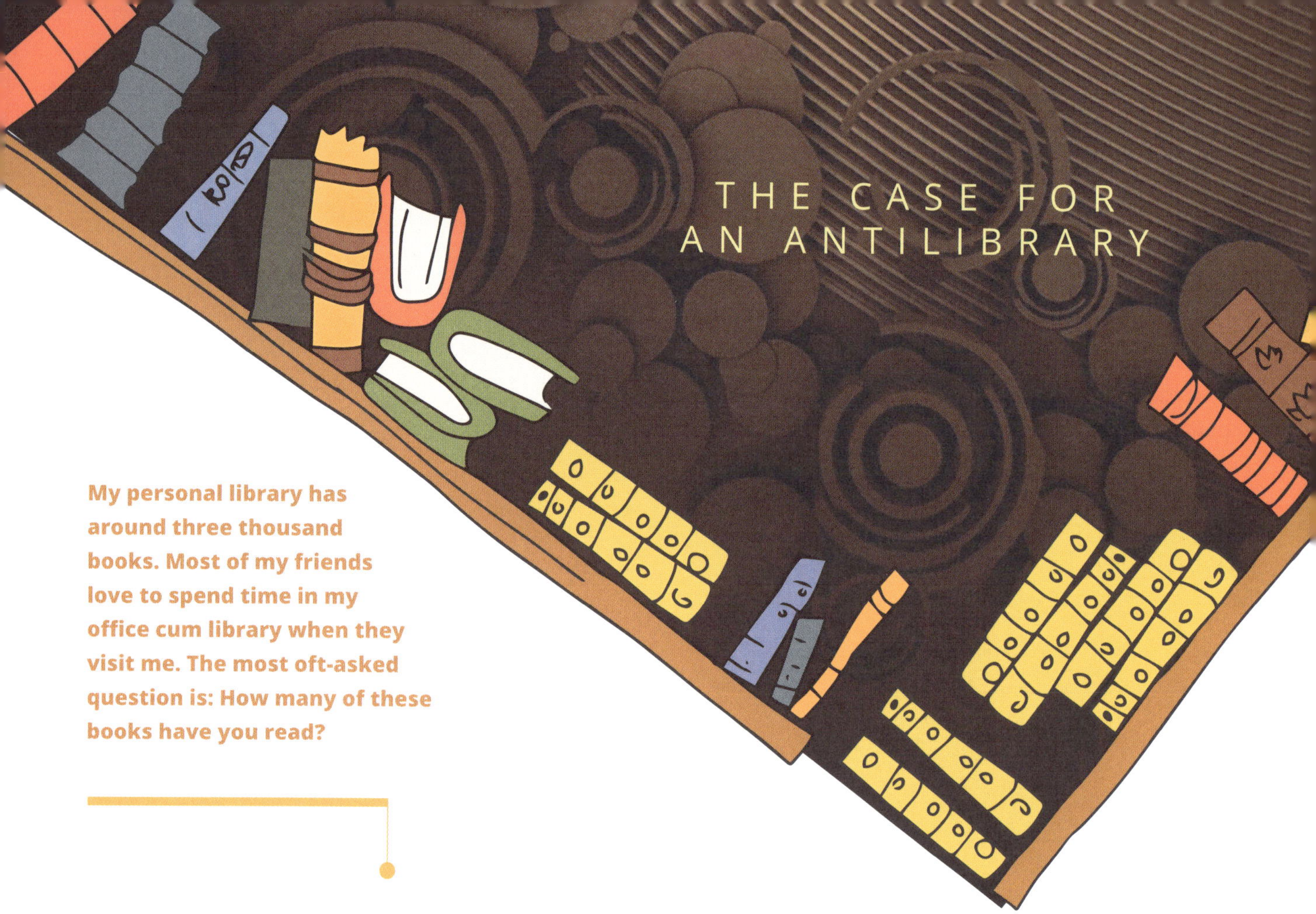

THE CASE FOR AN ANTILIBRARY

My personal library has around three thousand books. Most of my friends love to spend time in my office cum library when they visit me. The most oft-asked question is: How many of these books have you read?

Building a library is not an ego-boosting exercise but a research tool I use for most of the books and columns I write. Hence, I have come to realize that 'read' books are far less valuable than 'unread' ones. In fact, I have started giving away my read books, unless they are a collectible or have a personal association.

THE JOY OF A LIBRARY OF UNREAD BOOKS

In the book *Black Swan,* Nassim Nicholas Taleb claims that your personal library should contain as many books as your finances allow. He shared, 'You will accumulate more knowledge and more books as you grow older, and the growing number of unread books on the shelves will look at you menacingly. Indeed, the more you know, the larger the rows of unread books.' In effect, Taleb is saying that the ratio of the library (existing knowledge) to 'antilibrary' (potential of unlearned knowledge) should decrease over time – which perhaps runs counter to conventional wisdom.

Interestingly, there is a term for this in Japanese, *tsundoku*, for leaving a book unread after buying it, typically piled up together with other unread books.

A good library should always have more books than you need or have use for – that's how you know a library is comprehensive. Also, why can't your library or collection also reflect the interests of your friends or family? Why should it be stocked with only the books you care for – why not books for the times when friends drop by wanting to borrow a book?

Italian novelist Umberto Eco who had a personal library of over thirty thousand books wrote an essay, 'How to Justify a Private Library'. Eco points out that many people 'consider a bookshelf as a mere storage for already-read books'. But there is no need to waste valuable space on what you already know; it is better suited for what you want to learn. Or, as Eco wittily answers when asked about his bookshelf: 'No, these are the ones I have to read by the end of the month. I keep the others in my office.'

So many book lovers have spoken of a time when a book that had remained unread on the shelf for years suddenly took on a new and urgent importance. You become interested in a topic that you previously had no interest in, and then remember you've had a book on this very subject in your collection that you had ignored until now. This happened to me very recently. I had bought *Loafing Along Death Valley Trails* by William Caruthers during one of my road trips a few years back and never bothered to read it until recently when I planned a vacation to Death Valley.

Kevin Mims, who works in a bookstore, wrote a wonderful piece in the *New York Times* about why Taleb's 'antilibrary' does not appeal to him: it fails to describe his library. He even moots the idea of 'the partially read book' rather than the unread book. He points out (and it's true for many avid readers) that there are so many books we never complete, and so many that are not meant to be completed. What he describes is especially true for non-fiction: we read a few chapters and feel we have read enough about a subject; or even an anthology: poetry, essays and short stories. Do we usually read every story or poem or essay? No. We dip into them when we can and read what we are drawn to.

Mims calls this 'the twilight zone of the partially read'. He notes: 'Nor do I typically read biographies all the way through. Biographers have a tendency to shoehorn every last tidbit of information they can into their books. I don't really care about the marks that Ogden Nash received on his third-grade report card or how many trunks of clothing Edith Wharton had shipped across the Atlantic when she moved to France. There are probably hundreds of biographies in my personal library. I have read parts of most of them, but I have read very few in their entirety. The same is true of collections of letters... the sight of a partially read book can remind you that reading is an activity that you hope never to come to the end of.'

Another interesting angle to having an antilibrary was provided by Jessica Stillman in her article, 'Why You Should Surround Yourself With More Books Than You'll Ever Have Time to Read', where she writes that an antilibrary can act as a counter to the Dunning–Kruger effect – a cognitive bias that leads ignorant people to assume their knowledge or abilities are more proficient than they truly are. Since people are not prone to enjoying reminders of their ignorance, their unread books push them towards an ever-expanding understanding of competence. Stillman writes: 'All those books you haven't read are indeed a sign of your ignorance. But if you know how ignorant you are, you're way ahead of the vast majority of other people.'

All through the long, hot summer of 2017, dry fires raged in California. For a while, those of us who were in Palo Alto felt safe, but soon, we were waking up each morning to the TV news that the fires were closing in.

SAVING THAT one

At the time of the 2017 California fires, we all feared for the safety of our families, but I had something else to be nervous about: my precious collection of rare books.

It had me wondering, if I had to make a choice, what books I would grab as I fled the fire. Later that year, I happened to be reading that well-known book about books, *A Pound of Paper* by John Baxter. It has a chapter titled 'If your house is on fire'. Inspired by it, I wrote to my friends asking one simple question: If their house was on fire and they could save only one book, which would that be and why?

Essayist and novelist Pico Iyer, it turned out, had actually been in a California fire some years ago and could speak firsthand: 'I must admit that my house did burn down once...I was surrounded by 70-foot flames and was caught in the middle of the conflagration for three hours, watching the flames pick through every last thing I owned... One thing I learned from that experience is that whatever has value... is, by definition, what can never be replaced. And whatever can be replaced... probably doesn't have great value. The beauty of books for me is that they can always be replaced in some form...' However, when his house caught fire, he wished he could have saved his own next three books, 'all the handwritten notes for which got reduced to ash, stripping me of a future as well as of a past'.

PRECIOUS BOOK

Columnist and editor of *Wisden India Almanack,* Suresh Menon, wrote: 'Close finish between autographed copies of books by V.S. Naipaul, Nelson Mandela and Don Bradman.' But ultimately, he would choose *The Bradman Albums*, he said. 'Bradman and I sat on his porch and he signed on four different pages. It is a reminder of a warm, affectionate session, of a time when I was young enough and reckless enough to land up at someone's place without an appointment and the thoughtfulness of a veteran who had spent a large part of his life avoiding the media.'

I was thrilled with author Gary Zukav's response: 'One book, its binding torn and pages yellow, is irreplaceable to me.' That was Rabindranath Tagore's *Gitanjali.* Author of *Gently Mad,* Nicholas A. Basbanes wrote that he had already given away most of his precious books, shipping five thousand of them to Cushing Library at Texas A&M University as part of their acquisition of his literary and professional archive. 'I kept a few things that I couldn't bear parting with, my collection of Winslow Homer wood engravings in particular... And I did keep my magnificent set of Thomas Frognall Dibdin's *The Bibliographical Decameron*, 3 vols, 1817.'

The author of *Bapu Kuti*, Rajni Bakshi, picked a book that held sentimental value. 'It's a collection of musings by a person I knew very briefly, Jayantilal Parekh Jayatibhai, who spent more than fifity years as a *sadhak* at the Aurobindo Ashram – working closely with the Mother.' The 'book' he gave her just before he passed away was actually photocopies of what he wrote over the years for the ashram's magazine.

As for my personal choice, it would be a hard choice between Tagore's *Letters to a Friend* (1929) with his: 'To Mahatmaji' and signed by the poet; and Gandhi's *Songs from Prison* (1934) with the inscription 'For Dear Gurudev' and signed by him.

Looking at all the responses, one thing was for sure – I got to know my friends a little better after this exercise.

Have you ever started reading a book and been simply unable to finish reading it, even though you intended to?

James Joyce's seven-hundred-page epic *Ulysses* is considered one of the most unread books of all time, i.e., most people who own the book have not read it in its entirety. James Latham, editor of the University of Tulsa-based *James Joyce Quarterly*, recently described *Ulysses* as probably 'the most purchased and least read book in the world'. I have personally taken a stab at reading *Ulysses* but gave up after a few chapters. Now I am waiting for the release of the graphic novel adaptation of the book!

The question that intrigued me was: How do we really know whether or not a person finished reading a book? Thanks to Kindle and other e-readers, some data might be available to reveal the answer. In 2014, Prof. Jordan Ellenberg from University of Wisconsin, Madison, invented the Hawking Index (HI), which uses Amazon e-book highlights data as a proxy for where people stopped reading the books they've purchased.

The HI uses the highlight function on the devices and apps to make a simple yet unscientific assumption: a book with popular passages marked all the way to the end indicates that many people made it through the entire story. On the contrary, if the most highlighted passages are clustered at the beginning of the book, the book is more likely to have been abandoned. *Ulysses* has a HI score of 1.7 per cent and *A Brief History of Time* has 6.6 per cent while *Harry Potter and the Sorcerer's Stone* has 95.9 per cent.

Even though I possess more books than I can ever read, I do intend to read most of them, though not in their entirety. I, for one, am comfortable with the idea that not all books need to be read in full, especially non-fiction business books (though I know many people deem it a sacrilege to not finish a book they've started reading). I have to admit that I did not finish Arundhati Roy's *The God of Small Things* or Thomas Piketty's *Capital in the 21st Century*. I have not even tried to read the Harry Potter series beyond the first book.

In the *Wall Street Journal*, clinical psychologist Matthew Wilhelm states his belief that personality has something to do with the way books are read and that certain types of people are more likely to finish reading a book. Dr Wilhelm theorizes that people with competitive Type-A personalities might be more likely to abandon a book because they tend to be motivated by reward and punishment, and 'if there are no consequences or public recognition, why finish?' Conversely, he says, more laidback Type-B personalities 'may never start a book they know they won't finish'.

'The more important motivator of finishing a book is social pressure', says Dr Wilhelm, which is why book clubs are so good at getting readers to the epilogue. We often underestimate the power of accountability in getting things done. For me, every deadline for a column is a trigger to finish reading a book so that I can meaningfully write about it.

At a time when attention spans are at an all-time low, getting through a book without getting distracted seems like a herculean task. While a no-quit attitude is a good thing, continuing to read a book you don't enjoy is like living in a bad relationship. At times, we might find ourselves less and less motivated to make it to the end.

ALTERNATE HISTORY

THE WHAT IF GENRE

Have you ever imagined how your life would be if some of the most important moments had turned out differently?

Say you followed a different profession, moved to a different country or married a different person. In the world of literature, this idea is explored in the context of history. Called alternate history, it is considered a sub-genre of fiction (mainly historical fiction or science fiction). It is a niche space with the most common theme being around the outcomes of wars and presidential elections – for example, what if Germany had won World War II (*Fatherland* by Robert Harris); what if Napolean had won the Battle of Waterloo; or what if Lincoln had lost the Civil War (Peter G. Tsouras's *Napoleon Victorious* and *Gettysburg: An Alternate History*). What if James A. Garfield had become the president instead of Abraham Lincoln (Benjamin T. Arrington's *The Last Lincoln Republican*). This particular

US election of 1880 has been one of the most popular themes related to the American presidential elections.

Two of the most popular books around alternate history are *The Guns of the South* by Harry Turtledove and *The Man in the High Castle* by Philip K. Dick (the latter was made into an OTT series by the same name).

However, an interesting twist to the concept of alternate history has been to explore different outcomes for fictional ideas – such as what if Superman sides with the British during the American Revolutionary War; Batman sailed the seas as the dreaded pirate Leatherwing; or the armoured hero Steel faced a vicious slavemaster on a Civil War-era plantation. These are the themes of the graphic novel *Superman Batman: Alternate Histories*, which comprises a bunch of stories collected from the 1994 *DC Elseworlds Annuals*. It's a great introduction to the what-ifs of the DC superhero universe. You take a history that was fiction to begin with and move it into an alternate possibility. Such narratives have spawned some of the most imaginative comics going round.

Another intriguing biographical tale is *Rodham* by Curtis Sittenfeld, which asks the question: What if Hillary Rodham had not married Bill Clinton but had achieved something significant on her own? The book imagines a timeline where a twenty-something Yale Law School graduate Hillary Rodham ultimately rejects Bill Clinton's marriage proposal (in reality, she accepted his proposal the third time!).

Harry Turtledove is considered 'the master of alternate history' and has been credited with bringing the sub-genre into the mainstream. He is known for creating original alternate history scenarios, such as the survival of the Byzantine Empire or an alien invasion in the middle of World War II. In addition, he has been credited with providing original treatment to alternate themes that had been dealt with by many others. Most of his books have a strong military theme. *Guns of the South*, where he imagines the rebels winning the Civil War, is his most popular book. When Turtledove was asked how he wrote alternate fiction, he replied, 'I use the same extrapolation techniques of a science fiction writer, except that instead of projecting it into the future I turned it into the past.'

A book that generated a lot of controversy in India was the 2009 book by Wendy Doniger, *The Hindus: An Alternative History*. The book was explicitly intended as an alternative history of Hinduism, the mainstream history being (in the author's view) written from the male Brahminical and white Orientalist perspectives. Doniger instead portrays the history of Hinduism from the point of view of women, dogs, horses and outcastes in a 'playful, iconoclastic, and inherently controversial' style.

I am waiting for someone to write a fictional account of what if Donald Trump had won the 2020 election instead of Joe Biden. Going by what Trump's fans believe, many may not consider this as fiction to begin with!

Constrained writing is a literary technique that sees the writer bound by a condition that forbids something or ensures a particular pattern. One of the most famous of these constraints is a 'lipogram', where a particular letter is forbidden. This seems easy when the letter in question is Q or Z, for example, but to really challenge yourself, you can ban the use of a much more common letter. Or the most common letter of all – E.

the quirky technique of constrained writing

Gadsby is a 50,000-word novel by Ernest Vincent Wright, which was published in 1939 and doesn't use the letter 'E' at all. Wright spent five-and-a-half months writing on a typewriter with the E key tied down so that it couldn't be used at all. A warehouse holding copies of the book burned down shortly after it was printed, destroying most copies of the ill-fated novel. The book was never reviewed, but by word-of-mouth it has become an underground cult classic. The book's scarcity and oddness has seen copies priced at $4,000 by book dealers. Over time, this peculiar masterpiece has opened up many curious readers to this unusual reading experience.

Later editions of the book have sometimes carried the alternative subtitle *50,000 Word Novel Without the Letter 'E'*. Despite Wright's claim, however, published versions of the book may contain a handful of uses of the letter 'E'.

A Void by Georges Perec is another of the most famous lipogrammatic novels, but even more impressive is the number of translations it has undergone. Originally published in 1969 in French as *La Disparition*, the novel follows a group of friends who are trying to find their companion Anton Vowl. The novel doesn't contain a single letter 'E' (except the four unfortunately found in his name). It has since been translated into various other languages, with a similar rule being imposed on every translator. Because 'E' is so prevalent in many languages, that's usually the one that gets removed, but the Spanish version removes the 'A', the Russian the 'O', and the Japanese the 'I'.

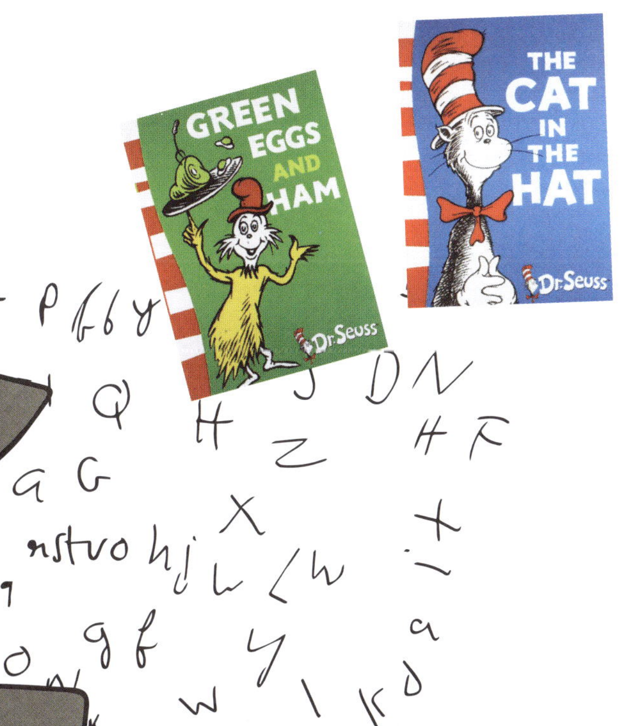

Dr Seuss was famous for books with simple language and catchy rhyme schemes, but perhaps his most famous title was written as the result of a bet between Seuss and his publisher, Bennett Cerf. Following on from *The Cat in the Hat*, which used 236 different words, Cerf bet Seuss that he couldn't complete one with even fewer. *Green Eggs and Ham* was published in 1960 with just fifty different words used in the whole text. Despite this stringent limitation, by 2001, it had become the fourth bestselling English language children's hardcover of all time.

And for those who are curious, some of the fifty words are: a, am, and, are, be, boat, box, car, dark, do, eat, fox, goat, green, ham, here, I, if, in, let, like, may, not, on, or, rain, Sam, say, see, that, the, them, there, they, train, tree, try, will, with, would, and lastly, you.

Another example of constrained writing is Peter Carey's book *True History of the Kelly Gang*, which doesn't use a single comma. In Walter Abish's *Alphabetical Africa*, every word in the first chapter begins with A. In the second chapter, words beginning with both A and B are allowed, and so on.

It seems to me that the only purpose of constrained writing is a good writing practice. For trivia and quiz junkies, it may provide some fun facts to remember.

THE BEST OF EXPERIMENTAL WRITING

***Lincoln in the Bardo* by George Saunders is not about President Abraham Lincoln but his son William, who died tragically at the age of twelve in 1862. It is also a book comprising quotes (accompanied by their citations).**

This 2017 Booker-winner was my first exposure to an experimental form of writing (though I had earlier read *Slaughterhouse-Five* and *Ulysses*, which were considered experimental in their times). The novel takes place during and after the death of Lincoln's son William 'Willie' Wallace Lincoln and deals with the president's grief at his loss.

'Experimental' literature utilizes unconventional or unorthodox forms to convey meaning and produce an impact. This can mean, for example, constructing a completely non-linear narrative, or creating characters that are aware that they are characters within a story. But bear in mind that a form is always experimental in relation to an earlier form. When Ernest Hemingway's early short stories were published, they caused a huge tumult because he was disrupting the earlier conventions of what constituted literary language. But now, Hemingway's clipped prose has influenced so many generations of writers around the world, that it has itself become conventional. 'Experimental writing' is therefore hard to define because no single definition suffices.

Experimentation in the literary arts is often considered inaccessible. If you are a fan of experimental writing, then you probably enjoy uncovering deep meaning in surprising texts. The plot is not subtle and often shakes up the reader. They bend genres and play with language and form to tell a story in a way it hasn't been told before. Often, it is defined by what it is not rather than what it is. It's fun because there are no rules and there are infinite possibilities.

If you are a writer and want to improve your skills, experimenting with the extremes of writing helps build confidence. Acknowledged as one of the most influential of modern French writers, Raymond Queneau's *Exercises in Style* has been part translated, partly adapted into over thirty languages. It contains ninety-nine versions of the same, very basic story employing a variety of styles, ranging from sonnet to cockney to mathematical formula. Every writer should read this to expand their understanding of literature and how they can go beyond first- and third-person narration. Translating this book would have been every translator's ultimate challenge. Another highly recommended book, especially for budding writers, is *The Mezzanine* by Nicholson Baker. What makes this 133-page book a classic is that nothing happens in the story. The plot, if you can call it one, is simple: a man buys a pair of shoelaces!

In Yann Martel's *Self*, the main character changes gender several times. (In Virginia Woolf's *Orlando* the eponymous character continually changes gender, location and historical period.). Martel uses the pages in the book in an interesting way: each page is divided into two, where on one side is the character's thoughts and on the other side, his description.

A novel that I did enjoy but which took a lot of effort to finish was *The Interrogative Mood: A Novel?* by Padgett Powell. Imagine a book that begins by asking a question – and then continues with one question after another. Many questions were peculiar, some a bit mad and some of them were very thought-provoking. Unlikely though it sounds, it's a work of real charm.

However, since experimental novels hinge upon innovative and clever forms rather than content, most are difficult to get through and need an open mind and a lot of patience to be enjoyed.

The phrase 'the book was better' is so oft-heard that we automatically fill in the rest of the sentence 'than the movie'. It is true that movies seldom do full justice to their source novels. But the reverse is also true. You might be disappointed after reading a book on which a great movie was made.

The book–movie relationship has taken strange turns. Take *Love Story* and *The Omen*. They began as screenplays and were then turned into books that unexpectedly became huge bestsellers. Another interesting reversion in the world of adaptations is that movies can lift books out of anonymity. Obscure books get a second life on bookstore shelves when their movie versions become hits. *The Martian*, the blockbuster Ridley Scott science fiction movie starring Matt Damon as an astronaut stranded on Mars, was based on a book that had a niche readership of sci-fi fans. *Lion,* a movie about a young man who goes looking for his home and parents using Google Earth, whetted our appetite to find out more about the life of Saroo in the book in *A Long Way Home* (which was, incidentally, retitled *Lion* in 2017). Another example is *Slumdog Millionaire*, which made the world take notice of author and diplomat Vikas Swarup's *Q&A* (upon which the movie was based) after the film won an Oscar.

Acclaimed books can find new readers when their movie adaptations become hits. Michael Ondaatje's *The English Patient* had won the Booker, but when the movie came out, it sent people rushing to buy copies. Yann Martel's *Life of Pi* had been popular for some years and had also won the Booker, but when Ang Lee adapted it into a beautiful, mystical film, book sales gained a fillip.

Milan Kundera's *The Unbearable Lightness of Being* was a cult novel, and when it was announced that it was going to be made into a movie, fans of the book gave a collective groan. Director Philip Kaufman wrote to Kundera assuring him that he would be faithful to the book. Kundera's reply was totally unexpected. He said that when he went to see the film, he did not want to

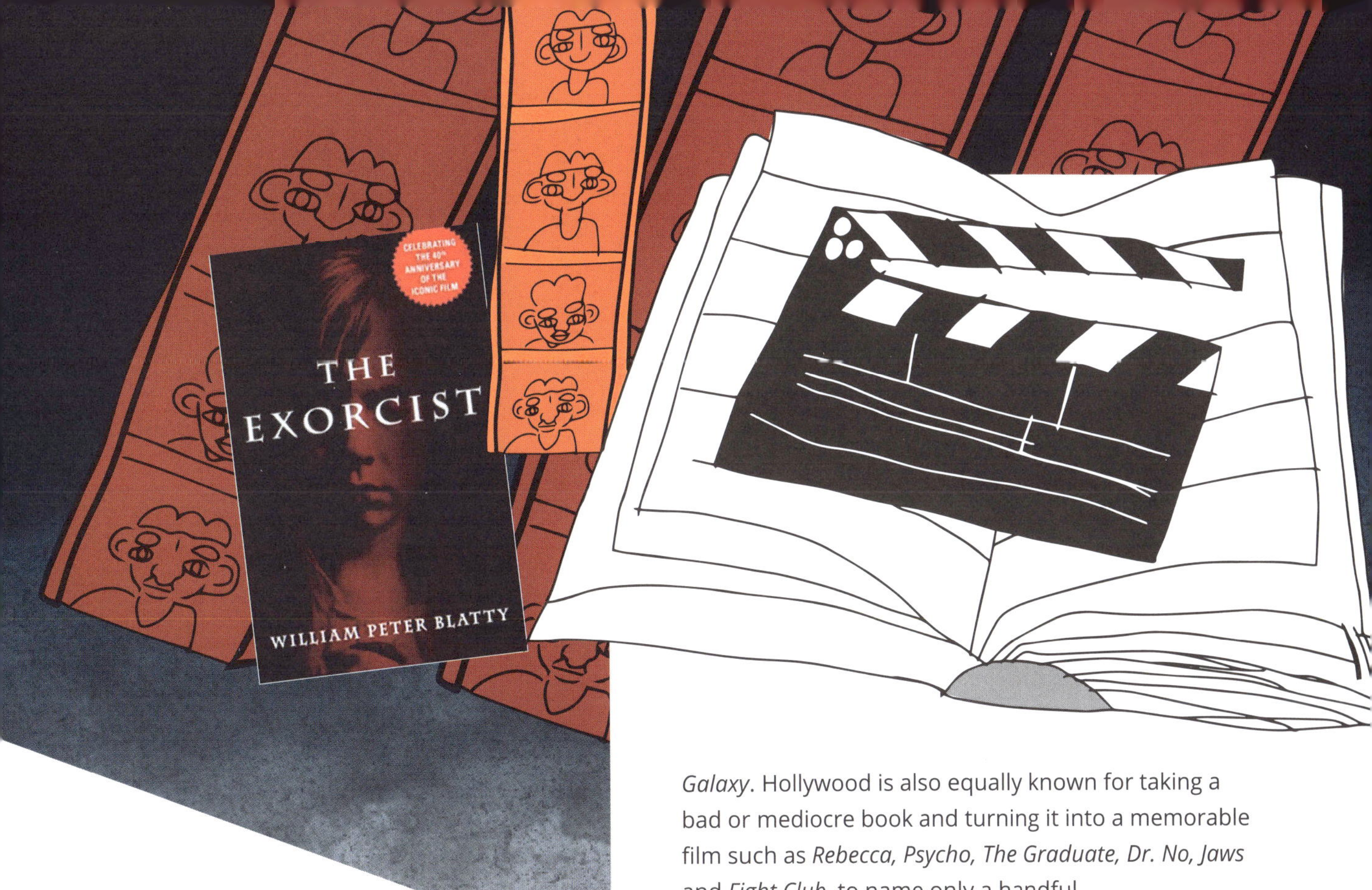

see the novel, and that he would be disappointed if Kaufman adapted it too faithfully!

This approach has been adopted by many modern screenwriters: instead of rigidly adhering to the plot, they attempt to capture the spirit of the book. I always think of filmaker Dev Benegal's *English, August* as a fine example. Somehow, without sticking too closely to the book, Benegal managed to please even diehard fans of Upamanyu Chatterjee's cult novel by transferring its idiosyncratic spirit onto celluloid. Another enjoyable Indian adaptation was *Parineeta.*

Hollywood is notorious for taking perfectly good books and ruining them for readers. Some examples: *The Great Gatsby* (both versions), *The Hobbit, Twilight, The Da Vinci Code* and *The Hitchhiker's Guide to the Galaxy*. Hollywood is also equally known for taking a bad or mediocre book and turning it into a memorable film such as *Rebecca, Psycho, The Graduate, Dr. No, Jaws* and *Fight Club*, to name only a handful.

Hollywood's newest source of inspiration has been graphic novels and comics. Every Marvel comic adaptation has been a box office success (*Black Panther* broke all records) while movies based on graphic novels have garnered critical acclaim, *Persepolis* was one such movie that was beautifully visualized and made the original graphic novel come alive.

On rare occasions, the book and the movie are equally good. They are so perfectly balanced that we can no longer decide which one is better. The finest examples are: *The Silence of the Lambs*, *The Firm, One Flew Over the Cuckoo's Nest, Gone with the Wind, The Exorcist, The Godfather, The Talented Mr. Ripley, Murder on the Orient Express,* and more recently, the Harry Potter movies. In these cases, some magic transpired, where the vision of the author and the vision of the director were in harmony. The magic of words was mirrored by the magic of moving images.

If you asked someone what their favourite Indian movie is, you would get a graded list plus a justification of their choices. But if you asked them to name their favourite book about movies, you would almost always get a blank. Unfortunately, we have not had books on movies that have captured the imagination the way our movies themselves have.

BEST *Bollywood* BOOKS

With more than sixteen hundred movies produced across various languages in 2019 (over eight hundred in Bollywood) and fourteen million Indians going to the movies daily, India has not produced high-quality literature to match those figures. Now, considering that Indians spend more time reading physical books (over ten hours per week) than citizens of any other country do, and produce the world's highest number of movies, it's a pity that the best biography of Bollywood is yet to be written. Mihir Bose's *Bollywood: A History* (2006) is a decent attempt, though. We need a social and cultural history of Bollywood on the lines of *A City Of Nets: A Portrait of Hollywood in the 1940's* by Otto Friedrich.

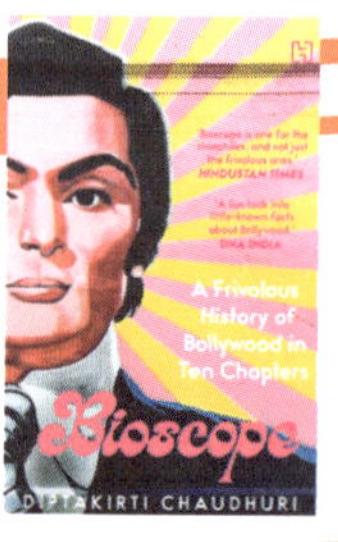

The earliest books I read on Bollywood movies were Anupama Chopra's *Sholay: Making of a Classic* and *Dilwale Dulhania Le Jayenge: A Modern Classic*, which provide you an entertaining, behind-the-scenes view of the making of these classics. My favourites that every Bollywood fan should read for its insights are *In a Cult of Their Own* by Amborish Roychoudhury and *Bioscope* by Diptakirti Chaudhuri.

While there are biographies of almost all the major stars (mostly male actors), I liked Lisa Ray's deeply personal memoir *Close to the Bone*. In her memoir, Ray, one of India's first supermodels at the age of sixteen, details her entry into Bollywood, brush with the Oscars, battle with cancer, and heartbreaks before she found love and embraced motherhood through surrogacy.

Amongst the superstars, Udaya Tara Nayar's biography *Dilip Kumar: The Substance and the Shadow* is probably the best. Naseeruddin Shah's memoir *And Then One Day* is a remarkable book about his personal and professional life up till the age of thirty-two. The most recent *Manto & I* by Nandita Das is as much about the making of the movie and Nandita's journey of years of research as about the protagonist, Saadat Hasan Manto.

Shamya Dasgupta's *Don't Disturb The Dead: The Story of the Ramsay Brothers* is a fascinating insight into the family name that remains synonymous with horror movies in India. *My Adventures With Satyajit Ray: The Making of Shatranj Ke Khiladi* is based on producer Suresh Jindal's memories of working with Ray on his first non-Bengali feature. It includes the letters that flew back and forth between director and producer, production stills and numerous anecdotes about Ray's film-making process. Bollywood's film posters have a long and illustrious history, and it is brilliantly celebrated in Jerry Pinto's coffee table book *Bollywood Posters*, which forefronts the industry's unsung heroes – graphic designers and artists of posters.

Bollywood often overshadows other regional cinema. *Beyond Bollywood: The Cinemas of South India* edited by M.K. Raghavendra, film critic and scholar, is an academic book comprising four essays on the major south Indian cinemas: Kannada, analysed by Raghavendra; Tamil by N. Kalyan Raman, a Chennai-based writer and translator; Telugu by author Elavarthi Sathya Prakash, who is a faculty member at the University of Hyderabad; and Malayalam by writer Meena T. Pillai, faculty member at the University of Kerala.

What I wish to read is a book that captures the history of the entire movie industry in India against the backdrop of the social and cultural history of the country. This is a gift awaiting every cinephile.

One of my personal high points in the journey of co-authoring the book *GIFTED* was when a friend messaged me excitedly, 'I saw your book *GIFTED* in the Tamil movie, *Taramani*!' He then sent me a screenshot of that scene.

BOOKS SEEN IN FILM SCENES

The reader in us thrills at the sight of bookshelves, bookshops and book-related objects in movies. European, American and Japanese films are full of such scenes while closer to home, Hindi films have only a smattering of them. In Malayalam and Bengali films, either a book of poetry or Marxist literature makes frequent appearances. English novels keep turning up in Bollywood movies. In

Rang De Basanti, it is the Mumbai thriller *Shantaram*, and in *Zindagi Na Milegi Dobara*, rather surprisingly for a mainstream film, it is Paul Auster's postmodern thriller *New York Trilogy*. More fittingly, Kajol is seen with a pulp romance, *The Scarlett Temptress*, in *Dilwale Dulhania Le Jayenge*. In fact, when movie characters are meant to sound a little pretentious, they are often seen carrying books by Ayn Rand and Paulo Coelho.

Sometimes, an in-joke makes an appearance in Indian films. In the Tamil remake of Stephen King's *Misery*, titled *Julie Ganapati*, a character is actually seen reading *Misery.* In the Hindi movie *Johnny Gaddaar,* which is based on a James Hadley Chase novel, one of the characters is seen reading his book. A neat Hollywood in-joke is when you see Nicholas Cage reading *The Orchid Thief* in *Adaptation,* a movie about adapting the very book into a movie.

Gone with the Wind is often seen held by characters, placed on tables, in libraries and living rooms, and occasionally making a cameo appearance, almost like a character in itself. Book lovers who also happen to be trivia buffs or quizzers at heart can't resist listing the sightings of great or cult books in movies. *1984, A Clockwork Orange, The Great Gatsby, 2001: A Space Odyssey, The Stranger* and *The Second Sex* appear frequently. In British movies, it is usually a P.G. Wodehouse novel, a mystery by P.D. James or a book by Agatha Christie.

In the fictional biography *Hitchcock*, where the titular character is played by Anthony Hopkins, he is seen reading Robert Bloch's *Psycho* (Hitchcock was just doing homework at that stage). A *Brief History of Time* turns up in *Donnie Darko*, a movie about time warps. In *10 Things I Hate about You*, the heroine thrusts *The Feminine Mystique* at the hero. In *Invasion of the Body Snatchers*, a science fiction nut is seen intensely reading the classic alien story *Worlds in Collision*. In *The Book of Eli,* Dan Brown's runaway bestseller turns up briefly in a scene. In the movie version of *The Book Thief*, the heroine reads *The Invisible Man*.

One movie where book lovers can feast their eyes on books, where books are the real stars, is *Fahrenheit 451*, François Truffaut's adaptation of the eponymous cult novel by Ray Bradbury. Books become forbidden objects in this futuristic world, and readers form an underground society of 'book people' who memorize at least one book each so that it remains preserved in their memory even if the government discovers and destroys all their copies.

One of my favourites is *Into the Wild* written by Jon Krakauer and made into a movie directed by Sean Penn. It is based on the travels of Christopher McCandless across North America in the early 1990s and his experiences in the Alaskan wilderness. The protagonist, played by Emile Hirsch, is seen reading, at different times, Leo Tolstoy's *Family Happiness*, Jack London's *The Call of the Wild,* Boris Pasternak's *Doctor Zhivago* and Priscilla Russell Kari's *Tanaina Plantlore: Dena'ina K'et'una*

On his travels, McCandless found company in books. He could summon up their words on any occasion. He certainly sounds like one of the 'book people'!

Today, my relationship to Shakespeare has taken a very different and exciting turn: that of a collector focused on the history and making of the first four *Folios* containing the complete works of Shakespeare.

My earliest memory of William Shakespeare is watching *Merchant of Venice* played out at my school annual day. The oft-quoted passage containing Portia's words to Shylock about 'a pound of flesh' has stayed with me for over three decades. While I have to thank our ICSE syllabus for introducing Shakespeare to me during my school years, I could not relate to the language or the characters. I would rather read all of Shakespeare now, when I have the understanding, ability and maturity to enjoy the narrative.

Over the years, my reintroduction to Shakespeare has been largely due to Vishal Bharadwaj's cinematic adaptations of Shakespeare's plays and parodies.

The four Shakespeare *Folios* have become some of the most valued books in the history of Western literature and printing. They were published in the seventeenth century for little more than a pound, and today, command anything from four to seven million dollars for an intact copy at auctions. Their full and original title is *Mr. William Shakespeare's Comedies, Histories, & Tragedies.*

If this interests you as much as it interests me, I would recommend a few books that make for fascinating reading. *Collecting Shakespeare: The Story of Henry and Emily Folger* by Stephen H. Grant, and *The Millionaire and the Bard* by Andrea E. Mays, both give a good idea of not only how the folios came into being but also the obsession of *Folio* collectors over the ages. Inspired by these collectors, I bought an original leaf from the *Fourth Folio* printed in the seventeenth century – the closest I will ever come to owning a piece of history.

One of the reasons the *Folios* have such an aura about them is because if they had not been printed, the world may perhaps have entirely lost several of the Bard's great plays to obscurity and time. Unpublished plays such as *Macbeth, Taming of the Shrew, Twelfth Night,* and *Julius Caesar* were all gathered here for the first time. If the two men responsible for the *Folios* – John Heminges and Henry Condell – had not been passionate enough about the project, many plays would have perished. I got the opportunity to see an original copy of the *First Folio* at the Morgan Library & Museum in New York, where it is kept on display.

When the *First Folio* was published, it was used by its owners just as if it were another book in the house. As a result, copies weren't particularly well taken care of, and when they began to be collected, perhaps fifty or hundred years after they were published, collectors noticed leaves torn or missing from the *Folio*. To complete their copy, the owners began the practice of having facsimile leaves made and carefully inserted. Thus, there is always the possibility that a leaf from a *First Folio* could be one of those facsimiles, which were of the highest quality and could almost stand in for the real thing.

While I was exploring Shakespeare in his published, physical editions, my wife, Deepali, was taking courses at Stanford University on him, the first of which was titled 'Shakespeare: The Invention of the Human'. Deepali shared with me what was implied by the notion that Shakespeare invented 'the human' by quoting from her course introduction: '...Shakespeare is the first literary writer to invent truly three-dimensional fictional human beings: characters who, in hearing themselves think, proceed to develop...They interact in a vibrant, global context, showing the extremities of the human condition. Betrayal, passionate first love, sibling rivalry, an unquenchable thirst for power, avarice, despair, madness – it's all there.'

Have you ever fallen in love with a book? Falling in love with a book is like discovering your best friend. They are special in their own unique way, and you can go back to them any time.

THE GOLDEN BOOK OF Tagore

It is hard for me to say in a few faltering words how I feel when voices greet me from my own country and from across the seas carrying to me the assurance that I have pleased many and have helped some and thus offering me the best reward of my life

Rabindranath Tagore

Dec. 27. 1931

As author Donald Miller says: 'Some people find beauty in music, some in painting, some in landscape, but I find it in words. By beauty, I mean the feeling you have suddenly glimpsed another world or looked into a portal that reveals a kind of magic or romance out of which the world has been constructed, a feeling there is something more than the mundane, and a reason for our plodding.'

While I always loved books and there are some in particular that I have re-read, there is one, in particular, that I fell in love with as soon as I had it in my hands. It was a copy of *The Golden Book of Tagore*. Printed in 1931 as a tribute to Rabindranath Tagore on his seventieth birthday, this privately produced book was brought out on the suggestion of Nobel laureate Romain Rolland. Rolland and Tagore had been in contact since 1919, but first met in Paris, in 1921. An important collection of writings, it was sponsored by leading intellectuals such as Mahatma Gandhi, Albert Einstein, Kostis Palamas and Rolland himself. The book goes to show how well-regarded Tagore was the world over. My copy is numbered 881 (out of fifteen hundred printed). What is special is not only that the almost ninety-year-old book is in great condition, but that it has a moving handwritten note by Tagore. The fifty-one words in Tagore's beautiful handwriting capture his gratitude as only a poet of his calibre can express.

Written on a Visva-Bharati University letterhead, an institute that Tagore founded in 1921 and became one of India's most renowned places of higher learning, the letter is addressed to no one in particular and begins '...It is hard for me to say in a few faltering words how I feel when voices greet me from my own country and across the seas...' The letter was signed and dated 27 December 1931.

The book has many portraits of Tagore in photogravure, including a picture by photographer Martin Vos as frontispiece. Of the remaining twenty-nine, many are tipped in colour plates (with tissue guards carrying title and artist's name), including Abanindranath Tagore, Nandalal Bose, A.D. Thomas, Gaganendranath Tagore and Samarendra Nath Gupta. Other plates are reproductions of works by Chinese and Japanese artists, portraits of Tagore by eminent Indian and Western artists and early photographs of Tagore.

What is even more interesting is to find the provenance of the book. This rare copy was given to me by my favourite bookseller, Krishna (owner of The Bookworm) who always gives me the first right of refusal to any rare book that comes his way. The book came from the estate of Jehangir Baba, better known as Homi Jehangir Bhabha, the father of India's nuclear programme. Another copy of the book had surfaced in Bengaluru many years ago, and the letter is now framed and kept at Blossom Book House, Church Street. I vividly remember looking at the letter, never imagining that in a couple of decades, a copy of the rare book would find its way into my hands.

THE RARE GANDHI-TAGORE ASSOCIATION COPY

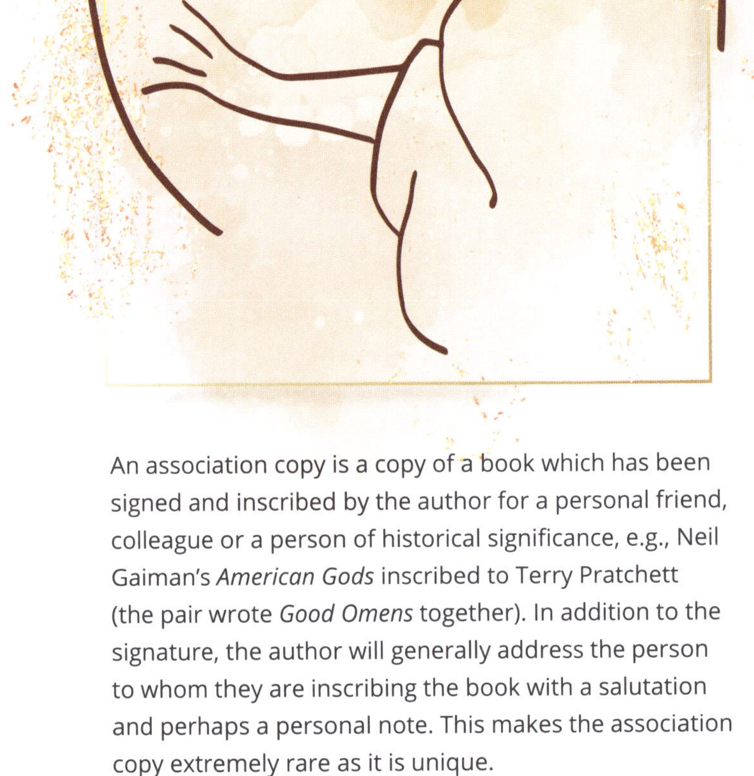

One of the most expensive books sold on biblio.com in 2021 was an association copy of *On Her Majesty's Secret Service* signed by Ian Fleming to Hugh Hefner (for $61,000).

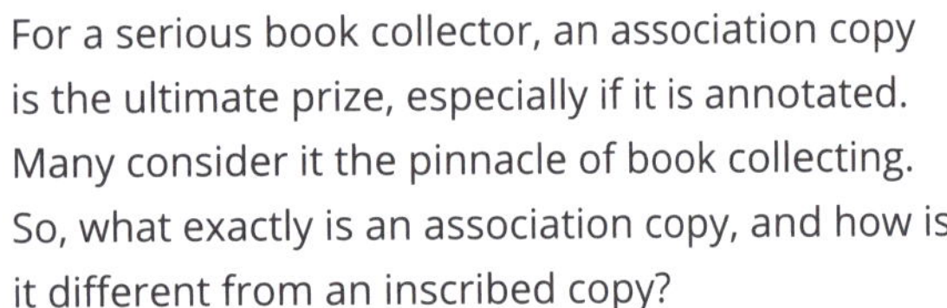

For a serious book collector, an association copy is the ultimate prize, especially if it is annotated. Many consider it the pinnacle of book collecting. So, what exactly is an association copy, and how is it different from an inscribed copy?

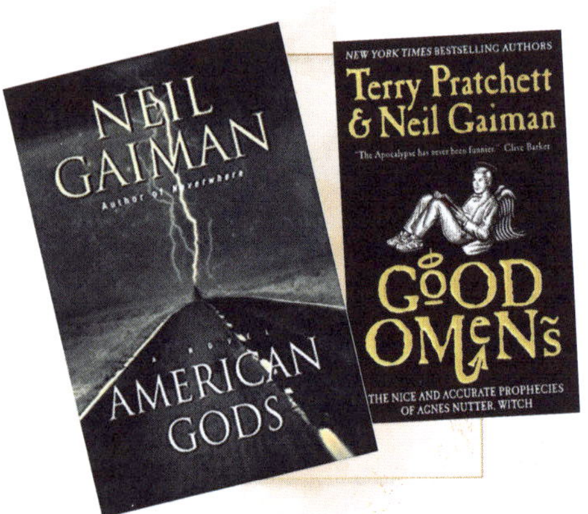

An association copy is a copy of a book which has been signed and inscribed by the author for a personal friend, colleague or a person of historical significance, e.g., Neil Gaiman's *American Gods* inscribed to Terry Pratchett (the pair wrote *Good Omens* together). In addition to the signature, the author will generally address the person to whom they are inscribing the book with a salutation and perhaps a personal note. This makes the association copy extremely rare as it is unique.

The more famous the author, the more valuable the copy, e.g., *Sunrise with Seamonsters: Travels and Discoveries* by Paul Theroux inscribed to V.S. Naipaul:

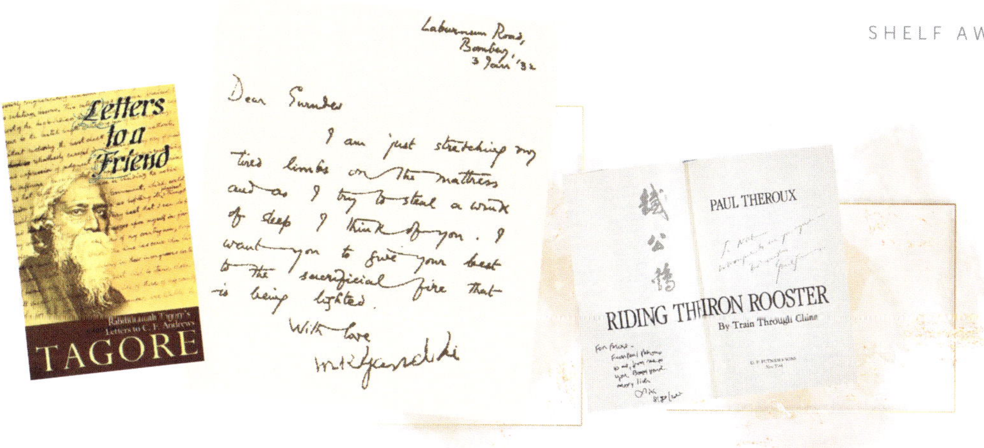

Laburnum Road,
Bombay,
3 Jan '32

Dear Sundar

I am just stretching my tired limbs on the mattress and as I try to steal a wink of sleep I think of you. I want you to give your best to the sacrificial fire that is being lighted.

With love
M.K.Gandhi

'For Vidia, To mark twenty years of friendship – if you only knew how your good influence has kept me on the straight and narrow, with love, Paul.'

A book owned by its author (Isaac Asimov's copy of *Foundation*) or a book owned by someone involved in its production, such as the illustrator or publisher (Dan Simmons's *Hyperion* inscribed to his editor) are examples of a prized association copy. However, if there is no connection between the two people mentioned in the book (say, a copy of *The Alchemist* owned by actor Al Pacino), then it is not an association copy.

While both the association copy and the inscribed book have signatures and inscriptions accompanying them, the difference lies in the association copy being inscribed to a person of social significance or of significance to the author, rather than to a random 'Raghu' or 'John'. Sometimes, accompanying materials such as an inlaid letter are necessary to identify and establish the provenance of an association copy claim.

The concept of association copies is rather new in the world of book collecting. It was first addressed from a bibliographic perspective in both *A Primer of Book Collecting* (1926) and *The Elements of Book Collecting* (1927). Since then, there has been growing acceptance of association copies in the trade and among collectors. Serious book collectors find them highly desirable because of their significance in understanding the broader context of the author's work and surrounding period of history, and also because of their comparative scarcity and uniqueness.

I was incredibly lucky to find not one but two presentation copies (a presentation copy can sometimes also be an association copy) from both my heroes – Mahathma Gandhi and Rabindranath Tagore. The first is a copy of Tagore's *Letters to a Friend* (1929) in a beautiful gold-tooled blue leather binding with the inscription: 'To Mahatmaji' and signed by the poet. The second is Gandhi's *Songs from Prison* (1934) with the inscription 'For Dear Gurudev' and signed by him. While it wasn't a bargain, it was every bit worth the price. These one-of-a-kind copies inspire fascination because they bring us a few degrees closer to the authors and personalities we admire.

Finally, a double association copy with an interesting story is a copy of *Riding the Iron Rooster* by Paul Theroux. It was first signed to Nicholas A. Basbanes, who had donated more than nine hundred association copies (received from authors in his career as a book reviewer) to the library of Texas A&M University. Knowing of the great admiration I have for the writing of Theroux, Nick chose to pass this copy on to me. Assured, he said, with the knowledge that a book that had been so special to him would have a good, welcoming home with me, on my shelves. The message from Paul Theroux to Nick read 'wonderful to see you again'. The message from Nicholas A. Basbanes to me read: 'From Paul Theroux to me, and from me to you. Books have many lives.'

Literary prizes, whether famous or lesser known, highlight quality literature, give credibility to the author and have the potential to increase sales worldwide. What are the book prizes that you follow?

THE BOOKER in the world of book prizes

I follow the Booker Prize every year but I must admit that I have never read a winning entry before it won the $50,000 prize.

Started in 1969, the Booker Prize is awarded to the best full-length novel written in English in the previous twelve months from 1 October to 30 August. Originally meant for authors from Commonwealth countries and the Republic of Ireland, the prize has been given to novels in English by writers of any nationality since 2015. From 2002–2019, it was known as the Man Booker Prize. Since 2005, the International Booker Prize has been given to a novel translated into English from any other language.

The first Indian to win the Booker was Salman Rushdie in 1981 for *Midnight's Children*. Others were Arundhati Roy for *The God of Small Things*, Kiran Desai for *Interpreter of Maladies* and Aravind Adiga for *The White Tiger.* Rushdie won the Booker of Bookers in the twenty-fifth year of the prize and Michael Ondaatje won the Golden Man Booker for *The English Patient* in the fiftieth year.

The Lost Man Booker Prize was a special edition of the prize awarded in 2010 by a public vote to a novel from 1970. Until 1970, books published in the previous year were eligible for the prize. However, from 1971 onwards, books published the same year as the award were eligible; thus 1970 was a 'lost year'. The Lost Man Booker Prize was won by J.G. Farrell for *Troubles*.

The *Guardian* started the Not the Booker Prize for books chosen through readers' votes. The Women's Prize for Fiction was started in 1996 in response to the all-male shortlist of the 1991 Booker despite more books being written by women than men that year. The Wainwright Prize has two categories, both focusing on nature: nature non-fiction and conservation non-fiction.

I also follow non-fiction prizes like the Wolfson History Prize. There are literary awards with a special focus such as the Lambda (LGBTQ+ writing), the Stella (for women writers in Australia), the Pushkin House (writing on Russia), and the Orwell (political writing) prizes. The BookTube Prize is a global award for YouTube content creators in the bookish community.

I must admit that I have not read most of the Booker winners, and there were many that I did not finish – including the longest winning novel in the prize's history, *The Luminaries* by Eleanor Catton, at 832 pages. My favourite has been Arvind Adiga's *The White Tiger*. Its movie adaptation was equally impressive although the most famous movie adaptation of a Booker novel, without a doubt, has been *Schindler's List* (based on *Schindler's Ark* by Thomas Keneally).

The highest selling Booker book is Yann Martel's *The Life of Pi*, which sold over ten million copies. Six authors have won the prize with their first novels: Keri Hulme, Arundhati Roy, D.B.C. Pierre, Aravind Adiga, George Saunders and Douglas Stuart. J.M. Coetzee, Hilary Mantel, Margaret Atwood and Peter Carey have won the Booker twice.

The Booker novels are more exploratory in their concerns and hence more universal. In 2022, *Tomb of Sand* became the first Hindi novel to win the International Booker. Written by Geetanjali Shree and translated by Daisy Rockwell, it was a surprise winner as it hardly got any attention from reviewers.

You might view self-publishing as either vanity publishing of a mediocre product or a means of liberation from the tyranny of publishers, but the truth lies in between.

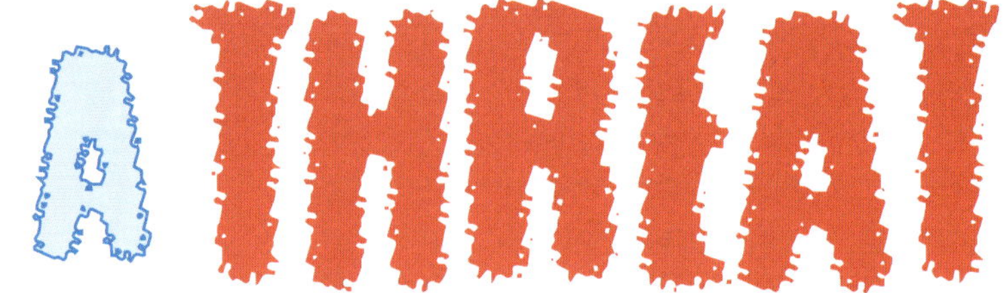

IS SELF-PUBLISHING A THREAT TO TRADITIONAL PUBLISHING?

Self-publishing in a simplistic analogy is to book publishing what blogging is to journalism. In short, self-publishing is an egalitarian way of giving every writer access to a readership. Eventually, what matters, though, is the quality of the content; the medium is incidental.

While there has been a threefold increase in the sale of self-published books in India in 2020 (compared to 2019), the absolute number of units sold were less than a hundred thousand. A large number was printed for private circulation, outside the monitored market. Most are sold either online or through local independent booksellers.

Self-publishing a book for the first time can be an overwhelming experience, especially if the author is a digital immigrant (as opposed to being a digital native). But avenues such as Amazon's Kindle Direct Publishing have made it easier for the author to seamlessly conduct the entire process, exercising control over every stage, from revisions to cover design and tagging of the book. With some exceptions, most self-published books that went on to achieve fame and wide readership were rejected by regular publishers.

Amish Tripathi's manuscript for *The Immortals of Meluha* was rejected by more than thirty-five publishing houses. Ashwin Sanghi had a similar experience with his bestselling novel *The Rozabal Line* that was self-published under his anagram-pseudonym, Shawn Higgins. A phenomenal self-publishing success (though it was panned by literary critics) was E.L. James's Fifty Shades of Grey trilogy. Conceived as fan fiction of the Twilight series, which James posted on fan fiction sites and her own website, it was later developed into an erotic trilogy. She then self-published the first e-book and print-on-demand copies through the Australia-based virtual publisher, the Writers' Coffee Shop. Similarly, Andy Weir started publishing excerpts of *The Martian* on his personal blog, and after a good reception from his readers, he published the book on Amazon US and sold it for 99 cents a copy – the rest is history.

The self-published book sold hundred thousand copies (23 million copies till date) and spent 165 weeks on the *New York Times* bestseller list. So, is self-publishing a threat to traditional publishing? Thomas Abraham, CEO of Hachette India, doesn't think so. There are good reasons why trade publishing has endured since 1768, shared Abraham. 'Authors, most of whom appreciate editorial intervention, realize the importance of imprints and the necessity of getting their work disseminated via the publishing framework structure of distribution as well as review mailouts.'

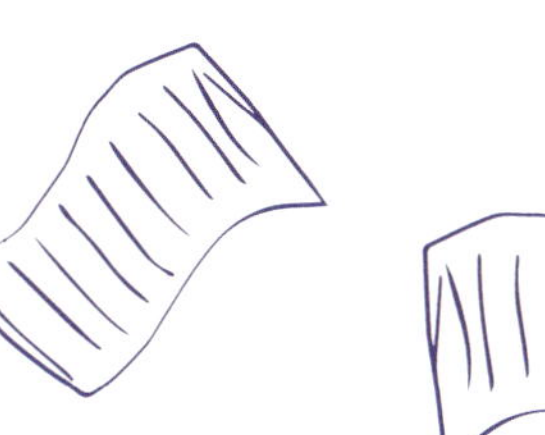

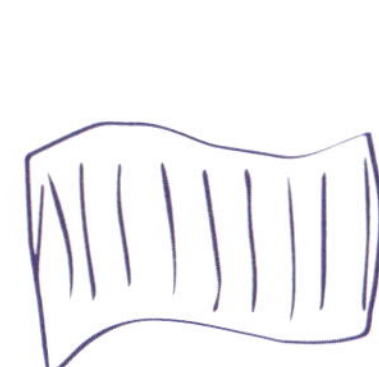

Tom Peters sold more than twenty-five thousand copies of his business book *In Search of Excellence* directly to consumers before he sold the rights to Warner; this edition sold more than 10 million copies. One of my favourite self-published books is *The Celestine Prophecy* by James Redfield, a first-person narrative of the author's spiritual awakening. Redfield set up Sartori publishing, named after a Zen term for instant enlightenment, and sank his life savings of $18,000 into printing 3,000 copies which he sold from the trunk of his car. The buzz built up and Warner stepped in.

There's ample room for both modes – self-published as well as those printed by mainstream publishers. With the bulk of self-published titles being non-competitive, they are often for private circulation and a way for writers to see their name in print, which is a very legitimate right according to Abraham. But today, they're not just two separate worlds as mainstream publishers are going in for self-publishing as well. However, the fundamental differentiator for a traditional publisher is whether their editorial team said yes to the self-published title and acknowledged it as being in keeping with their list and their imprint philosophy.

how authors sign books

Book scholars and bibliographers in the West have been looking at inscribed copies of books as an exciting new source to learn more about the mind and sensibility of an author.

As someone who has been collecting signed books by Indian authors, I have become rather intrigued by how our authors autograph or inscribe their books. I couldn't help but notice that some of them had a pattern or style in the way they always signed or inscribed their books. Once I caught on to this, I began to look more carefully at all the signed and inscribed copies in my collection. I even began looking forward to the next signed book that would come my way to see if a pattern emerged, or a style was present.

For instance, V.S. Naipaul signs above his printed name on the title page (while others more commonly sign below their names), Salman Rushdie on the blank front endpapers rather than the title page, Amartya Sen on the top right corner of the page and Sarnath Banerjee signs with a caricature doodle. I love Arundhati Roy's flowing, calligraphic signature. Amitav Ghosh signs with

a flourish too. Pavan K. Varma is probably one of the few writers in English who signs in Hindi. I also discovered that some authors, William Dalrymple for example, won't sign pirated copies. Another interesting way authors sign is a line that plays off the book title: when signing a copy of *Bookless in Baghdad* for me, Shashi Tharoor wrote, 'May you never remain bookless.' Kapil Sibal once wrote a line to rhyme with the title.

Many authors add brief messages above the signature. Dr Kiran Bedi likes to sign off with 'Blessings' and the late Abdul Kalam with 'Greetings'. Once, Vikram Chandra wrote that he generally does 'the very boring "With best wishes" '... while Suresh Menon shared that the tone of his message depends on whether the reader is a stranger or a friend.

Crossing out the printed name seems to be a common practice among many authors. Pico Iyer has always done this, he shared: 'And somehow, when I first began signing books, way back in 1988, I got in the habit of putting the name of the place where the signing took place and the month and year.' Menon sometimes cancels the printed name, adding the date and often the venue.

Something else that I find fascinating is the kind of pen they use – or in some cases, pencil. There is a tradition in the West of deliberately signing in pencil: many authors, poets and fine-press printers think this is a more elegant and individual way of signing books. But Indian authors, however, would sign in pencil only if a pen wasn't available at the time. On one occassion, Arun Shourie told me he prefers the pen to have black ink. And Anita Nair said: 'I usually use a fountain pen to sign. I discover that I make spellos when I sign with anything else.'

Of the two copies of the autobiography of Milkha Singh I have, one is signed by Singh and the other by Farhan Akhtar, who played him in *Bhaag Milkha Bhaag*. I should add here that Singh's autograph is truly unique; there is no way that anyone can guess from the signature that it is his.

Around the time I was doing a book tour for my (co-authored) book *Gifted: Inspiring Stories of People with Disabilities*, I would sign each copy with 'You are Gifted.' Not only does the title lend itself to this pun, but I also wanted each reader to think of themselves, like the people in the book, as being really gifted.

In the West, scholars look at inscribed copies of books as a new source to learn more about the authors. I feel that signed and inscribed copies by Indian authors can one day, similarly, be a useful, revealing and charming insight into our literary heroes and their connection with us, their readers.

What would make the dinner interesting would be to see how each would react to the predictions of the other.

One of my favourite sections of the *New York Times* Book Review is the column: 'By the Book: The Dinner Party'. It asks the question: You are organizing a literary dinner party. Which three writers, dead or alive, do you invite? In a recent poll, the top three dinner guests who received the maximum votes were: William Shakespeare, James Baldwin and Mark Twain.

This got me thinking about the three authors that I would like to have dinner with and why.

I would rate American science fiction author Frank Herbert, Canadian novelist Margaret Atwood and Israeli historian Yuval Noah Harari as my three favourite conversationalists (not just writers). They are original thinkers who provide interesting insights through their writings as well as their lives. I discovered Herbert very late, after watching the

2021 movie *Dune*. I am not a sci-fi fan, but once I started reading the book, published in 1965, I found that not only does it tell a fascinating story but also imparts some profound lessons.

I first read the graphic novel version of *Dune*, so I got a hang of the storyline and the characters before reading the novel, which is one of the longest and most difficult books I've ever read. The core message of the book is that every leader is flawed and so one should not trust leaders blindly. Herbert said, 'I wrote the Dune series because I had this idea that charismatic leaders ought to come with a warning label on their forehead: May be dangerous to your health.' If I had him over for dinner, I would ask, 'Since power attracts corruptible people, what virtue would attract noble ones?'

I have long been a fan of Atwood for being an outspoken feminist and environmentalist. To know her position on various issues, I recommend her book *Burning Questions*. I love her predictions for the future and her take on science and technology; she has warned us sternly against developments in biotechnology. We 'can make embryos out of skin cells' which, she said, could lead to a society where we are all women or where women are no longer needed.

She often comments about her relationship with her partner Graeme Gibson. She said: 'He wasn't an egotist, so he wasn't threatened by anything I was doing. He said to our daughter towards the end of his life, "Your mum would still have been a writer if she hadn't met me, but she wouldn't have had as much fun." My question to Atwood would be, 'What role does a man play in a woman's success?'

What makes Harari interesting is that he has answers for the future even though he is a historian. He shared, 'History is the study of change, not just the study of the past. So, it covers the future as well.' His blockbuster *Sapiens* is a sweeping saga of the human species – from our humble beginnings as apes to a future where we will sire the algorithms that will dethrone and dominate us.

All of Harari's books and talks are worth going through. I relate to his worry that 'the basis of the future, not only of humankind, the future of life, is now in the hands of a very small group of entrepreneurs'. He views modernity as a 'deal' whose 'entire contract can be summarised in a single phrase: humans agree to give up meaning in exchange for power'. My question to him would be, 'Is a moral life in conflict with power?'

What would make the dinner interesting would be to see how each would react to the predictions of the other. I wonder if they would all say the same thing!

Here is a comprehensive list of twenty-two books across many genres that have left a great impression upon me.

22 BOOKS THAT CHANGED MY LIFE (AND HOW)

It is very hard to pick your favourite books because your choices are fluid and can change over time. However, the easiest way is to just go with your memory – pick the ones that touched a deep chord, were very personal and have had a lasting impression. I wouldn't be surprised if they don't mean as much if I read them today because the context would have changed. So here is my list of top twenty-two books, some of which I've re-read and some not, but all of which played a role in making me who I am today. Why twenty-two? Well, when I started listing them off the top of my head, that's the number I stopped at!

1. *Man's Search for Meaning* by Viktor Frankl: If you asked me to pick just one book, it would be this. I have re-read it so often that I quote from the book on every possible occasion. One of my favorite videos is a five-minute YouTube recording of Victor Frankl teaching students and explaining 'the meaning and purpose of life'.

2. *The Class* by Erich Segal: The book was gifted to me by my then-girlfriend (and now wife) in college. I had an idea for a book about my college friends, and since I foresaw remarkable careers for many of them but not for me, I thought I could take on the role of the storyteller. When I told her about it, she mentioned that *The Class* had a similar premise.

3. *The Story of My Experiments with Truth* by Mohandas Karamchand Gandhi: This has been my bible. Time and again, I have read excerpts from it, just to allow the messages from Gandhi's life to soak into mine. I believe the book's title is the best.

4. *Riot* by Shashi Tharoor: This book meant a lot to me when I was dating my wife. Our lives were stressful and uncertain because we came from different religions and our families opposed our marriage. The book mirrors the complex times we live in and what it means to be in a Hindu–Muslim relationship.

5. *Maverick* by Ricardo Semler: This book deeply impacted me during my formative years in the IT industry. While the idea of employees deciding their own salary and rating their managers seemed far-fetched, I was drawn towards it. I have tried following many of the book's principles throughout my career as a people manager.

6. *I Dare!* by Dr Kiran Bedi: I have multiple editions of this book, which was one of the first biographies I read. Calling Dr Kiran Bedi my mentor, guide and friend has been a privilege and an honour.

7. *The Medici Effect* by Frans Johansson: Citing this book's mantra, I have often declared: 'Magic happens at the intersection of science and humanities'. Or, as the book suggests, at the intersection of ideas and disciplines.

8. *The Groaning Shelf* by Pradeep Sebastian: Pradeep has been a friend, mentor and guide in my journey of becoming a bibliophile. By sharing his unparalleled knowledge of books, he helped me become a columnist on books and acquire some of the rarest books in my collection.

9. *The Picador Book of Cricket* by Ramachandra Guha: Guha (besides Gideon Haigh) has been one of my favourite cricket writers. I spent a decade collecting the top fifty books mentioned in a chapter of this book called 'The Addict's Archive'.

10. *The Mahatma and the Poet* by Sabyasachi Bhattacharya: I love the now-lost art of letter writing. This rare book is a collection of the letters exchanged between two of my favourite intellectuals, Gandhi and Rabindranath Tagore, and contains the remarkable debates they engaged in. Every letter is a lesson in how two people can have deep respect for one another while disagreeing on many topics.

11. *Highway Dharma Letters* by Rev. Heng Sure and Heng Chau: I learnt about Buddhist teachings from this book. When I met Rev. Heng Sure, he deepened my understanding of the pilgrimage he undertook from Los Angeles to Mendocino County, doing the 'three steps and a bow' – an astounding exercise in inner transformation. I visited the City of 10,000 Buddhas in Mendocino to get a sense of life in the Buddhist monastery. As Huston Smith said, 'This is the most neglected book of the twentieth century... and one of the most inspiring.'

12. *Gitanjali* by Rabindranath Tagore: My favourite is Poem No 50. '...I bitterly wept and wished that I had had the heart to give thee my all.'

13. *Grit* by Angela Duckworth: This book played a huge role in assembling the pieces of a puzzle that I had always struggled with. It made me realize that grit is the most important predictor of success in the long run.

14. *Scaling Excellence* by Robert Sutton and Hayagreeva Rao: This book is special not only because of its insights on scaling but also because both Bob and Huggy are dear friends. They have often helped me navigate complex scaling challenges in my work.

15. *Give and Take* by Adam Grant: I heard Adam Grant speak at Davos, Switzerland, before I read his books. And, boy, is he a rock star! At twenty-eight, he became one of the youngest tenured professors at Wharton. *Give and Take* remains my favourite among his books because, while I was researching the topic of giving, I found that he had already published his book on it after a decade of research.

16. *The Seat of the Soul* by Gary Zukav: The book is about authentic power, the alignment of the personality with the soul. Its message about intention resonated deeply with me. My friendship with Gary and Linda has made me a better person over the years.

17. *Letters of Note* by Shaun Usher: A well-researched and produced collection of some of the most remarkable letters ever written, this book makes us realize how much we have lost in the digital age. No one ever stores an email for posterity.

18. *The Bhagavad Gita* by Eknath Eswaran: This brilliant translation introduced me to the Gita. Its message about equanimity has stayed with me the longest.

19. *The Reason I Jump* by Naoki Higashida: While I have read many books on autism, this opened my world to the mind of my non-verbal son, Vivaan. Every time I read it, I get new insights into Vivaan's incredible mind. The documentary on the book is amazing too.

20. *A Promised Land* by Barack Obama: Obama made me fall in love with words. Needless to say, I have been a fan of his, having watched his inauguration from the hospital when my son was three days old, and closely followed his journey (Vivaan even shares his birthday with Michelle Obama – 17 January). I was most excited when this book was released on Audible, narrated by Obama himself. I finished listening to it in one go. I also managed to get the deluxe signed edition of the book, thanks to a bookseller friend.

21. *Bibliophile* by Jane Mount: While I am a bibliophile and have read a lot of books on books, this one ranks high because of its simplicity and beautiful artwork. It's a book I would have loved to have written myself. I am grateful to know Jane and for her agreeing to create a personalized artwork of my list of twenty-two favourite books.

22. *Zen and the Art of Motorcycle Maintenance* by Robert M. Pirsig: I was introduced to this cult classic (written the year I was born) very late in life, yet it profoundly impacted me. I learnt that Zen can be found in everyday activity (I found my 'motorcycle maintenance' while dishwashing) and that the best writing happens through pure boredom. These notions were particularly relevant to the pandemic times, during which I first encountered the book. I heard it on Audible along with my son on our daily drives – like the author who wrote it during his motorcycle journeys with his son. His message, 'It is better to travel than arrive – because you never stop travelling and you never arrive,' resonated with me. The book that was once rejected by more than hundred and twenty publishers still rings true after forty-eight years of the seventeen-day motorcycle ride from Minnesota to California, even after the demise of the author and son.

AFTERWORD

A Collector's Homage to the Book

Pradeep Sebastian

One day while I was at The Bookworm, a secondhand bookshop in Bengaluru, Krishna, the owner, took out from a locked cupboard a copy of the Limited Editions Club's *Lysistrata* with Picasso's signature in pencil at the colophon. I had hardly expected to come across something as fine as this in a bookshop in India, and congratulated him. 'Actually, it's not for sale – this has been loaned to the bookshop by the collector, V.R. Ferose,' he replied. 'Really? But why?' I couldn't help exclaiming. 'Because he feels it will just sit on his shelf, whereas, here browsers can enjoy looking at it. Not only this book, but Ferose sir has given us other rare books also from his collection – such as the recent limited edition signed by Harper Lee.'

What collector would, after having spent a lakh or so on a single book, gladly proceed to remove it from his shelf and place it in the custody of another to display? He is, as friends, family and colleagues will readily testify, a generous collector. Too modest to speak of his generous gestures in collecting, it will have to be left to others to speak of this. Unforgettable to me was the time, when I barely knew him, when he parted with a rarity from his collection without even thinking for a second about it. I had given him something small, and he simply grabbed a book signed by Nehru from his shelf and thrust it at me, saying, 'Well, then, you must have this.' When I protested, he waved me off, saying he had two signed copies. Of course, he did! But is that any reason to part with a second copy of such a high spot, where expensive signed books from famous Indians are concerned?

There was that time when a friend – spotting a signed Tagore photograph in his office – expressed his admiration for it, and Ferose gifted it to him right away. An enduring habit with him is the extra signed copies he buys at every book signing event for anyone he thinks will be interested in a signed copy from that particular author. Typically, he will return from a book signing with an armful of copies to be distributed to family, colleagues, friends and fellow collectors.

Another time in the San Francisco Bay Area, while browsing through the rare books section of an antiquarian bookstore, he spotted a first edition of Agatha Christie's *The Thirteen Problems*. 'I decided immediately,' Ferose said, 'to pick it up for my wife, Deepali, who is a great fan of Christie, as her birthday was approaching. It was the best possible birthday gift I could give her!' His ambition is to be India's most significant book collector, and the focus and speed and resources he is putting into making that happen will soon bring him closer to fulfilling this goal.

He is a fearless collector – this is the second striking quality as a collector after his generosity that has impressed me deeply. And I have seen this at every turn and phase of his collecting. I recall this at one time, perhaps some three years ago, when a desirable and sumptuous collection of high-end books, made up mostly of limited signed editions, came up for sale rather unexpectedly in India for a lakh and a half, and no one wanted to take the plunge and buy it; it was only Ferose who stepped up. Quite a few collectors were interested in the collection but were dithering. This was so typical of Indian book collectors – a lot of talk and no action. Boasting was what turned them on more than actually making significant acquisitions. However, no one had brought the collection to Ferose's notice, but the moment he was sounded out on it, he didn't need any cajoling or persuading: he snapped it up at once. This, at once, demonstrated to all of us in the collecting world his high ambition, his vision, his commitment and his genuine passion for building a formidable collection.

It also showed his wisdom: because that collection of books, studded with many wonderful signed and fine editions was worth at least twice the price he paid for it. And this would hold good for a large part of his collection: that they will only increase in value over the years. Rare books only get rarer. Another remarkable feature of this intrepid collector is the variety he seeks: most collectors eventually settle into one or two areas of collecting, limiting themselves to a specialized focus. While this can and often is a good thing, it held no appeal for Ferose. He wanted to explore as many forms and areas of collecting as there were to taste and sample, and as a result, his collection is sweeping, studded with many intriguing examples of rarities and beauties.

Not just a wide-ranging collector but also a very creative one, he would think up of new areas of collecting – zine magazines, landmark graphic novels, collectible joke books, cartoon strips, movie posters, great speeches – or invent fascinating sub-categories of collecting: best books on technology, on autism or books that changed the world. Like the best collectors, he collected what mirrored his concerns, the subjects and people and themes that engaged him deeply. But he was also at the same time open to things that preoccupied or fascinated others, always with the belief and trust that there was more to learn, more to discover.

His other passion – as his cricket-loving friends know very well – is collecting cricket bats signed by cricketing legends, with many in the collection being miniature bats, a collectible in its own right, signed or otherwise. His desire to own priceless signed material is only half for the aura of a bespoke, legendary signature: the real passion is for the person, for what the signature stands for – the work and accomplishment of these people he admires so much. The adventure for Ferose, I realized, is really about the people. His yearning for signed books is also a yearning for letting the people he admires touch his life.

Interestingly, though, when acquiring a signed copy to add to his collection, he prefers books that are flat-signed by authors to inscribed copies. I assumed this was for the usual reason – the antiquarian market's preference for flat-signed copies – but it turned out to be for the most human of reasons. 'I feel every inscribed book has a personal story behind it. If someone had to give away an inscribed book, it would mean either the person did not value it any more or had to give it away for some reason, or the book has outlived the person. Whatever the case, it is all rather sad.' More recently, though, he has made an exception for association copies, seeing them in a different light, as possibly the most desirable copies, precisely because they carry a telltale inscription.

For Ferose, rare and fine books are not about money or prestige but, in his words, 'The adventure of building a library, book by book, is what the fun is all about, so there's a story behind every book!' And here, in this book, as he shares with us, chapter after chapter, all of these enthralling stories behind every book he collected, he has also managed to immerse us in not only in his personal collecting adventure, but in the adventure of editions, unravelling the individual stories of unique editions and how they came into his possession. This book itself came into being because he thinks it significant, thinks it enormous fun to lavish such attention and care and resources on the printed book. Whether beautiful or rare or just a common edition, for him there is no better way of paying homage to 'The Book' than acquiring, preserving and curating the best that the world of books has to offer us.

And now that you've reached the end of Ferose's collecting saga – well, at least the journey until now – you've no doubt seen for yourself the high quality of beautiful and rare books he pursued and acquired over the years, but what you may not realize is the guts and commitment it took to make this happen. Because being a serious collector means committing to buy books even when your finances are strapped or tight, and this is how it has always been with Ferose. Whether it was when he was just starting out as a collector with little funds at his disposal to buy the more common signed editions he was hankering after, or during his peak phase of collecting expensive high-end books with more funds at his disposal, it has always involved some sacrifice, some tension, some cutting into either personal or household resources. I would often hear him say, when confronted with either forking out the high price being asked for a coveted book or having to let it go: 'I think I'll go ahead and get it – it means I probably won't be able to buy any more books for at least a month or two, but I'm not going to pass this up.'

He has turned the activity of collecting into an adventure. Never have I heard him quibble about how much this is costing him, or that he is bored or fed up with it, or that he is now going to slow down. On the other hand, he is always spirited about the next collecting adventure, on his toes and ready to snap up new acquisitions, miraculously producing the funds for a stunning rarity that has just come his way or that he has stumbled on, or finding the funds needed for an entire set of rarities waiting to burn a deep hole in his pocket. Ferose will always remain for me the book collector extraordinaire because while India has its fair share of leaders, humanitarians and innovators, there are only a few book collectors of his stature, taste and accomplishment.

Best of all is how he includes *you* – that is anyone interested and charmed enough to buy rare and beautiful books – to join him in this adventure (even in his collecting life, he is inclusive). He does not like to play the book collecting game alone (as is common with possessive collectors) and would rather have you collaborate or participate in his quest, creating a sense of camaraderie and community in book collecting.

ABOUT THE AUTHOR

V.R. Ferose

V.R. Ferose is the founder of the India Inclusion Foundation, a Bengaluru-based nonprofit that aims to bring inclusion to the forefront in all sectors across India. He has co-authored several bestsellers, most notably *The Invisible Majority: India's Abled Disabled*, *Gifted: Inspiring Stories of People with Disabilities*, and the GRIT series. Ferose has been included in various international lists of significance, such as 'India's Top 40 under 40' in 2014 by *Economic Times* and Spencer Stuart, and was conferred 'Young Global Leader' in 2012 by the World Economic Forum. He currently heads the SAP Academy for Engineering in San Ramon and writes the bi-weekly column 'Flyleaf' for *New Indian Express*. A passionate bibliophile, he has over three thousand rare books in his collection and is a member of The Grolier Club. In June 2023, he joined the board of the California publishing house Heyday Books.

ABOUT THE ARTISTS

Angeline S. Pradhan

Back in the '90s, during our art college years, my friend Akshayee and I had been inseparable as we had bonded over the feeling of being outsiders in a place that neither of us had much of a choice but to be in. However, after two years, I found that the place was too limiting for me, and I moved out to work at an animation studio, where I could pursue my passion. Akshayee continued her studies there, and we managed to keep in touch intermittently despite our different paths.

As time went on, we were swept away by the hustle and bustle of earning a living and gradually lost touch. I started The Other Design Studio with my husband, Upesh, and was consumed by the work and the need to establish the studio.

Our paths crossed once again through a serendipitous encounter at an art and craft event. It was during this reunion that Akshayee shared the incredible venture she had embarked upon – a school for autism and Asperger's Syndrome – that she had co-founded to provide neurodivergent individuals with art education. She asked for my assistance in designing their annual report, and from that moment on, our involvement deepened. What moved me profoundly was witnessing Akshayee working with children with autism, who embraced art with a unique and extraordinary perspective. Both Upesh and I became incredibly invested in the programme, ultimately becoming managing trustees.

It was during our involvement in this endeavour that Akshayee introduced me to V.R. Ferose, explaining, 'Listen, there's this individual who wants my artists to illustrate his book on books, and I don't know where to start.' Fascinated by the project, I viewed it as an intriguing experiment and decided to take it on. The endeavour proved to be a brilliant undertaking, demanding patience as we conceptualized and eagerly anticipated the surprises the artists would bring. Fortunately, with Upesh's animation and artistic skills complementing my background in graphic design, we formed an exceptional team alongside the artists. It was an enlightening journey, during which we truly got to know each and every one of them.

Over the last year, I have come to know Ferose remarkably well through the process of reading his articles and translating them into concepts for my artists. These concepts were then given their own interpretations by the artists as pencil sketches. After selecting the most appropriate one for each article, I had the task of going over them with a digital pen and creating vector artwork of the sketches. The look of each article was primarily dictated by the artwork and embellished with design elements. It has been challenging, but I can proudly say that I have thoroughly absorbed the contents of all the hundred articles after going through them multiple times.

As fellow book lovers and collectors, we connected with Ferose's perspective and understood the influences that shaped his ideas. What's truly captivating is his boundless enthusiasm for books and book collecting.

The true stars of *Shelf Aware* are our artists who, despite the challenges that they face every day, have diligently worked on the project and provided all the necessary work to see it to completion. They have been our inspiration and continue to be so every day.

Allow me to provide you with a brief bio of each of these exceptional artists.

At 28, **ADARSH**, an autistic firecracker at Sense Kaleidoscopes, defies limitations. Seizures and challenges in communication and cognition are no match for his artistic spirit. Overcoming school rejections, he's become a self-taught linguist in 12 languages! Diverse interests fuel his creativity. From sculptures to theatre, Adarsh's art shines at the Kochi-Muziris Biennale and Outsider Art Fair in Paris. Unwavering and always smiling, he's a visual art force, challenging norms and showcasing the power of neurodiversity.

ANSHIKA is a brilliant 16-year-old artist at Sense Kaleidoscopes. Her journey is a testament to the transformative power of embracing neurodiversity in artistic expression. Anshika's natural flair for art, especially in cartoons, illuminates her unique perspective of the world. Despite challenges in communication and social interactions, her artistic skills have blossomed under the nurturing guidance at Sense Kaleidoscopes. Her journey showcases that with support and understanding, individuals with neurodivergent traits can overcome challenges and thrive.

PRANAV, at 23, is an abstract artist whose creative soul thrives on the symphony of order, structure and intricate patterns woven through geometric shapes. Resonating with Kandinsky's artistic essence, Pranav's vibrant palette mirrors his contagious zest for life. Despite grappling with barriers and challenges brought about by societal and institutional attitudes towards his autism, his exceptional empathy and unwavering optimism have propelled him forward. Beyond the canvas, he is honing his barista skills and indulging in his love for exploration and music in his leisure time. His story is one of resilience, creativity and the pursuit of happiness.

At 23, **ROHIT**, a whirlwind of artistic talent, finds solace at Sense Kaleidoscopes. Though challenged by an education system ill-prepared for his brilliant mind, he navigates the complexities of fitting in while embracing his uniqueness. Art is his powerful voice. He channels his struggles into mesmerizing, Dali-esque creations exhibited globally, even gracing the prestigious Outsider Art Fair in Paris. Rohit was presented the National Disability Artist Award at an event jointly organized by Youth4Jobs, UNESCO and HSBC (HDPI) in 2019. His journey exemplifies unwavering determination and his story, brimming with resilience and artistic fire, disrupts societal norms, urging the world to celebrate the genius of neurodiversity.

TANUSH is an effervescent 22-year-old luminary in our creative constellation. She dances, sings, plays the keyboard and excels in visual arts, sculpture, pottery, theatre and print arts at Sense Kaleidoscopes. Navigating young adulthood, she grapples with the complexities of societal expectations that trigger occasional anxiety. Despite sensory challenges, she dedicates hours to each piece, showcasing a meticulous eye for detail. Tanush stands out for her exceptional talent and work ethic, inspiring us all to appreciate the richness neurodiversity brings to the creative tapestry.

We thank the parents of the artists for sharing the bios.

ACKNOWLEDGEMENTS & ATTRIBUTIONS

Acknowledgements are made to the following publications, in which the stories in this collection first appeared; some differently titled or in slightly different form:

The New Indian Express ©: 'Collector's Piece'; 'Fine Press Books'; 'Book Covers'; 'Miniature Books as Tiny Treasures'; 'Big Little Books'; 'The Origin of Illuminated Manuscripts'; 'Chatting in the Margins'; 'When Politicians Write Memoirs'; 'Political Satire in the Age of Trump'; 'The Rise of Fascism'; 'The Fragility of Democracy'; 'Why Reading Banned Books Becomes an Act of Rebellion; 'Literature That Sprouted from Prison Cells'; 'The Spirit of the Games'; 'The Story of Philosophy'; 'Books on Spirituality'; 'Eye-Opening Books About Buddhism'; 'Bhagvad Gita and its Timeless Appeal'; 'Keeping a Healthy Mind'; 'Read to Lead'; 'The Art of Empathy'; 'Books on Science for the Lay Person'; 'Analog Sea: A Counter to the Digital World'; 'Math Matters'; 'Manga Magic'; 'The Nostalgia of Comics'; 'Classics in Graphics'; 'A Sketchy Affair'; 'Strokes of Creativity'; 'Is the Future of Books 'Phygital''; The Emotional Turmoil of Decluttering'; 'Norway: A Publisher's Paradise'; 'Documenting the Bookstore'; 'Krishna Gowda: The Bookman of Bengaluru'; 'Exploring the Genre of Books on Books'; 'Books About Bookstores'; 'The Sub-Category of Ephemera Collecting'; 'Women and Writing'; 'The Power of Poetry'; 'The Climate of Crisis'; 'Of Mystery and Magic'; 'The Oddity of Cult Books'; 'Special Tales'; 'Essay on Essays'; 'Writing Around Wars'; 'Death by the Book'; 'Not Just Child's Play'; 'Being Funny is No Joking Matter'; 'Books As Gifts'; 'Romance of the Railways'; 'The Great Domestic Cooking Renaissance'; 'Regional Bestsellers in English'; 'Sniffing Out Some 'Pawsome' Books'; 'Zooming in on Photojournalism'; 'Books on Creating Social Impact'; 'Diving Into Bibliomysteries'; 'The Life Contained in an Obituary'; 'The Thriving Self-Help Industry'; 'Why Public Libraries Need to be Revived'; 'The Joy of a Library of Unread Books'; 'Calling it Quits'; 'Alternate History: The What-If Genre'; 'The Quirky Technique of Constrained Writing'; 'The Best of Experimental Writing'; 'Best Bollywood Books'; 'The Golden Book of Tagore'; 'The Rare Gandhi–Tagore Association Copy'; 'The Booker in the World of Book Prizes'; 'Is Self-Publishing a Threat to Traditional Publishing'; '3 Writers for Dinner and a Question'.

Swarajya ©: 'An Ode to Odd Books'; 'Landmarks in Printing History'; 'Capturing All Sides of a Beautiful Game'; 'Timeless Books on Technology'; 'The Authentic and Powerful Gary Zukav'; 'Of Books and Bookshelves'; 'The Chase for My Alice'; 'The Case for Lefties'; 'The Stories That Letters Reveal'; 'What's in a Name?'; 'Saving That One Precious Book'; 'Books to Movies'; 'Books Seen in Film Scenes'; 'An Ode to the Bard'; 'How Authors Sign Books'.

Mint ©: 'On the Gentle Madness of Bibliophilia'.

Wisden India Almanack ©: 'Signs of a Good Cricket Book'.

PICTURE CREDITS: INSIDE PHOTOGRAPHS

(i) A portrait of Nicholas A. Basbanes © V.R. Ferose (Foreword); **(ii)** V.R. Ferose with Nicholas A. Basbanes © V.R. Ferose (Foreword); **(iii)** V.R. Ferose (Preface); **(iv)** L to R: Adarsh, Pranav, V.R. Ferose, Tanush and Rohit © V.R. Ferose (Acknowledgements); **(v)** V.R. Ferose with Ramachandra Guha © V.R. Ferose ('Signs of a Good Cricket Book'); **(vi)** V.R. Ferose with Jonathan Simons © V.R. Ferose ('Analog Sea: A Counter to the Digital World'); **(vii)** V.R. Ferose with Gary Zukav © V.R. Ferose ('The Authentic and Powerful Gary Zukav'); **(viii)** A portrait of Nicholas A. Basbanes © V.R. Ferose ('My Nicholas A. Basbanes Library'); **(ix)** V.R. Ferose with Nicholas A. Basbanes © V.R. Ferose ('My Nicholas A. Basbanes Library'); **(x)** In the frame: Nicholas A. Basbanes's copy of *A Gentle Madness*, which he gifted to V.R. Ferose, *GRIT: The Major Story* by D.P. Singh, V.R. Ferose and Sriram Jagannathan, and *America's Greatest Library* by John Y. Cole © V.R. Ferose ('My Nicholas A. Basbanes Library'); **(xi)** V.R. Ferose with wife Deepali Kulkarni and their son Vivaan © V.R. Ferose ('Living With a Collector'); **(xii)** A photograph of Premier Book Shop owner, T.S. Shanbhag © Mahesh Bhat ('Documenting the Bookstore'); **(xiii)** A photograph of Blossom Book House owner, Mayi Gowda © Mayi Gowda ('Documenting the Bookstore'); **(xiv)** The Bookman of Bengaluru, Krishna Gowda © V.R. Ferose ('Documenting the Bookstore'); **(xv)** Store front, The Monkey's Paw © V.R. Ferose ('The Monkey's Paw Springs a Surprise'); **(xvi)** Inside the store, The Monkey's Paw © V.R. Ferose ('The Monkey's Paw Springs a Surprise'); **(xvii)** V.R. Ferose with Stephen Fowler © V.R. Ferose ('The Monkey's Paw Springs A Surprise'); **(xviii)** Store front, Bell's Books, Downtown Palo Alto © V.R. Ferose ('The Bell Hasn't Tolled For This Bookstore'); **(xix)** V.R. Ferose with Faith Bell © V.R. Ferose ('The Bell Hasn't Tolled For This Bookstore'); **(xx)** Inside the store, Powell's City of Books, Portland © V.R. Ferose ('The World's Largest Independent Bookstore'); **(xxi)** Inside the store, Powell's City of Books, Portland © V.R. Ferose ('The World's Largest Independent Bookstore'); **(xxii)** Inside the store, Powell's City of Books, Portland © V.R. Ferose ('The World's Largest Independent Bookstore'); **(xxiii)** Inside the store, Powell's City of Books, Portland © V.R. Ferose ('The World's Largest Independent Bookstore'); **(xxiv)** A picture of *TIME* magazine's 2016 article, 'The Death of the Bookstore Was Greatly Exaggerated' inside the Powell's City of Books, Portland © V.R. Ferose ('The World's Largest Independent Bookstore'); **(xxv)** Store front, John K. King Used & Rare Books, Detroit © V.R. Ferose ('The Story of a Multi-Storey Bookstore'); **(xxvi)** Inside the store, John K. King Used & Rare Books, Detroit © V.R. Ferose ('The Story of a Multi-Storey Bookstore'); **(xxvii)** Inside the store, John K. King Used & Rare Books, Detroit © V.R. Ferose ('The Story of a Multi-Storey Bookstore'); **(xxviii)** Inside the store, John K. King Used & Rare Books, Detroit © V.R. Ferose ('The Story of a Multi-Storey Bookstore'); **(xxix)** V.R. Ferose with Alexendre Freiman © V.R. Ferose ('Shakespeare and Company'); **(xxx)** Store front, Mystery Pier Books ('Hidden Mysteries in Los Angeles'); **(xxxi)** V.R. Ferose with Harvey Jason, co-owner of Mystery Pier Books © V.R. Ferose ('A Hidden Mystery in Los Angeles'); **(xxxii)** Harvey Jason at work, co-owner of Mystery Pier Books © V.R. Ferose ('A Hidden Mystery in Los Angeles'); **(xxxiii)** Inside the store, The Mysterious Bookshop, New York City © V.R. Ferose ('The Mysteries Within the Mysterious Bookstore'); **(xxxiv)** Inside the store, The Mysterious Bookshop, New York City © V.R. Ferose ('The Mysteries Within the Mysterious Bookstore'); **(xxxv)** Inside the store, The Mysterious Bookshop, New York City © V.R. Ferose ('The Mysteries Within the Mysterious Bookstore'); **(xxxvi)** V.R. Ferose with his father V.A. Rasheed © V.R. Ferose ('Romance of the Railways'); **(xxxvii)** V.R. Ferose with Mother Fathima © V.R. Ferose ('The Great Domestic Cooking Renaissance'); **(xxxviii)** Coco and Vivaan © V.R. Ferose ('Sniffing out Some 'Pawsome' Books'); **(xxxix)** V.R. Ferose with C.K. Meena and Anshu Gupta © V.R. Ferose ('Books on Creating Social Impact').

PICTURE CREDITS: BOOK COVERS

Hay House India: I.K. Gujral, *Matters of Discretion*; Dilip Kumar, *The Substance and the Shadow: An Autobiography*.

Rupa Publications: Rabindranath Tagore, *Letters to a Friend*; L.K. Advani, *My Country, My Life*; P. Chidambaram, *Speaking Truth to Power: My Alternative Truth*; Pranab Mukherjee, *The Turbulent Years: 1980–1996*; Amborish Roychoudhury, *In a Cult of Their Own: Bollywood Beyond Box Office*; Rajendra B. Aklekar, *A Short History of the Indian Railways*; Milkha Singh, *The Race of My Life: An Autobiography*.

Chelsea Green Publishing: David Peter Stroh, *Systems Thinking for Social Change*.

Beacon Press: Edited by Robert Bly, *Kabir: Ecstatic Poems*; Thich Nhat Hanh; *The Miracle of Mindfulness: An Introduction to the Practice of Meditation*.

Diversion Books: Geoffrey A. Moore, *Zone to Win: Organizing to Compete in an Age of Disruption*.

Atlantic Books: Christian Wolmar, *Fire and Steam*.

Blaft Publications: Appupen, *Moonward*; edited by Rakesh Khanna, translated and compiled by Pritham K. Chakravarthy, *The Blaft Anthology of Tamil Pulp Fiction*; Charu Nivedita, *Zero Degree* (Kindle edition cover used).

HarperCollins Publishers India: Shamya Dasgupta, *Don't Disturb the Dead: The Story of the Ramsay Brothers*; Chimamanda Ngozi Adichie, *We Should All be Feminists*; Gene Zion, *Harry the Dirty Dog*; Margaret Thatcher, *The Path to Power*; Aravind Adiga, *The White Tiger*; Arun Shourie, *Does He Know a Mother's Heart?*; Pavithra K Mehta and Suchitra Shenoy, *Infinite Vision*; Gary Zukav, *The Dancing Wu Li Masters*; Paul Bloom, *Against Empathy*; James L. Swanson, *Manhunt*; Carl Sandburg, *Abraham Lincoln: The Prairie Years and the War Years*; Paulo Coelho, *The Alchemist*; Paul Roberts, *The End Of Food*; Alissa Nutting, *Tampa*; Tom Peters, *In Search of Excellence*; William Peter Blatty, *The Exorcist*; Translated by Coleman Barks, *The Essential Rumi*; Garth Stein, *The Art of Racing in the Rain*; Christina Hunger, *How Stella Learned to Talk*; Neil Gaiman, *American Gods*; Neil Gaiman, Terry Pratchett, *Good Omens: The Nice and Accurate Prophecies of Agnes Nutter, Witch*; Mark Manson, *The Subtle Art of Not Giving a F*ck*; Padgett Powel, *The Interrogative Mood: A Novel?*; Abhinav Bindra and Brijnath Rohit, *A Shot At History*; Boria Majumdar, *Dreams of a Billion: India and the Olympics Story*; Dave Sobel, *Longitude: The True Story of a Lone Genius Who Solved the Greatest Scientific Problem of his Time*; Lars Kepler, *The Hypnotist*; Simon Singh, *Fermat's Last Theorem*; Ellen Fitzpatrick, *Letters to Jackie: Condolences from a Grieving Nation*; Paulo Coelho, *The Alchemist: A Graphic Novel*; Harper Lee, *To Kill A Mockingbird* (Graphic Novel); Umberto Eco, *Name of the Rose*; Arturo Pérez-Reverte, *The Club Dumas*; Liz Wiseman, *Multipliers*; Edward Dolnick, *The Rescue Artist*; Venki Ramakrishnan, *Gene Machine: The Race to Decipher the Secrets of the Ribosome*; Amruta Patil, *Kari*; Anupama Chopra, *Dilwale Dulhaniya Le Jayenge*; Lisa Ray, *Close to the Bone*; edited by M.K. Raghavendra, *Beyond Bollywood: The Cinemas of South India*.

HarperCollins UK: Dr Seuss, *The Cat in the Hat*; Dr Seuss, *Green Eggs and Ham*; Madeleine Albright, *Fascism: A Warning*.

HarperCollins Publishers Australia: John Green, *Looking for Alaska*.

Harvard Business Review Press: Clayton M. Christensen, *The Innovators Dilemma: When New Technologies Cause Great Firms to Fail*; Frans Johansson, *The Medici Effect: What Elephants and Epidemics Can Teach Us About Innovation*.

Jaico Publishing House: Charles Freer Andrews, *Mahatma Gandhi: His Life and Ideas*; Eknath Eswaran, *The Bhagavad Gita*; Nirad C. Chaudhuri, *Autobiography of an Unknown Indian*.

Akshaya.io: Vikas Khanna, *Sacred Foods of India*.

University Press of Kansas: Benjamin Arrington, *The Last Lincoln Republican*.

Buddhist Text Translation Society: Heng Chau, Heng Sure, *Highway Dharma Letter*.

Verso Books: Felix Weinberg, *Boy 30529*.

Wordsworth Editions: Rudyard Kipling, *Collected Poems of Rudyard Kipling*.

Koehler Books: Whitney Ellenby, *Autism Uncensored: Pulling Back the Curtain*.

Bloomsbury Publishing: George Saunders, *Lincoln in the Bardo*; Rutger Bregman, *Utopia for Realists*; Kevin Birmingham, *The Most Dangerous Book: The Battle for James Joyce's Ulysses*; Wendy Lower, *The Ravine*.

Lisette Verhagen: Arundhati Roy, *My Seditious Heart*.

Europa Editions: Elena Ferrante (Author), Ann Goldstein (Translator), *My Brilliant Friend*.

Hachette India: V.R. Ferose and C.K. Meena, The *Invisible Majority: India's Abled Disabled*; Indra Nooyi, *My Life in Full: Work, Family, and Our Future*; Diptakirti Chaudhuri, *10 Bioscope*; Major D.P. Singh, V.R. Ferose and Sriram Jagannathan, *GRIT: The Major Story*; Pradeep Sebastian, *The Book Beautiful*; Pradeep Sebastian; *The Book Hunters of Katpadi: A Bibliomystery*; Pradeep Sebastian, *The Groaning Shelf*; Sadaf Hussain, *Daastan-e-Dastarkhan*.

Black Kite and Hachette India: Edited by Arvind Krishna Mehrotra, *The Book of Indian Essays*.

Photographs from Ferose's home library in Palo Alto, California © V.R. Ferose

COASTS OF CALIFORNIA
THE NAZI HUNTERS
ELEVEN SPRING
GUTENBERG BIBLE
TASCHEN
TOO MUCH COFFEE MAN
SILICON VALLEY
Manto & I
OTTOLENGHI FLAVOR
writers
THE VIETNAM WAR
WOODSTOCK
I don
Go
my WIFE Kn
THE BAREFOOT COACH
SACHIN TENDULKAR
WIZARDS
1,000 PLACES TO SEE BEFORE YOU DIE
JOE SACCO FOOTNOTES IN GAZA
DRAWN AND QUARTERED
WITCHES
NeuroTribes
UNSTOPPABLE
Switched On
PONTING
Sabi
Nobuo Suzuki
TUTTLE
Holding Things
MASTER EDITION
THE GROLIER CLUB
Museum of Innocence
Museum